REUBEN SACHS

broadview editions
series editor: L.W. Conolly

REUBEN SACHS
A Sketch

Amy Levy

edited by Susan David Bernstein

broadview editions

Library and Archives Canada Cataloguing in Publication

Levy, Amy, 1861–1889.
  Reuben Sachs : a sketch / Amy Levy ; edited by Susan David Bernstein.

(Broadview editions)
Includes bibliographical references.
ISBN 1-55111-565-4

  I. Bernstein, Susan David   II. Title.   III. Series.

PR4886.L25R49 2006   823'.8   C2006-900224-X

Broadview Editions
The Broadview Editions series represents the ever-changing canon of literature in English by bringing together texts long regarded as classics with valuable lesser-known works.

Advisory editor for this volume: Rebecca Conolly

Broadview Press is an independent, international publishing house, incorporated in 1985. Broadview believes in shared ownership, both with its employees and with the general public; since the year 2000 Broadview shares have traded publicly on the Toronto Venture Exchange under the symbol BDP.

We welcome comments and suggestions regarding any aspect of our publications—please feel free to contact us at the addresses below or at broadview@broadviewpress.com.

North America
Post Office Box 1243, Peterborough, Ontario, Canada K9J 7H5
Post Office Box 1015, 3576 California Road, Orchard Park, NY, USA 14127
Tel: (705) 743-8990; Fax: (705) 743-8353
email: customerservice@broadviewpress.com

UK, Ireland, and continental Europe
NBN International, Estover Road, Plymouth PL6 7PY UK
Tel: 44 (0) 1752 202300   Fax: 44 (0) 1752 202330
enquiries@nbninternational.com

Australia and New Zealand
UNIREPS, University of New South Wales
Sydney, NSW, 2052 Australia
Tel: 61 2 9664 0999; Fax: 61 2 9664 5420
email: info.press@unsw.edu.au

www.broadviewpress.com

Typesetting and assembly: True to Type Inc., Mississauga, Canada.

PRINTED IN CANADA

For Daniel

Contents

Acknowledgements • 9
Introduction • 11
Amy Levy: A Brief Chronology • 45
Anglo-Jewish History: A Brief Chronology • 49
A Note on the Text • 51

Reuben Sachs: A Sketch • 53

Appendix A: Contemporary Reviews of *Reuben Sachs*
1. "Critical Jews," *The Jewish Chronicle* (25 January 1889) • 159
2. "Reuben Sachs," *The Spectator* (16 February 1889) • 161
3. John Barrow Allen, "New Novels," *The Academy* (16 February 1889) • 163
4. "The Deterioration of the Jewess," *Jewish World* (22 February 1889) • 164
5. "Literary: Amy Levy's Reuben Sachs," *The American Hebrew* (5 April 1889) • 166
6. Oscar Wilde, "Amy Levy," *The Woman's World* (1890) • 167

Appendix B: Other Writing by Levy
1. "Jewish Women and 'Women's Rights,'" *The Jewish Chronicle* (7 February 1879, 28 February 1879) • 171
2. "The Jew in Fiction," *The Jewish Chronicle* (4 June 1886) • 175
3. "Middle-Class Jewish Women of To-Day," *The Jewish Chronicle* (17 September 1886) • 178
4. "Cohen of Trinity," *The Gentleman's Magazine* (May 1889) • 181
5. Poetry • 189

Appendix C: Literary Contexts
1. From George Eliot, "The Modern Hep! Hep! Hep!," *The Impressions of Theophrastus Such* (1878) • 193
2. From Mathilde Blind, "Daniel Deronda," *George Eliot* (1883) • 198
3. From Israel Zangwill, *Children of the Ghetto* (1892) • 202
4. From Vernon Lee, "A Dialogue on Novels," *The Contemporary Review* (September 1885) • 209
5. From Oscar Wilde, "The Decay of Lying: A Dialogue," *The Nineteenth Century* (January 1889) • 212

Themes: marriage, oppression of women by Jewish community, wealth, class

Appendix D: The Jewish Question in Victorian Culture
1. The Jewish Type: The New Race Sciences
   a. From Robert Knox, "Of the Coptic, Jewish, and
      Phœnician Races," *The Races of Men* (1862) • 215
   b. Joseph Jacobs, "The Jewish Type, and Galton's
      Composite Photographs," *The Photographic News* (24
      April 1885) • 218
2. Political and Social Contexts
   a. From Goldwin Smith, "Can Jews Be Patriots?"
      The Nineteenth Century (May 1878) • 224
   b. From Hermann Adler, "Recent Phases of Judaeophobia,"
      The Nineteenth Century (December 1881) • 226
   c. From Laurence Oliphant, "The Jew and the Eastern
      Question," *The Nineteenth Century* (August 1882) • 229

Appendix E: The New Woman Question
1. From Clementina Black, "On Marriage: A Criticism," *Fortnightly Review* (April 1890) • 235
2. From Grant Allen, "The Girl of the Future," *The Universal
   Review* (1890) • 238

Appendix F: Map of Levy's London from *Bacon's New Map of
London* (1885) • 243

Select Bibliography • 247

Acknowledgements

I am indebted to several Levy scholars, many of whom I met at the colloquium on Amy Levy held at the University of Southampton in July 2002, especially Linda Hunt Beckman, Naomi Hetherington, Ana Parejo Vadillo, and Nadia Valman. Linda and Ana shared with me invaluable archival advice and research materials. I am grateful to Christine Pullen for similar generosity. I also thank Michael Galchinsky and Cynthia Scheinberg for their suggestions on this edition.

My gratitude to Camellia Plc, now part of Linton Park Plc in Kent, which owns Levy's unpublished manuscripts, letters, diaries, scrapbooks, and sketches. The present curator, Mary Ann Prior, assisted me in my two visits to Linton Park. Anne Thomson, librarian at the Newnham College Archive, facilitated my research on Levy at Cambridge. I also appreciate Keith Feldman's assistance during my research in the archives of *The Jewish Chronicle* in London.

The University of Wisconsin Graduate School has provided me with research grants that funded my work on this edition, including my project assistants. Elizabeth Evans proofread the entire novel with a dexterous eye. Julia Chavez carried on with this work and discovered material for some of the most stubbornly arcane of references for the novel and the appendix items. She also deserves credit for her digital prowess in assembling the map of Levy's London in *Reuben Sachs*. With the support of the Department of English at the University of Wisconsin, Catherine Price accomplished the sometimes frustrating task of converting the novel into electronic format, and Karin Heffel worked diligently on formatting, editing, and proofreading the documents. Thanks also to Trevor Coe. The Center for Jewish Studies at the University of Wisconsin provided support for the cover photograph from The Jewish Museum, London.

I am grateful to several people who replied to queries posted on the Victoria discussion list, and to colleagues at the University of Wisconsin. In particular, David Sorkin was my constant bibliographic guide and ready resource on all matters pertaining to European Jewish history, and he provided excellent comments on the Introduction. Emily Auerbach gave me another venue to introduce Levy on "University of the Air" on 5 October 2003. I would also like to thank my graduate and undergraduate students who have offered stimulating readings of *Reuben Sachs* in our work together; their insights have not only extended and nourished mine but also persuaded me time and again of the intellectual pleasures of teaching Levy's work.

Melvyn New's 1993 edition *The Complete Novels and Selected Writings of Amy Levy 1861-1889* has made available the publications of Amy Levy to a broad audience today. I have selected for the appendices several items by Levy that are not included in New's edition, including her correspondence with *The Jewish Chronicle* over "women's rights," "The Jew in Fiction," and poems.

This edition would not be possible without the many kinds of love, diversion, and food shared with me by my family, Flora Claire Berklein and Daniel Lee Kleinman.

Introduction

In "The Jew in Fiction," published in *The Jewish Chronicle* in 1886, Amy Levy observed, "There has been no serious attempt at serious treatment of the subject; at grappling in its entirety with the complex problem of Jewish life and Jewish character. The Jew, as we know him to-day, with his curious mingling of diametrically opposed qualities; his surprising virtues and no less surprising vices; leading his eager, intricate life; living, moving, and having his being both within and without the tribal limits; this deeply interesting product of our civilisation has been found worthy of none but the most superficial observation."[1] According to Levy, English literature portrays Jewish characters as either too virtuous or villainous, from "bad fairies" like Charles Dickens's Fagin in *Oliver Twist* (1837-38) to his "good fairy" Riah in *Our Mutual Friend* (1864-65). "The Jew in Fiction" focuses on Levy's nineteenth-century antecedents, including Dickens, William Makepeace Thackeray, Sir Walter Scott, and George Eliot, as well as a few contemporary writers of fiction no longer in print. None of the authors Levy cites was Jewish, although there were several Anglo-Jewish Victorian novelists and poets to embrace Jewish subjects, including Grace Aguilar, Celia and Marian Moss, Emily Harris, and Benjamin Farjean.[2] By constructing "the Jew in fiction" through this catalogue of English writers for her Anglo-Jewish audience, Levy implies her own acculturated identity "both within and without the tribal limits," where her literary models did not encompass her co-religionists.

How successfully did Levy carry out this portrayal of "the complex problem" of contemporary Anglo-Jewry in her treatment of her title character as a "mixed, imperfect human creature"? When *Reuben Sachs* first appeared in print early in 1889, a critic in the *Jewish World* castigated Levy for invoking anti-Jewish stereotypes circulating in Victorian culture: "She is not ashamed of playing the *role* of an accuser of her people."[3] After Levy's suicide later that year at the age of 27, *The Jewish Standard* com-

---

1 See Appendix B2.
2 See Michael Galchinsky, *The Origin of the Modern Jewish Woman Writer: Romance and Reform in Victorian England* (Detroit: Wayne State UP, 1996) and Linda Gertner Zatlin, *The Nineteenth-Century Anglo-Jewish Novel* (Boston: G.K. Hall, 1981).
3 See Appendix A4.

mended the novel for its "acute diagnosis of the spiritual blight that has come over well-fed Judaism,"[1] while Oscar Wilde viewed *Reuben Sachs* as the pinnacle of Levy's literary achievement: "Its directness, its uncompromising truth, its depth of feeling, and, above all, its absence of any single superfluous word, make it, in some sort, a classic.... The strong undertone of moral earnestness, never preached, gives a stability and force to the vivid portraiture, and prevents the satiric touches from degenerating into mere malice."[2] More recently, Bryan Cheyette has celebrated *Reuben Sachs* as "the most influential and underrated Anglo-Jewish novel of its time" for inaugurating the modern "novel of revolt" instead of the apologist tradition in which Jewish writers idealized their co-religionists.[3] Yet Emma Francis finds Levy's representations of Anglo-Jewry "profoundly politically unsanitary" despite her "sophisticated sexual politics."[4] Thus *Reuben Sachs* continues to stir its readers in diverse ways, as it did when it was published.

In responding to this daunting task of "grappling" with "Jewish life and Jewish character," Levy blurs perspectives "within and without the tribal limits" of Anglo-Jewishness. The lines between inside and outside depictions of Jews were not so firmly drawn for an acculturated, middle-class woman who received a progressive education beyond the London Jewish community in which she spent her childhood, and later moved in vibrant intellectual circles in London and Cambridge. As Nadia Valman has noted, "That Jews could figure in Victorian culture—from historical and romance novels to poetry and cultural criticism—as both self *and* other underlies the range of contradictory Jewish representations of the period."[5] Levy suggests that an insider's view must necessarily be alloyed with these "other" visions. W.E.B. Du Bois's theory of double-consciousness, from his 1904 book on African

---

1 "Retrospect," *The Jewish Standard* (25 September 1889): 9.
2 See Appendix A6.
3 Bryan Cheyette, "From Apology to Revolt: Benjamin Farjeon, Amy Levy and the Post-Emancipation Anglo-Jewish Novel," *Transactions of the Jewish Historical Society of England* (January 1985): 260.
4 Emma Francis, "Amy Levy: Contradictions?—Feminism and Semitic Discourse," *Women's Poetry, Late Romantic to Late Victorian: Gender and Genre*, eds. Isobel Armstrong and Virginia Blain (Basingstroke: Macmillan, 1999) 201.
5 Nadia Valman, "'A Fresh-Made Garment of Citizenship': Representing Jewish Identities in Victorian Britain," *Nineteenth-Century Studies* 17 (2003): 39.

American identity, *The Souls of Black Folk*, resonates with the hyphenated character of Levy's Anglo-Jewishness: "It is a peculiar sensation, this double-consciousness, this sense of always looking at one's self through the eyes of others, of measuring one's soul by the tape of a world that looks on in amused contempt and pity."[1] Anticipating Du Bois's theory, Levy's fiction of Jewish identity in *Reuben Sachs* and in her short story "Cohen of Trinity" is imbued with "the tape of the world," with the discourses of her time that regarded Jews as a foreign race, nation, a throwback to a "tribal" religion predating the culture of Christianity. To understand Levy's project to treat this "complex problem" of representing Jewish double-consciousness, this Introduction considers her biographical background, the multiple cultural spheres of Levy's London, and the scientific and political discourses of her day that shaped meanings of Jewishness.

A Brief Biography

On 10 November 1861 Amy Judith Levy was born in South London, to Lewis and Isabelle Levy. Her ancestors had arrived in England in the eighteenth century, and like many diasporic "port Jews" of European coastal cities, her maternal great-grandfather conducted trade between Falmouth in Cornwall and Spain.[2] Taking advantage of the financial opportunities British colonialism afforded, Levy's father and uncles were export merchants in Australia, and later, after returning to London and marrying, Lewis Levy worked as a stock broker. Amy Levy was the second of seven children, the second of three daughters and four younger sons. Like other acculturated Jews of the late Victorian era, the Levys were thoroughly English in speech, manners, taste, and thought.[3] Given that her family was well-established in England, Levy's childhood resembled that of gentile middle-class children. She had a non-Jewish governess, an aunt who had a Christmas tree, and she was evidently familiar with both Hebrew and Christian biblical texts.[4] While it is not known to what extent Levy

---

1 W.E.B. Du Bois, *The Souls of Black Folk* (New York: Penguin, 1989) 5.
2 David Sorkin, "The Port Jew: Notes Toward a Social Type," *Journal of Jewish Studies* L.1. (Spring 1999): 87-97.
3 Todd M. Endelman, *Radical Assimilation in English Jewish History, 1656-1945* (Bloomington: Indiana UP, 1990) 73.
4 See Linda Hunt Beckman, *Amy Levy: Her Life and Letters* (Athens: Ohio UP, 2000) 13-14.

received a formal Jewish education, as a girl, she would not have been expected to master Hebrew or participate fully in synagogue services. Levy's letters to her mother and older sister suggest that there was some minimal observance of the weekly Jewish sabbath and synagogue attendance at least once a year at Yom Kippur, the Day of Atonement, along with the customary practice of fasting.

Levy's family were members of the West London Synagogue of British Jews, the first congregation established in London's West End in 1841 to draw together Anglicized Jews who were reluctant to attend the more traditional and less convenient synagogues located in the East End where poorer, immigrant Jews first settled. Tellingly, this was a religious institution of "British Jews," the first assembly in Great Britain of both Ashkenazim, whose ancestors came chiefly from Germany and Poland, and Sephardim, descended from Jews of the Iberian Peninsula, where reformed services included a modified prayer book, sermons in English, and shorter hours of worship compatible with secular timetables. The West London Synagogue performed the burial services at Balls Pond Cemetery for the first Jewish man cremated in England in 1887, a controversial change that reinterpreted the scriptural command of "unto dust shalt thou return," yet it coincided with modern ideas of science and hygiene.[1] The same synagogue officiated at the burial of the ashes of the first Jewish woman to be cremated in England—Amy Levy—who had made this explicit request.[2] While these modifications were considered so radical as to incur briefly a bill of excommunication from the orthodox London Jewish community, much tradition was still maintained.[3] For instance, genders were segregated in the sanctuary, with women relegated to the remote balconies where their participation was far more limited, a practice that continued in England well into the twentieth century.

The education Levy received indicates that her parents were more forward-thinking than many of their co-religionists in this regard. In 1876 at the age of 15 Levy entered the Brighton High School for Girls, part of the Girls' Public Day School Company,

---

1 On the question of cremation, see *The Jewish Chronicle* (20 April 1888): 5-6; (4 May 1888): 11.

2 "Death of a Jewish Authoress," *The Pall Mall Gazette* (14 September 1889): 5.

3 See Peter Renton, *The Lost Synagogues of London* (London: Tymsder Publishing, 2000) and James Picciotto, *Sketches of Anglo-Jewish History*, rev. and ed. Israel Finestein (London: The Soncino Press Ltd., 1956).

founded in 1871 by feminists Emily and Maria Shirreff. The school implemented a rigorous academic curriculum equivalent to the training boys received in preparation for university enrollment. Edith Creak, the head of Brighton High School when Levy attended, was a member of the very first class of five students at Newnham College in 1871, one of two colleges at Cambridge University expressly designed to accommodate women.[1] No doubt Levy's own feminist beliefs were shaped by this unusual educational experience. In her last year at Brighton, she wrote a letter to *The Jewish Chronicle* in which she advocated for the expansion of Jewish women's horizons beyond their relegated place in the domestic sphere as wives and mothers: "... there has sprung up a large class of intelligent, capable women who are willing and able to perform work from which they find themselves shut out by the tradition of ages—women ... whose aims lie outside the circle which convention has marked out for them."[2]

Levy herself was the first Jewish student at both Brighton High School and later at Newnham College, where she enrolled in 1879. In a letter to her sister Katie while at Brighton, Levy describes a "pious" Christian classmate and her family "who did not like to visit Jews, no orthodox persons *did*."[3] Like women, Jews at Cambridge were a recent phenomenon. The University Tests Act of 1871, abolishing the religious test of faith, made possible the admission of Jewish and Catholic students. Since Oxford and Cambridge were established institutions for training the Anglican Church ministry, Christian culture continued to define both universities even after 1871, and so Jewish students remained a decided minority, not exceeding a dozen undergraduates, far into the twentieth century.[4] Levy's short story "Cohen of Trinity" narrates the tragic career of a male Jewish student at Trinity College, Cambridge, from the perspective of a fascinated gentile classmate who views Cohen as a freakish curiosity, "the uncouth figure with the glowing face, the evil reputation, and that strange suggestion of latent force that clung to him."[5] The entire

---

1 Anne Phillips, ed., *A Newnham Anthology* (Cambridge: Newnham College, 1988) 1-4.
2 See Appendix B1.
3 Quoted in Linda Hunt Beckman, *Amy Levy: Her Life and Letters* (Athens: Ohio UP, 2000) 225.
4 Todd M. Endelman, *Radical Assimilation in English Jewish History, 1656-1945* (Bloomington: Indiana UP, 1990) 77-80.
5 See Appendix B4.

story is framed by the narrator's gaze, which mimics the new race-scientist classifying the Jewish "type." Like character descriptions in *Reuben Sachs*, Cohen's depiction reflects the ambiguity inherent in stereotypes of Jews. In the end, the narrator is no more able to understand Cohen than he can make sense of Cohen's bestseller, described as "half poem, half essay, wholly unclassifiable, with a force, a fire, a vision, a vigour and felicity of phrase that carried you through its glaring inequalities, its most appalling lapses of taste, the book fairly took the reader by storm."

While at Cambridge for two years, Levy studied classical and modern languages, and she published her first collection of poems, *Xantippe and Other Verse*. The title poem, a dramatic monologue in the style of Robert Browning, showcases the anger of Socrates's intellectually stifled wife, whose "high philosopher" husband "deigned not to stoop to touch so slight a thing/As the fine fabric of a woman's brain." This poem mingles classical and modern themes, just as her studies did, and again manifests Levy's feminism, a perspective she carried over into both short fiction and novels, including *Reuben Sachs*. Whether her doubly marginalized position as a Jewish woman was a factor, Levy left Cambridge in 1881 and returned to live with her family in London, punctuated with travels on the European continent. But she sustained her Newnham friendships with classmates and teachers, such as Ellen Crofts, who became a Fellow and Lecturer at Newnham before she married Charles Darwin's son Francis in 1886.[1]

Having launched a literary career with the publication of *Xantippe*, Levy continued to write and to publish across different genres in the remaining eight years of her short life, including two additional collections of poems, several short stories, three novels, and a few translations from French and German. Her stories, essays, and poems appeared in many different periodicals, including *The Woman's World*, Oscar Wilde's magazine, and *The Jewish Chronicle*, in which she published five short essays in 1886: "The Ghetto in Florence," "The Jew in Fiction," "Jewish Humour," "Jewish Children," and "Middle-Class Jewish Women of To-Day."[2] These two magazines encapsulate two realms of Levy's London life: the world of modern women writers, artists, and social

---

1 Gwen Raverat, *Period Piece: A Cambridge Childhood* (London: Faber and Faber, 1987) 101.
2 See Appendices B2 and B3.

reformers tasting unprecedented independence, and an established Anglo-Jewish community where traditional values, including gender roles, helped to preserve a Jewish identity in an era of declining religious belief and amid the pressures of assimilation.

Given Levy's remarkable literary career at an early age and her stimulating intellectual circle, along with the companionship of family and friends, it is difficult to grasp what motivated her suicide from charcoal asphyxiation on 10 September 1888 as she was correcting the page proofs for her third collection of poems, *A London Plane-Tree, and Other Verse*. Suicidal despair is a motif in several of Levy's poems and short fiction, and readers both immediately after her death and more recently have understood Levy to suffer from longstanding despondency. Her close friend Clementina Black wrote a letter to *The Athenaeum* in which she refuted the diverse rumors circulating in the press that her suicide was a consequence of estrangement from her family, or alienation from the West London Jewish community following the publication of *Reuben Sachs*, or of failing eyesight, or the strain from East End charity work. Instead, Black attributes Levy's suicide to "fits of depression, the result of ... her lack of physical robustness and of the exhaustion produced by strenuous brain work."[1] Another column a few years later in the *Pall Mall Gazette* characterizes Levy's melancholy as "constitutional, and had little relation to outward events. It was constantly increased by a tendency to deafness, which is frequent among Jews, and by a degree of ill-health that seldom enabled her to realize the joy of mere living."[2] This idea of an innate weakness bespeaks what Sander Gilman has called "the Jewish disease," the nineteenth-century medical construction whereby Jews were considered pathologically predisposed to physical infirmities, such as debilitating nervousness.[3]

Heinrich Heine, a German-Jew who converted to Christianity for career purposes, was a Romantic poet whose protracted illness captures this cultural linking of physical and emotional morbidity with Jewishness.[4] The trenchant ambivalence toward life that emerges in his writing is often read as the irreconcilable doubleness of his German and Jewish identities. Heine was one of Levy's literary models; she translated his poems for Lady Katie

---

1 *The Athenaeum* 3232 (5 October 1889): 457.
2 "The Tragedy of Amy Levy," *Pall Mall Gazette* (25 September 1891): 3.
3 Sander Gilman, *The Jew's Body* (New York: Routledge, 1991) 55.
4 Gilman, 132.

Magnus's *Jewish Portraits*, she wrote about his ironic style as a hallmark of Jewish wit that mixes humor with suffering in her essay "Jewish Humour," and she explicitly acknowledged his influence by titling one of her poems "After Heine."[1]

If Heine suffered from the incompatibilities of his hyphenated German-Jewishness, Levy's minority status was complicated not only by her gender but also, according to much speculation, by her sexuality. Recent scholars have commented on the same-sex eroticism suffusing her poetry, and her biographer Linda Hunt Beckman believes that Levy's despair may have been exacerbated by an unrequited love for Vernon Lee, who was a lesbian. In her note to a mutual friend, Lee too participated in the widespread hypothesis of an inherited malady accounting for Levy's suicide: "she learned in the last 6 weeks that she was on the verge of a horrible & loathsome form of madness apparently running in the family, & of which she had seen a brother of hers die."[2] Such an account of Levy's suicide illuminates the ways in which Jewishness was regarded through the new race science as subject to inherited infirmities due to inbreeding, and the title character of *Reuben Sachs* likewise suffers from this kind of impaired health: "'More than half my nervous patients are recruited from the ranks of the Jews,' said the great physician whom Reuben consulted. 'You pay the penalty of too high a civilization'" (56). As this opinion insinuates, Jewishness was an identity inflected in the Victorian era by ideas of race, nation, and culture as well as religion.

Gender and sexuality also informed interpretations of Levy's death. Grant Allen, with whom Levy visited in the last months of her life, made sense of her suicide through the lens of social Darwinism, evolutionary theory applied to social phenomena. Writing on feminism as a hazard to the perpetuation of the human race, Allen believed that intellectual pursuits compromised women's ability to procreate and, ultimately, to survive. In "The Girl of the Future," written shortly after Levy's death, Allen sardonically identifies her as a victim of the modern movement for women's higher education: "A few hundred pallid little Amy Levys sacrificed on the way are as nothing before the face of our fashionable Juggernaut. Newnham has slain its thousands, and

---

1 See Appendix B5.
2 Quoted in Linda Hunt Beckman, *Amy Levy: Her Life and Letters* (Athens: Ohio UP, 2000) 208. Levy's brother Alfred Lewis died in 1887 at the age of 24.

Girton its tens of thousands...."[1] Allen likewise reflected in verse about Levy's death, in which he figures her fate as a compounded consequence of feminine infirmity and feminist ideals:

This bitter age that pits our maids with men
   Wore out her woman's heart before its time:
         Too wan and pale,
         She strove to scale
The icy peaks of unimagined rhyme.[2]

These several representations of Levy's suicide make evident that gender, Jewish inheritance, and social transformation were construed as biological liabilities. Yet it is too simple to read her death as an effect of her own perceived condition of an inherited malady or even what we might today term depression. No one can ultimately know what prompted a young and accomplished woman to take her life, although how her contemporaries viewed her death gives us purchase on the beliefs shaping her culture. A poem privately circulated 25 years after Levy's suicide contemplates the contemporary set of English culture with traditional religion and gender roles on the wane.[3] "A Ballad of Religion and Marriage" opens with Christianity and Judaism "swept into limbo," as the first stanza poses the central question of the poem: "Shall marriage go the way of God?" In speculating on sexuality outside of the constraints of religion and monogamous marriage, the poem imagines that for men in the near future "perennial shall his pleasures flow," yet for women this idyllic vision is deferred indefinitely in the concluding stanza:

Grant, in a million years at most,
      Folk shall be neither pairs nor odd—
Alas! We sha'n't be there to boast
      "Marriage has gone the way of God!"

The offset "Grant" might be read as an address to Grant Allen, as the speaker ironically comments on the slow pace of social

---

1 See Appendix E2.
2 Grant Allen, "For Amy Levy's Urn," *The Lower Slopes* (London: E. Mathews & John Lane, 1894) 21. For two other poetic tributes to Levy, see Melvyn New, *The Complete Novels and Selected Writings of Amy Levy, 1861-1889* (Gainesville: UP of Florida, 1993) 53-55.
3 See Appendix B5.

progress rendered here in evolutionary time, "in a million years at most," when women especially will not be rated according to marital and sexual status, "neither pairs nor odd." Whether Levy saw herself in an unreconcilable position "outside the circle which convention has marked out"—to quote from her *Jewish Chronicle* letter—as Jewish, as a lesbian or in other ways as "odd," as unable or unwilling to marry, these lines convey a sensibility "all out of tune in this world's instrument," as Levy phrased this in "A Minor Poet." The dilemmas of both gender and Jewishness offer not only a context for viewing Levy's suicide but also for reading the ways *Reuben Sachs* is inflected by contemporary discourses about women and Jews. Given that the novel is set in London, a place of central importance in her poetry and short fiction as well, how did gender and Jewishness also accent Levy's daily urban life?

Levy's Londons: Modern Women and Jewish Geography

According to her 1889 calendar book, Levy followed a regular schedule of reading and writing at home or at the Reading Room of the British Museum in Bloomsbury, not far from her family's home in Endsleigh Gardens.[1] At the British Museum Levy met up with other women and men writers, and she published an essay in a girls' magazine on the importance of this egalitarian venue for "all sorts and conditions of men and women" with intellectual aspirations.[2] Besides devoting her time to her work, including meetings with publishers, Levy visited with a variety of friends and associates, including Clementina Black, Olive Schreiner, and Eleanor Marx, who translated *Reuben Sachs* for its German publication in 1890. On evenings spent circulating in literary salons in Bloomsbury, Levy mingled with Oscar Wilde, Thomas Hardy, and William Butler Yeats, as well as Vernon Lee, Mary Robinson, and other aspiring young women poets. Another landmark in Levy's London was the University Club for Ladies in New Bond Street, established in 1887, where Levy was a

---

1 For details from this calendar, see Linda Hunt Beckman, *Amy Levy: Her Life and Letters* (Athens: Ohio UP, 2000) 175-78.
2 Levy, "Readers at the British Museum," *Atalanta* (April 1889): 449-54. Reprinted in Amy Levy, *The Romance of a Shop*, ed. Susan David Bernstein (Peterborough, ON: Broadview Press, 2006).

member.[1] Her social calendar also includes attendance at concerts, theatre, art galleries and museums, walks in parks, meals at restaurants, and shopping.

Levy's London life and literary career attest to the image of the modern woman in fiction and in essays of the 1880s and 90s, dubbed "the new woman," a moniker (like "feminist" today) that triggered a cultural ambivalence about changing gender roles. Often affiliated with the pedantic "Girton girl," named for the first women's college to open in Cambridge, "the new woman" was thoroughly modern in dress, in expressing sexual desires outside of marriage and sometimes towards other women, in pursuing a career outside of the home, and was often outfitted in media caricatures with her signature props—spectacles for reading, a bicycle for mobility, and a cigarette connoting masculine appetites and habits. As Levy began writing *Reuben Sachs* in 1888, she was also finishing her first novel, *The Romance of a Shop*, about four sisters who manage their own home and a photography business in London, socialize with men they meet through their work, attend "private shows" at galleries, and travel by themselves about the city on foot, by underground train, and on omnibuses, much as Levy herself did.

Levy's place in the Jewish geography of London is more difficult to discern from her 1889 diary, but demographics provide a backdrop. Native Jews, like the Levy family, who had resided as British citizens for a few generations, numbered only 60,000 in 1880.[2] Jews were banished from England in 1290 and readmitted in 1656.[3] Gradually over two centuries the Anglo-Jewish community obtained civil rights, punctuated by occasional parliamentary debates over Jewish disabilities. With Catholic Emancipation in 1829, Jews became the only recognized religious group without full civil and political rights, but because they did enjoy freedom of occupation and mobility, this partial inequality—largely based on the belief that England was a Christian

---

1   See Appendix F for a map of Levy's London. Levy's "Women and Club-Life" appeared in *The Woman's World* (1888): 364-67; it is reprinted in Amy Levy, *The Romance of a Shop*, ed. Susan David Bernstein (Peterborough, ON: Broadview Press, 2006).

2   Todd Endelman, "Native Jews and Foreign Jews in London, 1870-1914," *The Legacy of Jewish Migration: 1881 and Its Impact*, ed. David Berger (New York: Social Science Monographs—Brooklyn College Press, 1983) 109.

3   Anglo-Jewish History: A Brief Chronology, p. 49.

nation—continued into the latter part of the nineteenth century. Three years before Levy's birth, Lionel de Rothschild became the first Jewish Member of Parliament to take his seat, and after that Jewish men increasingly gained public offices throughout the 1860s and 70s. Regarded as "English people of the Jewish persuasion," Anglo-Jews began to matriculate at Cambridge and Oxford in the early 1870s, and doors to various posts in the legal profession opened to them. Levy's own childhood, then, coincided with the most visible period of Anglo-Jewish emancipation.

However, in the 1880s, the Jewish population in England doubled when poor Jewish immigrants, fleeing persecution in Russia and Poland, flooded East End London. The response of established Anglo-Jewish Londoners was ambivalent to the arrival of their co-religionists. On the one hand, many participated in philanthropic work on behalf of impoverished Jewish foreigners through various institutions such as the Jewish Board of Guardians and the Anglo-Jewish Association. Levy depicts this support of East End Jews by West End Jewry with Reuben Sachs serving on these organizations because, as he puts it, "it consolidates one's position both ways to stand well with the Community, and I am a very good Jew at heart" (106). On the other hand, acculturated Jews sought to distance themselves from their unnaturalized counterparts who spoke Yiddish and clung to the orthodox Judaism of isolated Eastern European shtetl communities. Native Jews feared a backlash, since these newly arrived "alien" Jews prompted fresh debates on the worthiness of all Jews as English citizens. To reconcile this contradiction of wanting to assist Jewish immigrants in need but also wanting to protect their own secure place as English, the Board of Guardians sent back to the Continent nearly 50,000 Eastern European immigrants.[1] This crude picture of Jewish geography in Levy's time divided London into prospering West End Anglo-Jews and impoverished East End Eastern European Jews.

Although West London consisted of native rather than immigrant Jews, it was far from homogeneous. Before Levy's family moved to Bloomsbury, they lived in Regent's Park, almost as close to the West London Synagogue in Upper Berkeley Street as their later Endsleigh Gardens address was to the British

---

1   Todd Endelman, "Native Jews and Foreign Jews in London, 1870-1914," *The Legacy of Jewish Migration: 1881 and Its Impact*, ed. David Berger (New York: Social Science Monographs—Brooklyn College Press, 1983) 113.

Museum. While the family's relocation may have affected their synagogue attendance, Levy herself makes no explicit mention of Jewish places or events in her 1889 calendar. Yet *Reuben Sachs* does provide a more detailed account of London Jewish geography, with the West End punctuated by a variety of synagogues that offer a key to the social subdivisions of London Anglo-Jewry in Levy's day.[1] The most Anglicized members of Reuben's family, including the Leunigers, attend the West London Synagogue. More orthodox in religious practice, yet less wealthy and less refined—in terms of English manners and language—relatives such as the Samuel Sachses are affiliated with St. John's Wood Synagogue, near Maida Vale, a section of North London associated with lower middle-class Jews like the Samuel Sachses and the Quixano family, in contrast to the Leunigers, who live in South Kensington. Solomon Sachs, the patriarch of the family, as well as Reuben's sister and brother-in-law, Adelaide and Montague Cohen, belong to the Bayswater Synagogue. Both of these institutions were part of the United Synagogue, an umbrella union of principal British synagogues of Ashkenazim. Often the political spokesman for English Jews, the Chief Rabbi of Great Britain was the spiritual supervisor of all synagogues incorporated in the United Synagogue.[2] Sephardic Jews in the West End, like Judith Quixano's parents and siblings, attended the Spanish and Portuguese Synagogue in Bryanston Street, a branch of Bevis Marks, the oldest synagogue in London, established in 1701 in the East End. That Reuben, Judith, the Leunigers, and Bertie Lee-Harrison, a convert from Christianity, all attend the West London Synagogue marks them as modern reform in their practice of Judaism in contrast to more traditionally observant members of their community. Thus, religious observance and class position are facets of Levy's Jewish geography.

Another landmark of late-Victorian Jewish London was the Anglo-Jewish Historical Exhibition in 1887, at Royal Albert Hall, across from Kensington Gardens. The exhibition mounted the first large-scale display of artifacts of Anglo-Jewish culture from antiquity, including synagogue records and personal documents, as well as Jewish ritual art objects from synagogues and homes. According to the catalogue the purpose of the exhibition was to preserve and promote a knowledge of a history of Jews in

---

1   See Appendix F for the location of synagogues in *Reuben Sachs* and Levy's London.
2   See Appendix D2b.

England.[1] Supported by the leaders of the Anglo-Jewish community, this Kensington show also attempted to fortify a sense of the historical presence of Jews in England at a time when foreign Jewish immigrants poured into East End neighborhoods.

The Jewish Question in Victorian Culture: Race Science and Nationalism

Recent scholars of modern Jewish identity have recognized the instability of the idea of Jewishness. For Jonathan Freedman, "the Jew" is a boundary figure that calls into question any viable model of racial, national, cultural, or religious identity. Instead, Freedman construes Jewishness as hybrid, complex, and vacillating, like any ethnic category today.[2] For Victorians, being Jewish carried the meaning of a "people" in the sense of a premodern national community developed from a discrete family that proliferated into affiliated tribes. Benjamin Disraeli, who was the Prime Minister of Great Britain for several years during Levy's life, identified religiously as Christian and racially as Jewish. Converted to the Church of England as a child, Disraeli endorsed Jews as "the mighty prototype which has fashioned Europe" and as "a pure race of the Caucasian organisation" in his 1844 novel *Coningsby*.[3] His political opponents read his Jewish origins as a liability that compromised his foreign policy, especially during the "Eastern Question" of the 1870s. Following the syntax Victorians favored for headlining contemporary issues, "the Jewish Question" encompassed debates around Anglo-Jewish identity and Jewish social, civil, and political rights.

With the rise of a new scientific discourse on race in the nineteenth century, the notion of Jews as originating from ancient tribes was increasingly understood as a biological phenomenon. In England, Robert Knox's *The Races of Men*, with its second edition appearing the year after Levy's birth, had a significant influence on racial thinking.[4] For Knox, "race, or hereditary

1 Joseph Jacobs and Lucien Wolf, *Catalogue of the Anglo-Jewish Exhibition* (London: F. Haes, 1888).
2 Jonathan Freedman, *The Temple of Culture: Assimilation and Anti-Semitism in Literary Anglo-America* (New York: Oxford UP, 2000) 23.
3 Benjamin Disraeli, *Coningsby or the New Generation* (New York: Oxford UP, 1982) 219.
4 Nancy Stepan, *The Idea of Race in Science: Great Britain, 1800-1960* (Hamden, CT: Archon Books, 1982) 41.

descent, is everything," by which he meant that racial determinism trumped environment in human destiny. Knox's racial theory was a fixed hierarchy with Saxons at the apex, and placed what he termed "darker races," including Jews, Irish Celts, and Africans, lower on the organic scale. As an example of Knox's racial essentialism, he insisted that the old clothes man of London, a staple of Jewish stereotypes in Victorian England, even though "assuming the air of a person of a different stamp," is unmistakable, "never to be confounded with any other race."[1] Where Disraeli imagined Jews as the quintessential Caucasian race, Knox contested that this was a specious racial designation designed to disguise or whitewash Jewish racial inferiority. Knox offered a profile of Jewish physiognomy characterized by a "want of proportion" with a "convex" profile, heavy lips and a "muzzle-shaped mouth," close-set eyes, and a "swarthy" complexion likened to an "African look."

In the early pages of *Reuben Sachs*, the narrator echoes this racialist profile of Jews through descriptions of a deformed, irregular embodiment from face to feet. If Levy sketched drawings of the visual stereotypes Knox outlines while she was attending university classes, as the only Jewish woman at Cambridge, she might have been especially conscious of such derogatory typing of Jews by non-Jews.[2] For Levy and her contemporaries, this racialized caricature was clearly a living discourse that nourished the double-consciousness of Anglo-Jews. In a letter written from Dresden in 1881 just after Levy left Cambridge, she described a visit to a synagogue as "a beastly place" with "Zion, unventilated & unrefreshed" and "crammed with evil-looking Hebrews." Levy added that "the German Hebrew makes me feel, as a rule, that the Anti-Semitic movement is a most just & virtuous one."[3] Like West End acculturated Jews distancing themselves from their alien East End co-religionists, Levy registered her antipathy toward a perceived strangeness of German Jews as "unventilated & unrefreshed."

This ambivalent identification with derogatory stereotypes of

---

1 See Appendix D1a.

2 Linda Hunt Beckman, *Amy Levy: Her Life and Letters* (Athens: Ohio UP, 2000) 111-12. For these sketches, see Linda Hunt [Beckman], "Leaving the Tribal Duckpond: Amy Levy, Jewish Self-Hatred, and Jewish Identity," *Victorian Literature and Culture* 27.1 (1999): 192.

3 Quoted in Linda Hunt Beckman, *Amy Levy: Her Life and Letters* (Athens: Ohio UP, 2000) 236.

Jews in race science functions differently for Joseph Jacobs, who made a career as a specialist in Jewish history, literature, and culture. Like Levy, Jacobs was one of the first Jewish students at Cambridge, where he graduated from St. John's College in 1876. Levy mentions in a letter to her mother from Cambridge in 1880 that Jacobs "has been down to try for his fellowship,"[1] which he did not obtain because he was Jewish. Like Levy too, Jacobs pursued a writing career in London, where he focused on Jewish topics, including a review essay of George Eliot's *Daniel Deronda*, and he organized and wrote the catalogue for the Anglo-Jewish Exhibition of 1887. Jacobs's approach to Judaism was multi-disciplinary, and after studying under Francis Galton, he asked his mentor to create a composite of "the Jewish type" based on photographs Jacobs collected of East End Jewish schoolboys.

Composite photography was a process in which several images were "compounded" by exposing a number of portraits on the same negative to produce not an individual, but a "type" supposedly revealing the average facial qualities of a group defined ultimately as a biological category. Photography had become a tool for collecting evidence of racial types, and T.H. Huxley spearheaded a project, supported by the colonial office, to assemble a photographic portfolio of races across the British Empire.[2] Galton's archive of composite types included the insane, the consumptive, the poor, criminals, and, with Jacobs's prompting, Jews. Galton's interest in evolution and degeneration led to his theory of eugenics, whereby a portion of society—typically an urban working-class population—constituted a reservoir of physical deficiencies and infirmities that threatened the decline of the nation. By segregating and sterilizing this segment, Galton argued that the inherited and racialized health of a nation might be preserved. As Freedman points out, "there is no such thing as a pure, unmediated Jewish identity"[3] because both non-Jews and Jews, whether assimilated or not, colluded in their imaginative efforts to construct this identity, much as Galton and Jacobs collaborated in assembling "the Jewish type."

---

1   Quoted in Linda Hunt Beckman, *Amy Levy: Her Life and Letters* (Athens: Ohio UP, 2000) 231.
2   Peter Hamilton and Roger Hargreaves, *The Beautiful and the Damned: The Creation of Identity in Nineteenth-Century Photography* (London: National Portrait Gallery Publications, 2001) 91.
3   Jonathan Freedman, *The Temple of Culture: Assimilation and Anti-Semitism in Literary Anglo-America* (New York: Oxford UP, 2000) 28.

Jacobs's 1885 essay, "The Jewish Type and Galton's Composite Photographs," suggests how firmly the Jew was a composite racial figure in the Victorian imagination. The first sentence asserts that "the Jewish type" is self-evident: "Most people can tell a Jew when they see one."[1] But Galton and Jacobs read these superimposed images differently. Whereas Galton sees "cold calculation" as a facet of the facial expressions, Jacobs finds "something more like the thinker and the dreamer than the merchant." Like Levy, Jacobs both reiterates and complicates some stereotypes of a physical "Jewish type." He refutes the idea of a recognizable "Jewish" nose, and instead insists on the flexibility of nostrils rather than the fixity of shape. In this regard we can better understand Levy's own quotation of an ethnological "Jewish type" as a science fiction that is itself imaginary, drawn from images and cultural stereotypes whose only reality is a reductive composite.

Just as Victorian Jewishness bore a racialized meaning, so did ideas of national identity play into the Jewish Question, the focus of a series of articles in the magazine *The Nineteenth Century* from 1878 to 1882, following Disraeli's support of the Ottoman Empire against the uprising of Christian nationalists in Bosnia.[2] Detractors of Disraeli's foreign policy believed that his politics were dictated by his allegiance as a Jew by birth if not by religious faith to Muslim Turks rather than Christian Bulgarians. In this spirit, an Oxford historian, Goldwin Smith, argued in "Can Jews Be Patriots?" against Jewish acculturation in modern England because he saw Jewishness as fundamentally a race descended from "a group of primaeval and tribal religions" in contrast to the "sun of modern civilization."[3] Smith's contention that "a Jew is not an Englishman ... he is a Jew with a special deity for his own race" renders Anglo-Jewish identity a contradiction. Further, Smith exploits the portrayal of Jews as an ancient "tribal race" with Judaism as outmoded, "a relic of the age before humanity," or in other words, before Christianity.

In response to Smith's insistence that Jews could not be loyal

---

1 See Appendix D1b, including the composite photographs of "the Jewish type." For a detailed discussion of Galton and Jacobs, see Daniel Novak, "A Model Jew: 'Literary Photographs' and the Jewish Body in *Daniel Deronda*," *Representations* 85 (Winter 2004): 58-97.

2 David Feldman, *Englishmen and Jews: Social Relations and Political Culture, 1840-1914* (New Haven: Yale UP, 1994) 97.

3 See Appendix D2a.

English citizens, Hermann Adler, the Chief Rabbi of Great Britain, countered that Jewish identity was based on religion, not race or nationality, and that Anglo-Jews "consider ourselves citizens of the country in which we dwell, in the highest and fullest sense of the term, and esteem it our dearest privilege and duty to labour for its welfare."[1] Laurence Oliphant, another contributor to the magazine forum on the condition of Jews in British society, refocused the tension between orthodox Eastern European Jews and acculturated Jews of the West on the idea of a return to the land of Zion. A philosemite interested in establishing Jewish settlements in the Ottoman Turkish colony of Palestine, Oliphant points out that for persecuted Russian Jews, "a restoration to their ancient home" is a compelling hope, whereas for "the Jew of the West" who has imbibed modern skepticism toward religious belief and who enjoys civil liberties in various countries, the idea of Palestine holds little appeal. One of Levy's characters in *Reuben Sachs* remarks on George Eliot's "elaborate misconception" in portraying London Jews intent on a quest for a Jewish homeland in "the East" in *Daniel Deronda*. Debates about the social and political condition of English Jews carried over into literature, most notably in Eliot's 1876 novel, published when Levy was 14.

Jewishness and Gender in Victorian Literature

In "The Jew in Fiction," Levy devotes several sentences to *Daniel Deronda*, which garnered accolades from Jewish readers in England and beyond for its sympathetic and substantial attention to Judaism.[2] But Levy assesses the novel as "no picture of Jewish contemporary life, that of the little group of enthusiasts, with their yearnings after the Holy Land and dreams of a separate nation.... As a novel treating of modern Jews, *Daniel Deronda* cannot be regarded as a success." Although many prominent Anglo-Jewish men, from Disraeli to Jacobs, praised *Daniel Deronda*, Levy was not the only Jewish woman to offer a more mixed reaction. Mathilde Blind likewise took issue with the novel's proto-Zionist zeal as "curiously repugnant to modern

---

1 See Appendix D2b.
2 A testament to this reception, a street in Jerusalem is named after George Eliot.

feelings" of assimilated Jews.[1] Described by Levy as "poet and writer of *belles lettres*,"[2] Blind came from a German-Jewish family that relocated in England when she was a child, and was part of the London salon culture that Levy inhabited. Instead of Eliot's separatist Jews in *Daniel Deronda*, Blind advocates for a "fresh blending of nationalities and races."[3] *Reuben Sachs* offers more ambivalent views on intermarriage and conversion through the match between Judith and Bertie; the Jewish community of the novel accepts "Bertie's veneer of Judaism as the real thing" as an example of "the degeneracy of the times," and the epilogue envisions an infelicitous scene of the marriage. While Levy criticized previous depictions in fiction of unambiguously "good" and "bad" Jews, Blind diagnoses a similar binary in Eliot's Jewish heroines with one character faultlessly devout, the other rebellious and selfish: "one set of motives are righteous, just, and praiseworthy, as well as that the others are mischievous and reprehensible." Lucidly articulated in *Daniel Deronda* by the "rebellious" Jewish heroine, it is gender oppression that propels Levy's first public statements on behalf of Jewish women's emancipation.

In 1879, *The Jewish Chronicle* published a letter from a correspondent under the heading "Jewish Women and 'Women's Rights'" that urged female readers to shun the call of recent feminists, and instead to adhere to traditional roles of wife and mother. Michael Galchinsky credits Anna Maria Goldsmid, whose family were founders of the West London Synagogue for British Jews, for bringing feminist awareness to the Anglo-Jewish community of London through a public lecture in 1874.[4] Galchinsky speculates that Goldsmid's campaign for women's education provoked the *Jewish Chronicle* anti-feminist letter, yet by signing her name to two letters directly responding to the initial correspondent, it is Levy who explicitly favors women's rights. Levy took issue with the emotional, intellectual, and social suffocation inherent in a life that precluded any aspirations

---

1 See Appendix C2.
2 See Appendix B3.
3 Blind does observe that Eliot's 1878 essay "The Modern Hep! Hep! Hep!" renders the "amalgamation" of Jews and gentiles inevitable in English culture. See Appendix C1.
4 Michael Galchinsky, *The Origin of the Modern Jewish Woman Writer: Romance and Reform in Victorian England* (Detroit: Wayne State UP, 1996) 198-200.

beyond domesticity: "But I doubt if even the great thought of becoming in time a favourable specimen of the genus 'maiden-aunt' would be sufficient to console many a restless, ambitious woman for the dreary performance of work for which she is quite unsuited, for the quenching of personal hopes for the develop-ment of her own intellect."[1] Detectable here is Levy's trademark irony, a rhetorical strategy of bridging opposed tones or points of view that she hones in much of her writing. This literary device seems particularly apt to Levy's double-consciousness as a uni-versity-educated Anglo-Jewish woman who intimated same-sex desires in her poetry. From the *Jewish Chronicle* letters and "Xan-tippe" to other poems, fiction, and essays, Levy's investment in expanding the horizons of modern women's lives complements her acute vision of the disabilities of gender as well as Jewishness. At this early age, Levy took a bold feminist stance, closing her letter by asserting that "those who pay taxes should also have some voice in deciding by whom those taxes should be imposed."

Writing seven years later in *The Jewish Chronicle*, Levy deplores the lot of acculturated Jewish woman "taught to look upon mar-riage as the only satisfactory termination to her career" and dis-couraged from "healthy, objective activities, of the natural employment of her young faculties, of anything in short which diverts her attention from what should be the one end and aim of her existence!"[2] Levy uses what Edward Said has termed "orien-talism" to advance women's rights by describing Jewish men as "oriental at heart." Orientalism refers to a variety of nineteenth-century discourses that represent Western fantasies about Eastern cultures.[3] With Hebrew as a semitic language, Jews throughout the European Diaspora were categorized as "Eastern" by ethnologists and academic "Orientalists" who studied the cultures of the near and far East. Arguing against restrictions placed on women in contrast to male privilege, Levy invokes orientalist images of gender relations in Anglo-Jewry where "the shadow of the harem has rested on our womankind" unlike more modern—equated here with Western European— attitudes toward women's lives. Inflected by the prevailing views of British ethnocentrism, Levy identifies this resistance to mod-ernizing gender roles among English Jews as an attribute of non-Western cultures.

---

1 See Appendix B1.
2 See Appendix B3.
3 Edward Said, *Orientalism* (New York: Vintage Books, 1979) 1-4.

Perceiving this entrenched opposition tinges Levy's expectations of broadening opportunities for her female co-religionists: "That a change is coming o'er the spirit of the communal dream cannot be denied; but it is coming very slowly and at the cost of much suffering to every one concerned. The assertion even of comparative freedom on the part of a Jewess often means the severance of the closest ties, both of family and of our race."[1] As with many minority cultures, the Anglo-Jewish community Levy depicts clings to customs of femininity and masculinity as a way to preserve Jewish identity in the face of assimilation. With her remarkable education at Brighton and Cambridge, and the network of intellectual women and men she knew in London, Levy was in the vanguard with her feminist interpretation of modern English Jewishness.

In the last decades of the nineteenth century, a variety of publications were replete with criticism of traditional, middle-class marriages, a thread in the "Woman Question" debates about the condition of contemporary women with regard to education, legal rights and representation, marriage, motherhood, occupation, and sexuality. Mona Caird's 1888 exposé on the history of marriage as a patriarchal institution recommends a "free union" for women and men outside of the law rather than legal matrimony.[2] Responding to Caird's analysis, Clementina Black acknowledged that the law denied married women "the freedom of action which more and more women are coming to regard not only as their just right but also as their dearest treasure; and this naturally causes a certain unwillingness on the part of thoughtful women to marry."[3] Levy reoriented contemporary critiques of marriage as an institution that belittled and stifled women to acculturated Anglo-Jewry. *Reuben Sachs* represents Levy's most intricate and impassioned elaboration of this argument.

Reuben Sachs As Feminist and Cultural Critique

Expanding upon the cameo critique of Jewish patriarchy and sexism in *Daniel Deronda*, *Reuben Sachs* conflates the "marriage plot" of Gwendolen Harleth and the "Jewish plot" of the title character in Eliot's novel. Where *Daniel Deronda* opens with

---

1 See Appendix B3.
2 Mona Caird, "Marriage," *Westminster Review* 130 (August 1888): 186–201.
3 See Appendix E1.

Gwendolen's story, overshadowed later by the narrative turn to Daniel's Judaism, *Reuben Sachs* reverses this focus by shifting the narrative attention from Reuben in the first half to Judith Quixano in the second part, who, like Gwendolen, is forced to "worship at the shrine of the great god Expediency" (139) and marry a man to whom she is indifferent: "Bertie, as Gwendolen Harleth said of Grandcourt, was not disgusting. He took his love, as he took his religion, very theoretically" (146). This blurring of plots epitomizes the double-consciousness of Levy's vision of an acculturated Jewish woman encumbered by the parochialism of "the tribal duck-pond" of West London Jewry in contrast to "the wider and deeper waters of society" (69). Implicitly the novel models how the defining gazes of gentile society infiltrate the narration and characters' representations of their Jewishness.

Conveying this double-consciousness in the opening pages of *Reuben Sachs*, the narrator portrays Reuben's female relatives talking in "rapid, nervous tones peculiar to them" and wearing ostentatious jewels that convey "the same relation to their owners as his pigtail does to the Chinaman." Reuben himself speaks in "unmistakably the voice of a Jew," with facial features that reveal "his Semitic origin," and a body described as "bad" with "awkward" movements, "unmistakably the figure and movements of a Jew." Such essentializing and unflattering descriptions beg the question of the narrator's relationship to the author, and many readers have charged Levy with holding and perpetuating the views—much like Knox's ethnological account of "the Jewish race"—that she represents early in the novel. A reviewer in *The Academy* comments, "Miss Levy gives one the impression of having laid bare the failings of her people with a rather merciless hand, assuming, perhaps, by right of kinship a freedom of description which might be resented as 'flat perjury' if indulged in by an unprivileged Gentile." The Victorian Anglo-Jewish press was united in its censure of *Reuben Sachs* and Julia Frankau's 1887 novel *Dr. Phillips: A Maida Vale Idyll*. Criticism from *The Jewish World* typifies the perception that Levy "apparently delights in the task of persuading the general public that her own kith and kin are the most hideous types of vulgarity; she revels in misrepresentations of their customs and modes of thought and she is proud of being able to offer her testimony in support of the anti-Semitic theories of the clannishness of her people and the tribalism of their religion."[1]

---

1 See Appendix A for these reviews of *Reuben Sachs*.

Both readers infer that Levy's own opinions are identical with the narrator's views.

However, this assumption that the narrator is a mouthpiece for the author's viewpoints, and that Levy is deliberately or unwittingly perpetuating pernicious stereotypes about Jews, discounts the stylistic ways in which Levy's writing negotiates the "complex problem" of imagining Jewishness at a historical moment in which particular discourses of nationalism and racism shape portraits of Jews in literature. Performing the double-consciousness of a nearly but not quite assimilated Jewish identity, the novel rehearses competing ways of representing Jews in late-Victorian England as a backcloth for Levy's feminist critique which revolves around the central female character, Judith, whose name means "Jewess" in Hebrew. As formal devices for conveying this cultural double-vision, Levy's innovations include overlapping gazes from "within and without the tribal limits," the fracturing of voice and narrative, and a spare and salient use of symbolism. Anticipating the "inward turn" of modernism, Levy's formal experiments in *Reuben Sachs* bespeak the inadequacy of realism for other "new woman" writers of the late nineteenth century. Elaine Showalter has observed that the short story offered "flexibility and freedom from the traditional plots of the three-decker Victorian novel" as well as "psychological intensity and formal innovation."[1] As a blurred genre, *Reuben Sachs* falls in between a short story and a novel, and Levy's subtitle "A Sketch" resonates with her literary impressionism.

The most crucial kind of boundary crossing that Levy investigates in the novel is the mingling of "inside" and "outside" visions of Jews. Published in the aftermath of the critical reception of *Reuben Sachs*, "Cohen of Trinity" portrays the anguished and at times unflattering title character through the detached and perplexed first-person narrator, who is a non-Jewish Cambridge graduate. With this division between narrator and character as a framework, the story functions as Levy's retrospective reading instructions for *Reuben Sachs*, with its narrator drawing upon varied discourses about Jews in the late nineteenth century. According to Cynthia Scheinberg, Levy's poetry and prose give ample evidence of the extent to which Victorian Anglo-Jewish

---

1 Elaine Showalter, *Daughters of Decadence: Women Writers of the Fin-de-Siècle* (Rutgers UP, 1993) viii-ix.

and Christian discourses were intertwined.[1] Like the narrator's framing eye in "Cohen of Trinity," the epigraph of the opening chapter of *Reuben Sachs*, "This is my beloved Son," taken from the Christian Gospels about Jesus Christ, implies that any depiction of Jewish culture and religion is necessarily focused through Christian texts and gentile perspectives. In a chapter on Jewish observance during Yom Kippur, the narrator comments on Esther Kohnthal's absence from synagogue: "She, poor soul, was of those who deny utterly the existence of the Friend of whom she stood so sorely in need" (91). Esther's spiritual salvation here depends on her belief in "the Friend," a familiar allusion to Christ. By inserting this missionary trope at the close of the novel's sole chapter devoted to synagogue practices, Levy implies that Christian typology—where Jewish texts are read as incomplete narratives that prefigure what the Gospels fulfill—imbues even depictions of contemporary Anglo-Judaism. In other words, there is no "outside" to or detachment from Christian interpretive frames. From the opening epigraph to the gilt cross on top of the Prince Albert Memorial that dominates the view from Judith's window in the novel's epilogue, Christian imagery punctuates Levy's portrayal of middle-class Anglo-Jewry.

This blurring of perspectives in *Reuben Sachs* accentuates the difficulties of cultural translation. First, the narrator calls attention to the exclusivity of insider knowledge in this London Anglo-Jewish community, "with its innumerable trivial class differences, its sets within sets, its fine-drawn distinctions of caste, utterly incomprehensible to an outsider" (69). In her 1886 essay "Jewish Humour" Levy offers a different instance of this inaccessible local knowledge: "a humour so fine, so peculiar, so distinct in flavour, that we believe it impossible to impart its perception to any one not born a Jew. The most hardened Agnostic deserter from the synagogue enjoys its pungency, where the zealous alien convert to Judaism tastes nothing but a little bitterness."[2] Second, the character of Bertie Lee-Harrison represents the outsider gaze of "one not born a Jew" and "the zealous alien convert." The novel's approximation of the English gentleman,

---

1   Cynthia Scheinberg, "Amy Levy and the Accents of Minor(ity) Poetry," *Women's Poetry and Religion in Victorian England* (Cambridge: Cambridge UP, 2003) 181-82.

2   "Jewish Humour" in *The Jewish Chronicle* (20 August 1886): 10. Reprinted in Melvyn New, *The Complete Novels and Selcted Writings of Amy Levy, 1861-1889* (Gainesville: UP of Florida, 1993) 523-24.

Bertie signifies the "alien presence" (96) lodged within Du Bois's theory of double-consciousness. With Bertie described as "gone over body and soul to the Jewish community," his conversion comes off as a chapter in the escapades of a dilettante with a "taste for religion" who previously "flirted with the Holy Mother," presumably Roman Catholicism, then "joined a set of mystics ... somewhere in Asia Minor. Now he has come round to thinking Judaism the one religion, and has been regularly received into the synagogue"[1] (64). Bertie searches for specimens that fit his cultural fantasy of orientalized Jews, and instead is baffled and disappointed by the acculturated younger members of the Sachs family because they lack "local colour."

Despite Bertie's fetishistic desire to master Judaism, the narrative reveals the cultural complexities of Jewishness that elude the convert's grasp. For instance, Bertie approaches the family gathering after Yom Kippur with an idealized reverence for Jewish rituals as Solomon Sachs commences to *bench*, to sing the grace after the meal. To Bertie, this "solemn moment" signifies the "performance of the ancient rites in the land of exile," yet he is puzzled by "the spirit of indifference, of levity even, which appeared to prevail" (97) as he fails to comprehend the generation gap between the Sachs patriarch and his more Anglicized grandchildren. Reversing the initial narratorial gaze in which Reuben and his relatives appear as peculiar orientalized specimens, now the narrator ridicules Bertie as the naive cultural tourist: "Bertie stared and Bertie wondered. Needless to state, he was completely out of touch with these people whose faith his search for the true religion had led him, for the time being, to embrace" (98). Here too Levy switches the vantage points of inside and outside, of minority and dominant gazes, by trivializing Bertie's vision as awestruck staring. In addition, Bertie's character offers a counterpoint to conversion narratives, a staple in English portrayals of Jews who are redeemed socially as well as spiritually through baptism, or who attempt to pass as Christians by masking their Jewish faith, in the tradition of crypto-Jews after the expulsion of Jews from the Iberian Peninsula.[2] At times, Bertie's language

---

1 Anthony Trollope's character Bertie Stanhope in *Barchester Towers* (1857) suggests a model for Levy's Bertie; both are dilettantish weak men with dubious interests in Catholicism and Judaism.

2 On conversion narratives in nineteenth-century Britain, see Michael Ragussis, *Figures of Conversion: "The Jewish Question" and English National Identity* (Durham: Duke UP, 1995).

approximates that of the ethnologist researching "the Jewish character ... the strongly marked contrasts; the underlying resemblances; the elaborate differentiations from a fundamental type—!" (98). Levy's choreography of gazes both reinforces the ubiquity of scientific discourse undergirding projects of social classification like "the Jewish type" of Galton's eugenics, and also renders race science a partial and inadequate form of knowledge. Just as the ethnologist gaze Bertie projects seeps into the novel's narrating voice, orientalized notions of Jewishness color Judith's view of Reuben with his "imperturbable air of Eastern gravity" (65), again demonstrating the infiltration of dominant discourses, even if uneven and diverse, into Anglo-Jewish self-representations.

That the novel both reinforces and derides "the Jewish character" as "a fundamental type" signifies another blending, the juxtaposition of sober and comic ways of portraying the objectifying gaze of Jews. This ambivalence qualifies Levy's assessment of the Jewish condition in "Jewish Humour" where she cites Heine's line "I am laughing, too—and dying," and then goes on to explain, "The Poet stretched on his couch of pain; the nation whose shoulders are sore with the yoke of oppression; both can look up with rueful humourous eyes and crack their jests, as it were, in the face of Fortune."[1] This vacillation between serious and comic depictions of Jewish persecution figures within Jewish culture, from Purim—the holiday that retells a story of oppression with humor—to Passover, the tragic variation on the same theme. In effect, *Reuben Sachs* makes clear that there is no neutral vantage point from which to portray Anglo-Jewishness, a necessarily blurred and ambiguous identity, the condition of diasporic double-consciousness.

Boundary crossing also occurs through Levy's use of free indirect discourse diluting borders between narrator and character. When Bertie appears at the Leunigers' dance party, he "remained transfixed a moment in excited admiration" (113). The next paragraph dissolves the narrator's gaze into Bertie's enthrallment with Judith: "What a beautiful woman was this cousin, or pseudo-cousin, of Sachs's! How infinitely better bred she seemed

---

1 "Jewish Humour" in *The Jewish Chronicle* (20 August 1886): 9.
   Reprinted in Melvyn New, *The Complete Novels and Selected Writings of Amy Levy, 1861-1889* (Gainesville: UP of Florida, 1993) 523-24.

than the people surrounding her!" In keeping with Bertie's obsession with Judaism, Judith's value derives from her "Sephardic mystique," the exotic status attributed to the Sephardim in contrast to the vulgarity affiliated with the Ashkenazim, and she becomes the representative fetish of his desires for Judaism. There are numerous instances like this, when the narrator's voice bleeds into a character's perspective, from Bertie and Reuben early in the novel to Esther and Judith later on as the focus shifts to the particular predicaments of Anglo-Jewish women.

Thus, the novel fractures any unified perspective on Jewish identity, and by doing so, articulates the problem of authentic Jewishness and, by extension, authentic Englishness. Diasporic Judaism of modern day has been, comments Reuben, "modified, as we ourselves have been modified, by the influence of western thought and western morality" (101). Just as the narration dissolves boundaries between insider and outsider, and between narrator and character, so do the lines between realism and romance, between pessimism and idealism, and between anti-Semitism and philo-Semitism also converge. Reuben's cousin Leo, educated at Cambridge, ventriloquizes pejorative stereotypes of Judaism as "the religion of materialism" where "steeped to the lips in sordidness, as we have all been from the cradle, how is it possible that any one among us, by his own effort, can wipe off from his soul the hereditary stain?" (101). In this dialogue at the heart of the novel, Reuben and Leo debate the "Jewish Question" in contemporary English culture, with Reuben claiming Jewish "virtues" to offset Leo's litany of Jewish "faults."

On the question of the future of English Jews, the novel again explores a double-consciousness. Leo anticipates Jewish "disintegration" through "absorption complete, inevitable" as "the price we are bound to pay for restored freedom and consideration," while Reuben believes "the tide" of assimilation "will ebb in the intervals of flowing."[1] For Leo, Jewish identity is represented through the lens of antisemitic realism, while for Reuben, Jewishness assumes a philosemitic, romanticized quality of "unspeakable mysteries, affinity and—love." Yet even these opposing views become less distinct. Leo's revulsion for Jewishness is mollified as a youthful "revolt" eventually to be displaced

---

1 For George Eliot's 1878 discussion of this issue, see Appendix C1.

by "love for his race," and Reuben's philosemitic vision of an intrinsic Jewish bond that transcends social exigencies remains illusionary, a metaphysical Judaism as vulnerable as his own survival. Reuben's romance of Judaism is synonymous with—and as unfeasible as—his love for Judith. Although Levy is ultimately interested in Judith's fate, she does suggest the dilemmas of the ambitious acculturated hero seeking a parliamentary career, whose unstable position as Jewish in the public sphere means that he must marry well, like Gwendolen Harleth and other heroines of domestic fiction. In this current of ambivalence that runs throughout the novel, there are fleeting moments of nostalgic reverence for an idealized Jewish spirituality lost in contemporary England. Judith's father, Joseph Quixano, the "dusty scholar" absorbed in his own world of past ideas as he researches for his "monograph on the Jews of Spain and Portugal," signifies the traditional link between Jewish piety and scholarship. In a brief epiphany, Judith sees her father as "one of the pure spirits of this world" (86). Yet Joseph Quixano remains in the background, shut in his "room at the back of the house" as "he let the world and life go by unheeded."

Where competing responses to Jewishness for men unfold in the novel, from Leo's racialized self-abhorrence and desire for complete assimilation to the philosemitic romances of both Joseph's reverie with Jewish scholarship and Reuben's spiritual sublimity, for women these attitudes are not viable. Through her characterizations of Esther and Judith, Levy demonstrates the necessity of new forms of representation to explore the multiple marginalizations of Anglo-Jewish women. Esther's voice is wry, satiric, and penetrating in contrast to Judith's naivety. With her ironic manner, like the serio-comic style Levy describes in "Jewish Humour," Esther is the crux of the novel's feminist double-consciousness.[1] Unlike Judith, who is imprisoned in the central marriage plot of the novel, Esther reads the world around her from a peripheral position that allows her the novel's vexed voice of truth. Freed from the need or ability to marry because she is "the biggest heiress and the ugliest woman in all Bayswater" (62), Esther, who has nothing to gain, can afford to be one "of those who walk naked and are not ashamed" (116). Expressing anger about the disabilities of Jewish women, Esther

---

1 For an analysis of Esther as "the novel's feminist," see Meri-Jane Rochelson, "Jews, Gender, and Genre in Late-Victorian England: Amy Levy's *Reuban Sachs*," *Women Studies* 25 (1996): 322.

represents an updated, converted version of Levy's Xantippe. As a liminal, caustic presence, Esther provides the reader with acute commentary on Judith's intellectual, social, and emotional suffocation as a dependent woman enclosed within the "tribal duckpond" of West London Anglo-Jewry. Acting as a feminist soothsayer, Esther understands the futility of Judith's love for Reuben and perceives that Bertie is "as obstinate as a mule, and as whimsical as a goat" (148), words that foretell the state of Judith's marriage in the novel's epilogue. In her most scathing accusation of sexism, Esther revises the traditionally gendered morning prayer accordingly, "Cursed art Thou, O Lord my God. Who hast had the cruelty to make me a woman" (129). Again speaking in legible codes, Esther directs these words to Judith in a scene marking Judith's dawning awareness of the impotence of her desires, her inability to effect her own destiny.

Interestingly, Esther's significance in Levy's novel is echoed by Israel Zangwill, who gives the name "Esther" to his leading female character in *Children of the Ghetto*, published a few years after *Reuben Sachs*. In Zangwill's novel, which compares immigrant poor Jews of East End London with their West London co-religionists, Esther Ansell writes *Mordecai Jacobs*, a story about the rank materialism and spiritual vacuity of acculturated Kensington Jewry and is assailed by her community for this betrayal.[1] In this fictional account that mimics—but with unusual sympathy—the reception to *Reuben Sachs*, Zangwill revised his initial 1889 responses to Levy's novel in *The Jewish Standard*. First he wrote in doggerel, "Dr. Reuben Green: A Study of the Maida Vale Jewish Colony," a conflation in three stanzas of the plots of *Reuben Sachs* and *Dr. Phillips*.[2] A week later he followed this comic diatribe with a more somber effort deploring these novels as "unflattering pictures of us" and as "the bipedal cuttle-fish squirting its nauseous black fluid on to clean paper and calling the result a picture."[3] Following Levy's death, however, Zangwill remarked about Levy and her controversial novel, "She was accused ... of fouling her own nest; whereas what she had really done was to point out that the nest was fouled and must be cleaned out."[4]

---

1 See Appendix C3.
2 "Dr. Reuben Green," *The Jewish Standard* (1 March 1892): 9-10.
3 "A Misunderstood Marshallik," *The Jewish Standard* (8 March 1889): 7.
4 Quoted in Bryan Cheyette, "From Apology to Revolt: Benjamin Farjean, Amy Levy and the Post-Emancipation Anglo-Jewish Novel," *Transactions of the Jewish Historical Society of England* (January 1985): 253-65.

Levy reserves her most stylistic innovations in *Reuben Sachs* to convey Judith's evolving double-consciousness about her social fate, which coincides with her sexual awakening. Striking instances of literary impressionism through symbolist imagery and terse, fragmented narration occur at moments of crisis for Judith when she loses Reuben twice, at the dance and at the close of the novel. Reacting against the dominant modes of realism and naturalism in literature, the symbolists, at first a group of French writers, emphasized the power of suggestion to evoke an emotional mood rather than explicit, detailed descriptions of mental states. Symbolist writers endowed the well-chosen image with the ability to distill a private mood that could never be wholly captured. Entering literary debates about artistic representation, Levy's friend Vernon Lee wrote on the disadvantages of the psychological realism of George Eliot's novels that attempt to expose "every little moral nerve and muscle" of their characters: "It is not morally correct, any more than it is artistically correct, to see the microscopic and the hidden." Lee's dialectic meditation on contemporary novels voices the position of a range of artists who experimented beyond realism at the end of the nineteenth century, from symbolists, new women writers, decadents, and aesthetes.[1] In a similar vein, Wilde's manifesto for aestheticism over realism in "The Decay of Lying" criticizes adherence to nature and reality in literature: "All bad art comes from returning to life and nature, and elevating them into ideals." Reversing the realist formula that art imitates life, Wilde maintains that "Life imitates Art far more" because "the desire of Life is simply to find expression" and that art facilitates this impulse.[2]

The symbol of "some chrysanthemums like snowflakes in her bodice" (121) furnishes a momentous example of Levy's literary investigation to intimate the emotions of Reuben and Judith. At this pivotal dance scene, Reuben's smoldering desire for Judith is exacerbated through his jealousy over Bertie's "unmistakable devotion" to Judith, who appears "to be devouring her with his eyes." After tearing up Judith's dance card crowded with Bertie's name, Reuben seizes the flowers with these words: "'I am going to commit a theft,' he said, and his low voice shook a little." The narrative devolves into imagistic shards to convey Judith's vulnerability to Reuben's sexual power to possess her and his professional ambitions that thwart this passion. The sensuous com-

---

1 See Appendix C4.
2 See Appendix C5.

plexity of this moment emerges through spare, charged language that affiliates different sensory perceptions, a trademark of Wilde's aestheticism: "It was like a dream to her, a wonderful dream, with which the whirling maze of dancers, the heavy scents, the delicious music were inextricably mingled. And mingling with it also was a strange, harsh sound in the street outside..." (121). Here the external public world of politics interrupts the promise of consummated love symbolized through the white chrysanthemums, figuring for Judith as pure, susceptible, and sexualized. Where the scene suggests Reuben's deflowering impulses here, his abandonment of this act as he pursues his parliamentary career is equally violent in its effect on Judith, again limned through the symbolism of the blossoms: "At her feet lay her own chrysanthemums, crushed by Reuben's departing feet."

Also through impressionistic fragments, the novel's epilogue flouts the conventional Victorian closure. Staccato-like images convey the hollowness of Judith's emotional life due to her marriage and her estrangement from Reuben and "her own people." Symbols once again hint at the incongruity of Judith's double-consciousness. Gazing outside from her Kensington Gardens home, Judith's "eyes mechanically fixed on the glistening gilt cross surmounting the Albert Memorial." Yet within the drawing-room is a medley of "costly, interesting, or merely bizarre" articles, with only two explicitly detailed: "an antique silver *Hanucah* lamp and a spice box, such as the Jews make use of in certain religious services, of the same metal" (152). As with the novel's opening epigraph, the epilogue shows the outside world of Christianity framing the interiority of Anglo-Jewish culture. The language implies that these objects of Jewish holiday rituals are "antique" relics on display rather than features integrated into everyday life. This description of Jewish artifacts recalls the 1887 Anglo-Jewish Historical Exhibition likewise housed in South Kensington, across from the Albert Memorial. Similarly, the narrative conveys Judith's connection to Jewish culture as remote, as she experiences "a strange fit of home-sickness, an inrushing sense of exile."

Judith's emotional atrophy in her bifurcated environment emerges fully in the last pages of the novel. Upon learning that Reuben is again lost to her, Judith "actually smiled," words that betoken a profound incongruity. As the narrative whirls to a close through formally fragmented pieces to represent the chaos of Judith's interiority, externally she becomes "the automatic woman." Eight sets of asterisks break this closure into a series of disjointed images that defy narrative coherence, ricocheting back and forth between interior and external worlds, and across time and space without transitions to the Leuniger dance scene, to Leo in Cambridge, to Reuben's mother on the other side of Kensington Gardens, back to Judith at the window, "a figure of stone." Where the prevailing tone of these proto-modernist images is one of dislocation and despair, the final sentence reasserts its central motif of ambivalence about Judith's future apart from Reuben and "her own people." The novel conveys that in leaving "the tribal duck-pond" of Anglo-Jewry, characters experience a paradoxical yearning for an impossible return. Judith's estrangement resonates with Levy's "Captivity" from her last collection, *A London Plane-Tree*, a poem figuring the perpetual sense of homelessness of diasporic identity:

> Shall I wander in vain for my country?
> Shall I seek and not find?
> Shall I cry for the bars that encage me,
> The fetters that bind?[1]

For Jewish women, Levy suggests, this ambivalence around home and freedom is especially fraught.

Levy's protest against the disenfranchisement of Anglo-Jewish women in *Reuben Sachs* as well as in her *Jewish Chronicle* letters and essay must be read in concert with her varied representations of the emotional, intellectual, social, and sexual complexities of late-nineteenth-century women in her poetry and her other novels, *The Romance of a Shop* and *Miss Meredith*, a retelling of the governess story. Although *Reuben Sachs* offers a slender, impressionistic "sketch" of Anglo-Jewry, Levy provokes difficult questions that defy easy answers about the knottiness of this hyphenated identity, just as she experiments with the borders of literary genre in this late-Victorian novel that anticipates modernism. This compatibility between formal innovations and social nuance makes manifest the ways the novel questions the demarcations between inside and outside perspectives. When Bertie marries Judith, the novel asks, does this finally secure him a place on the "inside" of Anglo-Jewish society? Is Judith left suspended between social identities? Levy's own project of representing English Jewishness is a dialectical process in which an array of

---

1 For the complete text of the poem, see Appendix B5.

discourses and genres forms a contextual landscape to re-imagine Jewish identity. If Jewishness has been ambivalently constructed across racial, religious, and national discourses, Levy's collected writing on Anglo-Jewry, culminating with *Reuben Sachs*, urges her readers to consider the double-consciousness impinging on Jewish women.

Amy Levy: A Brief Chronology

1861   Amy Judith Levy is born on 10 November at 16 Percy Place, Clapham, the second of seven children, to Isabelle Levin Levy and Lewis Levy.

1872   Levy family moves to Regent's Park. Levy and her siblings produce a family magazine, *The Poplar Club Journal*, with articles, short stories, and sketches.

1875   Levy wins junior prize in *Kind Words Magazine for Boys and Girls* for her essay on Elizabeth Barrett Browning's *Aurora Leigh*. Levy's first published poem, "The Ballad of Ida Grey (A Story of a Woman's Sacrifice)," appears in *The Pelican*, a feminist magazine.

1876   Levy enrolls at the new High School for Girls at Brighton, under headmistress Edith Creak, one of the original students at Newnham College, Cambridge.

1879   In February Levy's letter to *The Jewish Chronicle* is printed under the heading, "Jewish Women and 'Women's Rights.'" Her poem "Run to Death: A True Incident of Pre-Revolutionary France" appears in the July issue of *Victoria Magazine*. Levy enrolls at Newnham College, Cambridge, in October.

1880   Levy publishes two short stories: "Euphemia" in *Victoria Magazine* and "Mrs. Pierrepoint" in *Temple Bar*. Female students at Cambridge granted admission to university examinations, although women are denied degrees.

1881   Levy publishes on daily life at Newnham College. *Xantippe and Other Verse* published. Levy leaves Cambridge and travels on the European Continent.

1882   Levy returns to London from Germany and Switzerland. She joins a discussion club for women and men intellectuals and artists, including Karl Pearson, Dollie Radford, Mary Robinson, and Eleanor Marx; the club disbands in 1885. In November she obtains admission to the Reading Room of the British Museum and meets Olive Schreiner, Margaret Harkness, and Beatrice Potter. She publishes translations of poems by Heinrich Heine and Nikolaus Lenau.

1883   "Between Two Stools" appears in *Temple Bar*. "The
        Diary of a Plain Girl" is published in September in
        London Society; this is the first of a series, many in episto-
        lary or diary form, appearing in *London Society* in 1883-
        86, featuring "Melissa."

1884   Levy travels to Germany and Switzerland. "Sokratics in
        the Strand" is published in *The Cambridge Review*, and
        "The New School of American Fiction" appears in
        Temple Bar. In June T. Fisher Unwin publishes *A Minor
        Poet and Other Verse*.

1885   Levy moves with her family to 7 Endsleigh Gardens,
        Bloomsbury. Several stories are published in *London
        Society*, including "Easter-Tide at Tunbridge Wells" and
        "Revenge."

1886   Levy spends a few months in Florence with Clementina
        Black at the Casa Guidi, where she meets Vernon Lee
        (Violet Paget). She returns to London and publishes five
        essays in *The Jewish Chronicle*: "The Ghetto in Florence,"
        "The Jew in Fiction," "Jewish Children," "Jewish
        Humour," and "Middle-Class Jewish Women of To-Day."

1887   The University Club for Ladies opens in New Bond
        Street. Two of Levy's sonnets appear in Elizabeth Sharp's
        *Women's Voices: An Anthology of the Most Characteristic
        Poems by English, Scottish, and Irish Women*.

1888   Levy begins publishing in *The Woman's World* with a short
        story, "The Recent Telepathic Occurrence at the British
        Museum," in the first issue, followed by "The Poetry of
        Christina Rossetti" and "Women and Club Life." *The
        Romance of a Shop* is published by T. Fisher Unwin in
        October. Levy submits the manuscript of *Reuben Sachs*
        to Macmillan and travels to Florence.

1889   *Reuben Sachs: A Sketch* is published by Macmillan in
        January, when Levy returns from Florence. In May *Miss
        Meredith* appears in the *British Weekly* and then in volume
        form. "Readers at the British Museum" is published in
        Atalanta, "Cohen of Trinity" is published in *The Gentle-
        man's Magazine*, and several publications appear in *The
        Woman's World*. On 10 September alone at her family's
        home in London, Levy commits suicide by charcoal
        asphyxiation after correcting proofs for *A London Plane-
        Tree, and Other Verse*, later published in the Cameo Series

of T. Fisher Unwin. Her body is cremated and her ashes buried at Balls Pond Cemetery under the auspices of the West London Synagogue for British Jews on 15 September 1889. Clementina Black's notice about Levy's death appears in *The Athenaeum* in October.

1890   Oscar Wilde's essay on Levy appears in *The Woman's World*. Also appearing in this magazine are four poems by Levy and her short story, "Wise in Her Generation."

1915   Levy's undated poem, "A Ballad of Religion and Marriage," is privately printed and circulated.

Anglo-Jewish History: A Brief Chronology

1144   Accusations of ritual murders (known as "blood libel") by Jews begin with the death of a boy in Norwich. Over the next centuries restrictions on Jews include wearing badges and confinement to "Jewries."

1189   Richard I, a crusader, accedes to the throne, followed by violent attacks against Jews in London that spread to the provinces, including the massacre of 150 Jews at Clifford's Tower in York.

1290   Edward I expels Jews from England.

1656   Jewish resettlement under Cromwell.

1701   Bevis Marks Synagogue opens in London.

1753   A bill (referred to as the "Jew Bill") proposing to naturalize foreign-born Jews is debated in Parliament and incites anti-Jewish outbursts. The bill is not passed.

1817   After severing his ties to the Bevis Marks Synagogue, Isaac D'Israeli permits his four children, including Benjamin, to be baptized in the Church of England.

1829   Catholic Emancipation Act passed.

1831   Thomas Babington Macaulay argues against Jewish disabilities in Parliament.

1833   The first Jewish lawyer is called to the bar.

1835   The first Jewish sheriff of London (David Salomons) is elected.

1841   Francis Goldsmid is the first practicing Jew to be given a baronetcy. The West London Synagogue of British Jews opens with reformed ritual.

1844   *The Jewish Chronicle* is established under Joseph Mitchell.

1847   Lionel de Rothschild is elected to Parliament for the City of London, but refuses to take the required Oath of Abjuration "on the true faith of a Christian."

1855   David Salomons elected first Jewish Lord Mayor of London.

1858   Permitted to omit the words "on the true faith of a Christian" in the Oath of Abjuration, Rothschild takes his seat in Parliament after being elected four times.

1868   Benjamin Disraeli, Jewish by birth and a convert to the Church of England, becomes Prime Minister during this year, and again from 1874 to 1880.

1870   Act of Parliament establishes the United Synagogue.

1871   University Tests Act abolishes membership in the Church of England and compulsory attendance of church services, resulting in the admission of Jews and Catholics to Cambridge, Oxford, and Durham Universities.

1873   Sir George Jessell becomes the first Jewish judge appointed to the High Court Bench.

1879   Amy Levy enters Newnham College as the first Jewish student. (Sarah Marks was the first Jewish student at Girton College, Cambridge, in 1876).

1885   Nathaniel de Rothschild becomes the first Jewish member of the House of Lords.

1887   The Anglo-Jewish Historical Exhibition opens at Royal Albert Hall.

1890   Full emancipation achieved with Jews permitted to occupy positions of Lord Chancellor or Lord Lieutenant for Ireland.

A Note on the Text

The text of *Reuben Sachs: A Sketch* is based on the first edition published in London and New York by Macmillan and Company in 1888. I have corrected inconsistencies in spelling and punctuation.

Reuben Sachs
A Sketch

CHAPTER I.

This is my beloved Son.[1]

Reuben Sachs was the pride of his family.

After a highly successful career at one of the great London day-schools,[2] he had gone up on a scholarship to the University, where, if indeed he had chosen to turn aside from the beaten paths of academic distinction, he had made good use of his time in more ways than one.[3]

The fact that he was a Jew had proved no bar to his popularity; he had gained many desirable friends and had, to some extent, shaken off the provincialism inevitable to one born and bred in the Jewish community.

At the bar, to which in due course he was called, his usual good fortune did not desert him.

Before he was twenty-five he had begun to be spoken of as "rising"; and at twenty-six, by unsuccessfully contesting a hard-fought election, had attracted to himself attention of another sort. He had no objection, he said, to the woolsack;[4] but a career of political distinction was growing slowly but surely to be his leading aim in life.

"He will never starve," said his mother, shrugging her shoulders with a comfortable consciousness of safe investments; "and he must marry money. But Reuben can be trusted to do nothing rash." In the midst of so much that was highly promising, his

---

1 Matthew 3.17, Mark 1.11. A phrase indicating Jesus Christ, usually spoken by God.

2 Typically an independent (not state-sponsored) school that students attended during the day. In a Jewish day school Hebrew and Jewish scripture would be part of the curriculum. The Jewish day schools of late-nineteenth-century West-End and middle-class London included the Westminster Jews' Free School and the Bayswater Schools (see Vivian Lipman, *Social History of the Jews in England, 1850-1950* [London: Watts & Co., 1954] 146-47, and Vivian Lipman, *A History of the Jews in Britain since 1858* [London: Leicester UP, 1990] 29).

3 See Levy's story "Cohen of Trinity" (Appendix B).

4 A seat stuffed with wool on which the Lord Chancellor sits. The Lord Chancellor is a high government official who presides over the House of Lords.

health had broken down suddenly, and he had gone off grumbling to the antipodes.

It was a case of over-work, of over-strain, of nervous breakdown, said the doctors; no doubt a sea-voyage would set him right again, but he must be careful of himself in the future.

"More than half my nervous patients are recruited from the ranks of the Jews," said the great physician whom Reuben consulted. "You pay the penalty of too high a civilization."

"On the other hand," Reuben answered, "we never die; so we may be said to have our compensations."

Reuben's father had not borne out his son's theory; he had died many years before my story opens, greatly to his own surprise and that of a family which could boast more than one nonogenarian in a generation.

He had left his wife and children well provided for, and the house in Lancaster Gate[1] was rich in material comfort.

In the drawing-room of this house Mrs. Sachs and her daughter were sitting on the day of Reuben's return from his six months' absence.

He had arrived early in the day, and was now sleeping off the effects of a night passed in travelling, and of the plentiful supply of fatted calf with which he had been welcomed.

His devoted womankind meanwhile sipped their tea in the fading light of the September afternoon, and talked over the event of the day in the rapid, nervous tones peculiar to them.

Mrs. Sachs was an elderly woman, stout and short, with a wide, sallow, impassive face, lighted up by occasional gleams of shrewdness from a pair of half-shut eyes.

An indescribable air of intense, but subdued vitality characterized her presence; she did not appear in good health, but you saw at a glance that this was an old lady whom it would be difficult to kill.

"He looks better, Addie, he looks very well indeed," she said, the dull red spot of colour on either sallow cheek alone testifying to her excitement.

"I have said all along," answered her daughter, "that if Reuben had been a poor man the doctors would never have found out that he wanted a sea-voyage at all. Let us only hope that it has done him no harm professionally." She emptied her tea-cup as

---

1 Northern entrance to Kensington Gardens and Hyde Park in Bayswater, London.

she spoke, and cut herself a fresh slice of the rich cake which she was devouring with nervous voracity.

Adelaide Sachs, or to give her her right title, Mrs. Montagu Cohen, was a thin, dark young woman of eight or nine-and-twenty, with a restless, eager, sallow face, and an abrupt manner. She was richly and very fashionably dressed in an unbecoming gown of green shot silk, and wore big diamond solitaires in her ears. She and her mother indeed were never seen without such jewels, which seemed to bear the same relation to their owners as his pigtail does to the Chinaman.

Adelaide was the eldest of the family; she had married young a husband chosen for her, with whom she lived with average contentment.

Reuben was scarcely two years her junior; no one cared to remember the age of Lionel, the youngest of the three, a hopeless ne'er-do-weel, who had with difficulty been relegated to an obscure colony.

"There is always either a ne'er-do-weel or an idiot in every Jewish family!" Esther Kohnthal had remarked in one of her appalling bursts of candour.

The mother and daughter sat there in the growing dusk, amid the plush ottomans, stamped velvet tables, and other Philistine splendours of the large drawing-room, till the lamp-lighter came down the Bayswater Road and the gilt clock on the mantel-piece struck six.

Almost at the same moment the door was flung open and a voice cried:

"Why *do* women invariably sit in the dark?"

It was a pleasant voice; to a fine ear, unmistakably the voice of a Jew, though the accents of the speaker were free from the cockney twang which marred the speech of the two women.

"Reuben! I thought you were asleep," cried his mother.

"So I was. Now I have arisen like a giant refreshed."

A man of middle height and slender build had made his way across the room to the window; his face was indistinct in the darkness as he stooped and put his arm caressingly about the broad, fat shoulder of his mother.

"Dressed for dinner already, Reuben?" was all she said, though the hard eye under the cautious old eyelid grew soft as she spoke.

Her love for this son and her pride in him were the passion of her life.

"Dinner? You are never going to kill the fatted calf twice over?

But seriously, I must run down to the club for an hour or two. There may be letters."

He hesitated a moment, then added: "I shall look in at the Leunigers on my way back."

"The Leunigers!" cried Adelaide in open disapproval.

"Reuben, there's the old gentleman. He won't like your going first to your cousins," said his mother.

"My grandfather? Oh, but my arrival isn't an official fact till to-morrow. We were sixteen hours before our time, remember. Good-bye, Addie. I suppose you and Monty will be dining in Portland Place[1] to-morrow with the rest of us. What a gathering of the clans! Well, I must be off." And he suited the action to the word.

"Why on earth need he rush off like that to the Leunigers?" said Mrs. Cohen as she drew on her gloves.

Her mother looked across at her through the dusk.

"Reuben will do nothing rash," she said.

CHAPTER II.

Whatever my mood is, I love Piccadilly.

London Lyrics.[2]

Reuben Sachs stepped into the twilit street with a distinct sense of exhilaration.

He was back again; back to the old, full, strenuous life which was so dear to him; to the din and rush and struggle of the London which he loved with a passion that had something of poetry in it.

With the eager curiosity, the vivid interest in life, which underlay his rather impassive bearing, it was impossible that foreign travel should be without charm for him; but he returned with unmixed delight to his own haunts; to the work and the play; the market-place, and the greetings in the market-place; to the innumerable pleasantnesses of an existence which owed something of its piquancy to the fact that it was led partly in the democratic

---

1 A street just south of Regent's Park in Marylebone, London.
2 Frederick Locker Lampson (1821-95), "Piccadilly," line 4, *London Lyrics* (1857).

atmosphere of modern London, partly in the conservative precincts of the Jewish community.

Now as he lingered a moment on the pavement, looking up and down the road for a hansom, the light from the street lamp fell full upon him, revealing what the darkness of his mother's drawing-room had previously hidden from sight.

He was, as I have said, of middle height and slender build. He wore good clothes, but they could not disguise the fact that his figure was bad, and his movements awkward; unmistakably the figure and movements of a Jew.

And his features, without presenting any marked national trait, bespoke no less clearly his Semitic origin.[1]

His complexion was of a dark pallor; the hair, small moustache and eyes, dark, with red lights in them; over these last the lids were drooping, and the whole face wore for the moment a relaxed, dreamy, impassive air, curiously Eastern, and not wholly free from melancholy.

He walked slowly in the direction of an advancing hansom, hailed it quickly and quietly, and had himself driven off to Pall Mall.[2] To every movement of the man clung that indescribable suggestion of an irrepressible vitality which was the leading characteristic of his mother.

There were several letters for him at the club; having discussed them, and been greeted by half a dozen men of his acquaintance, he dined lightly off a chop and a glass of claret, and gave himself up to what was apparently an exceedingly pleasant reverie.

The club where he sat was not, as he himself would have been the first to acknowledge, in the front rank of such institutions; but it was respectable and had its advantages. As for its drawbacks, supported by his sense of better things to come, Reuben Sachs could tolerate them.

It was nearly half past eight when Reuben's cab drew up before the Leunigers' house in Kensington Palace Gardens,[3] where a blaze of light from the lower windows told him that he had come on no vain errand.

---

1   For a historical context here, see Robert Knox on Jews in *The Races of Men* and Joseph Jacobs on "the Jewish type" in composite photography (both in Appendix D) as examples of the scientific discourse on race in Victorian culture.

2   Near St. James Park and Charing Cross, Pall Mall was the central location of men's clubs in London.

3   Neighborhood adjacent to the west side of Kensington Park.

Israel Leuniger had begun life as a clerk on the Stock Exchange, where he had been fortunate enough to find employment in the great broking firm of Sachs & Co. There his undeniable business talents and devotion to his work had met with ample reward. He had advanced from one confidential post to another; after a successful speculation on his own account, had been admitted into partnership, and finally, like the industrious apprentice of the story books, had married his master's daughter.

In these days the reins of government in Capel Court[1] had fallen almost entirely into his hands. Solomon Sachs, though a wonderful man of his years, was too old for regular attendance in the city, while poor Kohnthal, the other member of the firm, and, like Leuniger, son-in-law to old Solomon, had been shut up in a madhouse for the last ten years and more.

As Reuben advanced into the large, heavily upholstered vestibule, one of the many surrounding doors opened slowly, and a woman emerged with a vague, uncertain movement into the light.

She might have been fifty years of age, perhaps more, perhaps less; her figure was slim as a girl's, but the dark hair, uncovered by a cap, was largely mixed with gray. The long, oval face was of a deep, unwholesome, sallow tinge; and from its haggard gloom looked out two dark, restless, miserable eyes; the eyes of a creature in pain. Her dress was rich but carelessly worn, and about her whole person was an air of neglect.

"Aunt Ada!" cried Reuben, going forward.

She rubbed her lean sallow hands together, saying in low, broken, lifeless tones: "We didn't expect you till to-morrow, Reuben. I hope your health has improved." This was quite a long speech for Mrs. Leuniger, who was of a monosyllabic habit.

Before Reuben could reply, the door opposite the one from which his aunt had emerged was flung open, and two little boys, dressed in sailor-suits, rushed into the hall.

One was dark, with bright black eyes; the other had a shock of flame-coloured hair, and pale, prominent eyes. "Reuben!" they cried in astonishment, and rushed upon their cousin.

"Lionel! Sidney!" protested their mother faintly as the boys proceeded to take all sorts of liberties with the new arrival.

The door by which they had come opened again, and a man's voice cried, half in fun:

---

1   The location of the London Stock Exchange, and thus identified with it, adjacent to the Bank of England in the City of London.

"Why on earth are you youngsters making this confounded row? Be off to bed, or you'll be sorry for it!"

Reuben was standing under the light of a lamp, a smile on his face, as he lifted little red-haired Sidney from the ground and held him suspended by his wide sailor-collar.

"It's Reuben, old Reuben come back!" cried the children.

An exclamation followed; the door was flung open wide; Reuben set down the child with a laugh and passed into the lighted room.

CHAPTER III.

How should Love,
Whom the cross-lightnings of four chance-met eyes
Flash into fiery life from nothing, follow
Such dear familiarities of dawn?
Seldom; but when he does, Master of all.

Aylmer's Field.[1]

The Leunigers' drawing-room, in which Reuben now found himself, was a spacious apartment, hung with primrose coloured satin, furnished throughout in impeccable Louis XV. and lighted with incandescent gas from innumerable chandeliers and sconces. Beyond, divided by a plush-draped alcove, was a room of smaller size, where, at present, could be discerned the intent, Semitic faces of some half-dozen card-players.

In the front room four or five young people in evening dress were grouped, but at Reuben's entrance they all came forward with various exclamations of greeting.

"Thought you weren't coming back till to-morrow!"

"I shouldn't have known you; you're as brown as a berry!"

"See the conquering hero comes!"

This last from Rose Leuniger, a fat girl of twenty, in a tight-fitting blue silk dress, with the red hair and light eyes *à fleur de tête*[2] of her little brother.

"I am awfully glad to see you looking so well," added Leopold Leuniger, the owner of the voice.

---

1 Alfred Lord Tennyson (1809-92), "Aylmer's Field" (1864), lines 128-32.
2 Prominent eyes (French).

He was a short, slight person of one or two-and-twenty, with a picturesque head of markedly tribal character.

The dark, oval face, bright, melancholy eyes, alternately dreamy and shrewd; the charming, humorous smile, with its flash of white even teeth, might have belonged to some poet or musician, instead of to the son of a successful Jewish stockbroker.

By his side stood a small, dark, gnome-like creature, apparently entirely overpowered by the rich, untidy garments she was wearing. She was a girl, or woman, whose age it would be difficult to determine, with small, glittering eyes that outshone the diamonds in her ears.

Her trailing gown of heavy flowered brocade was made with an attempt at picturesqueness; an intention which was further evidenced by the studied untidiness of the tousled hair, and by the thick strings of amber coiled round the lean brown neck.

This was Esther Kohnthal, the only child of poor Kohnthal; and, according to her own account, the biggest heiress and the ugliest woman in all Bayswater.[1]

Shuffling up awkwardly behind her came Ernest Leuniger, the eldest son of the house, of whom it would be unfair to say that he was an idiot. He was nervous, delicate; had a rooted aversion to society; and was obliged by his state of health to spend the greater part of his time in the country.

Esther used to shrug her shoulders and smile shrewdly and unpleasantly whenever this description of what she chose to consider the family skeleton was given out in her hearing; she told every one, quite frankly, that her own father was in a madhouse.

Judith Quixano came up a little behind the others, with a hesitation in her manner which was new to her, and of which she herself was unconscious.

She was twenty-two years of age, in the very prime of her youth and beauty; a tall, regal-looking creature, with an exquisite dark head, features like those of a face cut on gem or cameo, and wonderful, lustrous, mournful eyes, entirely out of keeping with the accepted characteristics of their owner.

Her smooth, oval cheek glowed with a rich, yet subdued, hue of perfect health; and her tight-fitting fashionable white evening dress showed to advantage the generous lines of a figure which was distinguished for stateliness rather than grace.

Reuben Sachs had looked straight at this girl on entering the

---

1 Area of West London including Edgeware Road and adjacent to the west side of Kensington Gardens.

room; but he shook hands with her last of all, clasping her fingers closely and searching her face with his eyes. They were not cousins, her relationship to the Leunigers coming from the father's side; but there had always been between them a fiction of cousinship, which had made possible what is rare all the world over, but rarer than ever in the Jewish community—an intimacy between young people of opposite sexes.

"I thought I had better come while I could. We were before our time," said Reuben as they sat down, the whole party of them grouped close together, with the exception of Ernest, who returned to his solitaire board, a plaything which afforded him perpetual occupation. After several years of practice he had never arrived at leaving the glass marble in solitary state on the board; but he lived in hopes.

"While you could! Before, in fact, fashion had again claimed Mr. Reuben Sachs for her own," cried Esther.

"I don't know about fashion," answered Reuben with perfect good temper; Esther was Esther, and if you began to mind what she said, you would never know where to stop; "but there are a hundred things to be attended to. I suppose every one is going to the grandpater's feed to-morrow?"

Every one was going; then, turning to Leo, Reuben said: "When do you go up?"

"Not till October 14th."

Leopold Leuniger was on the eve of his third year at Cambridge.

"What have you been doing this Long?"[1]

"Oh.... staying about."

"Leo has been stopping with Lord Norwood, but we are not allowed to mention it," cried Rose in her loud, penetrating voice, "in case it should seem that we are proud."

Leo, who was passing through a sensitive phase of his growth, winced visibly, and Reuben said in a matter-of-fact way: "Oh, by the by, I came across a cousin of Lord Norwood's abroad—Lee-Harrison;[2] a curious fellow, but a good fellow."

"A howling swell," added Esther, "with a double-barrelled name."

---

1 I.e., the Long Vacation, the summer break between school year terms.
2 Amy Levy's friend, the poet Vernon Lee, had a brother, Eugene Lee-Hamilton, who was also a poet, although not very accomplished.

"Exactly. But the point about him is that he has gone over body and soul to the Jewish community."[1]

There was an ironical exclamation all round. The Jews, the most clannish and exclusive of peoples, the most keen to resent outside criticism, can say hard things of one another within the walls of the ghetto.

"He says himself," went on Reuben, "that he has a taste for religion. I believe he flirted with the Holy Mother for some years, but didn't get caught. Then he joined a set of mystics, and lived for three months on a mountain, somewhere in Asia Minor. Now he has come round to thinking Judaism the one religion, and has been regularly received into the synagogue."

"And expects, no doubt," said Esther, "to be rejoiced over as the one sinner that repenteth.[2] I hope you didn't shatter his illusions by telling him that he would more likely be considered a fool for his pains?"

Reuben laughed, and with an amused expression on his now animated face went on: "He has a seat in Berkeley Street,[3] and a brand new *talith*,[4] but still he is not happy. He complains that the Jews he meets in society are unsatisfactory; they have no local colour. I said I thought I could promise him a little local colour; I hope to have the pleasure of introducing him to you all."

They all laughed with the exception of Rose, who said, rather offended: "I don't know about local colour. We don't wear turbans."

Reuben put back his head, laughing a little, and seeking Judith's eyes for the answering smile he knew he should find there.

She had been keeping rather in the background to-night, quietly but intensely happy.

---

1 While the conversion of Jews to Christianity was an established and long-held practice in the nineteenth century, this reversal, whereby a Christian converts to Judaism, was rare. Although England permitted this practice, in many European countries it was illegal for Christians to convert.

2 See Luke 15.7, 15.10.

3 The West London Synagogue of British Jews, located in Upper Berkeley Street, Edgeware Road, was established in 1840 to reform Anglo-Jewish observance by introducing sermons in English, shortened prayers, later start to sabbath and festival services, a choir, and the abolishment of the second days of festivals. Levy's family were members of this congregation.

4 Prayer shawl; *tallit* (Hebrew) or *tallis* (Yiddish).

Reuben was back again! How delightfully familiar was every tone, every inflection of his voice! And how well she knew the changes of his face: the heavy dreaminess, the imperturbable air of Eastern gravity; then lo! the lifting of the mask; the flash and play of kindling features; the fire of speaking eyes; the hundred lights and shades of expression that she could so well interpret.

"What do his people say to it all?" asked Leo.

"Lee-Harrison's? Oh, I believe they take it very sensibly. They say it's only Bertie," answered Reuben, rising and holding out his hand to his uncle, who sauntered in from the card-room.

He was a short, stout, red-haired man, closely resembling his daughter, and at the present moment looked annoyed. The play was high and he had been losing heavily.

"Let's have some music, Leo," he said, flinging himself into an arm-chair at some distance from the young people. Rose, who was a skilled musician, went over to the piano, and Leopold took his violin from its case.

Reuben moved closer to Judith, and, under cover of the violin tuning, they exchanged a few words.

"I can't tell you how glad I am to get back."

"You look all the better for your trip. But you must take care and not overdo it again. It's bad policy."

"It is almost impossible not to."

"But those committees and meetings and things" (she smiled), "surely they might be cut down?"

"They are often very useful, indirectly, to a man in my position," answered Reuben, who had no intention of saying anything cynical.

There was a good deal of genuine benevolence in his nature, and an almost insatiable energy.

He took naturally to the modern forms of philanthropy: the committees, the classes, the concerts and meetings. He found indeed that they had their uses, both social and political; higher motives for attending them were not wanting; and he liked them for their own sake besides. Out-door sports he detested; the pleasures of dancing he had exhausted long ago; the practice of philanthropy provided a vent for his many-sided energies.

The tuning had come to an end by now, and the musicians had taken up their position.

Immediately silence fell upon the little audience, broken only by the click of counters, the crackle of a bank-note in the room beyond; and the sound of Ernest's solitaire balls as they dropped into their holes.

Mrs. Leuniger, at the first notes of the tuning, had stolen in and taken up a position near the door; Esther had moved to a further corner of the room, where she lay buried in a deep lounge.

Then, all at once, the music broke forth. The great, vulgar, over-decorated room, with its garish lights, its stifling fumes of gas, was filled with the sound of dreams; and over the keen faces stole, like a softening mist, a far-away air of dreamy sensuousness. The long, delicate hands of the violinist, the dusky, sensitive face, as he bent lovingly over the instrument, seemed to vibrate with the strings over which he had such mastery.

The voice of a troubled soul cried out to-night in Leo's music, whose accents even the hard brilliance of his accompanist failed to drown.

As the bow was drawn across the strings for the last time, Ernest's solitaire board fell to the ground with a crash, the little balls of Venetian glass rolling audibly in every direction.

The spell was broken; every one rose, and the card-players, who by this time were hungry, came strolling in from the other room.

Reuben found himself the centre of much handshaking and congratulation on his improved appearance. He was popular with his relatives, enjoying his popularity and accepting it gracefully.

"No airs, like that stuck up Leo," the aunts and uncles used to say.

"There's a spread in the dining-room; won't you stay?" said Rose, as Reuben held out his hand in farewell.

"Not to-night." He turned last of all to Judith, who stood there silent, with smiling eyes.

"To-morrow in Portland Place," he said, clasping her hand with lingering fingers.

As he walked home in the warm September night he had for once neither ears nor eyes for the city pageant so dear to him.

He heard and saw nothing but the sound of Leo's violin, and the face of Judith Quixano.

CHAPTER IV.

The full sum of me
Is an untutored girl, unschooled, unpractised.

Merchant of Venice.[1]

Judith Quixano had lived with the Leunigers ever since she was
fifteen years old.

Her mother, Israel Leuniger's sister, had been thought to do
very well for herself when she married Joshua Quixano, who
came of a family of Portuguese merchants, the *vieille noblesse* of
the Jewish community.[2]

That was before the days of Leuniger's prosperity; now here,
as elsewhere, the prestige of birth had dwindled, that of money
had increased. The Quixanos were a large family, and they had
grown poorer with the years; very gratefully did they welcome the
offer of the rich uncle to adopt their eldest daughter.

So Judith had been borne away from the little crowded house
in a dreary region lying somewhere between Westbourne Park
and Maida Vale[3] to the splendours of Kensington Palace
Gardens.

Here she had shared everything with her cousin Rose: the
French and German governesses, the expensive music lessons,
the useless, pretentious "finishing" lessons from innumerable
masters.

Later on, the girls, who were about of an age, had gone
together into such society as their set afforded; and here, again,
no difference had been made between them. The gowns and
bonnets of Rose were neither more splendid nor more abundant
than those of her poor relation, nor her invitations to parties
more numerous.

---

1 Shakespeare, *The Merchant of Venice* III.ii.157–59.
2 By *vieille noblesse* or old élite (French), Levy refers to the Sephardim,
  Jews and their descendants from Asia Minor and the Iberian Peninsula,
  in contrast to the *Ashkenazim*, Jews of the Franco-German traditions
  and Eastern Europe. The Sephardim, a much smaller portion of the
  Anglo-Jewish population, were viewed as more scholarly and genuinely
  devout in contrast to prejudice against the Ashkenazim.
3 Westbourne Park is west of Paddington and north of Kensington
  Gardens; Maida Vale is north of Edgeware Road.

Rose, it is true, had a fortune of £50,000; but it was a matter of common knowledge that her uncle would settle £5000 on Judith when she married.

The cousins were good friends after a fashion. Rose was a materialist to her fingers' ends; she was lacking in the finer feelings, perhaps even in the finer honesties. But on the other hand she was easy to live with, good-tempered, good-natured, high-spirited; qualities which cover a multitude of sins.

It will be seen that in their own fashion, and according to their own lights, the Leunigers had been very kind to Judith. She had no ground for complaint; nor indeed was there anything but gratitude in her thoughts of them. If, at times, she was discontented, she was only vaguely aware of her own discontent. To rail at fate, to cry out against the gods, were amusements she left to such people as Esther and Leo, for whom, in her quiet way, she had considerable contempt.

But the life, the position, the atmosphere, though she knew it not, were repressive ones. This woman, with her beauty, her intelligence, her power of feeling, saw herself merely as one of a vast crowd of girls awaiting their promotion by marriage.

She had, it is true, the advantage of good looks; on the other hand she was, comparatively speaking, portionless; and the marriageable Jew, as Esther was fond of saying, is even rarer and shyer than the marriageable Gentile.

To marry a Gentile would have been quite out of the question for her. Mr. Leuniger, thorough-going pagan as he was, would have set his foot mercilessly on such an arrangement; it would not have seemed to him respectable. He was no stickler for forms and ceremonies; though while old Solomon lived a certain amount of observance of them was necessary; you need only marry a Jew and be buried at Willesden or Balls Pond;[1] the rest would take care of itself.

But, her uncle's views apart, Judith's opportunities for uniting herself to an alien were small.

The Leunigers had of course their Gentile acquaintance, chiefly people of the sham "smart," pseudo-fashionable variety,

---

1 Nineteenth-century cemeteries where Jews were allowed to be buried. Levy's ashes were interred at Balls Pond under the auspices of the West London Synagogue; she was the first Jewish woman to be cremated in England.

whose parties at Bayswater or South Kensington they attended. But the business of their lives, its main interests, lay almost entirely within the tribal limits. It was as Hebrews of the Hebrews that Solomon Sachs and his son-in-law took their stand.

In the Community, with its innumerable trivial class differences, its sets within sets, its fine-drawn distinctions of caste, utterly incomprehensible to an outsider, they held a good, though not the best position. They were, as yet, socially on their promotion. The Sachses and the Leunigers, in their elder branches, troubled themselves, as we have seen, little enough about their relations to the outer world; but the younger members of the family, Reuben, Leo, even Adelaide and Esther in their own crude fashion, showed symptoms of a desire to strike out from the tribal duck-pond into the wider and deeper waters of society. Such symptoms, their position and training considered, were of course, inevitable; and the elders looked on with pride and approval, not understanding indeed the full meaning of the change.

But as for Judith Quixano, and for many women placed as she, it is difficult to conceive a training, an existence, more curiously limited, more completely provincial than hers. Her outlook on life was of the narrowest; of the world, of London, of society beyond her own set, it may be said that she had seen nothing at first hand; had looked at it all, not with her own eyes, but with the eyes of Reuben Sachs.

She could scarcely remember the time when she and Reuben had not been friends. Ever since she was a little girl in the schoolroom, and he a charming lad in his first terms at the University, he had thought it worth while to talk to her, to confide to her his hopes, plans and ambitions; to direct her reading and lend her books.

Books were a luxury in the Leuniger household. We all have our economies, even the richest of us; and the Leunigers, who begrudged no money for food, clothes or furniture, who went constantly into the stalls of the theatre, without considering the expense, regarded every shilling spent on books as pure extravagance.

Reuben indeed was the only person who had any conception of Judith's possibilities, or, of those surrounding her, who even estimated at its full her rich and stately beauty. Their friendship, unusual enough in a society which retains, in relation to women at least, so many traces of orientalism,[1] had sprung up at first unnoticed in the intimacy of family life.

It was not till the last year or two that it had attracted any serious attention. Adelaide Cohen openly did everything in her power to check it; and even Mrs. Sachs, with her rooted belief in her son's discretion, her conviction that he would never fail to act up to his creed of doing the very best for himself, grew anxious at times, and was almost glad of the chance which had sent him off to the antipodes.

Aloud to her daughter, she scouted the notion of any serious cause for alarm.

"It is for the girl's sake I am sorry. That sort of thing does a girl a great deal of harm. It is time she was married."

"She has no money. Very likely she won't marry at all," cried Adelaide, who was dyspeptic and subject to fits of bad temper.

Meanwhile Judith, acquiescent, receptive, appreciative, took the good things this friendship offered her, and shut her eyes to the future. Not, as she believed, that she ever for a moment deceived herself. That would scarcely have been possible in the atmosphere in which she breathed.

She had known from the beginning, how could she fail to know? that Reuben must do great things for himself in every relation of life; must ultimately climb to inaccessible heights where she could not hope to follow.

Her pride and her humility went hand in hand, and she prided herself on her own good sense which made any mistake in the matter impossible. And that he was so sensible, was what she particularly admired in Reuben.

Leo was clever, she knew; and Esther after a fashion; but these two people had an uncomfortable, eccentric, undignified method of setting about things, from the way they did their hair, upwards.

But Reuben had sacrificed none of his dignity as a human

---

1 As Edward Said clarifies in *Orientalism* (1978), nineteenth-century British culture developed ideas of the East (which included Semitic people, both Jewish and Arab) such as what Levy describes here where women are valued chiefly as exotic sexual objects. "Orientalism" also referred to the academic discipline in Britain and France that focused on the cultures, languages, and literatures of "the Orient" (including Hebrew and Arabic). This use of "orientalism" is possibly an allusion to harems in Eastern cultures, a popular stereotype used by Westerners to portray supposedly inferior social practices of non-Western cultures.

being to his cleverness; he was eminently normal, though cleverer than any one she knew.

For the long-haired type of man, the professional person of genius, this thorough-going Philistine, this conservative ingrain, had no tolerance whatever. She never could understand the mania among some of the girls of her set, Rose Leuniger included, for the second-rate actors, musicians, and professional reciters with whom they came into occasional contact at parties.

She had, it is seen, distinct if unformulated notions as to the sanity of true genius.

And she herself? She was so sensible, oh, she was thoroughly sensible and matter-of-fact!

Esther fell in love half-a-dozen times a season, loudly bewailing herself throughout. Even Rose was not without her *affairs de coeur*; but she, Judith, was utterly free from such sentimental aberrations.

That was why perhaps a man like Reuben, who had not much opinion of women in general, considering them creatures easily snared, should find it possible to make a friend of her.

She understood perfectly Adelaide's snubs, Mrs. Sachs's repressive attitude, Esther's clumsily veiled warnings.

She understood and was indignant. Did they think her such a fool; a person incapable of friendship with a man without misinterpretation of his motives?

But Reuben knew that it was not so; and therein of course lay her strength and her consolation.

It was this openly matter-of-fact attitude of hers which had not only added piquancy to his intercourse with her, but had made Reuben less careful with her than he would otherwise have been.

He had no wish to hurt the girl, either as regarded her feelings or her prospects; nor was the danger, he told himself, a serious one.

She liked him immensely, of course, but she was unsentimental, like most women of her race, and would settle down happily enough when the time came.

He told himself these things with a secret, pleasant consciousness of a subtler element in their relationship; of unsounded depths in the nature of this girl who trusted him so completely, and whom he had so completely in hand. Nor did he hide from himself that she charmed him and pleased his taste as no other woman had ever done.

A man does not so easily deceive himself in these matters, and during the last year or two he had been fully aware of a quickening in his sentiments towards her.

Yes, Reuben knew by now that he was in love with Judith Quixano. The situation was full of delights, of dangers, of pains and pleasantnesses.

A disturbing element in the serene course of his existence, it added a charm to existence of which he was in no haste to be rid.

CHAPTER V.

Quand il pâlit un soir, et que sa voix tremblante
S'éteignit tout à coup dans un mot commencé;
Quand ses yeux, soulevant leur paupière brûlante,
Me blessèrent d'un mal dont je le crus blessé;

★ ★ ★ ★ ★ ★

Il n'aimait pas—j'aimais.

M. Desbordes Valmore.[1]

Old Solomon Sachs awaited his guests in the drawing-room of his house in Portland Place.

It was the night after Reuben's arrival, in honour of which the feast was given.

Such feasts were by no means rare events, the old man liking to assemble his family round him in true patriarchal fashion. As for the family, it always grumbled and always went.

He was a short, sturdy-looking man, with a flowing white beard, which added size to a head already out of all proportion to the rest of him. The enormous face was both powerful and shrewd; there was power too in the coarse, square hands, in the square, firmly-planted feet.

You saw at a glance that he was blest with that fitness of which survival is the inevitable reward.[2]

---

1 Marceline Desbordes-Valmore (1786-1859), "Souvenir," *Elégies et Poésies nouvelles* (1825). Translation from the French: "When he grew pale one evening, and his trembling voice died suddenly on a half-formed word; when his eyes, raising their burning lids, pierced me with a wound with which I thought him pierced; ... he did not love, I loved!" See *French Poetry 1820-1950*, trans. William Rees (London: Penguin, 1990) 17.

2 "Survival of the fittest" comes from Herbert Spencer's *First Principles* (1862), and by the 1880s had become a phrase invoking social Darwinism.

He wore a skull-cap,[1] and, at the present moment, was pacing the room, performing what seemed to be an incantation in Hebrew below his breath.

As a matter of fact, he was saying his prayers, an occupation which helped him to get rid of a great deal of his time, which hung heavily on his hands, now that age had disabled him from active service on the Stock Exchange.

His daughter Rebecca, a woman far advanced in middle-life, stitched drearily at some fancy-work by the fire. She was unmarried, and hated the position with the frank hatred of the women of her race, for whom it is a peculiarly unenviable one.

Reuben's mother, her daughter and son in-law, were the first to arrive.

Old Solomon shook hands with them, still continuing his muttered devotions, and they received in silence a greeting to which they were too much accustomed to consider in any way remarkable.

"Grandpapa saying his prayers," was an everyday phenomenon. Perhaps the younger members of the party remembered that it had never been allowed to interfere with the production of cake; the generous slices had not been less welcome from the fact that they must be eaten without acknowledgment.

Montague Cohen, Adelaide Sachs's husband, belonged to that rapidly dwindling section of the Community which attaches importance to the observation of the Mosaic and Rabbinical laws in various minute points.

He would have half-starved himself sooner than eat meat killed according to Gentile fashion, or leavened bread in the Passover week.[2]

Adelaide chafed at the restrictions imposed by this constant making clean of the outside of the cup and platter; but it was a point on which her husband, amenable in everything else, remained firm.

He was an anæmic young man, destitute of the more brilliant qualities of his race, with a rooted belief in himself and every thing that belonged to him.

---

1 A covering of a man's head in accordance with orthodox Jewish custom; *yarmulke* (Yiddish) or *kippah* (Hebrew).

2 Jewish dietary laws, kosher or *kashrut* (Hebrew), detail how animals should be slaughtered for meat and that no leavened breads are consumed during the festival of Passover. The laws also involve restrictions on the use of dishes for either dairy or meat in order to observe the strict separation of these two categories of food in any meal.

He was proud of his house, his wife and his children. He was proud, Heaven knows why, of his personal appearance, his mental qualities, and his sex; this last to an even greater extent than most men of his race, with whom pride of sex is a characteristic quality.

"Blessed art Thou, O Lord my God, who hast not made me a woman."[1]

No prayer goes up from the synagogue with greater fervour than this.

This fact notwithstanding, it must be acknowledged that, save in the one matter of religious observation, Montague Cohen was led by the nose by his wife, whose intelligence and vitality far exceeded his own. Borne along in her wake, he passed his life in pursuit of a shadow which is called social advancement; going uncomplainingly over quagmires, into stony places, up and down uncomfortable declivities; following patiently and faithfully wherever the restless, energetic Adelaide led.

Esther and her mother were the next to arrive. Mrs. Kohnthal was old Solomon's eldest child, a stout, dark, exuberant-looking woman, between whom and her daughter was waged a constant feud.

The whole party of the Leunigers, with the exception of Ernest, who never dined out, was not long in following: Mrs. Leuniger, dejected, monosyllabic, untidy as usual; Mr. Leuniger, cheerful, pompous, important; Rose, loud-voiced, overdressed, good-tempered; Judith, blooming, stately, calm, in her fashionable gown, which assorted oddly, a close observer might have thought, with the exotic nature of her beauty. Leo dragged in mournfully in the rear of his party; he was in one of his worst moods. He hated these family gatherings, and had only been prevailed on with great difficulty to put in an appearance.

"We are all here," cried Adelaide, when greetings had been exchanged, "with the exception of the hero of the feast."

"Who has evidently," added Esther, "a sense of dramatic propriety."

"Reuben is at his club," explained Mrs. Sachs, looking under

---

1 One of the three negative Morning Benedictions (*Birkhot ha-Shahar*) blessing God for not making oneself (i.e., Jewish men) a heathen, a slave, or a woman. This prayer was modeled after similar Greek prayers, and has been revised recently in non-orthodox prayer books in positive and egalitarian terms to thank God "who made me a Jew" or "who made me free."

her eyelids at Judith, who had taken a seat opposite her.

She admired the girl immensely, and at the bottom of her heart was fond of her.

Judith, on her part, would have found it hard to define her feelings towards Mrs. Sachs.

With Reuben she was always calm; in his mother's presence she was conscious of a strange agitation, of the stirrings of an emotion which was neither love, nor hate, nor fear, but which perhaps was compounded of all three.

They had not long to wait before the door was thrown open and the person expected entered.

He came straight across the room to old Solomon, a vivifying presence—Reuben Sachs, with his bad figure, awkward movements, and charming face, which wore tonight its air of greatest alertness.

The old man, who had finished his prayers and taken off his cap, greeted the newcomer with something like emotion. Solomon Sachs, if report be true, had been a hard man in his dealings with the world; never over-stepping the line of legal honesty, but taking an advantage wherever he could do so with impunity.

But to his own kindred he had always been generous; the ties of race, of family, were strong with him. His love for his children had been the romance of an eminently unromantic career; and the death of his favourite son, Reuben's father, had been a grief whose marks he would bear to his own dying day.

Something of the love for the father had been transferred to the son, and Reuben stood high in the old man's favour.

The greater subtlety of ambition which had made him while, comparatively speaking, a poor man, prefer the chances of a professional career to the certainties of a good berth in Capel Court, appealed to some kindred feeling, had set vibrating some responsive cord in his grandfather's breast. Such a personality as Reuben's seemed the crowning splendour of that structure of gold which it had been his life-work to build up; a luxury only to be afforded by the rich.

For poor Leo's attainments, his violin-playing, his classical scholarship, he had no respect whatever.

They went down to dinner without ceremony, taking their places, for the most part, as chance directed; Reuben sitting next to old Solomon, on the side of his best ear; Judith at the far end of the table opposite.

Conversation flagged, as it inevitably did at these family gatherings, until after the meal, when crabbed age and youth, separating by mutual consent, would grow loquacious enough in their respective circles.

Reuben, his voice raised, but not raised too much, for his grandfather's benefit, recounted the main incidents of his recent travels, while doing ample justice to the excellent meal set before him.

It might have been thought that he did not show to advantage under the circumstances; that his introduction of "good" names, and of his own familiarity with their bearers was a little too frequent, too obtrusive; that altogether there was an unpleasant flavour of brag about the whole narration.

Esther smiled meaningly and lifted her shoulders. Leo frowned and winced perceptibly, his taste offended to nausea; there were times when the coarser strands woven into the bright woof of his cousin's personality affected him like a harsh sound or evil odour.

But, these two cavillers apart, Reuben understood his audience.

Old Solomon listened attentively, nodding his great head from time to time with satisfaction; Mrs. Sachs, while apparently absorbed in her dinner, never lost a word of the beloved voice; Monty and Adelaide who, when all is said, were naïve creatures, were frankly impressed, and revelled in a sense of reflected glory.

As for Judith, shall it be blamed her if she saw no fault? She sat there silent, now and then lifting her eyes to the far-off corner of the table where Reuben was, divided between admiration and that unacknowledged sense of terror which came over her whenever the fact of Reuben's growing importance was brought home to her. Shall it be blamed her, I say, that she saw no fault, she who, where others were concerned, had sense of humour and critical faculty enough? Shall it be blamed her that she had a kindness for everything he said and everything he did; that he was the king and could do no wrong?

Only once during the meal did their eyes meet, then he smiled quietly, almost imperceptibly—a smile for her alone.

"Mr. Lee-Harrison," said Adelaide, stretching forward her sallow, eager, inquisitive face, on either side of which the diamonds shone like lamps, and plunging her dark, ring-laden fingers into a dish of olives as she spoke; "Mr. Lee-Harrison was staying at our hotel one year at Pontresina. He was a High Churchman in those days, and hardly knew a Jew from a Mohammedan."

"He is a cousin of Lord Norwood's," added Monty, who cultivated the acquaintance of the peerage through the pages of *Truth*.[1] After several years' study of that periodical he was beginning to feel on intimate terms with many of the distinguished people who figure weekly therein.

"A friend of yours, Leo!" cried Adelaide nodding across to her cousin.

She had a great respect for the lad, who affected to despise class distinctions, but succeeded in getting himself invited to such "good" houses.

"I know Lord Norwood," answered Leo with an impassive air, that caused Reuben to smile under his moustache.

"He was at this year's Academy private view,[2] don't you remember, Monty, with that sister of his, Lady Geraldine?" went on Adelaide, undisturbed.

"They are both often to be seen at Sandown," chimed in the faithful Monty, "and at Kempton."[3]

The Montague Cohens, those two indefatigable Peris[4] at the gate, patronized art, and never missed a private view; patronized the turf, and at every race-meeting, with any pretensions to "smartness," were familiar figures.

There was but a brief separation of the sexes at the end of dinner, the whole party within a short space of time adjourning to the ugly, old-fashioned splendours of the drawing-room, where card-playing went on as usual.

A game of whist was got up among the elders for the benefit of old Solomon, the others preferring to embark on the excitements of Polish bank with the exception of Leo, who never played cards, and Judith, who was anxious to finish a piece of embroidery she was preparing for her mother's birthday.

Reuben, who had dutifully offered himself as a whist-player and been cut out, lingered a few moments, divided between the expediency of challenging fortune at Polish bank, and the pleasantness of joining the girlish figure at the far end of the room.

Adelaide, shuffling her cards with deft, accustomed fingers,

---

1 A weekly newspaper.
2 The annual art exhibition at the Royal Academy of Arts offered a preview before opening to the public.
3 Sandown Park and Kempton Park were racecourses near London established in the nineteenth century.
4 Supernatural, fairy-like creatures in Persian folklore who are the descendants of fallen angels.

looked up and read something of his indecision in her brother's face.

"There's a place here, Reuben," she called out, drawing her silken skirts from a chair on to which they had overflowed.

She was not a person of tact; her remark, and the tone of it, turned the balance.

"No, thanks," said Reuben, dropping his lids and assuming his most imperturbable air.

It was not his custom to single out Judith for his attentions at these family gatherings, but to-night some irresistible magnetism drew him towards her. It only wanted that little goad from Adelaide to send him deliberately to the ottoman where she sat at work, her beautiful head bent over the many-coloured embroidery.

Leo, lounging discontentedly a few paces off, with something of the air of a petulant child who is ashamed of itself, twisted a bit of silk in his long brown fingers and hummed the air of *Ich grolle nicht*[1] below his breath.

"Judith," said Reuben, taking a seat very close beside her and looking straight at her face, "poor Ronaldson, the member for St. Baldwin's, is dangerously ill."

She looked up eagerly.

"Then you will be asked to stand?"[2]

He smiled; partly at her readiness of comprehension, partly at the frank, feminine hard-heartedness which realizes nothing beyond the circle of its own affections.

"You mustn't kill him off in that summary fashion, poor fellow."

"I meant, of course, if he should die."

"Under those circumstances I believe they will ask me to stand. That's the beauty of you, Judith," he added, half-seriously, half jestingly, "one never has to waste one's breath with needless explanation."

She blushed, and smiled naïvely at the little compliment with its studied uncouthness.

---

1   *Ich grolle nicht* (German), "I bear no grudge, even when my heart is breaking," is based on a poem by Heinrich Heine (1797-1856) from his collection *Dichterliebe*, and adapted to song by many composers, including Felix Mendelssohn and Robert Schumann.
2   British idiom for running for election for public office, here for the position of Member of Parliament, House of Commons, representing a specific British district.

There was something incongruous in the girl's rich and stately beauty, in the deep, serious gaze of the wonderful eyes, the severe, almost tragic lines of the head and face, with her total lack of manner, her little, abrupt, simple air, her apparent utter unconsciousness of her own value and importance as a young and beautiful woman.

"Judith is not a woman of the world, certainly," Reuben had said on one occasion, in reply to a criticism of his sister's; "but neither is she a bad imitation of one." And Adelaide, scenting a brotherly sarcasm, had allowed the subject to drop.

Leo, who had broken his bit of silk and hummed his song to the end, rose at this point, and went from the room without a word.

"Leo is in one of his moods," said Judith looking after him. "I am sure I don't know what is the matter with him."

Reuben, who understood perhaps more of Leopold's state of mind than any one suspected, of the struggles with himself, the revolt against his surroundings which the lad was undergoing, answered slowly: "He is in a ticklish stage of his growth. Horribly unpleasant, I grant you. But I like the boy, though he regards me at present as an incarnation of the seven deadly sins."

"You know he is very fond of you."

"That may be. All the same, he thinks I keep a golden calf in my bedroom for purposes of devotion."

Judith laughed, and Reuben, his face very close to hers, said: "Can you keep a secret?"

"You know best."

"Well, that poor boy is head over heels in love with Lord Norwood's sister."

She looked up with her most matter-of-fact air.

"He will have to get over *that!*"

"Judith!" cried Reuben, piqued, provoked, inflamed by her manner; "I believe there isn't one grain of sentiment in your whole composition. Oh, I know it's a fine thing to be calm and cool and have one's self well in hand, but a woman is not always the worse for such a weakness as possessing a heart."

There was a note in his voice new to her; a look in the brown depths of his eyes as they met hers which she had never seen there before. It seemed to her that voice and eyes entreated her, cried to her for mercy; that a wonderful answering emotion of pity stirred in her own breast.

A moment they sat there looking at one another, then came a rustle of skirts, the sound of a penetrating, familiar voice, and

Adelaide was sitting beside them. She had lost her part in the game for the time being, and, full of sisterly solicitude, had borne down on the pair with the object of interrupting that dangerous *tête-à-tête*.

"Reuben," she cried gaily, "I want you to dine with me to-morrow."

"I don't know that I can," he answered ungraciously, the mask of apathy falling over his features which a moment before had been instinct with life.

"Caroline Cardozo is coming. She has £50,000, and will have more when her father dies. You see," turning to Judith, "I am a good sister, and do not forget my duty."

Judith made some commonplace rejoinder, and went on stitching, outwardly calm.

Reuben, bitterly annoyed, tugged at the silks in the basket with those broad, square hands of his, which, in spite of their superior delicacy, were so much like his grandfather's.

"And, by the by," went on Adelaide, nothing daunted, "you must bring Mr. Lee-Harrison to see me, and then I can ask him to dinner."

"I don't know about that," answered Reuben slowly, looking at her from under his eyelids; "he might swallow your Jews; he walks by faith as regards *them* just at present. But as for the rest—a man doesn't care to meet bad imitations of the people of his own set, does he?"

Having planted this poisoned shaft, and feeling rather ashamed of himself, Reuben rose sullenly and went to the card-table, where Rose was winning steadily, and Esther, who always sat down reluctantly and ended by giving herself up completely to the excitement of the game, fingered with flushed cheeks her own diminishing hoard.

Adelaide and Judith, each in her way shocked at this outburst of bad temper from the urbane Reuben, plunged into lame and awkward conversation. Only somewhere in the hidden depths of Judith's being a voice was singing of triumph and delight.

CHAPTER VI.

He had a gentle, yet aspiring mind;
Just, innocent, with varied learning fed.

Shelley: Prince Athanase.[1]

Judith rose early the next morning and put the finishing touches to her embroidery. It was her mother's birthday, and she had planned going to the Walterton Road[2] after breakfast with her gift.

But Rose claimed her for purposes of shopping, and the two girls set out together for the region of Westbourne Grove. It was a delicious autumn morning; Whiteley's[3] was thronged with familiar, sunburnt faces, and greetings were exchanged on all sides.

The Community had come back in a body from country and seaside, in time for the impending religious festivals; the feast of the New Year would be celebrated the next week, and the great fast, or Day of Atonement, some ten days later.[4]

"How glad every one is to get back," cried Rose. "I know I hate the country; so do most people, only it isn't the fashion to say so."

And she nodded in passing to Adelaide, who, with her gloves off, was intently comparing the respective merits of some dress lengths in brocaded velvet.

Judith smiled rather dreamily, and remarked that they had better go first to the glove-department, that for the sale of dress-materials, for which they were bound, being so hopelessly over-crowded.

---

1 Percy Bysshe Shelley (1792-1822), "Prince Athanase" (1817), lines 22-23.
2 In Maida Vale, just north of Westbourne Grove.
3 William Whiteley opened his first shop in Westbourne Grove in 1863; by the late 1870s it had grown into London's first department store, rivaling similar stores in New York and Paris. Situated in Bayswater, an inner London suburb in Levy's day, Westbourne Grove became a shopping emporium for middle-class women.
4 *Rosh ha-Shanah*, the Jewish New Year, and *Yom Kippur*, the day of atonement, which follows ten days later, are the most important Jewish religious festivals, and usually occur in September or early October, on 1 and 10 *Tishrei* in the Jewish calendar.

"Very well," cried Rose. Then, in an undertone: "Look the other way; there's Netta Sachs. What a howling cad!" as a bouncing, gaily-attired daughter of Shem passed them in the throng.

Rose was in her element; she was an excellent shopping-woman, loving a bargain for its own sake, grudging no time to the matching of colours and such patience-trying operations, going through the business from beginning to end with a whole-hearted enjoyment that was good to see.

Judith, who had all a pretty girl's interest in dress, and was generally willing enough for such expeditions, followed her cousin from counter to counter, with a little amiable air of abstraction.

Was there some magic in the autumn morning, some intoxication in the hazy, gold-coloured air, that she, the practical, sensible Judith, went about like a hashish-eater under the first delightful influence of the dangerous drug?

"What a crowd!" ejaculated Adelaide, coming up to them as she turned from the contemplation of some cheap ribbons in a basket.

She had, to the full, the gregarious instincts of her race, and Whiteley's was her happy hunting-ground. Here, on this neutral territory, where Bayswater nodded to Maida Vale, and South Kensington took Bayswater by the hand, here could her boundless curiosity be gratified, here could her love of gossip have free play.

"We are going to get some lunch," said Rose, moving off; "Judith has to go and see her people."

She, too, loved the social aspects of the place no less than its business ones. Her pale, prominent, sleepy eyes, under their heavy white lids, saw quite as much and as quickly as Adelaide's dancing, glittering, hard little organs of vision.

The girls lunched in the refreshment room, having obtained leave of absence from the family meal, then set out together from the shop.

At the corner of Westbourne Grove they parted, Rose going towards home, Judith committing herself to a large blue omnibus.[1]

The Walterton Road is a dreary thoroughfare, which, in

---

1 The Atlas Omnibus Company used blue vehicles. See Levy's poem, "Ballade of an Omnibus" in *London Plane-Tree, and Other Verse* (London: T. Fisher Unwin, 1889) 21-22.

respect of unloveliness, if not of length, leaves Harley Street, condemned of the poet, far behind.[1]

It is lined on either side with little sordid gray houses, characterized by tall flights of steps and bow-windows, these latter having for frequent adornment cards proclaiming the practice of various humble occupations, from the letting of lodgings to the tuning of pianos.

About half way up the street Judith stopped the omnibus, and mounted the steps to a house some degrees less dreary-looking than the majority of its neighbours. Fresh white curtains hung in the clean windows, while steps, scraper and doorbell bore witness to the hand of labour.

Mrs. Quixano herself opened the door to her daughter, and drew her by the hand into the sitting-room, across the little hall to which still clung the odour of the mid-day mutton.

"Many happy returns of the day, mamma," said Judith, kissing her and offering her parcel.

"I am sure it is very good of you to remember, my dear," answered her mother, leaning back in her chair and taking in every detail of the girl's appearance; her gown, her bonnet, the tinge of sunburn on her fresh young cheek, a certain indescribable air of softness, of maidenliness which was hers to-day.

Israel Leuniger's sister was a stout, comely woman of middle-age; red-haired, white-skinned, plump, with a projecting under-lip and comfortable double chin.

She was disappointed with her life, but she made the best of it; loving her husband, though unable to sympathize with him; planning, working unremittingly for her six children; extracting the utmost benefit from the narrowest of means; a capable person who did her duty according to her own lights.

"So Reuben Sachs has come back," she said, after some conversation.

Judith glanced up quickly with a bright, gentle look.

"Yes, and he is ever so much better; quite himself again."

Mrs. Quixano grumbled some inarticulate reply. Personally, she would not have been sorry if he had failed to return from the antipodes.

As may be imagined, she had been one of the first people whom the gossip about Reuben and her daughter had reached.

---

1 Tennyson writes of nearby Wimpole Street as "the long unlovely street" (*In Memoriam*, stanza 7, line 2) where Arthur Hallam died. This location in the élite section of central London contrasts with Maida Vale, a lower-middle class suburban area where Judith's parents live.

She had begun to be jealously conscious that there was no one to protect Judith's interests; that, after all, it might have been better for the girl to take her chance in the Walterton Road, than waste her time among a set of people too greedy or too ambitious to marry her.

Twenty-two, and no sign of a husband; only a troublesome flirtation that kept off the rest of the world, and was not in the least likely to end in anything but smoke.

And yet, thought Mrs. Quixano, with a sudden burst of maternal pride and indignation, any man might be proud of such a wife.

With her beauty, her health, and her air of breeding, surely she was good enough, and more than good enough, for such a man as Reuben Sachs, his enormous pretensions, and those of his family on his behalf notwithstanding?

The door opened presently to admit two little dark-eyed, foreign-looking children—children such as Murillo[1] loved to paint—who had just returned from a walk with a very juvenile nursemaid.

They were Judith's youngest brothers, and as she knelt on the floor with her arm round one of them, administering chocolate and burnt almonds, she was conscious of a new tenderness, of a strange yearning affection for them in her heart.

"The girls will be so sorry to miss seeing you," said Mrs. Quixano, taking in the picture before her with her shrewd glance; "they are at the High School, and Jack, of course, is in the City."[2]

Jack Quixano, the eldest of the family, was also its chief hope and pride.

He had taken to finance as a duck to water, and from the humblest of berths at Sachs and Co.'s, had risen in a few years to the proud position of authorized clerk.

It had been evident, almost from the cradle, that he had inherited the true Leuniger ambition and determination to get on in the world, qualities which had shone forth so conspicuously in the case of his uncle Israel, and, unlike the ambition and deter-

---

1 Bartolomé Esteban Murillo (1617-82), a Spanish painter of religious subjects, especially the lives of the saints and the Madonna; his genre paintings of impoverished children were particularly influential in nineteenth-century realism. Levy's description here draws out the likeness between the Quixanos, as Sephardic Jews, and Murillo's subjects.
2 The financial district located in what was the original area of medieval London.

mination of the Sachs family, were unrelieved by any touch of imagination or self-criticism.

"It is disappointing not to see the girls," answered Judith, who was fond of her sisters, when she remembered them. "But papa, he is at home? I shall not be disturbing him?"

A moment later she was standing with her hand on the door of the room at the back of the house, where her father was accustomed to pass his time.

Turning the handle, in obedience to a voice from within, she entered slowly, a suggestion of shyness and reluctance in her manner, and found herself in a tiny apartment, into which the afternoon sun was streaming. It was lined and littered with books, all of them dusty and many dilapidated.

From the midst of this confusion of dust and sunlight rose a tall, lean, shabby figure: a middle-aged man, with stooping shoulders, a very dark skin, dark, straight, lank hair, growing close round the cheek-bones, deep-set eyes, and long features.

"Why, Judith, my dear," he said, with his vague, pleasant smile, as she came forward and submitted her fresh cheek to his lips.

"I hope I don't disturb you, papa. And how is the treatise getting on?"

He shook his head and smiled, and Judith was content with this for an answer. She only asked after the treatise from politeness, not from any interest in the subject.

Long ago in Portugal there had been Quixanos doctors and scholars of distinction.[1] When Joshua Quixano had been stranded high and dry by the tides of modern commercial competition, he had reverted to the ancestral pursuits, and for many years had devoted himself to collecting the materials for a monograph on the Jews of Spain and Portugal.

Absorbed in close and curious learning, in strange genealogical lore, full of a simple, abstract, unthinking piety, he let the world and life go by unheeded.

Judith remained with her father for some ten minutes. Conversation between them was never an easy matter, yet there was affection on both sides.

---

1   "Quixano" was the name of a prominent Sephardic family in Levy's Jewish community. A marble plaque below the pulpit at the West London Synagogue, where Levy's parents held seats, reads: "In Memory of David Quixano Henriques 1804-1870" in honor of one of the founders of the synagogue.

Quixano's manners and customs were accepted facts, unalterable as natural laws, over which his children had never puzzled themselves. Some of them indeed had inherited to some extent the paternal temperament, but in most cases it had been overborne by the greater vitality of the Leunigers. But to-day the dusty scholar's room, the dusty scholar, struck Judith with a new force. She looked about her wistfully, from the book-laden shelves, the paper-strewn tables, to her father's face and eyes, whence shone forth clear and frank his spirit—one of the pure spirits of this world.

★★★★★

When Judith reached home it was already dusk, and afternoon tea was going on in the morning-room.

Mrs. Leuniger was absent, and Rose officiated at the tea-table, while Adelaide, her feet on the fender, her gloves off, was preparing for herself an attack of indigestion with unlimited muffins and strong tea.

She had been paying calls in the neighbourhood, clad in the proof-mail of her very best manners, an uncomfortable garment which she had now thrown off, and was reclining, metaphorically speaking, in dressing-gown and slippers.

A burst of laughter from both young women greeted Judith's ears as she entered.

"How late you are," cried Rose. "What filial piety!"

Judith knelt down by the fire smiling, and took her part with spirit in the girlish jokes and gossip.

It was six o'clock before Adelaide rose to go, by which time the attack of indigestion had set in. Her vivacity died out suddenly; her features looked thick, strained, and lifeless; her sallow skin took a positively orange tinge.

"Dear me," she cried ill-temperedly, "I had no idea it was so late. I must fly. I have one or two people dining with me to-night: the Cardozos, the Hanbury-ffrenches—oh, and Reuben finds he can come."

Judith felt suddenly as though a chill wind had struck her; but she called out gaily to Rose, who was escorting Adelaide to the door, that there was time before dinner to practise the new duet.

CHAPTER VII.

On this day shall He make an atonement for
you, to purify you; you shall be clean from all
your sins.

Leviticus xvi. 30.[1]

Herbert, or, as he was generally spoken of, Bertie Lee-Harrison,
called at Lancaster Gate on the day of the New Year, to make
acquaintance with Reuben's people and offer his best wishes for
the year 564—.[2]

He was a small, fair, fluent person, very carefully dressed,
assiduously polite, and bearing on his amiable, commonplace,
neatly modelled little face no traces of the spiritual conflict which
any one knowing his history might have supposed him to have
passed through.

Esther, who happened to be calling on her aunt at the time of
Bertie's visit, classified him at once as an intelligent fool; but Adelaide professed herself delighted with the little man, and had had
the joy of informing him that she had once met his sister, Lady
Kemys, at a garden-party.

"Lady Kemys is charming," Reuben said when the matter was
being discussed. "Sir Nicholas, too, is a good fellow. They have a
place some miles out of St. Baldwin's."

His mind ran a good deal on St. Baldwin's in these days, and
on poor Ronaldson, its Conservative member, lying hopelessly ill
in Grosvenor Place.

Reuben, it may be added, was true to the traditions of his race,
and wore the primrose;[3] while Leo, who knew nothing about politics, gave himself out as a social democrat.

---

1   In Leviticus, the third book of the Torah, God imparts to Moses various
    laws, including those pertaining to the annual *Yom Kippur*, where the
    high priest makes atonement for the people. Levy seems to substitute a
    divine "He" in this epigraph in contrast to the scriptural text: "for on
    this day shall atonement be made for you, to cleanse you; from all your
    sins you shall be clean before the Lord."
2   In the Jewish calendar, 5640-49 corresponds to the 1880s. To omit
    digits of a date was a Victorian convention to convey ambiguity.
3   Symbol of the Conservative Party, later affiliated with the Primrose
    League, established in 1883 to mix politics with social activities. Benjamin
    Disraeli, a leader of the Conservative Party, and Prime Minister from
    1874 to 1880, was converted from Judaism to Christianity as a boy.

Mr. Lee-Harrison was to break his fast in Portland Place on the evening of the Day of Atonement, when it was old Solomon's custom to assemble his family round him in great numbers.

Adelaide objected to this arrangement.

"It will give him such a bad impression," she said.

"He asked for local colour, and local colour he shall have," answered Reuben, amused.

"It is disloyal to your own people to assume such an attitude regarding them to a stranger. After all, he is not one of us," cried Adelaide, taking a high tone.

"Your accusations are a little vague, Addie; but to tell you the truth I had no choice in the matter. I took him up yesterday to Portland Place, and the old man gave him the invitation. He simply jumped at it."

"Those dreadful Samuel Sachses!" groaned Adelaide.

"Oh, they are a remarkable survival. You should learn to take them in the right spirit," answered her brother.

He was dining that night at the house of an important Conservative M.P., and was disposed to take a cheerful view of things.

★★★★★

The Fast Day, or Day of Atonement, is the greatest national occasion of the whole year.

Even those lax Jews who practise their callings on Saturdays and other religious holidays, are withheld by public opinion on either side the tribal barrier from doing so on this day of days.

The synagogues are thronged; and if the number of people who rigidly adhere to total abstinence from food for twenty-four hours is rapidly diminishing, there are still many to be found who continue to do so.

Solomon Sachs, his daughter Rebecca, and the Montague Cohens worshipped in the Bayswater synagogue;[1] the rest of the family had seats in the Reformed synagogue in Upper Berkeley Street, an arrangement to which the old man was too liberal-minded to take objection.

The Quixano family attended the synagogue of the Spanish

---

1 Established in 1863 in Chichester Place, Harrow Road. In 1870, an act of Parliament established the United Synagogue, which incorporated a union of synagogues of the London Ashkenazim, and was under the auspices of the Chief Rabbi of Great Britain. Bayswater Synagogue was part of the United Synagogue.

and Portuguese Jews in Bryanston Street,[1] with the exception of Judith, who shared with her cousins the simplified service, the beautiful music, and other innovations of Upper Berkeley Street.

The morning of the particular Day of Atonement of which I write dawned bright and clear; and from an early hour, in all quarters of the town, the Chosen People—a breakfastless band— might have been seen making their way to the synagogues.

Many of the women were in white, which is considered appropriate wear for the occasion; and if traces of depression were discernible on many faces, in view of the long day before them, it is scarcely to be wondered at.

It was about ten o'clock when the Leunigers, who had all breakfasted, made their way into the great hall of the synagogue in Upper Berkeley Street, where the people were streaming in, in great numbers. As they paused a moment at the bottom of the staircase leading to the ladies' gallery, for their party to divide according to sex,[2] Reuben came up to them with Bertie Lee-Harrison in his wake.

There was a general hand-shaking, and Reuben, as he pressed her fingers, smiled a half-humorous, half-rueful smile at Judith— a protest against the rigours and *longueurs*[3] of the day which lay before them.

She managed to say to him over her shoulder:

"How is Mr. Ronaldson?"

"He has taken a turn for the better."

They laughed in one another's faces.

Bertie, struck by the effect of that sudden, rapidly checked wave of mirth passing over the beautiful, serious face, remarked to Reuben as they turned towards the entrance to their part of the building, that the Jewish ladies were certainly very lovely. Reuben said nothing; they were by this time well within the synagogue, but he glanced quickly and coldly under his eyelids at Bertie picking his way jauntily to his seat.

Ernest Leuniger, who was very devout, and who loved the

---

1 The Spanish and Portuguese Synagogue of Bryanston Street, West London, was established in 1866 as a branch of the Bevis Marks Synagogue located in the City of London, the main house of worship for the Sephardic Jewish community.

2 Although the West London Synagogue incorporated various reforms, in the 1880s women were still expected to sit in a separate area, an upper balcony, following the traditional Jewish practice.

3 Lengthy textual passages, part of the extensive services of *Yom Kippur*.

exercise of his religion even more than the game of solitaire, had already enwound himself in his *talith*, exchanged his tall hat for an embroidered cap, and was muttering his prayers in Hebrew below his breath.

Leo, his small, slight, picturesque figure swathed carelessly in the long white garment, with the fringes and the border of blue, his hat tilted over his eyes, leaned against a porphyry column, lost to everything but the glorious music which rolled out from the great organ.

He had come to-day under protest, to prevent a definite break with his father, who exacted attendance at synagogue on no other day of the year.

The time was yet to come when he should acknowledge to himself the depth of tribal feeling, of love for his race, which lay at the root of his nature. At present he was aware of nothing but revolt against, almost of hatred of, a people who, as far as he could see, lived without ideals, and was given up body and soul to the pursuit of material advantage.

Behind him his two little brothers were quarrelling for possession of a prayer-book. Near him stood his father, swaying from side to side, and mumbling his prayers in the corrupt German-Hebrew of his youth[1]—a jargon not recognized by the modern culture of Upper Berkeley Street.

Reuben and his friend had seats opposite; seats moreover which commanded a good view of the ladies of the Leuniger household in the gallery above: Mrs. Leuniger, in a rich lace shawl, very much crumpled, and a new bonnet hopelessly askew; Rose, in a tight-fitting costume of white, with blue ribbons; Judith, in white also, her dusky hair, the clear, soft oval of her face surmounted by a flippant French bonnet—the very latest fashion.

It was a long day, growing less and less endurable as it went on; the atmosphere getting thicker and hotter and sickly with the smell of stale perfume.

The people, for the most part, stuck to their posts throughout. A few disappeared boldly about lunch time, returning within an hour refreshed and cheerful. Some—these were chiefly men—fidgeted in and out of the building to the disturbance of their neighbours. One or two ladies fainted; one or two others gossiped

---

1 Yiddish was the vernacular language among Ashkenazi Jews from Central and Eastern Europe.

audibly from morning till evening; but, on the whole, decorum was admirably maintained.

Judith Quixano went through her devotions upheld by that sense of fitness, of obedience to law and order, which characterized her every action.

But it cannot be said that her religion had any strong hold over her; she accepted it unthinkingly.

These prayers, read so diligently, in a language of which her knowledge was exceedingly imperfect, these reiterated praises of an austere tribal deity, these expressions of a hope whose consummation was neither desired nor expected, what connection could they have with the personal needs, the human longings of this touchingly ignorant and limited creature?

Now and then, when she lifted her eyes, she saw the bored, resigned face of Reuben opposite, and the respectful, attentive countenance of Mr. Lee-Harrison, who was going through the day's proceedings with all the zeal of a convert.

Leo had absented himself early in the day, and was wandering about the streets in one of those intolerable fits of restless misery which sometimes laid their hold on him.

Esther was not in synagogue. She had had a sharp wrangle with her mother the night before, which had ended in her staying in bed with *Good-bye, Sweetheart!*[1] for company.

She, poor soul, was of those who deny utterly the existence of the Friend of whom she stood so sorely in need.

CHAPTER VIII.

My lord, will't please you to fall to?

Richard II.[2]

A limp, drab-coloured group was assembled in the drawing-room at Portland Place.

It was nearly half-past seven, and it only wanted the arrival of the Samuel Sachses—who came from the St. John's Wood syna-

---

1   Rhoda Broughton (1840-1920), *Good-bye, Sweetheart* (1872). The novel ends with the heroine's lingering death following a disappointing love. Broughton's novels were considered sensational bestsellers.
2   Shakespeare, *Richard II* V.v.98.

gogue[1]—for the whole party to descend into the dining-room, where the much-needed meal awaited them.

The Leunigers were there, of course, with the exception of Ernest and his mother, who had gone home; the Sachses; the Montague Cohens; Mrs. Kohnthal and Esther, who had left her bed at the eleventh hour prompted by a desire for society; Judith; Mr. and Mrs. Quixano, their son Jack, and two young sisters.

Bertie Lee-Harrison, who had come in with Reuben, pale, exhausted, but prepared to be impressed by every thing and every one he saw, confided to his friend that the twenty-four hours' fast had been the severest ordeal he had as yet undergone in the service of religion—his experiences in Asia Minor not excepted.

Leo, whose mood had changed, overheard this confidence with an irresistible twitching of the lips. He was sitting on the big sofa with his two little brothers, making jokes below his breath to their immense delight; while Rose, at the other end of the same piece of furniture, was maintaining an animated conversation with her cousin Jack.

Jack Quixano was a spruce, dapper, polite young man of some twenty-four or twenty-five years of age. Perhaps he was a little too spruce, a little too dapper, a little too anxious to put himself *en évidence* by his assiduity in picking up handkerchiefs and opening doors. But few of his family noticed these defects, least of all Rose, on whom he was beginning to cast aspiring eyes, and whom he closely resembled in personal appearance.

The door opened at last, to every one's relief, to admit the expected guests: a party of six—father, mother, grown-up son and daughter, a little girl and a little boy.

Samuel Sachs was the unsuccessful member of his family.

From the beginning, the atmosphere of the Stock Exchange had proved too strong for his not very strong brains, and his career had been inaugurated by a series of gambling debts.

His father paid his debts and forbade him the office, and he had gone his own way for many years, settling down ultimately in a humble way of business as a lithographer.

He had married a Polish Jewess with some money of her own, and in these latter days old Solomon made him an allowance, so there was enough and to spare in the home in Maida Vale where he and his family were established.

---

1   St. John's Wood Synagogue, Abbey Road, was established in 1876 under the auspices of the United Synagogue in response to the growing Jewish population in West London.

They came now into the crowded drawing-room with a curious mixture of deference and self-assertion.

To their eminently provincial minds, the Bayswater Sachses, the Leunigers and the Kohnthals were very great people indeed, and they derived no little prestige in Maida Vale from their connection with so distinguished a family.

But as regarded their occasional admittance into the charmed circle, that was a privilege which, though they would on no account have foregone it, was certainly not without its drawbacks.

It was splendid, but it was not comfortable.

Mrs. Sachs was a stout, dark-haired matron, who entirely overshadowed her shambling, neutral-tinted husband. Netta, the eldest daughter, was a black-eyed, richly coloured, bouncing maiden of two or three-and-twenty, wearing a white dress, with elbow sleeves, cut open a little at the neck, and a great deal of silver jewellery.

Alec, her brother, was a short, fair, exuberant-looking youth, with a complexion both glossy and florid, in whom the Sachses fitness for survival had reasserted itself. He practised painless dentistry with great success in the heart of Maida Vale, and was writing a manual—destined to pass through several editions—on *Diseases of the Teeth and Gums.*

Adèle and Bernard (pronounced Adale and Bernàrd), the two children, strutted in behind the others, in all the glory of white cambric and black velveteen, respectively, much impressed by the situation, but no less on the defensive than the elder members of their family.

There was languid greeting all round; languor, under the circumstances, was excusable; and then the whole party poured down into the dining-room, where an abundant meal was set out.

Old Solomon prided himself on his hospitality, and the great table, which shone with snowy linen, gleaming china, and glittering silver, groaned, as the phrase goes, with good things to eat.

There were golden-brown blocks of cold fried fish in heavy silver dishes; rosy piles of smoked salmon; saffron-tinted masses of stewed fish; long twisted loaves covered with seeds;[1] innumer-

---

1 *Challah,* a braided loaf often topped with poppy or sesame seeds, is a traditional part of Jewish Sabbath and festival meals; fish (excluding shellfish) is pareve ("neutral"—being or containing neither meat nor dairy) according to Kosher laws and therefore can be consumed with either dairy or meat dishes. For this reason, fish has often been a mainstay of Ashkenazi holiday meals.

able little plates of olives, pickled herrings, and pickled cucumbers; and the quick eyes of Lionel and Sidney had lighted at once on the many coloured surfaces of the almond puddings, which awaited the second course on the sideboard.

Aunt Rebecca, faint and yellow, behind the silver urns, dispensed tea and coffee with rapid hand; while old Solomon, none the worse for his rigid fast, wielded the fish slice at the other end of the table.

Bertie, respectful, wondering, interested through all his hunger, was seated between Reuben and Mrs. Kohnthal.

Adelaide had chosen her seat as far as possible from the Samuel Sachses, whose presence was an offence to her. They, on their part, regarded her with a mixture of respect and dislike. She never gave them more than two fingers[1] in her grandfather's house, and ignored them altogether when she met them anywhere else. This conduct impressed them by its magnificence, and they followed the ups and downs of her career, as far as they were able, with a passionate interest that had in it something of the pride of possession.

Nor was Adelaide above taking an interest in the affairs of her humbler relatives behind their backs. I cannot help wishing that they had known this; it would have been to them the source of so much innocent gratification.

Reuben, who had his cousin Netta on the other side of him, and whose vanity was a far subtler, more complicated affair than his sister's, was making himself agreeable with his accustomed urbanity, beneath which the delighted maiden was unable to detect a lurking irony.

The humours of the Samuel Sachses, their appearance, gestures, their excruciating method of pronouncing the English language, the hundred and one tribal peculiarities which clung to them, had long served their cousins as a favourite family joke into which it would have been difficult for the most observant of outsiders to enter.[2]

They were indeed, as Reuben had said, a remarkable survival.

Born and bred in the very heart of nineteenth century London, belonging to an age and a city which has seen the throwing down of so many barriers, the levelling of so many distinc-

---

1 Adelaide's "two fingers" rather than her entire hand conveys her reluctant social contact with relatives beneath her in class position.

2 See Levy's essay "Jewish Humour," *The Jewish Chronicle* (20 August 1886): 9-10.

tions of class, of caste, of race, of opinion, they had managed to retain the tribal characteristics, to live within the tribal pale to an extent which spoke worlds for the national conservatism.

They had been educated at Jewish schools, fed on Jewish food, brought up on Jewish traditions and Jewish prejudice.

Their friends, with few exceptions, were of their own race, the making of acquaintance outside the tribal barrier being sternly discouraged by the authorities. Mrs. Samuel Sachs indeed had been heard more than once to observe pleasantly that she would sooner see her daughters lying dead before her than married to Christians.

Netta tossed her head defiantly at these remarks, but contented herself with sowing her little crop of wild oats on the staircases of Bayswater and Maida Vale, where she "sat out" by the hour with the very indifferent specimens of Englishmen who frequented the dances in her set.

Generally speaking, the race instincts of Rebecca of York are strong, and she is less apt to give her heart to Ivanhoe, the Saxon knight, than might be imagined.[1]

Bernard Sachs, a very smug-looking little boy, with inordinately thick lips and a disagreeable nasal twang, had been placed between the two young Leunigers, who regarded him with a mixture of disgust and amusement, which they were at small pains to conceal.

"Did you fast all day?" he said, by way of opening the conversation. "I did. I was *bar-mitz-vah* last month. Is either of you fellows *bar-mitz-vah?*"[2]

"I am thirteen, if that's what you mean," said Lionel, with his most man-of-the-world air. He considered the introduction of the popular tribal phrases very bad form indeed.

"I suppose you were in *shool*[3] all day?" went on Bernard unabashed, and much on his dignity.

---

1 Sir Walter Scott (1771-1832), *Ivanhoe* (1819). Rebecca of York, a Jewess who resists the dishonorable advances of a crusading knight and eventually leaves England to flee Ivanhoe with whom she has fallen in love, became a popular model of a Jewish woman alluded to in many nineteenth-century literary depictions, including George Eliot's *Daniel Deronda* (1876). See William Makepeace Thackeray's parody, *Rebecca and Rowena* (1850), first serialized in *Fraser's Magazine* in 1846.

2 *Bar Mitzvah* (Hebrew), son of the commandment. At age 13 a Jewish boy becomes a *bar mitzvah*, marked by a ceremony in which he is recognized as an adult member of the community and thus obligated to perform the commandments, including fasting on *Yom Kippur*.

3 *Shul* (Yiddish), i.e., synagogue.

"I was only in synagogue in the morning," answered Lionel. Then he kicked Sidney violently under the table, and the two little brothers went off into a series of chuckles; while Bernard, with a vague sense of being insulted, turned his attention to his fried salmon and Dutch herring.

Meanwhile Alec, who had been rather subdued at the beginning of the evening, was regaining his native confidence as the meal proceeded.

He happened to be sitting opposite Bertie, and having elicited from his neighbour, Mrs. Quixano, the explanation of an alien presence among them on such an occasion, had fixed his attention with great frankness on the stranger.

Very soon he was leaning across the table, and with much use of his fat red hands, and many liftings of his round shoulders, was expatiating to the astonished Bertie on the beauties and advantages of the faith which he had just embraced.

"Mr. Harrison," he cried at last—he preferred to skip the difficulties of the double-barrelled name—"Mr. Harrison, take my word for it, it is the finest religion under the sun. Those who have left it for reasons of their own have always come back in the end. They're bound to, they're bound to!" (He pronounced the word "bound" with an indescribable twang.) "Look at Lord Beaconsfield"[1]—he pointed with his short forefinger—"everyone knows he died with the *shemang*[2] on his lips!"

There was a sudden stifled explosion of laughter from Leo's quarter of the table; and Judith glanced across rather anxiously at Reuben, on whose polite, impassive face she at once detected a look of annoyance.

She was sitting next to her father in the close-fitting white gown which displayed to advantage the charming lines of her arms and shoulders.

Now and then she caught the glance of Mr. Lee-Harrison, who was far too well-bred to obtrude his admiration by staring, fixed momentarily on her face.

The hunger and weariness natural, under the circumstances, to her youth and health had in no way marred the perfect freshness of

---

1 Benjamin Disraeli (1804-81), Conservative statesman and first Earl of Beaconsfield. See p. 87, note 3.

2 *Shema Yisrael* (Hear, O Israel), from Deuteronomy 6.4., the most common Hebrew prayer as a declaration of faith, and traditionally uttered on one's deathbed.

her appearance; and there was a gentle kindliness in her manner to her father which added a charm, not always present, to her beauty.

Perhaps she felt instinctively, what Quixano himself was far too much in the clouds to notice, that no one made much account of him, that it behoved her to take him under her protection. He was one of this world's failures; and the Jewish people, so eager to crown success in any form, so determined in laying claim to the successful among their number, have scant love for those unfortunates who have dropped behind in the race.

The meal came to an end at last, and there was a pushing back of chairs on the part of the men.

Bertie, about to rise, felt himself held down by main force; Reuben was gripping him hard by the wrist with one hand, and with the other was engaged in fishing out his hat from under the table; while Netta, leaning across her cousin, explained with her most fascinating smile that grandpa was going to *bench*.[1]

Bertie, at a sign from Reuben, rose to the situation, and stooping for his own hat with alacrity, drew it from its place of concealment and placed it on his head. By this time all the men had unearthed and assumed their head-gear, with the exception of Samuel Sachs, whose hat by some mischance was not forthcoming; however, to avoid delay, he covered his head in all gravity with his table-napkin.[2]

Bertie glanced round him, from one face to another, puzzled and inquiring.

It seemed to him a solemn moment, this gathering together of kinsfolk after the long day of prayer, of expiation; this offering up of thanksgiving; this performance of the ancient rites in the land of exile.

He could not understand the spirit of indifference, of levity even, which appeared to prevail.

A finer historic sense, other motives apart, should, it seemed, have prevented so obvious a display of the contempt which familiarity had bred.

Alec had put his hat on rakishly askew, and was winking across to him re-assuringly, as though to intimate that the whole thing was not to be taken seriously.

---

1 *Bench* (Yiddish), to recite or sing benedictions or grace after meals (*Birkat ha-Mazon*).

2 For all blessings, adult Jewish men would be obligated to cover their heads.

Rose, led on by Jack Quixano, giggled hysterically behind her pocket-handkerchief.

Leo and Esther took on airs of aggressive boredom. Judith, lifting her eyes, met Reuben's in a smile, and even Montague Cohen permitted himself to yawn.

Only old Solomon at the head of the table, mumbling and droning out the long grace in his corrupt Hebrew—his great face impenetrably grave—appeared to take any interest in the proceeding, with perhaps the exception of his son Samuel, who joined in now and then from beneath the drooping shelter of his table-napkin.

Bertie stared and Bertie wondered. Needless to state, he was completely out of touch with these people whose faith his search for the true religion had led him, for the time being, to embrace.

Grace over, the women went up stairs, the men, with the exception of old Solomon, remaining behind to smoke.

Bertie, who was thoroughly tired out, soon rose to go.

"I will make your excuses up stairs," said Reuben.

But the polite little man preferred to go to the drawing-room and perform his farewells in person.

"Thanks so much," he said in the hall, where Leo and Reuben were speeding him.

"I hope you have been edified—that's all." Reuben laughed.

"I am deeply interested in the Jewish character," answered Bertie; "the strongly marked contrasts; the underlying resemblances; the elaborate differentiations from a fundamental type—!"

"Ah, yes," broke in Reuben, secretly irritated, his tribal sensitiveness a little hurt, "you will find among us all sorts and conditions of men."[1]

"Except perhaps Don Quixote, or even King Cophetua,"[2] added Leo.

"King Cophetua," repeated Reuben in a slow, reflective tone,

---

1 Walter Besant's novel *All Sorts and Conditions of Men* (1882) describes a young woman graduate of Cambridge who pursues social reforms in impoverished East End London. Levy extends this phrase to include "and women" in her essay "Readers at the British Museum" (*Atalanta: Every Girl's Magazine* [April 1889]: 449-54).

2 Legendary ancient African king who was immune to love until he fell instantly in love with a beggar girl and made her his queen. A popular Victorian subject, such as Tennyson's 1842 poem "The Beggar Maid" or Edward Burne-Jones's 1884 painting *King Cophetua and the Beggar Maid*, based on the poem.

as the door closed on Mr. Lee-Harrison; "King Cophetua had an assured position. It isn't every one that can afford to marry beggar-maids."

CHAPTER IX.

Never by passion quite possessed,
And never quite benumbed by the world's sway.

Matthew Arnold[1]

The party was never prolonged to a late hour on these occasions, and by ten o'clock there was no one left in the drawing-room in Portland Place except Mrs. Sachs, Mr. Leuniger, Mrs. Kohnthal and the young people in their respective trains.

The elders had got up a game of whist for the amusement of old Solomon, the termination of which their juniors awaited in conclave at the other end of the room.

Lionel and Sidney meanwhile, sleepy and overfed, quarrelled in a corner over the possession of a bound volume of the *Graphic*.[2]

"Judith," said Reuben, who had taken a seat opposite her, "do you know that you have made a conquest?"

"Is that such an unheard-of occurrence?"

Reuben laughed gently, and Rose cried:

"It is Mr. Lee-Harrison! I know it from the way he looked at supper."

"Yes, it is Bertie." Reuben looked straight in Judith's eyes. "He says you exactly fulfil his idea of Queen Esther."

"Ah," cried Esther Kohnthal, "I have always had a theory about *her.* When she was kneeling at the feet of that detestable Ahasuerus,[3] she was thinking all the time of some young Jew

---

1 Matthew Arnold (1822-88), "A Summer Night," lines 32-33.
2 An illustrated weekly newspaper established in 1869 that ran serialized novels such as Wilkie Collins's *The Law and the Lady* (1875) and Thomas Hardy's *Tess of the d'Urbervilles* (1891).
3 The story from the *Book of Esther* about the Persian king Ahasuerus (Xerxes), who had his first wife, Vashti, deposed for disobeying him, and then married Esther, who hid her Jewish identity from her husband until his chief minister, Haman, issued a decree of genocide against the Jews. While this story forms the basis of the festival of *Purim* to celebrate this victory over the persecution of the Jews, Esther and Vashti have occasioned many feminist interpretations as well.

whom she mashed,[1] and who mashed her, and whom she renounced for the sake of her people!"

A momentary silence fell among them, then Reuben, looking down, said slowly: "Or perhaps she preferred the splendours of the royal position even to the attractions of that youth whom you suppose her to—er—have mashed."

He was not fond of Esther at the best of times; now he glanced at her under his eyelids with an expression of unmistakable dislike.

"I wonder," cried Rose, throwing herself into the breach, "what Mr. Lee-Harrison thought of it all."

"I think," said Leo, "that he was shocked at finding us so little like the people in *Daniel Deronda*."[2]

"Did he expect," cried Esther, "to see our boxes in the hall, ready packed and labelled *Palestine?*"

"I have always been touched," said Leo, "at the immense good faith with which George Eliot carried out that elaborate misconception of hers."

"Now Leo is going to begin," cried Rose; "he never has a good word for his people. He is always running them down."

"Horrid bad form," said Reuben; "besides being altogether a mistake."

"Oh, I have nothing to say against us at all," answered Leo ironically, "except that we are materialists to our fingers' ends. That we have outlived, from the nature of things, such ideals as we ever had."

"Idealists don't grow on every bush," answered Reuben, "and I think we have our fair share of them. This is a materialistic age, a materialistic country."

"And ours the religion of materialism. The corn and the wine and the oil; the multiplication of the seed; the conquest of the hostile tribes—these have always had more attraction for us than the harp and crown of a spiritualized existence."

---

1   I.e., flirted with.
2   George Eliot (1819-80), *Daniel Deronda* (1876). Eliot's novel concerns a young Englishman who becomes fascinated with Judaism and then discovers that his own Jewish identity has been concealed from him. At the end of the novel, Deronda departs on a proto-Zionist quest to restore "a political existence to my people, making them a nation again, giving them a national centre, such as the English have" (chapter 69). The "Jewish plot" of the novel was praised by the Anglo-Jewish community, but criticized by other reviewers.

"It is no good to pretend," answered Reuben in his reasonable, pacific way, "that our religion remains a vital force among the cultivated and thoughtful Jews of to-day. Of course it has been modified, as we ourselves have been modified, by the influence of western thought and western morality. And belief, among thinking people of all races, has become, as you know perfectly, a matter of personal idiosyncrasy."

"That does not alter my position," said Leo, "as to the character of the national religion and the significance of the fact. Ah, look at us," he cried with sudden passion, "where else do you see such eagerness to take advantage; such sickening, hideous greed; such cruel, remorseless striving for power and importance; such ever-active, ever-hungry vanity, that must be fed at any cost? Steeped to the lips in sordidness, as we have all been from the cradle, how is it possible that any one among us, by any effort of his own, can wipe off from his soul the hereditary stain?"[1]

"My dear boy," said Reuben, touched by the personal note which sounded at the close of poor Leo's heroics, and speaking with sudden earnestness, "you put things in too lurid a light. We have our faults; you seem to forget what our virtues are. Have you forgotten for how long, and at what a cruel disadvantage, the Jewish people has gone its way, until at last it has shamed the nations into respect? Our self-restraint, our self-respect, our industry, our power of endurance, our love of race, home and kindred, and our regard for their ties—are none of these things to be set down to our account?"

"Oh, our instincts of self-preservation are remarkably strong; I grant you that."

Leo tossed back his head with its longish hair as he spoke, and Reuben went on:

"And where would you find a truer hospitality, a more generous charity than among us?"

"A charity whose right hand is so remarkably well posted up in the doings of its left!"

"Oh, come, that's a libel—and not even true."

"There is one good thing," cried Leo, taking a fresh start, "and that is the inevitability—at least as regards us English Jews—of our disintegration; of our absorption by the people of the country. That is the price we are bound to pay for restored

---

1 Leo's remarks capture the prevalent view of Jewishness as not only an ancient religion and people, but also a racial identity. See p. 59, note 1 and Appendix D1.

freedom and consideration. The Community will grow more and more to consist of mediocrities, and worse, as the general world claims our choicer specimens for its own. We may continue to exist as a separate clan, reinforced from below by German and Polish Jews for some time to come: but absorption complete, inevitable—that is only a matter of time. You and I sitting here, self-conscious, discussing our own race-attributes, race-position—are we not as sure a token of what is to come as anything well could be?"

"Yours is a sweeping theory," said Reuben; "and at present, I don't feel inclined to go into the rights and wrongs of it; still less to deny its soundness. I can only say that, should I live to see it borne out, I should be very sorry. It may be a weakness on my part, but I am exceedingly fond of my people. If we are to die as a race, we shall die harder than you think. The tide will ebb in the intervals of flowing. That strange, strong instinct which has held us so long together is not a thing easily eradicated. It will come into play when it is least expected. Jew will gravitate to Jew, though each may call himself by another name. If prejudice died, if difference of opinion died, if all the world, metaphorically speaking, thought one thought and spoke one language, there would still remain those unspeakable mysteries, affinity and—love."

Reuben's voice sounded curiously moved, and in his eyes, as he spoke, glowed a dreamy flame, as of some deep and tender emotion.

Judith, leaning forward with parted lips, lifted her shining eyes to his face in a long, unconscious gaze. Reuben with his sword in his hand, fighting the battle for his people, seemed to her a figure noble and heroic beyond speech.

In her own breast was kindled the flame of a great emotion; she felt the love of her race grow stronger at every word.

Reuben, conscious to the finger-tips of Judith's presence, of her gaze, which he did not return, was stirred, on his part, with a new enthusiasm.

He praised her in the race, and the race in her; and this was conveyed in some subtle manner to her consciousness.

Thus they acted and reacted on one another, deceiving and deceived, with that strange, unconscious hypocrisy of lovers.

★★★★★

The game of whist had come to an end, and every one rose, preparatory to departure.

"Good-night, uncle Solomon," said Reuben's mother. She, too, was a Sachs, who had married her cousin.

"Come along, mamma," cried Esther yawning, "I am dead beat. The domestic habits of the cobra are not adapted to the human constitution, that is clear."

Reuben was standing in the hall with his mother, as Rose and Judith came down stairs in their outdoor clothes.

"Your carriage is at the door," said Israel Leuniger to Mrs. Sachs as he lit his cigar.

Mrs. Sachs turned to her son:

"Aren't you coming, Reuben?"

"No, but I do not expect to be late." He answered gently and seriously, stooping down and folding a shawl about her shoulders as he spoke.

Mrs. Sachs raised her wide, sallow, wrinkled face to her son's, looked at him a moment, then, with a sudden impulse of tenderness, lifted her hand and stroked back the hair from his forehead.

Ah, what had come to Judith, standing in a corner of the hall watching the little scene?

Ah, what did it mean, what was it, this beating and throbbing of all her pulses, this strange, choked feeling in her throat, this mist that swam before her eyesight?

The dining-room door, near which she stood, was ajar; moved by the blind impulse of her terror, she pushed it open; and trembling, ashamed, not daring to analyse her own emotions, she sought the shelter of the darkness.

★★★★★

While Judith was being driven to Kensington Palace Gardens, lying back pale and tired in a corner of the carriage, Reuben was sauntering towards Piccadilly with a cigar in his mouth.

For the moment, his mind dwelt on the fact that he had not been able to say good-night to Judith.

"Where did she make off to?" he asked himself persistently.

He was strangely irritated and baffled by the little accident.

As he went slowly down Regent Street, which was full of light and of people returning from the theatres, the thought of Judith took more and more possession of him, till his pulses beat and his senses swam.

Ah, why not, why not?

Children on his hearth with Judith's eyes, and Judith there

herself amongst them: Judith, calm, dignified, stately, yet a creature so gentle withal, so sweet, so teachable!

He looked again and again at this picture of his fancy, fascinated, alarmed at his own fascination.

Whatever happened, he would never be a poor man. There was the money which would come to him at his grandfather's death, and at his mother's: no inconsiderable sums. There was his own little income, besides what his practice brought him.

But it was not altogether a question of money. He had no wish to fetter himself at this early stage of his career; his ambition was boundless; and the possibilities of the future looked almost boundless too.

He had an immense idea of his own market value; an instinctive aversion to making a bad bargain.

From his cradle he had imbibed the creed that it is noble and desirable to have everything better than your neighbour; from the first had been impressed on him the sacred duty of doing the very best for yourself.

Yes, he was in love; cruelly, inconveniently, most unfortunately in love. But ten years hence, when he would still be a young man, the fever would certainly have abated, would be a dream of the past, while his ambition he had no doubt would be as lusty as ever.

Thus he swayed from side to side, balancing this way and that; pitying himself and Judith as the victims of fate; full of tenderness, of sentiment for his own thwarted desires.

He believed himself to hesitate, to waver; but at the bottom of Reuben's heart there was that which never wavered.

He put the question by at last, wearied with the conflict, and gave himself up to pleasant dreams.

He thought of the look in Judith's eyes, of the vibration in her voice when she spoke to him.

"Ah, she does not know it herself!"

Triumph, joy, compunction, an overwhelming tenderness, set his pulses beating, his whole being aglow.

It was late when, tired and haggard, he reached his home and let himself in with the key.

His mother came out on the landing with a candle.

She did not present a charming spectacle *en déshabillé*,[1] her large, partially bald head deprived of the sheltering, softening

---

1 In a state of undress (French).

cap, her withered neck exposed, the lines of her figure revealed by a dingy old dressing-gown.

She gave an exclamation as she saw him; the wide, yellow expanse of her face, with its unwholesome yet undying air, lighted up by the twinkling diamonds on either side of it, looked agitated and alarmed.

"My dear boy, thank God it is you! I have been dreaming about you—a terrible dream."

CHAPTER X.

Dusty purlieus of the law.

Tennyson.[1]

Leopold Leuniger came slouching down Chancery Lane,[2] his hat at the back of his head, a woe-begone air on his expressive face, dejection written in his graceless, characteristic walk, and in the droop of his picturesque head, which was, it must be owned, a little too large for his small, slight figure. He turned up under the archway leading to Lincoln's Inn, and made his way to New Square, where Reuben's chambers were situated.

Reuben, the clerk told him, was in court, but was expected every minute, and Leo passed into the inner room, which was his cousin's private sanctum. It was two or three days after the Day of Atonement, and in less than a week he would be back in Cambridge.

He paced restlessly to and fro in the little dingy room with its professional litter of books and papers, pausing now and then to look out of window, or to examine the mass of cards, photographs, notes and tickets which adorned the mantelpiece.

Leo was by no means free from the tribal foible of inquisitiveness.

It was not long before the door burst open, and Reuben rushed in, in his wig and gown. The former decoration imparted

---

1 Tennyson, *In Memoriam* (1850), stanza 89, line 12. The full stanza reads: "He brought an eye for all he saw; / He mixt in all our simple sports; / They pleased him, fresh from brawling courts / And dusty purlieus of the law."

2 A street in Holborn, central London, associated with the law profession; adjacent to the Royal Courts of Justice.

a curious air of sageness to his keen face, and brought out more strongly its peculiarities of colour: the clear, dark pallor of the skin, the red lights in the eyes and moustache.

"Hullo!" said Leo, still standing by the mantelpiece, his hat tilted back at a very acute angle, his restless fingers busy with the cards on the mantelpiece, "a nice gay time you appear to be having, old man: Jewish Board of Guardians,[1] committee meeting; Anglo-Jewish Association,[2] committee meeting; Bell Lane Free Schools,[3] committee meeting—shall I go on?"

Reuben laughed.

"You see, it consolidates one's position both ways to stand well with the Community; and I am a very good Jew at heart, as I have often told you. But if you continue your investigations among my list of engagements you will find a good many meetings of all sorts, which are not communal; not to speak of first nights at the Terpischore and the Thalian."[4]

Leo, abandoning the subject, flung himself into a chair and said: "Ah, by the by, how is Ronaldson?"

"Much the same as ever. It may be a long business. The doctors have left off issuing bulletins."

Reuben took the chair opposite his cousin, then said shortly: "You have come to tell me something."

"Yes. I have been having it out with my governor."

"Ah?" interrogatively.

"I told him," went on Leo, leaning forward and speaking with some excitement, "that I hadn't the faintest idea of going on the Stock Exchange, or even of reading for the bar; that my plan was this: to work hard for my degree, and then stay on, on chance of

---

1   An organization created in 1859 responsible for poor relief among London Jews, many of them immigrants in the East End.

2   British Jews established this organization in 1871 to defend religious and political liberty for oppressed Jews throughout the Diaspora.

3   A school welfare program funded by wealthier Anglo-Jews was provided for poor Jewish children of East End London. Many students were immigrants or children of immigrants from Eastern Europe. The Free Schools helped to assimilate poor Jewish children into English culture through education. For information on middle-class Jewish day schools of London, see p. 55, note 2.

4   Terpischore, a daughter of Zeus and mother of the Sirens, was the muse of choral songs and dancing, and Thalia was the muse of dancing. In this context the Terpischore and the Thalian were most likely theatres of dance and drama.

a fellowship. Every one up there seems to think the matter lies virtually in my own hands."[1]

"What did my uncle say to that?"

"Oh, he was furious; wouldn't listen to reason for a moment. I think"—with a boyish, bitter laugh—"that he rather confounds a fellow of Trinity with the assistant-master at a Jewish boarding-school. The word 'usher' figured very largely in his arguments."

"I think," said Reuben slowly, "that you are making a mistake."

"Ah," cried Leo, flinging out his hand, "you don't understand. I can't live—I can't breathe in this atmosphere; I should choke. Up there, somehow, it is freer, purer; life is simpler, nobler."

Reuben looked down: "I quite agree with you on that point. All the same, you were never cut out for a University don. Do you want me to tell you that you are a musician?"

Leo blushed like a girl, and his face quivered. He did not altogether approve of Reuben, but Reuben's approval was very precious to him.

Moreover he greatly respected his cousin's intelligent appreciation of music.

"Do you think so?" he cried. "That's what Norwood says. But there is plenty of opportunity for cultivating music; we have Silver up there, remember. He is immensely kind."

"You might talk it over with Silver. But think it well over and do nothing rash. There is plenty of time between now and taking your degree."

He rose and proceeded to take off his wig and gown.

"I don't know that my advice is worth much," he said, "but I should say a year or two in Germany—Leipsic, Berlin, Vienna—and if by then you feel justified in setting your face against the substantial attractions of Capel Court, no doubt your governor can be brought round."

"You will have to put it to him, Reuben. He believes in no one as he does in you."

"Very handsome of him. But doubtless he will welcome the idea after the usher scheme."

"You will have to paint the splendours of a musical success,"

---

1   Levy's unpublished story, "Leopold Leuniger: A Study," describes the conflicts of a Jewish student at Cambridge, including his father's criticism of his academic aspirations. (See Linda Hunt Beckman, *Amy Levy: Her Life and Letters* [Athens: Ohio UP, 2000] 69-74.) Levy's story "Cohen of Trinity" is based on this earlier study. (See Appendix B4.)

cried Leo, his spirits rising, his white teeth flashing as he smiled. "You must employ rather crude colours, and go in for obvious effects—such as the Prince of Wales, the Lord Mayor, and the Archbishop of Canterbury seated in the front row of the stalls at St. James's Hall."

Reuben laughed as he put on his well brushed hat before the glass.

"I will impress upon him how fashionable is the pursuit of the arts in these democratic days." He added slowly, looking furtively at the lad: "And shall I tell him that one of these days you will marry very well indeed?"

Leo rose hastily, jarred, discomposed.

"Aren't you coming to lunch, Reuben?"

"Yes, I am ready." He smiled to himself, and the two young men passed out together into the paved court-yard of the old inn.

They made their way up Chancery Lane into Holborn. Leo hated London almost as vehemently as his cousin loved it. It was the place, he said, which had succeeded better than any other in reducing life to a huge competitive examination. Its busy, characteristic streets, which Reuben regarded with an interest both passionate and affectionate, filled him with a dreary sensation of disgust and depression.

As they sat down to lunch at the First Avenue Hotel, Lord Norwood came into the dining-room. He was a tall, fair, aristocratic-looking young man, with a refined and thoughtful face, which, as he advanced towards his friend, broke into a peculiarly charming smile.

Leo exclaimed with impetuosity: "Oh, there's Norwood!" But as the latter approached he stiffened into self-consciousness; somehow, he did not welcome the juxtaposition of his cousin and his friend. Acting on a sudden impulse he rose and met the latter half-way, and the two young men stood talking together in the middle of the room.

Reuben, after a moment's hesitation, rose also and joined them. He greeted Lord Norwood, whom he had met once or twice before, with a little emphasis of deference, which was not lost on poor Leo, who hated himself at the same time for noticing it. Lord Norwood returned Reuben's greeting with marked *hauteur*; that cousin of Leuniger's was a snob, was not a person to be encouraged. In the young nobleman's delicate, fastidious, but exceedingly *borné*[1] mind there was no mercy for such as he.

---

1   Limited, confined (French).

Reuben, though he showed no signs of it, was keenly alive to the fact that he had been snubbed; was alive no less keenly to the many points in favour of the offender.

The Norwoods were people whom it hurt the subtler part of his vanity not to stand well with.

They were not rich, not "smart," not politically important; but in their own fashion they were people of the very best sort, true aristocrats, such as few remain to us in these degenerate days.

For generations they had borne the reputation of high personal character and of scholarly attainment. They were, in the true sense of the word, exclusive; and their pride was of that nature which, as the poet has it, asserts an inward honour by denying outward show.[1]

The friendship existing between Lord Norwood and Leo was founded on mutual admiration.

The Jew's many-sided talent, his brilliant scholarship, his mental quickness and versatility, above all, his musical genius, had fairly dazzled the scholarly young Englishman, who loved art, but had not a drop of artist's blood in his veins.

Leo, on his part, had fallen down before the other's refinement of mind and soul and body, and before the delicate strength of his character.

It was a strange friendship perhaps, but one which had stood, and was destined long to stand, the test of time.

Meanwhile Reuben, who knew that it is half the battle not to know when you are vanquished, quietly invited Lord Norwood to join them at table.

He pleaded, coldly, an appointment with a friend, and after a few words with Leo withdrew to a further apartment.

Leo had taken in the slight, brief, yet significant episode in all its bearings, hating himself meanwhile for his own shrewdness, which he considered a mark of latent meanness.

Reuben returned thoughtfully, if quite composedly, to the discussion of his roast pheasant and potato chips.

His method of wiping out a snub was the grandly simple one of making a conquest of the snubber. Persons less completely equipped for the battle of life have been known to prefer certain defeat to the chances of such a victory.

But Reuben was possessed of a bottomless fund of silent

---

1 Compare with Shakespeare, *Hamlet* I.ii.85-86: "But I have that within which passes show, / These but the trappings and the suits of woe."

energy, of quiet resistance and persistence, which had stood him ere now in good stead under like circumstances.

He appraised Lord Norwood very justly; recognized instinctively the charms of mind and manner which had cast such glamour over him in his cousin's eyes; recognized also his limitations, with an irritated consciousness that he, Reuben, was being judged at a far less open-minded tribunal. In such cases, it is always the more intelligent person who is at a disadvantage—he appreciates, and is not appreciated.

I have no intention of following out Reuben's relations with Lord Norwood, throughout which, it may be added, he had little to gain, even in the matter of social prestige, for he numbered people far more important among his acquaintance. But it was not long before an invitation to Norwood Towers was given and accepted. By one at least of the people concerned however, the circumstances which had marked the earlier stages of their acquaintance were never forgotten.

★★★★★

A few days later saw Leo back at Trinity with his lexicon, his violin, and the friend of his heart. Here he alternately worked furiously and gave himself up to spells of complete idleness; to sauntering, sociable days spent in cheerful, excited discussion of the vexed problems of the universe, or long days of moody solitude. At these latter times he pondered deeply on the unsatisfactoriness of life in general, and of his own life in particular, and underwent a good many uncomfortable sensations which he ascribed to a hopeless passion for his friend's sister.

Lady Geraldine Sydenham was a gentle, kindly, cultivated young woman, who had not the faintest idea of having inspired any one with hopeless passion, least of all young Leuniger.

She was two or three years older than Leo—a thin, pale person, with faint colouring, a rather receding chin, and slightly prominent teeth.

She dressed dowdily, and even Leo did not credit her with being pretty. Indeed he took a fanciful pleasure in dwelling on the fact that she was plain, and in quoting to himself the verse from Browning's *Too Late*:

".... There never was to my mind
Such a funny mouth, for it would not shut;
And the dented chin too—what a chin! ...

You were thin, however; like a bird's
Your hand seemed—some would say the pounce
Of a scaly-footed hawk—all but!
The world was right when it called you thin."[1]

Meanwhile in London Bertie Lee-Harrison was celebrating
the Feast of Tabernacles[2] as best he could.

He had given up with considerable reluctance his plan of living
in a tent, the resources of his flat in Albert Hall Mansions not
being able to meet the scheme.

He consoled himself by visits to the handsome *succouth*[3] which
the Montague Cohens had erected in their garden in the Bayswater Road.

CHAPTER XI.

I do not like this manner of a dance,
This game of two and two; it were much better
To mix between the pauses than to sit
Each lady out of earshot with her friend.

Swinburne: Chastelard.[4]

The Leunigers were giving a dance at the beginning of November, and the female part of the household was greatly taken up
with preparations for the event.

---

1 Robert Browning (1812-89), "Too Late" (1864), lines 124-26, 129-32.
2 Jewish festival of *Sukkot*. The name highlights the custom of dwelling in
   a *sukkah* or booth during this ancient harvest and pilgrimage festival
   that lasts nine days. The eighth day is *Shemini Atseret*, when a prayer for
   rain is recited, and the ninth day is *Simchat Torah*, when the Torah
   reading cycle concludes and begins again. These festivals follow immediately after *Yom Kippur*. In the following passages the narrator notes the
   challenges of adapting these customs in a modern urban environment.
3 Variant of *sukkah* (plural is *sukkot*). Such discrepancies are common
   given the transliteration from Hebrew.
4 Algernon Charles Swinburne (1837-1909), *Chastelard* (1866). Swinburne was associated with the Pre-Raphaelite Brotherhood through his
   acquaintance with D.G. Rossetti, with whom he was named a member
   of "The Fleshly School of Poetry" (1871), the title of Robert
   Buchanan's critique.

There was much revising of invitation lists, discussion of the social claims of their friends and acquaintance, and the usual anxious beating up of every available dancing-man.

"Addie will bring Mr. Griffiths, and Esther Mr. Peck," said Rose. "They go well, look nice, and one sees them everywhere, although Reuben calls them 'outsiders.'"

Rose loved dances, as well she might, for from the first she had been a success.

Rose, with her fair, plump shoulders and blonde hair, her high spirits and good-nature, her nimble feet and nimble tongue; Rose with her 50,000 and twenty guinea ball-gowns; Rose went down—magic phrase!—as not one girl in ten succeeds in doing.[1]

"I suppose," said Judith, "that the Samuel Sachses will have to be asked?"

She, though of course she had her admirers, was by no means such a success as her cousin.

"Yes, isn't it a nuisance?" cried Rose; "and the Lazarus Harts."

If there is a strong family feeling among the children of Israel, it takes often the form of acute family jealousy.

The Jew who will open his doors in reckless ignorance to every sort and condition of Gentile is morbidly sensitive as regards the social standing of the compatriot whom he admits to his hospitality.

The Leunigers, as we know, were not people of long standing in the Community, and numbered among their acquaintance Jews of every rank and shade; from the Cardozos, who were rich, cultivated, could almost trace their descent from Hillel,[2] the son of David, and had a footing in English society, to such children of nature as the Samuel Sachses.

"We must have Nellie Hepburn and the Strettel girls," went on Rose, consulting her list; "the men all rush at them, though I don't see that they are so pretty myself."

"I suppose they make a change from ourselves," answered Judith smiling, "whose faces are known by heart."

Judith was entering with spirit, with a zeal that was almost feverish, into the preparations for the forthcoming festivity.

She and Reuben had scarcely spoken to one another since the

---

1 To "go down" is a colloquialism for how someone or something fares or turns out. In this context, "Rose went down" implies she is received well in society.

2 First century BCE rabbinic authority and scholar; an innovator in biblical interpretation and teaching the Torah.

Day of Atonement. They had met once or twice at family gatherings, at which, either by accident, or design on Reuben's part, there had been no opportunity for private conversation.

Perhaps an instinctive feeling that the old relations were imperilled and that no new ones could ever be so satisfactory held them apart.

Meanwhile Judith unconsciously fixed her mind on the one definite fact that Reuben would be at the Leunigers' dance. It was in the crowded solitude of ball-rooms that they had hitherto found their best opportunity.

The night so much prepared for came round at last, and the house in Kensington Palace Gardens became for the time being the scene of ceaseless activity.

Ernest had gone away into the country with the person who was always talked of as his valet; and Leo, of course, was in Cambridge; but the rest of the family—not excepting Lionel and Sidney, who handed programmes—had mustered in great force to do honour to the event.

From an early hour poor Mrs. Leuniger had taken up her station in the doorway of the primrose-coloured drawing-room, where she stood dejectedly welcoming her guests. She was wearing a quantity of valuable lace, very much crumpled, and had a profusion of diamonds scattered about her person, but had apparently forgotten to do her hair.

Rose, in short, voluminous skirts of pink tulle, and a pale pink satin bodice fitting close about her plump person, defining the lines of her ample hips, was performing introductions with noisy zeal, with the help of Jack Quixano, whom she had constituted her *aide-de-camp*. The Montague Cohens had come early, and Adelaide, in a very grand gown, scrutinized the scene with breathless interest, secretly wondering why more people had not asked her to dance.

Judith was looking very well. Her short, diaphanous white ball-gown, with its low-cut, tight-fitting satin bodice was not exactly a dignified garment, but she managed to maintain, in spite of it, her customary air of stateliness.

Moreover to-night some indefinable change had come over the character of her beauty, heightening it, intensifying it, giving it new life and colour. The calm, unawakened look which many people had found so baffling, had left her face; the eyes, always curiously mournful, shone out with a new soft fire.

Bertie Lee-Harrison, tripping jauntily into the ball-room, remained transfixed a moment in excited admiration.

What a beautiful woman was this cousin, or pseudo-cousin, of Sachs's! How infinitely better bred she seemed than the people surrounding her!

The Quixanos, as Reuben had told him, were *sephardim*,[1] for whose claim to birth he had the greatest respect. But as for that red-headed young man, her brother—there were no marks of breeding about *him*!

Bertie was puzzled, as the stranger is so often puzzled, by the violent contrasts which exist among Jews, even in the case of members of the same family.

Judith was standing some way off, where Bertie stood observing her, while two or three men wrote their names on her dancing-card.

She was one of the few people of her race who look well in a crowd or at a distance. The charms of person which a Jew or Jewess may possess are not usually such as will bear the test of being regarded as a whole.

Some quite commonplace English girls and men who were here to-night looked positively beautiful as they moved about among the ill-made sons and daughters of Shem,[2] whose interesting faces gain so infinitely on a nearer view, even where it is a case of genuine good-looks.

Bertie waited a minute till the men had moved off, then advanced to Miss Quixano and humbly asked for two dances. Judith gave them to him with a smile. He was a poor creature, certainly, but he was Reuben's friend, and she knew that, in one way at least, Reuben thought well of him: he was one of the few Gentiles of her acquaintance whom he had not stigmatized as an "outsider."

Moreover Bertie's little air of deference was a pleasant change from the rather patronizing attitude of the young men of her set, whose number was very limited, and who were aggressively conscious of commanding the market.

Bertie, his dances secured, moved off regretfully. He would have liked to sue for further favours, but his sense of decorum restrained him. Had he but known it, he might without exciting notice have claimed a third, at least, of the dances on Judith's card. Hard flirtation was the order of the day, and the chaperons,

---

1 See p. 67, note 2 and p. 85, note 1.
2 According to Genesis 10-11, Noah had three sons, Shem, Ham, and Japheth. The descendents of Shem include the Jewish patriarch and matriarch, Abram and Sarai.

who were few in number, gossiped comfortably together, while their charges sat out half the night with the same partner.

Rose fell upon Bertie at this point, and fired him off like a gun at one or two partnerless damsels; while Judith, her partner in her wake, moved over to the doorway, where Adelaide was standing with Caroline Cardozo.

It was eleven o'clock and Reuben had not come. Judith had, it must be owned, changed her position with a view to consulting the hall-clock, and perhaps Adelaide had some inkling of this, for she said very loudly to her companion:

"It is a first night at the Thalian; my brother never misses one. I don't expect we shall see him to-night. Young men have so many ways of amusing themselves, I wonder they care about dances at all."

The musicians struck up a fresh waltz, and Bertie came over to claim the first of his dances with Judith.

He danced very nicely, in a straightforward, unambitious way, never reversing his partner round a corner without saying, "I beg your pardon."

Esther, her sharp brown shoulders shuffling restlessly in and out of a gold-coloured gown of *moiré*[1] silk, and with a string of pearls round her neck worth a king's ransom, surveyed the scene with shrewd, miserable eyes, while rattling on aimlessly to her partner and *protégé* Mr. Peck.

It was indeed a motley throng which was whirling and laughing and shouting across the music, in the bare, bright, flower-scented apartment.

The great majority of the people were Jews—Jews belonging to varying shades of caste and clique in that socially sensitive Community. But besides these, there was a goodly contingent of Gentile dancing men—"outsiders," according to Reuben, every one—and a smaller band of Gentile ladies who were the fashion of the hour among the sons of Shem.

("Bad form" was the label affixed by Reuben to these attractive maids and matrons.)

To give distinction to the scene, there were a well-known R.A.,[2]

---

1 Watered (French); obtained by passing the fabric through engraving rollers, producing crushed "watermark" patterns that reflect light differently.

2 Member of the Royal Academy of Art, the most prestigious institution of visual arts in Victorian England, with an annual summer exhibition of juried paintings; "last year's Academy" refers to this show.

who had painted Rose's portrait for last year's Academy; two or three pretty actresses; an ex-Lord Mayor, who had been knighted while in office; and last, though by no means least in the eyes of the clannish children of Israel, Caroline Cardozo and her father.

"'What a pretty girl' did you say?" remarked Esther as the music died away. "Yes, Judith Quixano is very good-looking, but I don't know that she goes down particularly well."

Mr. Peck made some complimentary remark, of a general character, as to the beauty of Jewish ladies.

"Yes, we have some pretty women," Esther answered; "but our men! No, the Jew, unlike the horse, is not a noble animal."

Esther, it will be seen, was of those who walk naked and are not ashamed.[1]

At this point, a fashionably late hour, a new arrival was announced, and in marched Netta and Alec Sachs, their heads very much in the air, the self-assertion of self-distrust written on every line of their ingenuous countenances.

Netta, who had had a new dress from Paris for the occasion, really looked rather well in her own style, which was of the exuberant, black-haired, highly-coloured kind, and was at once greeted by one of the "outsiders" as an old friend.

This was no less a person than Adelaide's particular *protégé*, Mr. Griffiths, who, ignorant of the fine shades of Community class-distinction, engaged Miss Sachs for several dances under the eyes of his mortified patroness. Mr. Griffiths indeed was an impartial person, who, so long as you gave him a good floor, a decent supper, and a partner who could "go," would lend the light of his presence to any ballroom whatever, whether situated in South Kensington or Maida Vale.

Alec Sachs was less fortunate than his sister. There were plenty of men, and the girls whom he thought worthy of inviting to dance for the most part declared themselves engaged.

This was a new experience to him. His skilful dancing—it was of the acrobatic or gymnastic order—his powers of "chaff" and repartee, above all, his reputation as a *parti*,[2] had secured him a high place among the maidens of Maida Vale.

He stood now, his back to the wall, an air of contempt for the whole proceeding written on his florid face, exclaiming loudly

---

1 Genesis 2.25: "And they were both naked, the man and his wife, and were not ashamed."

2 A match or choice, i.e., a " catch" (French).

and petulantly to his sister; whenever he had an opportunity: "They don't introduce, they don't introduce!"

Twelve o'clock was striking as Reuben Sachs stepped into the hall, which by this time was filled with couples "sitting out"; a few of them really enjoying themselves, the great majority gay with that rather spurious gaiety, that forcing of the note, which is so marked a characteristic of festivities. Sounds of waltz music were borne from the drawing-room, and the draped aperture of the doorway—the door itself had been removed—showed a capering throng of dancers of varying degrees of agility.

Reuben advanced languidly; his face wore the mingled look of exhaustion and nerve-tension which with him denoted great fatigue.

It had been a long day: in and out of court all the morning; two committee meetings, political and philanthropical, respectively, later on; a hurried club dinner; and an interminable first night, with hitches in the scene-shifting, and long waits between the acts.

He had told himself over and over again that he would "cut" the dance at his uncle's, and here he was—alleging to himself as an excuse the impossibility of getting to sleep directly after the theatre.

It was little more than a month that he had been home, and already his old enemy, insomnia, showed signs of being on the track.

Reuben made his way to a position near the foot of the stairs, which afforded a good view of the ball-room.

He could not see Judith, a circumstance which irritated him, as he did not wish to go in search of her.

Beyond, in the crowded refreshment room, he had a glimpse of Rose, who was exceedingly *friande*,[1] giggling behind a large pink ice, while Jack Quixano, a look of conscious waggishness on his face, dropped confidential remarks into her ear. Esther, on the stairs behind him, was delivering herself freely of cheap epigrams to an impecunious partner; and in a rose-lit recess was to be seen Montague Cohen, his pale, pompous, feeble face wreathed in smiles, enjoying himself hugely with a light-hearted matron from the Gentile camp.

The whole scene was familiar enough to Reuben, who from his boyhood upward had taken part in the festivities of his tribe,

---

1 Dainty (French).

with their gorgeously gowned and bejewelled women, elaborate floral decorations and costly suppers.

The Jew, it may be remarked in passing, eats and dresses at least two degrees above his Gentile brother in the same rank of life.

The music came to an end, and the dancers streamed out from the ball-room.

Alec Sachs, who had been dancing with his sister, brushed past Reuben in the throng, and the latter was mechanically aware of hearing him say to his partner:

"Mixed, very mixed! A scratch lot of people *I* call it."

Lionel Leuniger came rushing up to him in all the glory of an Eton suit and a white gardenia.

"So you've come at last, Reuben! You are very late, and all the pretty girls are engaged. Have a programme?"

Reuben did not answer. By this time the ball-room was almost empty, and he could see clearly into the room beyond, where a red cloth recess had been built in from the balcony.

CHAPTER XII.

There are flashes struck from midnights, there are
    fire-flames noondays kindle,
Whereby piled-up honours perish, whereby swollen
    ambitions dwindle....

★★★★★★

Oh, observe! Of course, next moment, the world's
    honours, in derision,
Trampled out the light for ever.

Browning: Christina.[1]

There were two people sitting there, to all appearance completely absorbed in one another. In the distance, Judith's head bending slightly forward, her profile, the curves of her neck and bosom,

---

1 Robert Browning, "Christina" (1842), lines 25-28, 49-51. Levy has revised the lines here.

and the white mass of her gown, were to be seen clearly outlined against the red. And another figure, in close proximity to the first, defined itself against the same background. Reuben started— Judith and Lee-Harrison!

His apathy, his fatigue, his uncertainty as to seeking Judith vanished as by magic. Outwardly he looked impassive as ever as he strolled into the all but deserted ballroom. It would have taken a close observer to perceive the repressed intensity of his every movement.

There was a draped alcove dividing the front and back drawing-rooms where Caroline Cardozo and Adelaide were standing as Reuben sauntered towards them.

"I hardly expected to see you," cried his sister as Reuben stopped and greeted the ladies. Adelaide was not enjoying herself. Her social successes, such as they were, were not usually obtained in the open competition of the ball-room.

"Am I too late for a dance?" asked Reuben, turning with deference to Miss Cardozo.

She handed him her card with a faint smile; there were two or three vacant places on it.

A great fortune (I am quoting Esther), though it always brings proposals of marriage, does not so invariably bring invitations to dance. Caroline Cardozo was a plain, thin, wistful girl, with a shy manner that some people mistook for stand-offishness, who was declared by the men of the Leunigers' set to be without an atom of "go."

Her wealth and importance notwithstanding, she was, as Rose in her capacity of hostess explained, difficult to get rid of.

Reuben, his dance duly registered, stood talking urbanely, while scrutinizing from beneath his lids the pair on the balcony.

A nearer view showed him the unmistakable devotion on Bertie's little fair face, which was lifted close to Judith's; he appeared to be devouring her with his eyes.

And Judith?

It seemed to Reuben that never before had he seen that light in her eyes, never that flush on her soft cheek, never that strange, indescribable, almost passionate air in her pose, in her whole presence.

His own heart was beating with a wild, incredulous anger, an astonished contempt. *He* to be careful of Judith; *he* to beware of engaging her feelings too deeply, *he*, who after all these years had never been able to bring that look into her eyes!

Bertie? it was impossible!

In any case (with sudden vindictiveness) it was unlikely that Bertie himself meant anything; and yet—yet—he was just the sort of man to do an idiotic thing of the kind.

The music struck up, and the dancers drifted back to the ballroom.

Reuben, bowing himself away, turned to see Judith and her escort standing behind him, while the latter, gathering courage, wrote his name again and again on her card.

Reuben remained a moment in doubt, then went straight up to her.

"Good-evening, Miss Quixano."

There was a note of irony in his voice, a look of irony on his pale, tense face; the glance that he shot at her from his brilliant eyes was almost cruel.

"Ah, good-evening, Reuben."

She gave a little gasp, thrilled, bewildered. Long ago, her searching glance travelling across the two crowded rooms had distinguished the top of Reuben's head in the hall beyond. She knew just the way the hair grew, just the way it was lifted from the forehead in a sidelong crest, just the way it was beginning to get a little thin at the temples.

Bertie moved off in search of his partner, with a bow and a reminder of future engagements.

"May I have the pleasure of a dance?"

Reuben retained his tone of ironical formality, but looking into her uplifted face his jealousy faded and was forgotten.

She held up her card with a smile; it was quite full.

Reuben took it gently from her hand, glanced at it, and tore it into fragments.

Judith said not a word.

To both of them the little act seemed fraught with strange significance, the beginning of a new phase in their mutual relations.

Reuben gave her his arm in silence; she took it, half frightened, and he led her to the furthermost corner of the crimson recess.

The dancers, overflowing from the ballroom beyond, closed about it, and they were screened from sight.

Reuben leaned forward, looking at her with eyes that seemed literally alight with some inward flame. The precautions, the restraints, the reserves which had hitherto fenced in their intercourse, were for the moment overthrown. Each was swept away on a current of feeling which was bearing them who knew whither?

To Judith, Reuben was no longer a commodity of the market

with a high price set on him; he was a piteous human creature who entreated her with his eyes, yet held her chained: her suppliant and her master.

A soft wind blew in suddenly through the red curtains and stirred the hair on Judith's forehead.

"Aren't you cold?"

Reuben broke the silence for the first time.

"No, not at all." She smiled, then holding back the red drapery with her hand, looked out into the night.

The November air was damp, warm, and filled full of a yellow haze which any but a Londoner would have called a fog.

Across the yard and a half of garden which divided the house from the street, she could see the long deserted thoroughfare with its double line of lamps, their flames shining dull through the mist.

Reuben watched her. The clear curve of the lifted arm, the beautiful lines of the half-averted face stirred his already excited senses.

"Judith!"

She turned her face, with its almost ecstatic look, towards him, letting fall the curtain.

There were some chrysanthemums like snowflakes in her bodice, scarcely showing against the white, and as she turned, Reuben bent towards her and laid his hand on them.

"I am going to commit a theft," he said, and his low voice shook a little.

Judith yielded, passive, rapt, as his fingers fumbled with the gold pin.

It was like a dream to her, a wonderful dream, with which the whirling maze of dancers, the heavy scents, the delicious music were inextricably mingled. And mingling with it also was a strange, harsh sound in the street outside, which, faint and muffled at first, was growing every moment louder and more distinct.

Reuben had just succeeded in releasing the flowers from their fastening; but he held them loosely, with doubtful fingers, realizing suddenly what he had done.

Judith shivered, vaguely conscious of a change in the moral atmosphere.

The noise in the street was very loud, and words could be distinguished.

"What is it they are saying?" he cried, dropping the flowers, springing to the aperture, and pulling back the curtain.

Outside the house stood a dark figure, a narrow crackling sheet flung across one shoulder. A voice mounted up, clear in discordance through the mist:

"Death of a Conservative M.P.! Death of the member for St. Baldwin's!"

"Ah, what is it?"

Cold, white, trembling, she too heard the words, and knew that they were her sentence.

He turned towards her; on his face was the look of a man who has escaped a great danger.

"Poor Ronaldson is dead. It has come suddenly at the last. No doubt I shall find a telegram at home."

He spoke in his most every-day tones, but he did not look at her.

She summoned all her strength, all her pride:

"Then I suppose you will be going down there to-morrow?"

Her voice never faltered.

"No; in any case I must wait till after the funeral."

He looked down stiffly. It was she who kept her presence of mind.

"Don't you want to buy a paper and to tell Adelaide?"

"If you will excuse me. Where shall I leave you?"

"Oh, I will stop here. The dance is just over."

He moved off awkwardly; she stood there white and straight, and never moving.

At her feet lay her own chrysanthemums, crushed by Reuben's departing feet.

She picked them up and flung them into the street.

At the same moment a voice sounded at her elbow:

"I have found you at last."

"Is this our dance, Mr. Lee-Harrison?"

CHAPTER XIII.

We did not dream, my heart, and yet
With what a pang we woke at last.

A. Mary F. Robinson.[1]

Rose, with a candle in her hand, stood at the top of the stairs and yawned.

It was half-past three; the last waltz had been waltzed, the last light extinguished, the last carriage had rolled away.

Bertie, on his road to Albert Hall Mansions, was dreaming dreams; and Reuben, as he tossed on his sleepless bed, pondering plans for the coming contest, was disagreeably haunted by the recollection of some white chrysanthemums which he had let fall—on purpose.

"It has been a great success," said Judith, passing by her cousin and going towards her own room.

Rose followed her, and sitting down on the bed, began drawing out the pins from her elaborately dressed hair.

"Yes, I think it went off all right. Caroline Cardozo stuck now and then, and no one would dance with poor Alec, so I had to take him round myself."

Judith laughed. She had danced straight through the programme, had eaten supper, had talked gaily in the intervals of dancing. Rose got up from the bed and went over to Judith.

"Please unfasten my bodice. I have sent Marie to bed."

Then, as Judith complied:

"What was Reuben telling Adelaide, and why did he make off so soon?"

"Mr. Ronaldson, the member for St. Baldwin's, is dead. A man came and shouted the news down the street."

Her voice was quite steady.

"What a ghoul Reuben is! He has been waiting to step into that dead man's shoes this last month and more.—'Reuben Sachs, M.P.'—'My brother, the member for St. Baldwin's'—'A man told me in the House last night'—'My son cannot get away while Parliament is sitting.'—The whole family will be quite unbearable."

---

1 A. Mary F. Robinson (1857-1944), "Semitones," *An Italian Garden: A Book of Songs* (1886), stanza 3, lines 1-2.

Judith bent her head over an obstinate knot in the silk dress-lace.

"He is not elected yet," she said.

Rose, her bodice unfastened, sprang round and faced her cousin.

"Reuben is as hard as nails!" she cried with apparent inconsequence. "Under all that good-nature, he is as hard as nails!"

"Undo my frock, please," said Judith, yawning with assumed sleepiness. "It must be nearly four o'clock."

Rose's capable fingers moved quickly in and out the lace; as she drew the tag from the last hole, she said: "Well, Judith, when are we to congratulate you?"

Judith did not affect to misunderstand the allusion. Bertie's open devotion had acted as a buffer between her and her smarting pride.

"Poor little person!" she said, and smiled.

"You might do worse," said Rose, gathering herself up for departure.

The mask fell off from Judith's face as the door closed on her cousin. She stood there stiff and cold in the middle of the room, her hands hanging loosely at her side.

Rose put her head in at the door—

"Do you know what Jack says?" she began, then stopped suddenly.

"Judith, don't look like that, it is no good."

"No," said Judith, lifting her eyes, "it is no good." Then she went over to the door and shut it.

She sat down on the edge of her little white bed, supporting one knee with a smooth, solid arm, while she stared into vacancy.

Nothing had happened—nothing; yet henceforward life would wear a different face for her and she knew it.

It was impossible any longer to deceive herself. Her wide, vacant eyes saw nothing, but her mental vision, grown suddenly acute, was confronted by a thronging array of images.

Yes, she was beginning to see it all now; dimly and slowly indeed at first, but with ever increasing clearness as she gazed; to see how it had all been from the beginning; how slowly and surely this thing had grown about her life; how in the night a silent foe had undermined the citadel.

She had been caught, snared in a fine, strong net of woven hair, this young, strong creature. Her strength mocked her in the clinging, subtle toils.

She got up from the bed slowly, stiffly, and stood again upright in the middle of the room. Forced into a position alien to her whole nature, to the very essence of her decorous, law-abiding soul, it was impossible that she should not seek to strike a blow in her own behalf.

"It is no good," Rose had said, and she had echoed the words. She did not put her thought into words, but her heart cried out in sudden rebellion, "Why was it no good?"

She went over mentally almost every incident in her intercourse with Reuben; saw how from day to day, from month to month, from year to year they had been drawn closer together in ever strengthening, ever tightening bonds. She remembered his voice, his eyes, his face—his near face—as she had heard and seen them a few short hours ago.

The conventions, the disguises, which she had been taught to regard as the only realities, fell down suddenly before the living reality of this thing which had grown up between her and Reuben. She recognized in it a living creature, wonderful, mysterious, beautiful and strong, with all the rights of its existence. It was impossible that they who had given it breath should do violence to it, should stain their hands with its blood—it was impossible.

She stood there still, her head lifted up, glowing with a strange exultation as her pride re-asserted itself.

Opposite was a mirror, a three-sided toilet mirror, hung against the wall, and suddenly Judith caught sight of her own reflected face with its wild eyes and flushed cheeks; her face which was usually so calm.

Calm? Had she ever been calm, save with the false calmness which narcotic drugs bestow? She was frightened of herself, of her own daring, of the wild, strange thoughts and feelings which struggled for mastery within her. There is nothing more terrible, more tragic than this ignorance of a woman of her own nature, her own possibilities, her own passions.

She covered her face with her hands, and in the darkness the thoughts came crowding (was it thought, or vision, or feeling?).

The inexorable realities of her world, those realities of which she had so rarely allowed herself to lose sight, came pressing back upon her with renewed insistence.

That momentary glow of exultation, of self-vindication faded before the hard daylight which rushed in upon her soul.

She saw not only how it had all been, but how it would all be to the end.

Then once more his low, broken voice was in her ear, his supplicating eyes before her; the music, the breath of dying flowers assailed once more her senses; she lived over again that near, far-off, wonderful moment.

Again Judith dropped her hands to her side; she clenched them in an intolerable agony; she took a few steps and flung herself face forwards on the pillow.

Shame, anger, pride, all were swept away in an overwhelming torrent of emotion; in a sudden flood of passion, of longing, of desolation.

Baffled, vanquished, she lay there, crushing out the sound of unresisted sobs.

From her heart rose only the cry of defeat:—

"Reuben, Reuben, have mercy on me!"

CHAPTER XIV.

Man's love is of man's life a thing apart;
'Tis woman's whole existence.

Byron.[1]

Judith slept far into the morning the sound, deep sleep of exhaustion; that sleep of the heavy-hearted from which, almost by an effort of will, the dreams are banished.

The first thing of which she was aware was the sound of Rose's voice, and then of Rose herself standing over her with a plate and a cup of coffee in her hand. Judith raised herself on her elbow; a vague sense of calamity clung to her; her eyes were heavy with more than the heaviness of sleep.

"It is ten o'clock," cried Rose. "I have brought you your breakfast. Rather handsome of me, isn't it?"

"Yes, very," said Judith, smiling faintly. "How came I to sleep so late?"

It was quite an event in her well-ordered existence; she realized it with a little shock which set her memory in motion.

Judith drank her coffee hastily and sprang out of bed. She

---

1 George Gordon, Lord Byron (1788-1824), *Don Juan* (1819-24), canto 1, stanza 194, lines 1-2.

went through her toilet with even more care and precision than usual; there is nothing more conducive to self-respect than a careful toilet.

Nothing had happened; everything had happened. Judith felt that she had grown older in the night.

All day long people came and went and gossiped; gossiped loudly and ceaselessly of last night's party; more cautiously and at intervals of Mr. Ronaldson's death.

In the evening Adelaide, Esther, and Mrs. Sachs came in, but not Reuben. Not Reuben—she knew her sentence.

That brief moment of clear vision, of courage, had faded, as we know, even as it came. Now she dared not even look back upon it—dared not think at all.

Nothing had happened—nothing.

She fell back upon the unconsciousness, the unsuspiciousness of her neighbours. For them the world was not changed; how was it possible that great things had taken place?

She talked, moved about, and went through all the little offices of her life.

Now and then she repeated to herself the formulæ on which she had been brought up, which she had always accepted, as to the unseriousness, the unreality of the romantic, the sentimental in life.

Two or three days went by without any event to mark them. On the fourth, Bertie Lee-Harrison paid a call of interminable length, when Judith, with bright eyes and flushed cheeks, talked to him with unusual animation.

In her heart she was thinking: "Reuben will never come again, and what shall I do?"

But the very next day Reuben came.

It was of course impossible that he should stay away for any length of time.

The Leunigers were at tea in the drawing-room after dinner when the door was pushed open, and he entered, as usual, unannounced.

Judith's heart leapt suddenly within her. The misery of the last few days melted like a bad dream. After all, were things any different from what they had always been?

Here was Reuben, here was she, face to face—alive—together.

He came slowly forwards, his eyelids drooping, an air of almost wooden immobility on his face. The black frock-coat which he wore, and in which he had that day attended Mr. Ronaldson's funeral, brought out the unusual sallowness of his complexion. There was a withered, yellow look about him to-night which forcibly recalled his mother.

Judith's heart grew very soft as she watched him shaking hands with her aunt and uncle.

"He is not well," she thought; then: "He always comes last to me."

But even as this thought flitted across her mind Reuben was in front of her, holding out his hand.

For a moment she stared astonished at the stiff, outstretched arm, the downcast, expressionless face, taking in the exaggerated, self-conscious indifference of his whole manner, then, with light-ning quickness, put her hand in his.

It was as though he had struck her.

She looked round, half-expecting a general protest against this public insult, saw the quiet, unmoved faces, and understood.

She, too, to outward appearance, was quiet and unmoved enough, as she sat there on a primrose-coloured ottoman, bending over a bit of work. But the blood was beating and surging in her ears, and her stiff, cold fingers blundered impo-tently with needle and thread.

Reuben finished his greetings, then sat down near his uncle. He had come, he explained, to say "good-bye" before going down to St. Baldwin's, for which, as he had expected, he had been asked to stand.

There was every chance of his being returned, Mr. Leuniger believed?

Well, yes. There was a small Radical party down there, cer-tainly, beginning to feel its way, and they had brought forward a candidate. Otherwise there would have been no opposition.

Sir Nicholas Kemys, who had a place down there, and who was member for the county of which St. Baldwin's was the chief town, had been very kind about it all. Lady Kemys was Lee-Har-rison's sister.

Judith listened, cold as a stone.

How could he bear to sit there, drawling out these facts to Israel Leuniger, which in the natural course of things should have been poured forth for her private benefit in delicious confidence and sympathy?

Esther, who was spending the evening with her cousins, came and sat beside her.

"You are putting green silk instead of blue into those corn-flowers," she cried.

Judith lifted her head and met the other's curious, penetrating glance.

"When I was a little girl," cried Esther, still looking at her, "a little girl of eight years old, I wrote in my prayer-book: 'Cursed art Thou, O Lord my God, Who hast had the cruelty to make me a woman.' And I have gone on saying that prayer all my life—the only one."[1]

Judith stared at her as she sat there, self-conscious, melodramatic, anxious for effect.

She never knew if mere whim or a sudden burst of cruelty had prompted her words.

"According to your own account, Esther," she said, "you must always have been a little beast."

Esther chuckled. Judith went on sewing, but changed her silks.

She wondered if the evening would never end, and yet she did not want Reuben to go.

He rose at last and made his farewells.

Judith put out her hand carelessly as he approached her, then, drawn by an irresistible magnetism, lifted her eyes to his.

As she did so, from Reuben's eyes flashed out a long melancholy glance of passion, of entreaty, of renunciation; and once again, even from the depths of her own humiliation, arose that strange, yearning sentiment of pity, with which this man, who was strong, ruthless and successful, had such power of inspiring her.

Only for a moment did their eyes meet, the next she had turned hers away—had in her turn grown cold and unresponsive.

How dared he look at her thus? How dared he profane that holiest of sorrows, the sorrow of those who love and are by fate separated?

---

1 See p. 74, note 1.

CHAPTER XV.

Wer nie sein Brod mit Thraenen ass,
Wer nie die kummervollen Naechte
Auf seinem Bette weinend sass,
Der Kennt euch nicht, ihr himmlische Maechte!

Goethe.[1]

There was a little set of shelves in Judith's bedroom which contained the whole of her modest library, some twenty books in all—*Lorna Doone*; Carlyle's *Sterling*; Macaulay's *Essays*; *Hypatia*; *The Life of Palmerston*; the *Life of Lord Beaconsfield*:[2] these were among her favourites, and they had all been given to her by Reuben Sachs.

Like many wholly unliterary people, she preferred the mildly instructive even in her fiction. It was a matter of surprise to her that clever creatures, like Leo and Esther for instance, should pass whole days when the fit was on in the perusal of such works as *Cometh Up as a Flower*, and *Molly Bawn*.[3]

---

1 Johann Wolfgang von Goethe (1749-1832), *Wilhelm Meister's Apprentice-ship* (1796), book 2, chapter 13: "The man who never ate his bread / With tears, nor spent nocturnal hours / In careworn weeping on his bed, / Cannot have known you, heavenly powers." See *Wilhelm Meister's Years of Apprenticeship*, trans. H.M. Waidson, vol. 1 (London: John Calder, 1977) 119.

2 R.D. Blackmore (1825-1900), *Lorna Doone* (1869), an historical novel about an ill-fated love; Thomas Carlyle (1795-1881), *Life of Sterling* (1851), a biography of John Sterling (1806-44), essayist, novelist, poet; Thomas Babington Macaulay (1800-59), statesman and historian, *Essays* (1843) on literary and historical subjects, including Jewish civil rights; Charles Kingsley (1819-75), *Hypatia, or New Foes with Old Faces* (1851), an historical novel about the Greek Neoplatonic philosopher; Henry Lytton Bulwer (1801-72), *The Life of Henry John Temple, Viscount Palmerston* (1870), on the eminent statesman whose career included foreign secretary and Prime Minister; Lewis Apjohn, *The Earl of Beaconsfield: His Life and Work* (1886) about Benjamin Disraeli, who died in 1881.

3 Rhoda Broughton, *Cometh Up as a Flower* (1867), a novel about a mildly scandalous romance of an outspoken narrator-heroine; Margaret Wolfe Hungerford (1855-97), *Molly Bawn* (1878), a light, frothy romance about an Irish girl.

But it was not novels, even the less frivolous ones, that Judith cared for.

Rose, whose own literary tastes inclined towards the society papers, varied by an occasional French novel, had said of her with some truth, that the drier a book was, the better she liked it. Reuben had long ago discovered Judith's power of following out a train of thought in her clear, careful way, and had taken pleasure in providing her with historical essays and political lives, and even in leading her through the mazes of modern politics.

Perhaps he did not realize, what it is always hard for the happy, objective male creature to realize, that if he had happened to be a doctor, Judith might have developed scientific tastes, or if a clergyman, have found nothing so interesting as theological discussion and the history of the Church.

Judith stood before her little library in the dark November dawn, with a candle in her hand, scanning the familiar titles with weary eyes. She was so young and strong, that even in her misery she could sleep the greater part of the night; but these last few days she had taken to waking at dawn, to lying for hours wide-eyed in her little white bed, while the slow day grew.

But to-day it was intolerable, she could bear it no longer, to lie and let the heavy, inarticulate sorrow prey on her.

She would try a book; not a very hopeful remedy in her own opinion, but one which Reuben, Esther, and Leo, who were all troubled by sleeplessness, regarded, she knew, as the best thing under the circumstances.

So she scanned the familiar bookshelves, then turned away; there was nothing there to meet her case.

She put on her dressing-gown and stole out softly across the passage to Leo's empty room, where she remembered to have seen some books.

Here she set down the candle, and, as she looked round the dim walls, her thoughts went out suddenly to Leo himself, went out to him with a new tenderness, with something that was almost beyond comprehension.

She knew, though she did not use the word to herself, that after some blind, groping fashion of his own, Leo was an idealist—poor Leo!

There were books on a table near, and she took them up one by one: some volumes of Heine, in prose and verse; the operatic score of *Parsifal*; Donaldson on the *Greek Theatre*; and then two books of poetry, each of which, had she but known it, appealed strongly to two strongly marked phases of Leo's mood—*Poems and Ballads*, and a worn green copy of the poems of Clough.[1]

She turned over the leaves carelessly.

Poetry? Yes, she would try a little poetry. She had always enjoyed reading Tennyson and Shakespeare in the schoolroom. So she put the books under her arm, went back to her room, and crept into her little cold bed.

She took up the volume of Swinburne and began reading it mechanically by the flickering candlelight.

The rolling, copious phrases conveyed little meaning to her, but she liked the music of them. There was something to make a sophisticated onlooker laugh in the sight of this young, pure creature, with her strong, slow-growing passions, her strong, slow-growing intellect, bending over the diffuse, unreserved, unrestrained pages. She came at last to one poem, the *Triumph of Time*, which seemed to have more meaning than the others, and which arrested her attention, though even this was only comprehensible at intervals. She read on and on:—

"I have given no man of any fruit to eat;
I have trod the grapes, I have drunken the wine.
Had you eaten and drunken and found it sweet,
This wild new growth of the corn and vine,
This wine and bread without lees or leaven,
We had grown as gods, as the gods in heaven,
Souls fair to look upon, goodly to greet,
One splendid spirit, your soul and mine.

"In the change of years, in the coil of things,
In the clamour and rumour of life to be,
We, drinking love at the furthest springs,
Covered with love as a covering tree,
We had grown as gods, as the gods above,
Filled from the heart to the lips with love,
Held fast in his arms, clothed warm with his wings,
O love, my love, had you loved but me!

---

1   Heinrich Heine (see p. 78, note 1), a much admired and anguished Jewish-German poet who converted to Christianity for career purposes; Levy translated his poems and was influenced by his work (see Appendix B5); Richard Wagner (1818-83), his last opera, *Parsifal* (1882); John William Donaldson (1811-61), *The Theatre of the Greeks* (1879); Algernon Charles Swinburne, *Poems and Ballads* (1887); Arthur Hugh Clough (1819-61), *Poems* (1862).

"We had stood as the sure stars stand, and moved
As the moon moves, loving the world; and seen
Grief collapse as a thing disproved,
Death consume as a thing unclean.
Twin halves of a perfect heart, made fast
Soul to soul while the years fell past;
Had you loved me once, as you have not loved;
Had the chance been with us that has not been."[1]

The slow tears gathered in her eyes, and forcing themselves forward fell down her cheeks.

Then there was, after all, something to be said for feelings which had not their basis in material relationships. They were not mere phantasmagoria conjured up by silly people, by sentimental people, by women. Clever men, men of distinction, recognized them, treated them as of paramount importance.

The practical, if not the theoretical, teaching of her life had been to treat as absurd any close or strong feeling which had not its foundations in material interests. There must be no undue giving away of one's self in friendship, in the pursuit of ideas, in charity, in a public cause. Only gushing fools did that sort of thing, and their folly generally met with its reward.

And this teaching, sensible enough in its way, had been accepted without question by the clannish, exclusive, conservative soul of Judith.

Where your interests lie, there should lie your duties; and where your duties, your feelings. A wholesome doctrine no doubt, if not one that will always meet the far-reaching and complicated needs of a human soul.

And if this doctrine applied to friendship, to philanthropy, to art and politics, in how much greater a degree must it apply to love, to the unspoken, unacknowledged love between a man and woman; a thing in its very essence immaterial, and which, in its nature, can have no rights, no duties attached to it?

It was the very hatred of the position into which she had been forced, the very loathing of what was so alien to her whole way of life and mode of thought that was giving Judith courage; if she could not vindicate herself, she must be simply crushed beneath the load of shame.

On one point, the nature and extent of her feeling for Reuben, there could no longer be illusion or self-deception; she would have walked to the stake for him without a murmur, and she knew it.

---

1   Swinburne, "The Triumph of Time," *Poems and Ballads* (1866).

She knew, too, that Reuben loved her as far as in him lay; knew, with a bitter humiliation, how far short of hers fell his love.

Yet deep in her heart lay the touching obstinate belief of the woman who loves—that she was necessary to him, that she alone could minister to his needs; that in turning away from her and her large protection, her infinite toleration, he was turning away from the best which life had to offer him.

In the first sharp agony of awakening, Judith, as we know, had recognized that which had grown up between her and Reuben as a reality with rights and claims of its own. And the conviction of this was slowly growing upon her in the intervals of the swinging back of the pendulum, when she judged herself by conventional standards and felt herself withered by her own scorn, the scorn of her world, and the scorn of the man she loved.

A great tear splashing down across the *Triumph of Time* recalled her to herself.

She shut the book and sat up in bed, sweeping back the heavy masses of hair from her forehead.

Often and often, with secret contempt and astonishment, had she seen Esther dissolved in tears over her favourite poets.

Should she grow in time to be like Esther, undignified, unreserved? Would people talk about her, pity her, say that she had had unfortunate love affairs?

Oh, yes, they would talk, that was the way of her world; even Rose who was kind, and her own mother who loved her; no doubt they had begun to talk already.

Then, with a sense of unutterable weariness, she fell back on the pillows and slept.

CHAPTER XVI.

....What help is there?
There is no help, for all these things are so.

A.C. Swinburne.[1]

"Come over here, Judith, and I will show you something," said Ernest Leuniger as he sat by the fire in the morning-room.

1   Swinburne, "A Leave-Taking," *Poems and Ballads* (1866), lines 10-11.

It was two days after Reuben's departure for St. Baldwin's, and Ernest had returned from the country that morning.

She went over to him, drawing a chair close to his. Judith was always very kind to him, and he admired her immensely, treating her at intervals with a sort of gallantry.

"Now look at me!" He had the solitaire board on his knee, and a little glass ball, with coloured threads spun into it, between his fingers.

"There, and there, and there!"

Judith bent forward dutifully, watching how he lifted the marbles, one after the other, from their holes.

"Don't you see?

He looked at her triumphantly, but a little irritated at her obtuseness.

"Oh, yes," said Judith vaguely.

"The figure eight—don't you see?"

He pointed to the balls remaining on the board.

"So it is! Where did you learn to do that?" she asked, smiling gently.

"Ah, that's telling, isn't it?" He chuckled slyly, swept the balls together with his hand, and announced his intention of going in search of his man, with a view to a game of billiards.

Judith sank back in her chair as the door closed on him. The fire-light played about her face, which, though not less beautiful, had grown to look older. She had been living hard these last few days.

The door opened, and Rose came in with her hat on and a parcel in her hand.

"No tea?" she cried, kneeling down on the hearthrug and holding out her hands to the fire.

"It isn't five o'clock yet."

There was an air of tension, of expectancy almost about Judith which contrasted markedly with her habitual serenity.

Rose turned suddenly. "When, Judith, *when?*" she cried with immense archness.

"I don't know," said Judith quietly.

There had been a dance the night before at the Kohnthals, where Bertie's unconcealed devotion to herself had been one of the events of the hour.

"Judith!"—Rose regarded her with excitement—"do you mean to say he has—spoken? Or are you humbugging in that serious way of yours?"

"Mr. Lee-Harrison has not proposed to me, if that is what you want to know."

Rose unfastened her fur mantle in silence. Something in Judith's manner puzzled her.

"He really is a nice little person," Rose went on after a pause; "such beautiful manners!"

"Oh, he hands plates and opens doors very prettily."

Judith spoke with a certain weary scorn, which Rose accepted as the tone of depreciation natural to a woman who discusses an undeclared admirer.

As a matter of fact, Judith recognized clearly the marks of breeding, the hundred and one fine differences which distinguished Bertie from the people of her set, whose manners were almost invariably tinged with respect of persons—that sure foe to respect of humanity. She recognized them and their value as hallmarks, wondering all the time with a dreary wonder, that any one should attach importance to such things as these.

For in her heart she despised the man. His intelligent fluency, his unfailing, monotonous politeness were a weariness to her.

His very readiness to fall down utterly before her, seemed to her—alas, poor Judith!—in itself a brand of inferiority.

"Tea at last," cried Rose, as the door opened. "And Adelaide. What a scent you have for tea, Addie."

Mrs. Montague Cohen swept in past the servant with the tray and took possession of the best chair.

"Mamma is here too," she cried; "she and aunt Ada will be in in a minute."

She drew off her gloves and the two girls rose to greet Mrs. Sachs, who at this point came with Mrs. Leuniger into the room.

Judith gave her hand very quietly to Reuben's mother, then took her seat at some distance from the group round the tea-table, occupying herself with cutting the leaves of a novel that had just arrived from Mudie's.[1]

"Reuben is nominated," cried Adelaide, as she helped herself liberally to tea-cake. "We had a telegram this morning."

"He expects to get in *this* time?" said Mrs. Leuniger, her pessimistic mind reverting naturally to her nephew's first unsuccessful attempt at embarking on a political career.

"It won't be for want of interest if he doesn't," said Mrs.

---

1 Mudie's Circulating Library (1842-1937), founded by Charles Edward Mudie, was the prominent lending library in Victorian England, where patrons paid annual subscriptions that entitled them to borrow books a volume at a time. The main establishment was located in Oxford Street.

Sachs; "Sir Nicholas Kemys and his wife are working day and night for him—day and night."

"And Miss Lee-Harrison, Lady Kemys' sister, *she* seems to be quite specially zealous in the good cause," put in Adelaide with meaning.

Secretly she was mortified at not having been asked down to St. Baldwin's for the campaign, Reuben having met her hints on the subject in a very decided manner. There was some satisfaction in venting her feelings on Judith, for whose benefit her last remark was uttered.

"When is the election?" said Rose, turning to her aunt.

"Not till to-day week. But I may safely say there is no real cause for anxiety."

"Did you see last night's *Globe?*" cried Adelaide, "and the *St. James's?* They cracked up Reuben no end."

Judith had seen them; she had seen also the *Pall Mall Gazette*, which expressed itself in very different terms.[1]

She had put back *Poems and Ballads* on its shelf, and had taken to reading all the articles respecting the prospects of the St. Baldwin's elections that she could lay hands on.

At least she had a right to be interested in what she had been told so much about, but there were times when she felt, as she read, that her interest was intrusive, a thing to be ashamed of.

"I suppose," said Rose, "that he is too busy to write much."

"We had a letter yesterday—just a line. He seemed in splendid spirits, and has promised to wire from time to time," answered Adelaide.

"A good son," said Mrs. Sachs half tenderly, half jestingly, very proudly, "who never forgets his mother."

So the talk went on.

Judith sat there listening, cutting open her novel, and throwing in a remark from time to time.

Every word that was uttered seemed a brick in the wall that was building between herself and Reuben.

In this crisis of his career, so long looked forward to, so often discussed, he had no need, no thought of her. Adelaide, Esther, Rose, all had more claim on him than she; she was shut out from his life.

Reuben, disappointed, defeated: in such a one she would

---

1 All three London daily newspapers: *The Globe* (1803-1921) and *The St. James's Gazette* (1880-1905) had a conservative orientation, while *The Pall Mall Gazette* (1865-present) had a broader appeal.

always, in spite of himself, have felt her rights. But Reuben, hopeful, successful, surrounded by admiring friends and relatives, fenced in more closely still by his mother's love: from the contemplation of this glittering figure, cruel, triumphant, she turned away in a stony agony of self-contempt.

There was a sound of carriage wheels outside, and Lionel, who had been reconnoitring in the hall, burst in with the announcement, "Grandpapa has come."

Mrs. Leuniger received the news with something like agitation. Old Solomon's visits were few and far between, and now as he came, with pompous uncertainty of step across the room, the whole group by the fireplace rose hastily and went to meet him.

"Reuben is nominated," cried Adelaide, when the old man had been established in a chair.

"Yes, yes," said Solomon Sachs, "so I hear."

He turned to his niece: "He ain't looking well, that boy of yours."

Mrs. Sachs shifted uneasily.

"You saw him just before he went, uncle Solomon, when he was tired out and not himself. He had been running from pillar to post all the week."

Mrs. Leuniger muttered dejectedly: "He is getting to look like his father."

Old Solomon raised his square hand to his beard, lifting his eyebrows high above the grave, shrewd, melancholy eyes.

Mrs. Sachs started; a sudden look of terror came into her face; the whites of her little hard eyes grew visible.

"Why don't he marry?" said Solomon Sachs after a pause; "why don't he marry that daughter of Cardozo's? She's not much to look at, certainly," he added, and a wave of whimsical amusement broke out suddenly over the large, grave face.

"Yes," put in Mrs. Leuniger, unusually loquacious, "his wife might see that he didn't work himself to death."

"I don't see how he can work less," cried Adelaide; "he has his way to make. And making your way, in these days, means pulling a great many strings."

"Yes," said Mrs. Sachs, relieved by this view of the case, "he must get on."

Judith began to feel that her powers of endurance had their limits. She rose slowly, went over to the fireplace for a moment, threw a casual remark to Rose, and went from the room.

As she made her way up stairs the postman's knock sounded

through the house, and then Lionel came running to her with a letter.

Her correspondence was very small, and she glanced with but faint interest at the little packet in her cousin's hand.

He was carrying it seal upwards, and suddenly her heart beat with a wild, mad beating, and the colour leapt to her pale cheeks.

She could see that it was sealed with wax. There was only one person that she knew who fastened his letters so. Reuben invariably made use of the signet ring which had belonged to his father, engraved with a crest duly bought and paid for at the Heralds' College.[1]

She took the precious thing in her hand, closing her fingers over it, and smiled radiantly at the little boy.

"Thank you, Lionel."

Her room gained, she locked the door, sat down on the bed, and looked at her letter—

"To Miss Judith Quixano."

The writing was certainly not Reuben's, and he never used the "To."

Then she turned it over and examined the seal, the seal that was totally unfamiliar. She felt a little sick, a little dazed, and leaned her head against the wall.

After a time she opened the letter and read it.

It was from Bertie Lee-Harrison, who asked her to be his wife.

It was a long letter, and stated, amongst other things, that he had already obtained his uncle's permission to address her.

Old Solomon's words as to his grandson's marriage flashed into her mind. It struck her that these plans for Reuben, for herself, were nothing less than an outrage.

It struck her also that she might marry Bertie.

All her courage had deserted her, all her daring of thought and feeling, in the face of a world where thought and feeling were kept apart from word and deed.

She too must fall down and worship at the shrine of the great god Expediency.

For how, otherwise, could she live her life?

Thrust out from Reuben's friendship, from all that made her happiness; shorn of self-respect, of the respect of her world; how could she bear to go on in the old track?

---

1 Chartered in 1483 by Richard III, its purpose is to trace lineages to determine heraldic privileges, and to assign new coats of arms.

To her blind misery, her ignorance, Bertie was nothing more than a polite little figure holding open for her a door of escape.

CHAPTER XVII.

O'Thursday let it be: o'Thursday, tell her,
She shall be married to this noble earl.

Romeo and Juliet.[1]

The news of Bertie's proposal spread like fire in the family.

Rose had a vision of bridesmaids' gowns and of belted earls at the wedding. Lionel and Sidney, who always knew everything without being told, scented wedding-cake from afar, and indulged in a great deal of chaff *sotto voce* at their cousin's expense.

Adelaide was so excited when the news reached her, that she flattened her nose with the handle of her parasol, and exclaimed with her usual directness: "I wonder if the Norwood people will receive her."

Like every one else, she took for granted that Judith would not be allowed to let slip so brilliant an opportunity.

A little maidenly hesitation, a little genuine reluctance perhaps—for Bertie was not the man to take a girl's fancy—and Judith would give further proof of her good sense; would open her mouth and shut her eyes and swallow what the Fates had sent her.

Poor Mrs. Quixano, greatly agitated, vibrated between the Walterton Road and Kensington Palace Gardens, expending quite a little fortune on blue omnibuses.

It took a long time for her brother to convince her that Bertie's spurious Judaism could for a moment be accepted as the real thing.

"He is not a Jew," she reiterated obstinately; "would you let your own daughter marry him?"

Israel Leuniger evaded the question.

---

1 Shakespeare, *Romeo and Juliet* III.iv.20-21.

"My dear Golda, he is as much a Jew as you or I. Her father is perfectly satisfied, as well he may be—it is a brilliant match."

Mrs. Leuniger realized perfectly the meaning of £5000 a year. Bertie's other advantages, such, for instance, as his connection with the Norwoods, had little weight with her. If he had been one of the Cardozos, or of the Silberheims—the great Jewish bankers—she could have understood all this fuss about his family.

"Who are the girls to marry in these days?" Mrs. Sachs said later on, as she, Mrs. Quixano, and Mrs. Leuniger sat in consultation. "If I had unmarried daughters I should tell them they would have to marry Germans."

The extreme nature of this statement did not fail to impress her hearers.

While the matrons sat in conclave in the primrose-coloured drawing-room, Judith up stairs in her own little domain was trying to come to a decision on the subject of their discussion.

She had asked for time, for a few days in which to make up her mind, and of these, three had already gone by. But from the first there had always been this thing in her mind, this thing from which she shrank—that she would marry Bertie.

Her loneliness, her utter isolation of spirit in that crowded house where she was for the moment a centre of interest, a mark for observation, are difficult to realize. A severance of home ties had been to a certain extent involved in her change of homes. Her nearest approach to intimate women friends were Rose and Esther. As for the one friend who had wound his way into her reserved, exclusive soul, who had made a path into her inclosed, restricted life, he was her friend no more.

Reuben, oh, humiliation! had shown her plainly that he was afraid of her; afraid of any claims she might choose to base on the friendship which had existed between them. There was always this thought in her mind goading her.

On the faces round her she read nothing but anxiety that she would make up her mind without delay. She knew what was expected of her.

Sometimes she thought she could have borne it better if some one had said outright:

"We know that you love Reuben; that Reuben loves you after a fashion. But it is no good crying for the moon; take your half loaf and be thankful for it."

It was this absolute, stony ignoring of all that had gone before which seemed to crush the life out of her.

She was growing to feel that in loving Reuben she had committed a crime too shameful for decent people even to speak of.

That Reuben had ever loved her she now doubted. It had all been a chimera of the emotional female brain, of which Reuben, who was subject, as we know, to occasional lapses of taste, had often confided to her his contempt. Yet even now there were moments when, remembering all that had gone before, it seemed to her impossible that Reuben should do long without her.

If she flew in the face of nature and said "Yes" to Bertie, surely he would come forward and protest against such an outrage.

Every day she devoured the scraps of news which the papers contained respecting the coming election at St. Baldwin's.

Sometimes her mind dwelt on the splendours of the prospect held out before her; splendours which, in her ignorance, she was disposed to exaggerate. Reuben, climbing to those social heights, which for herself she had always deemed inaccessible, Reuben reaching the summit, would find her there before him. That would impress him greatly, she knew.

Let this thought be forgiven her; let it be remembered who was her hero, and how little choice there had been for her in the matter of heroes.

Yet such are the contradictions of our nature, that had the Admirable Crichton[1] stood before her, Don Quixote, or Sir Galahad himself, I cannot answer for Judith that she would not have turned from them to the mixed, imperfect human creature—Reuben Sachs.

So she sat there swaying this way and that, and then the door opened and her mother came in. Mrs. Quixano, we know, was not pleased at heart, but she had become very anxious for the marriage.

Judith listened passively as the advantages of her future position were laid before her.

Then she made her protest, fully conscious of its weakness.

"I do not like Mr. Lee-Harrison."

"Of course not," said Mrs. Quixano. "I should be sorry to hear that you did. No girl likes her intended—at first."

Judith bowed her head, conscious, ashamed.

Only that afternoon Rose had said to her: "We all have to

---

1   James Crichton (1560-82), a Scotsman descended from royalty and known as "the Admirable Crichton" for his remarkable travels and knowledge of 12 languages.

marry the men we don't care for. I shall, I know, although I have a lot of money. I am not sure that it is not best in the end."

And she sighed, as a red-headed, cousinly vision rose before her mental sight.

"You are coming home with me," went on Mrs. Quixano, "then we can talk it over comfortably. You mustn't keep the poor man waiting much longer."

Mrs. Leuniger came in as Judith was tying her bonnet strings.

"Judith is coming with me," said her mother.

Aunt Ada drifted slowly across the room to where Judith was standing. She looked at her with her miserable eyes, rubbing her hands together as she said:

"You had better write to Mr. Lee-Harrison before you go. You won't get such an opportunity as this every day."

Judith stared at her aunt in a sort of desperation.

She, too? Aunt Ada, who all the days of her life had known wealth, splendour, importance, and, as far as could be seen, had never enjoyed an hour's happiness!

She looked at the dejected, untidy figure, with the load of diamonds on the fingers, the rich lace round neck and wrists, the crumpled gown of costly silk.

Aunt Ada still believed in these things then; in diamonds, lace and silk? Did not wring her hands and cry, "all is vanity!"

Hers was truly an astonishing manifestation of faith.

★★★★★

Judith sat in her father's study in the Walterton Road.

On the desk before her lay the letter which she had written and sealed to Mr. Lee-Harrison, containing her acceptance of his offer.

A certain relief had come with the deed. She had opened up for herself a new field of action; she would be reinstated in the eyes of her world, in Reuben's eyes, in her own.

She was so strong, so cruelly vital that it never for an instant occurred to her that she might pine and fade under her misery. She would have laughed to scorn such a thought.

Not thus could she hope for escape. A new field of action— there lay her best chance.

Her father came up to her and put his hand on her shoulder. She lifted her mournful glance to his; the kind, vague regard was inexpressibly soothing after the battery of eyes to which she had been recently exposed.

"I hope, my dear," said Joshua Quixano, "that you are quite happy in this engagement?"

"Oh, yes, papa," answered Judith; but suddenly, as she spoke, the tears welled to her eyes and poured down her face.

Such a display of feeling on her part was without precedent. Both father and daughter were exceedingly shy, though in neither case with that shyness which manifests itself in outward physical flutter.

Mr. Quixano, deeply moved, stretched out his arms, and putting them about her, drew her close against him.

"My dear girl, my dear girl, you are not to do this unless you are sure it is for your happiness. Remember, there is always a home for you here. You can always come back to us."

She let her face lie on his breast, while the tears flowed unchecked. His words, the kind, timid, caressing movements with which he accompanied them were sweet to her, though in the depths of her heart she knew that there was no turning back.

Material advantage; things that you could touch and see and talk about; that these were the only things which really mattered, had been the unspoken gospel of her life.

Now and then you allowed yourself the luxury of a fine sentiment in speech, but when it came to the point, to take the best that you could get for yourself was the only course open to a person of sense.

The push, the struggle, the hunger and greed of her world rose vividly before her. Wealth, power, success—a flaunting success for all men to see; had she not believed in these things as the most desirable on earth? Had she not always wished them to fall to the lot of the person dearest to her? Did she not believe in them still? Was she not doing her best to secure them for herself?

But she was Joshua Quixano's daughter—was it possible that she cared for none of these things?

CHAPTER XVIII.

The essence of love is kindness; and indeed it
may be best defined as passionate kindness.

R.L. Stevenson[1]

There is nothing more dear to the Jewish heart than an engagement; and when, four days after the events of the last chapter,
that between Judith and Bertie was made public, congratulations
flowed in, people called at all hours of the day, and the house in
Kensington Palace Gardens presented a scene of cheerful activity and excitement.

The Community, after much discussion, much shaking of
heads over the degeneracy of the times, had decided on accepting Bertie's veneer of Judaism as the real thing, and the engagement was treated like any other. If Mr. Lee-Harrison had continued in the faith of his fathers this would not have been the case.
Though both engagement and marriage would in a great number
of instances have been countenanced, their recognition would
have been less formal and public, and of course a fair proportion
of Jews would never have recognized them at all.

As it was, the brilliancy of the match was considered a little
dimmed by the fact of Bertie's not being of the Semitic race. It
showed indifferent sportsmanship, if nothing else, to have failed
in bringing down one of the wily sons of Shem.

The Samuel Sachses came over at the first opportunity to *wish
joy*, as they themselves expressed it, and inspect the new *fiancé*.

It is possible that they were not well received, for Netta gave
out subsequently, whenever the Lee-Harrisons were in question:
"We don't visit. Mamma doesn't approve of mixed marriages."

The day on which the engagement was announced happened
also to be that of the election, and in the course of the afternoon
Adelaide burst in, much excited by the double event.

"An overwhelming majority!" she cried; "Reuben is in by an
overwhelming majority."

Then going up to Judith, she gave her a sounding kiss.

"I am so glad, dear," she said gushingly.

---

1   Robert Louis Stevenson (1850-94), "On Falling in Love," *Virginibus
    Puerisque* (1881).

Judith submitted to this display of affection with a good grace. For the last four days she had been living in a dream; a dream peopled by phantoms, who went and came, spoke and smiled, but had about as much reality as the figures of a magic lantern.[1]

As before Bertie's proposal she had been too much preoccupied to be much aware of him, so now she continued to accept his attentions in the same spirit of amiable indifference and unconsciousness. Bertie, as Gwendolen Harleth said of Grandcourt, was not disgusting.[2] He took his love, as he took his religion, very theoretically. There was something not unpleasant in the atmosphere of respectful devotion with which he contrived to surround her.

"Where is your young man?" went on Adelaide, taking a seat close to Judith, and noting with admiration the rich colour in her face, the wonderful brilliance of her eyes.

She felt very friendly towards the girl, who was safely out of her brother's way, and was doing so remarkably well for herself.

Afterwards she observed to her husband: "Judith looked quite good-looking. I always say there is nothing like being engaged for improving a girl's complexion."

"Am I my young man's keeper?" answered Judith lightly. "But I believe he is at Christie's."[3]

"When can you come and dine with us?" went on Adelaide, who had never asked Judith to dinner before. "I will get some pleasant people to meet you. You shall choose your own night. Reuben must come as well—if he is not too jealous."

Adelaide did not mean to be cruel. She honestly believed that before the solid reality of an engagement, such vapour as unspoken, unacknowledged feeling must at once have melted.

And Judith was beyond being hurt by her words.

"I don't know exactly when we can come. Blanche Kemys wants us to go down there for a day or two next week. And we are half promised to Geraldine Sydenham for the week after."

She pronounced these distinguished names thus familiarly

---

1 A forerunner of the modern slide projector, a device of optical projection related to the camera obscura, shadow shows, and the magic mirror; a popular form of Victorian entertainment.

2 Levy is comparing Judith to Eliot's heroine Gwendolen in *Daniel Deronda* (chapter 28), who repeatedly comments on her suitor's manner of detachment in this fashion.

3 The famous London auction house, established in 1766, dealing in art treasures as well as all manner of objects, including the 1882 sale of Hamilton Palace in Scotland.

with a secret amusement, a sense that there was really a great deal of fun to be got out of Adelaide.

Mrs. Cohen stared open-mouthed, frankly impressed.

She had no idea that Bertie's people would come round without any difficulty in that way, and visions of herself and Monty honoured guests at Norwood Towers began to dance before her mental vision.

Esther, noting the little comedy, smiled to herself. She had perhaps a clearer view of Judith's state of mind than any one else.

Judith indeed had almost succeeded in banishing thought during the last few days.

The persistent questions: "What will Reuben think?" "When will he know?" were the nearest approach to thought she had allowed herself.

Rose, who was thoroughly enjoying the engagement, and had confided to Judith that, once married, "she would be all right," came in at this point, and in her turn was made acquainted with the results of the election.

"Reuben comes back to-night by the last train, the 12.15," added Mrs. Cohen.

Judith thought: "He knows now."

Lady Kemys would certainly have told him what that morning had been a public fact.

People streamed in and out all the afternoon, greatly disappointed at not finding Bertie.

At six Judith, at the instigation of Rose, went to dress for dinner. Bertie had announced his intention of coming early.

As she shut the drawing-room door behind her, the muscles of her face relaxed, she stood a moment at the foot of the stairs like a figure of stone.

Mrs. Sachs, emerging from Mr. Leuniger's private room, where she had been imparting the news of her son's triumph, came upon her thus.

"My dear!" she cried, going up to her.

Judith roused herself at once, and held out her hand with the comedy-smile which she had learned to wear these last few days.

Mrs. Sachs looked up at her, curiously moved. "My dear, I have to congratulate you."

"And I to congratulate you, Mrs. Sachs."

Their eyes met.

Hitherto Judith had been too proud to make the least advance to Reuben's mother, to respond even to any advance the latter might choose to make. But things were changed between them now.

She looked down at the sallow face, the shrewd eyes lifted to hers, almost, it seemed, in deprecation, in sympathy almost.

Her beautiful face quivered; stooping forward, she pressed her lips with sudden passion to the other's wrinkled cheek.

CHAPTER XIX.

....This life's end, and this love-bliss have been
    lost here. Doubt you whether
This she felt, as looking at me, mine and her souls
    rushed together?

Browning: Christina[1]

Esther sat a little apart, watching the lovers.

"Does she think he is a cardboard man to play with, or an umbrella to take shelter under?" she reflected. "A lover may be a shadowy creature, but husbands are made of flesh and blood. Doesn't she see already that he is as obstinate as a mule, and as whimsical as a goat?"

And she repeated the phrase to herself well pleased with it.

It was Sunday, the day following that of the election. A great family party had dined in Kensington Palace Gardens, and now were awaiting Reuben in the primrose-coloured drawing-room.

Judith, side by side with Bertie, was listening amiably to a fluent account of his adventures in Asia Minor, in which he dwelt a great deal on his state of mind and state of health at the time; while Rose played scraps of music for the benefit of Jack Quixano, who had a taste for comic opera.

Judith was in such a state of tension as scarcely to be conscious of pain. Her duties as *fiancée* were clearly marked out; anything was better than those days of chaos, of upheaval, which had preceded her engagement.

Esther's favourite phrase, that marriage was an opiate, had occurred to her more than once during the past week.

"I sat up all night long, and read every word of it. I was determined to make up my mind once for all," Bertie was saying.

Rose, at the piano, put her hand on her hip and hummed

---

1 Robert Browning, "Christina," lines 45-48.

a scrap from a music-hall song, while Jack whistled an accompaniment:

"Stop the cab,
Stop the cab,
Woh, woh, woh!"

The hall-door banged to with some violence.

The voices of Lionel and Sidney were heard upraised without: "Vote for Sachs! Vote for Sachs, the people's friend!"

Then came the sound of another voice—

"My head was like a live coal, and my feet were as cold as stones..." went on Bertie.

Judith looked sympathetic, and her heart leaped suddenly within her: it had not yet unlearnt the trick of leaping at the sound of Reuben's voice. Lionel flung open the door and capered into the room.

Behind him came Reuben Sachs.

Judith knew nothing more till she and Reuben were standing face to face, holding one another's hands.

Whatever had happened before, whatever happened afterwards, she will remember to the day of her death that in that one moment, at least, they understood one another.

No need for question, for answer, for explanation of motives and feelings.

It was all as clear as daylight, in that strange, brief, interminable moment which to the onlookers showed nothing more than a pale, tired-looking gentleman offering his congratulations on her engagement to a flushed, bright-eyed lady.

Even that sharp battery of eyes could discover nothing more than this.

It was not long before the hall-door closed again upon Reuben.

He flung out into the night.

"Good God, good God!" he said to himself. Not till he had actually seen her had he been able to realize what had happened; to understand what manner of change had come into his life; to see what might have been, and what was.

He had so many things to tell her, which might never now be told. The blind, choking rage of a baffled creature came over him; he sped on, stifled, through the darkness.

Judith, sitting dazed and smiling in the gaslight, said over and over again in her heart:

"Oh my poor Reuben, my poor, poor Reuben!"
At the piano Rose and Jack sang in chorus:

"For he's going to marry, Yum Yum,
    Yum Yum.
Your anger pray bury,
For all will be merry,
I think you had better succumb,
    cumb—cumb!"[1]

★★★★★

At the beginning of January there was a wedding at the synagogue in Upper Berkeley Street[2] which excited unusual interest.
The beautiful bride in her white silk dress was greatly
admired. She was very pale, certainly, and in her wide-open eyes
an acute observer might have read an expression of something
like terror; but acute observers, fortunately, are few and far
between. The bridegroom, to all appearance, enjoyed himself
immensely, going through the whole pageant with great exact-
ness, smashing the wine-glass vigourously with his little foot, and
sipping the wine daintily from the silver cup.[3]

Old Solomon Sachs, whose own daughters had been married
in the drawing-room at Portland Place, but who had no prejudice
against the new fashion of weddings in the synagogue, occupied
a prominent place near the ark, surrounded by his family.

Reuben Sachs stood close to Leopold Leuniger, a little in the
background. His face was absolutely expressionless, unless weariness may be allowed to count as expression. He wanted yet a year
or two of thirty, and already he was beginning to lose his look of
youth. Leo, it must be owned, paid little attention to the ceremony. His eyes roved constantly to where the bridegroom's
family, the Lee-Harrisons and the Norwoods, stood together in a

1 W.S. Gilbert (1836-1911) and Arthur Sullivan (1842-1900), *The
    Mikado* (1885), a comic opera about an ill-fated romance, first per-
    formed at the Savoy Theatre in London in March 1885. Levy quotes
    from the finale song, "He's Gone and Married Yum-Yum."
2 See p. 64, note 3.
3 In traditional Jewish weddings, the ceremony concludes with the groom
    smashing a glass with his foot to recall the destruction of the ancient
    temple in Jerusalem; the early part of the ceremony when the bride is
    betrothed to the groom includes a blessing over and tasting of wine typi-
    cally in a silver kiddush cup.

rather chilly group; to where, in particular, Lady Geraldine Sydenham, in her unassertive, unaccentuated costume, leaned lightly against a porphyry column.

Bertie's people had accepted the situation with philosophy, and were really fond of Judith, but they found her family, especially in its collateral branches, uncongenial, if not worse.

On the outskirts of this group hovered Montague Cohen, absolutely rigid with importance. Near him Adelaide tossed her head in its smart new bonnet from side to side, her sallow face and diamond earrings flashing this way and that throughout the ceremony.

She knew that such restlessness was not good manners, but for the life of her she could not resist the temptation of seeing all that was to be seen.

Poor Mrs. Quixano, proud, but vaguely distressed, stood near her husband; while Jack, the picture of nimble smartness, ushered every one into their places and made himself generally useful.

The wedding was followed by a reception; and afterwards, amid showers of rice from Lionel and Sidney, the newly-married pair set out *en route* for Italy.

EPILOGUE.

It was the beginning of May, a bright, balmy evening, and the London season was in full swing.

The trees in Kensington Gardens wore yet that delicate brilliance of early spring, which, a passing glory all the world over, is in London the glory of an hour.

Under the trees children were playing and calling; out beyond in the road a ceaseless stream of cabs, carriages, carts, and omnibuses rolled by.

The broad back of the Prince Consort, gold beneath his golden canopy, shone forth with unusual splendour; the marble groups beneath stood out clearly against the soft background of pale blue sky.[1]

And in the air—the London air—lingered something of the

---

1 The Albert Memorial, located on the south side of Kensington Gardens, was completed in 1876, 15 years after Prince Albert's death. Near the steps around the base are four sculpted groups representing the expanse of the British Empire: Europe, Africa, America, and Asia.

freshness of evening and of spring, mixed though it was with the odour of dinners in preparation, and with that of the bad tobacco which rose every now and then from the tops of the crowded road-cars rolling by.

The windows of a flat in the Albert Hall Mansions opposite were open, and a lady who was standing by one of them could smell the characteristic London odour, and could hear the sound of the children's voices, the rolling and turning of the wheels, and the shuffle and tramp of footsteps on the pavement below. She stood there a moment, one bare, beautiful hand and arm resting on the back of an adjacent couch, her eyes mechanically fixed on the glistening gilt cross surmounting the Albert Memorial, then she turned away suddenly, the thick, rich folds of her white silk dress trailing heavily behind her. The room across which she moved was small, but bright, and fitted up with the varied and elaborate luxury of a modern fashionable drawing-room. Among the articles of *bric à brac*, costly, interesting, or merely bizarre which adorned it, were an antique silver *Hanucah* lamp and a spice box, such as the Jews make use of in certain religious services, of the same metal.[1]

Judith Lee-Harrison, for it was she, went over to the mantel-piece and consulted a little carriage-clock which stood upon it.

It was barely three months since her marriage, though to judge from the great, if undefinable change which had passed over her, it might have been the same number of years.

Her beauty indeed had ripened and deepened, so that it would have been impossible for the least observant person to pass it by, and the little over emphasis of fashion which had hitherto marred the perfect distinction of her appearance, had vanished.

"Mrs. Lee-Harrison would be a beauty if she cared about it," is the verdict of the world to which she had been introduced little more than a month ago.

But it was sufficiently evident that Mrs. Lee-Harrison did not care.

There was something almost austere in the pose of the head and figure, the lines of the mouth, the look in the wonderful eyes.

---

1   The main feature of the celebration of *Hanukkah*, or the Festival of Lights, is the kindling of the eight-branched menorah; on each of the eight nights of the festival one additional candle is lit. A spice box is part of the ceremony of *Havdalah*, which concludes festivals and the sabbath (*Shabbat*). The sweet smell of the spices (*b'samim*) is meant to refresh the soul.

Those eyes, to a close observer indeed, told that Judith had learnt many things, had grown strangely wise these last three months.

Yes, she knew now more clearly what before she had only dimly and instinctively felt: the nature and extent of the wrong which had been perpetrated; which had been dealt her; which she in her turn had dealt herself and another person.

She stood idly by the mantelpiece, staring at the mass of invitation cards stuck into the mirror above it.

One of them told that Lady Kemys would be at home that night in Grosvenor Place[1] at nine o'clock. It was to be a political party, and like all such gatherings would begin early, for which reason she had dressed before dinner.

She took the card from its place and read it over. Reuben would be there of course.

Well, they would shake hands perhaps; she, for one, would be very amiable; they might even talk about the weather; and would he ask her to have an ice?

She put back the card indifferently; it mattered so little.

She had been home a month from Italy, and, as it happened, she and Reuben had not yet met.

The Lee-Harrisons had dined duly in Kensington Palace Gardens, but Reuben had been unavoidably detained that night at the House.

He had called on her some weeks ago, and she had been out.

But rumours of him had reached her. He had addressed his constituents with great *éclat* in the recess, and was already beginning to attract attention from the leader of his party.

As for more intimate matters, there were reports current connecting his name with Caroline Cardozo, with Miss Lee-Harrison, and with a chorus girl at the Gaiety.[2]

Some people said he was only waiting for old Solomon's death to marry the chorus girl.

The last month, which had been full of new experiences, of social events for Judith, seemed curiously long as she stood there looking back on it.

It came over her that she was in a fair way to drift off completely from her own people; they and she were borne on dividing currents.

---

1 Adjacent to Palace Gardens, near Buckingham Palace.
2 The Gaiety Theatre was built in The Strand in 1868. The first Gilbert and Sullivan collaboration, *Thespis; or, the Gods Grown Old*, appeared there in December 1871.

A sudden longing for the old faces, the old ties and associations came over her as she stood there; a strange fit of home-sickness, an inrushing sense of exile.

Her people—oh, her people!—to be back once more among them! When all was said, she had been so happy there.

A servant entered with a letter.

Judith, glancing again at the clock, saw that it was nearly eight, and said, as she opened the envelope,

"Has Mr. Lee-Harrison come in?"

He had come in half an hour ago, when she had been dressing, and had gone straight to his room.

The gong sounded for dinner as the man spoke, and a few minutes afterwards Bertie came tripping in, fully equipped for the festivities of the evening.

"Blanche expects us early," said Judith as she swept across to the dining-room and took her place at the little round table.

Bertie looked across at her doubtfully, then put his spoon into the excellent white soup before him.

It was the first time for some weeks that they had dined alone together, and conversation did not flow freely.

Bertie looked up again, fixing his eyes, not on her face, but on the row of pearls at her throat.

"My dear, you will be very much shocked."

"Yes?" said Judith interrogatively, eating her soup.

"Reuben Sachs is dead."

"It is not true," said Judith, and then she actually smiled.

★★★★★

The room was whirling round and round, a strange, thick mist was over everything, and through it came the muffled sound of Bertie's voice:

"It occurred this afternoon, quite suddenly. I heard it at the club. He had not been well for some time, and had collapsed more or less the last week. But no one had any idea of danger. It seems that his heart was weak; he had been overdoing himself terribly, and cardiac disease was the immediate cause of his death—cardiac disease," repeated Bertie, with mournful enjoyment of the phrase, and pulling a long face as he spoke.

Judith, sitting there like an automaton, eating something that tasted like sawdust, something that was difficult to swallow, was vividly conscious of only this—that Bertie must be silenced at any cost. Anything else could be borne, but not Bertie's fluent regrets.

Another woman would have fainted: there had never been any mercy for her: but at least she would not sit there while Bertie talked of it.

So she lifted up her face, her stony face, and turned the current of his talk.

★★★★★

Dinner came to an end at last and the automatic woman passed across to the sitting-room.

Her husband followed her; she stared at him.

"You must take my excuses to Blanche. It is due to my family that I should not appear to-night in public."

"Certainly, certainly; a mark of respect, Blanche will understand. We will neither of us go."

She looked at him in horror, all her force of will gathered to a point: "Go—go! Blanche will expect it. There is no reason for you to stop here."

"My dear girl, do you think I can't stand an evening alone with you? It will be a change, quite a pleasant change."

★★★★★

He had gone at last, and she stood there motionless by the mantelpiece, staring at the card for Lady Kemys' "At home."

"Infinite æons"[1] seemed to divide the present moment from that other moment, half an hour ago, when she had told herself carelessly, indifferently, that she would meet Reuben that night.

---

1 A phrase connoting evolutionary time, the extinction and succession of species, in "The City of Dreadful Night" (1874), an epic poem about London of great importance to Levy, by James Thomson (1834-82). These words come from the following stanza in chapter 14:

> We finish thus; and all our wretched race
> Shall finish with its cycle, and give place
>   To other beings with their own time—doom:
> Infinite æons ere our kind began;
> Infinite æons after the last man
>   Has joined the mammoth in earth's tomb and womb.

Levy's "A Ballad of Religion and Marriage" (see Appendix B5) resonates with this stanza.

It struck her now that all the sorrow of her life, all the suffering she had undergone would be wiped out, would be as nothing, if only she could indeed meet Reuben—could see his face, hear his voice, touch his hand. Everything else looked trivial, imaginary; everything else could have been forgotten, forgiven; only this thing could never be forgiven him, this inconceivable thing— that he was dead.

★★★★★

She knew that her agony was not yet upon her, that she was dazed, stunned, without feeling. A dim foreshadowing of what that agony would be was slowly creeping over her.

She moved across to a chair by the open window, and sat down.

The children's voices were silent; the iron gates were shut; the gold cross above the Memorial shone like fire as the rays of the setting sun fell upon it.

And below in the roadway the ceaseless stream of carriages moved east and west. On the pavement the people gathered, thicker and thicker. A pair of lovers moved along slowly, close against the park railings, beneath the shadow of the trees.

The pulses of the great city beat and throbbed; the great tide roared and flowed ever onwards.

London, his London, was full of life and sound, a living, solid reality; not—oh, wonder!—a dream city that melted and faded in the sunset.

★★★★★

Across the great gulf she could never stretch a hand. Death had thrown down no barriers, had brought them no nearer to one another. Wider and deeper—though before it had been very wide and deep—flowed the stream between them.

★★★★★

Nearer and nearer came the sound, nearer and nearer. Where had she heard it before?

There was music in her ears now, the dreamy monotony of a waltz; the scent of dying flowers—tuberose, gardenia—was wafted in from some unseen region. It was a November night, not springtime sunset, and the harsh sound struck upwards through the mist:

"Death of a Conservative M.P.! Death of the member for St. Baldwin's!"

★★★★★

Away in Cambridge Leo paced beneath the lime-trees, a sick, blank horror at his heart.

Nearer, across that verdant stretch of twilit park, sat a wrinkled image of despair, surely a mark for the mirth of ironical gods.

And here by the open window sat Judith, absolutely motionless—a figure of stone.

Before the great mysteries of life her soul grew frozen and appalled.

It seemed to her, as she sat there in the fading light, that this is the bitter lesson of existence: that the sacred serves only to teach the full meaning of sacrilege; the beautiful of the hideous; modesty of outrage; joy of sorrow; life of death.

★★★★★

Is life indeed over for Judith, or at least all that makes life beautiful, worthy—a thing in any way tolerable?

The ways of joy like the ways of sorrow are many; and hidden away in the depths of Judith's life—though as yet she knows it not—is the germ of another life, which shall quicken, grow, and come forth at last. Shall bring with it no doubt, pain and sorrow, and tears; but shall bring also hope and joy, and that quickening of purpose which is perhaps as much as any of us should expect or demand from Fate.

Appendix A: Contemporary Reviews of Reuben Sachs

1. "Critical Jews," *The Jewish Chronicle* (25 January 1889): 11

Recent events[1] in the community have called renewed attention to a characteristic of Jews which has always played a great part in their history from the earliest times. Jerusalem fell through the dissensions of the Jewish leaders, and polemics have formed a large part of the published activity of Jewish scholars from the time of SAADIA[2] to the present. Wherever there are two Jews, there are two critics. Jews are nothing if not critical.

This failing, for failing it is, is perhaps a necessary accompaniment of the marked individuality of the Jewish nature which gives so much character to it. There cannot be great energy without great self-confidence, and it is rarely indeed that this confidence in one's own power fails to degenerate into vanity. Hence some Jews are proud of their vanity as being in some way a measure of their capacity. So it is, but they forget that it also measures their capacity in another way by showing that there is a lurking suspicion on the part of the vain person that this capacity is not sufficiently recognised. So that ultimately vanity is after all but an uneasy sense of insufficiency compared with the masterly indifference to popular opinion with which the truly strong man goes about his work in sublime unconsciousness of everything else than his work.

So much for vanity in its individual aspects. But what will happen when two such natures clash? That is the public interest in vanity. It is obvious that an amount of personal feeling and hypercriticism will be introduced into public affairs in which public interest must necessarily be subordinated to private animosities. Hence it happens that in Jewish affairs there is never anything done for the communal good which does not suffer from the most extreme form of criticism. To a certain extent this is an advantage, since the slightest lapse in a public institution is liable to be pointed out by someone who has a personal inter-

---

1 *Reuben Sachs* was published in mid-January 1889. *The Jewish Chronicle* typically reviewed books by Anglo-Jewish authors, but did not explicitly review *Reuben Sachs*. This article appears to be a veiled criticism of *Reuben Sachs* and Julia Frankau's *Dr. Phillips*.

2 Saadia ben Joseph Al-Fayyumi (892-942), Egyptian Jewish philosopher.

est in the working of the institution, not so much from a disinterested love of the objects of the institution, as from friendly emulation, to call it by no other name, with its ruling spirits.

The spirit of criticism has its advantages, we have said. But it has likewise its disadvantages of no small extent. It introduces into controversy a personal and a petty element which obscures greater issues. It often serves to disgust the better minds with communal work altogether. It tends to narrow the interest of those who are affected by the criticism; they desire to vindicate themselves rather than to advance their cause. It lowers the dignity of public life, and introduces entirely foreign issues into the discussion of public subjects. A. votes against a certain proposal, not because he has impartially considered it, but because it is proposed by B., who once criticised A.'s conduct or ability with reference to an entirely foreign matter.

Not that Jews are alone in these manifestations of sensitive vanity and hypercriticism. In every small community, where there is a well developed spirit of public usefulness combined with only a limited scope for its development, the clash of personal interests must exist. Novelists, those careful observers of life, make a great point of the quarrels of dissenters in small communities. Mrs. OLIPHANT,[1] for example, began her career with the "Chronicles of Carlingford," a series of novels entirely devoted to the petty quarrels of the dissenting and Low Church communities. But among Jews the contest is the more keen, and the criticism more intense owing to the inherent sense of power so frequent in Jewish natures and so frequently manifested in a peculiar kind of vanity.

If we are not mistaken English Jews are somewhat less apt to fall into this failing than their foreign brethren. English Jews are perhaps somewhat livelier than their fellow countrymen of other faiths. But the natural reserve of the English nature has had its effect on them too, and there is a sense of personal dignity in the English Jews of the old stock which contrasts at times unfavourably, at times favourably, with the unreserve of the foreign Jew, who is good enough to enliven us by his presence. Still, it is worth noting that a certain acrimonious tone which has been of late imported into public discussion, is somewhat removed from English conceptions of the proper modes of living the collective life. In one case the acrimoniousness passed into a deplorable lampoon in the worst possible taste.

---

1 Margaret Oliphant (1828-97), Scottish novelist and literary critic.

There is another kind of Jewish criticism of Jews which has begun to be unpleasantly frequent recently. Jewish *littérateurs*, finding a ready interest in descriptions of Jewish life among the general novel-reading public, have gone to the pains of renewing their acquaintance with Jewish society for a few weeks in order to obtain local colour. On the strength of this, they produce super-ficial sketches of the aspects of Jewish manners that strike them unpleasantly. In non-Jewish authors this might be innocuous, especially as want of sympathy invariably results in faulty art not likely to win belief. But with the outside world the effect of such performances by Israelites is the more deleterious as it is impos-sible for the general public to know on what superficial knowl-edge of Jewish society such ill-natured sketches are founded.

It is a curious point that the tendency to an over-acuteness of intercommunal criticism is counterbalanced among Jews by a remarkable absence of critical measurement of the external credit won by Jews. Let a Jew but get renown for anything—chess or football, music or acting, engineering or the press—and all Jews are proud of him without any minute inquiries into the grounds of their pride. Thus, it too often happens that those who give up to Judaism what is meet for mankind are much more sharply crit-icised and less honoured than men, who in the very creditable desire to better themselves, have gained some reputation in an outside sphere. Many a career that might have been diverted into spheres of communal usefulness has been diverted into other channels owing to the over-acuteness of communal criticism.

Altogether it would seem from the above consideration that the evil aspects of the Jewish tendency to criticism greatly out-weigh the good it may do at times. It would be well, therefore, if those who are prone to it should check it in themselves, while those who are happily free from it should discourage it as much as possible in others. The dignity of communal life must not be endangered by the vagaries of too critical Jews.

2. "Reuben Sachs," *The Spectator* 62 (16 February 1889): 234-35

This is certainly much more of "a sketch," as it is called on the title-page, than either a novel or even a story, for there is exceed-ingly little story in it, and the merit of the book, which is great, consists in the extraordinary power with which the writer describes the general character of the Jewish group with which the sketch concerns itself. No one can say that Miss Levy underrates the materialistic element in the tendencies of modern Israel. She gives us, indeed, by way of contrast to the idolatry of material wealth and luxury in which most of her characters are plunged,— and only the deeper plunged, it would seem, the more miserable they find themselves under the galling yoke which it imposes upon them,—three characters who heartily loathe this materialism. Yet one even of these three, the heroine of the sketch, makes just the same sacrifice to the idol as she would have made if she had loved instead of loathing it; the second one, who loathes without bowing the knee to it, is rescued from its fascinations only by that passionate rapture which the power of music has always seemed to awaken in certain chosen sons of Israel, as the one idealistic pursuit which more than counterpoises for them the magnetism of wealth and luxury; and third, who is a mere student, is just outlined and no more, for Joshua Quixano is a nobody among the Israelites, just because he is incapable of appreciating the might of Mammon. All the rest of the characters, the women even more than the men, are Mammon-worshippers, or World-worshippers, or Fashion-worshippers, some of them wholly given up to that worship, some of them with sufficient variety of faculty and insight to be capable of lucid intervals, though they regard the lucid intervals as, in fact, the intervals when their mind, far from being at its serenest, is most disturbed. The Jews have, it would seem, somehow divined that if in modern days the power of materialism can be resisted successfully at all, it can be most successfully resisted by a sort of idealism which makes no claim to be definite, but which, like the power of music, causes all sorts of vague chords to vibrate in the heart, though the owner of the heart is quite unable to interpret even the general meaning of the vibrations thus produced. The vaguer the idealism is, if it makes its appeal through the senses at all, the more chance it has of coping successfully with the sordid realism of our time. Any definite ideal is at a disadvantage as compared with those rushes of glorious sensation witnessing to something higher than the glories even of the most exalted sensations themselves, but not defining in any way in what fashion this vague elevation of drift, by which music contrives to dispute with material enjoyments the control of human life, ought to be construed. How well Miss Levy understands that one mighty ideal influence which is still so potent in Jewish circles, and its power to dispel when it lists even the vulgar tyranny of ostentatious luxury.... The women of the sketch, if we except the heroine, who is made profoundly interesting without being made very visible to us, are better delineated than the men.

The lazy, untidy Jewess, who has been sated with wealth all her life, and who has never enjoyed it in the least, yet who goes on idolising it with the most disinterested worship, holding that everything should give way to the acquisition of it, in spite of its joylessness; the fat, pretty, fair-complexioned daughter who admits with a sigh that she is certain not to like the man she marries, but who is quite too rich to marry the man she likes; the rich, malicious, gnome-like daughter of a mad father who proclaims aloud that there is always either an idiot or a ne'er-do-weel in every Jewish family; the greedy, dyspeptic, and eager devotee of fashion who knows herself to be distinctly second-rate, and yet cannot control her desire to force her way to the circles where she is well aware that she will be snubbed,—these and several other such figures are dashed off with a vigour which, in spite of the slightness of the sketching, greatly impresses the reader. Nor is the picture of the hero, as we suppose we must call him,—unheroic except in his power of work though he certainly is,—at all wanting in vividness. His absorbing ambition, his vast delight in work, his genuine philanthropy, his determination to overcome those who snub him and make them feel that he is worth cultivating, his sincere doubt as to the depth of his own love for Judith, and the deliberation with which at its very crises he coldly sacrifices it to his worldly prospects, as well as the despair with which he afterwards recognises what he has done,—are all painted with a force which more than makes up for the complete absence of plot.

The hold of the world of luxury and fashion on a certain class of minds is stamped upon this little volume with the same sort of power with which Crabbe[1] stamped upon his poems the sordid misery of humbler life; but, in contrast to it, the idealising yearnings of the heart are also painted, though with a sort of hopelessness,—indeed, a despair of giving them their true rights over human life,—and yet painted with a strength which is all the more impressive for that obvious despair.

3. John Barrow Allen, "New Novels," *The Academy* 35 (16 February 1889): 109

Reuben Sachs is a novel exclusively descriptive of Jewish life, written by a lady who, at least by birth, is a member of that

---

1 George Crabbe (1754-1832) wrote poetry about the evils of alcohol, about madhouses, and about his opium addiction.

community. In this respect the book is, as a novel, perhaps unique; for the occasional portraiture of Hebrew personalities or customs that occurs in the works of Disraeli, George Eliot, and other writers of fiction, may have successfully illustrated prominent types of character or notable tribal peculiarities, but is in no way an exposition of the day-to-day life of a people of whom the outside world is permitted to know but little. It must be confessed that the glimpse of the social *régime* peculiar to the children of Israel which is here unveiled to us is far from prepossessing. Miss Levy gives one the impression of having laid bare the failings of her people with a rather merciless hand, assuming, perhaps, by right of kinship a freedom of description which might be resented as "flat perjury" if indulged in by an unprivileged Gentile. The novel, appears, however, to have a purpose quite distinct from the mere gratification of alien curiousity. Reuben Sachs, the hero, is a man who, after enjoying all the opportunities of culture afforded by English institutions, as embodied in Oxford, the Inns of Court, and the House of Commons, nevertheless remains the slave of inherited instincts, and deliberately breaks away from the grand passion of his life from mercenary or ambitious motives. Herein seems to be intended a moral and a warning. Miss Levy is apparently conscious of a certain soullessness and absence of ennobling ideals in the national character, and deplores her kinsmen's sordid devotion to material interests and lack of any yearning for a higher life. The book, though crude in parts, is, on the whole, cleverly written; and we shall be glad to see further revelations from the same pen.

4. "The Deterioration of the Jewess," *Jewish World* (22 February 1889): 5

Some months ago a Jewish lady wrote a novel in which a jaundiced picture of Jewish life was painted according to the canons of Zolaesque art.[1] The book was exceedingly malicious and nasty; but there was one feature about it which pleased us, and that was that the authoress exhibited a saving remnant of decency in the adoption of a Gentile pseudonym. Of course, everyone

---

1 Émile Zola (1840-1902), leading novelist in the French school of naturalism, focused his writing on the vice and misery of contemporary working-class and middle-class life, conveying a spirit of pessimism.

knows who wrote "Dr. Phillips"[1] and the writer herself does not deny her responsibility; but the mere fact that she hesitated, if only for a moment, to blazon her name to the world shows a lurking sense of the impropriety of her work and gives hope that the normal instincts of her Jewish womanhood may one day reassert themselves. "Dr. Phillips" has recently been followed by another novel of Jewish life constructed on the lines of a more humdrum art, but exhibiting an equally malicious desire to libel the community and all its belongings. In one respect, however, the authoress of "Reuben Sachs" stands in strong contrast to the lady who hides her creditable blushes under the mask of "Frank Danby." She is not ashamed of playing the *role* of an accuser of her people. The unpleasant reproach, derived from ornithological observations, which persons in her position incur, has no terrors for her. She apparently delights in the task of persuading the general public that her own kith and kin are the most hideous types of vulgarity; she revels in misrepresentations of their customs and modes of thought and she is proud of being able to offer her testimony in support of the anti-Semitic theories of the clannishness of her people and the tribalism of their religion. At least, so we gather from the fact that her peculiarly Hebraic name appears in prominent capitals on both the title page and cover of her very infelicitous romance.

Our aim in directing public attention to these books is not to discuss their literary merits or to contest the accuracy of the impressions they seek to convey. Anything in the shape of serious criticism would be paying them far too high a compliment. To us they are not so much books as they are symptoms of moral disease, which call for diagnosis in the interest of community at large. It seems to us a serious thing that, in a small body like our own, it should be possible to find two women so devoid of sympathy and taste as to be capable of writing and publishing books like these. We are almost disposed to believe that Lady MAGNUS[2] argued from a shrewd knowledge of her sex when she declaimed

---

1 Julia Frankau (1859-1916) under the name "Frank Danby," published two novels that capture racist views of Jews in England, *Dr. Phillips: A Maida Vale Idyll* (1887) and *Pigs in Clover* (1903).

2 Lady Katie Magnus (1844-1924) wrote on Jewish topics, including *Outlines of Jewish History* (1888). In her essay "Heinrich Heine: A Plea" (*Macmillan's Magazine* 47 [November 1882]: 59-67), on the German-Jewish poet, Magnus included Levy's translation of one of Heine's poems. The essay was included in Magnus' *Jewish Portraits* (1888).

last month against the higher education of women. But it is not in over-education that the fault is to be found. The truth is, as any reader may gather from the ridiculous slips in Jewish allusions in both books, that, in the particular direction in which it was required, these ladies have received no education whatever. They are illustrations, and very lamentable ones, of the neglected state of specifically Jewish female education among the middle-classes in our community, and the consequent deterioration of the English Jewess. It has been a matter of common observation for some time that the Jewish woman, as she was known to our fathers, with her strong racial sympathies, her unaffected piety, her devotion to her children, her delight in a purely Jewish home, and the modest virtues of her thorough womanliness, does not tend to reproduce herself. The demon of *Chukath Hagoyim*[1] has got at her even more completely than at her brother. Nor is this surprising, for if the Jew is vain, the Jewess has the superadded vanity of the female, and when her Jewish sympathies remain uncultivated she hunts the *Goyische*[2] tuft *au grand galop*.[3] This is a very lamentable phenomenon; for, as we may see by the books which have suggested these observations, the effect is not only to produce inferior Jewesses, but a low type of womanhood in which the finer feelings are blunted to the extent almost of obliterating all sense of decency.

5. "Literary: Amy Levy's Reuben Sachs," *The American Hebrew* 88 (5 April 1889): 142

"The Romance of a Shop" by the same author afforded a promise that has been amply fulfilled by this her latest production. In many respects it is a notable advance upon her previous performance. It is more skillfully constructed upon lines more definitely laid out. The authoress has also gained considerable more mastery over her vocabulary and utilizes a much more agreeable style. The accession of power gained by Miss Levy is best evinced by the really brilliant manner in which she has managed the crucial episode of her novel that in which Reuben Sachs expresses to Judith his love, without speaking, and then renounces the hopes of both for ambition, again without speak-

---

1 Following the practices of non-Jewish nations (Hebrew).
2 Non-Jewish, Gentile (Yiddish).
3 At full gallop (French).

ing. It is certainly very cleverly done. In fact as a novel it is one that takes very high rank among some of the best productions in the field of fiction.

The story it tells is that of an Englishman who is in love with a poor girl. His political ambition is about to be crowned with success in the shape of a seat in Parliament. The necessities of the situation require that he should marry a rich woman, and renders it necessary for him to give up the poor girl. Now, the fatal blunder that Amy Levy makes is that she makes this Englishman a Jew as well, for no earthly reason whatever. She must know of course that there are Episcopalians and Dissenters in England who would have acted exactly as Sachs did and with as little, if not with less compunction. In fact, there are a number of other people in the book called Jews, for no other evident reason than to say ill-natured things about them. It is a Jewish novel only in that sense that the characters are ostentatiously labelled with the name of their race. There is certainly no Judaism in the book.

An antipodal ethnological student reading Miss Levy's novel would infer that all manner of ungraceful and ungracious habits including curiosity were the exclusive property of the Jewish "race." He would think that Thackeray and Dickens had either maligned the English people or that they had all since then become transformed perfect angels, compared with the Jews. Perhaps Miss Levy set out—we will give her the benefit of the doubt—with the idea of reforming her people, and of leading them up to her exalted plane of etiquette.

We would in all sincerity advise her before she attempts another Jewish novel, to study something of Judaism, at least as diligently as she reads her Browning. Then perhaps she will, too, acquire somewhat of that master's reverence for her ancestral faith and for the literature the sages of Israel created. Feeble, petty, idle sneers are not his tribute to Judaism, they certainly should not be hers, a daughter of the race. His appreciation, however, is the outcome of knowledge. If Amy Levy would strive to learn what Judaism is, she might produce works that would be not simply entertaining to the world, but elevating and helpful for her coreligionists.

6. Oscar Wilde, "Amy Levy," *The Woman's World* 3 (1890): 51–52

The gifted subject of these paragraphs, whose distressing death has brought sorrow to many who knew her only from her writings, was born at Clapham, and spent the greater part of her short and outwardly uneventful life in London. Her family was Jewish, but she herself, as she grew up, gradually ceased to hold the orthodox doctrines of her nation, retaining, however, a strong race feeling. At a very early age she showed a marked turn for writing, and some of her childish verses, still preserved, are both correct and original. During the years 1880 and 1881 she was a student at Newnham College, Cambridge, and while still in residence published her first volume of verse, "Xantippe." The modest little paper-covered book, which contains only thirty pages, was published in Cambridge, and was, we believe, never advertised. Its merit, however, attracted a good deal of attention, and the whole edition was sold out. "Xantippe," the longest and most important poem, had been written three years earlier, and had already appeared (in May, 1880) in the *University Magazine*. Xantippe on her death-bed relates the disappointment of her life, beginning with her love for her husband, and her longing to share his thoughts:—

"I guided by his wisdom and his love,
Led by his words, and counselled by his care,
Should lift the shrouding veil from things which be.
And at the flowing fountain of his soul
Refresh my thirsting spirit."

But Socrates wanted no such companion or disciple in his wife, and gradually her love turned to bitterness:—

"Then faded that vain fury: hope died out;
A huge despair was stealing on my soul:
A sort of fierce acceptance of my fate—
He wished a household vessel—well! 'twas good
For he should have it . . . . . .
. . . . . . till at last I grew
As ye have known me—eye exact to mark
The texture of the spinning; ear all keen
For aimless talking when the moon is up
And ye should be a sleeping; tongue to cut,
With quick incision, thwart the merry words
Of idle maidens."

This poem—surely a most remarkable one to be produced by a girl still at school—is distinguished, as nearly all Miss Levy's work is, by the qualities of sincerity, directness, and melancholy. In expression it is less simple and lucid than some of her later verse, far less so, for instance, than the two short poems which we publish in this issue; but its spirit is the same, and no intelligent critic could fail to see the promise of greater things.

"A Minor Poet, and other Verse," published in 1884, showed a distinct advance. This, too, is but a thin volume, with no single superfluous line in it. The two epitaphs with which it closes, and the dedication "to a dead poet"[1] with which it opens, are perhaps the most perfect and complete things in it; these, if they stood alone, would be enough to mark their writer as a poet of no mean excellence.

A third volume of poems was nearly ready for publication at the time of her death, and is to appear immediately.[2] Some of the pieces to be included in it have appeared already in various papers and magazines, and two or three of these are among her very best work.

Her prose work consists almost entirely of fiction. The few magazine articles which she wrote are good of their kind, but they lack that special individuality which makes the value of her other writing. Of her short stories, two or three are slight and careless, written from a very superficial stratum of thought or feeling, and produced with the utmost facility. Of these stories she herself was the first to speak slightingly, and she would never have sanctioned their republication. But even these are marked by a strong vitality. They are careless, but not dull; they show how much the touch of the real artist tells, even in second-rate work. But besides these there are a few other short stories which are by no means second-rate. Among these may be named "Cohen of Trinity,"[3] "Eldorado at Islington," "Addenbrooke," "Wise in her Generation"—one of her latest, which we give in our present number—and "The Recent Telepathic Occurrence at the British Museum." This last is a good example of Miss Levy's extraordinary power of condensation. The story occupied only about a page of this magazine, and it gives the whole history of a wasted and misunderstood love. There is not so much as a name in it, but the

---

1 Levy published an essay on James Thomson (1834-82) entitled, "James Thomson: A Minor Poet" in 1883; the dedication suggests that Thomson's *The City of Dreadful Night* (1874) inspired the title poem as well as her own poetic career as a female bard of London.

2 *A London Plane-Tree, and Other Verse* was published in late 1889.

3 See Appendix B4 for "Cohen of Trinity."

relation of the man and woman stands out vivid as if we had known and watched its growth.

Miss Levy's two novels, "The Romance of a Shop" and "Reuben Sachs," were both published last year. The first is a bright and clever story, full of sparkling touches; the second is a novel that probably no other writer could have produced. Its directness, its uncompromising truth, its depth of feeling, and, above all, its absence of any single superfluous word, make it, in some sort, a classic. Like all her best work it is sad, but the sadness is by no means morbid. The strong undertone of moral earnestness, never preached, gives a stability and force to the vivid portraiture, and prevents the satiric touches from degenerating into mere malice. Truly the book is an achievement.

To write thus at six-and-twenty is given to very few; and from the few thus endowed their readers may safely hope for yet greater things later on. But "later on" has not come for the writer of "Reuben Sachs," and the world must forego the full fruition of her power. The loss is the world's, but perhaps not hers. She was never robust; not often actually ill, but seldom well enough to feel life a joy instead of a burden; and her work was not poured out lightly, but drawn drop by drop from the very depth of her own feeling. We may say of it that it was in truth her life's blood.

Appendix B: Other Writing by Levy

1. "Jewish Women and 'Women's Rights,'" *The Jewish Chronicle* (7 February 1879): 5

[The following letter marks Levy's debut at age 17 in the pages of *The Jewish Chronicle*, the oldest and still publishing weekly Jewish newspaper, first published in London in 1842. In 1886 she published several essays in *The Jewish Chronicle*, including "Jewish Humour," "Middle-Class Jewish Women of To-Day," "The Jew in Fiction," and "Jewish Children."]

To the Editor of the "Jewish Chronicle."

Sir,—Will you allow me to make a few remarks in your columns on a letter which appeared last week in the *Jewish Chronicle*, bearing on the subject of "Women's Rights"? Your correspondent (while owning himself ignorant of the full meaning of the term) starts with a deprecation, and, at the same time, desires a definition of it. His impression that, "what is claimed" is "perfect equality ... with Man," is to a great extent a correct one: but, beyond this, he appears to have misconstrued the question.

Thus, he is mistaken in thinking that "coercion into marriage" (as he expresses it) is the great ground of complaint among women; it is rather the obstacles which are placed to hinder "from attaining higher culture," and "sharing in the sterner struggles of life," those women, who, from circumstance or temperament, do not marry. "Marriage," writes your correspondent, "has been defined in Parliament as the principal means of livelihood at present open to women": some people might be inclined to regard this as a melancholy statement, with the hard fact of—I should not like to say how many—millions of surplus women (in the British Isles alone) staring us in the face. What is to become of this surplus? With regard to working-women, " ש "[1] suggests, for "the higher classes" the "imparting of education" (in plain words, "governessing," a notoriously ill-paid drudgery, for which

---

1 ש is a letter in the Hebrew alphabet, pronounced either "shin" or "sin" depending on the vowel. It was not unusual for correspondents of *The Jewish Chronicle* to sign with an initial, either Hebrew or English. Levy's signature of her full name without a title ("Miss" or "Mrs.") was far more unusual.

only peculiar minds are really fitted), and, "to a certain extent," the medical profession; which latter is barred and blocked to the sex (in this country) by about every means which the ingenuity of man could devise. Would it be "inconsistent with the reserve that the social experience of generations imagines," if the broad field of free competition were opened to both sexes? If woman be, indeed, "the weaker," she will not fail to "go to the wall." Without daring to make any positive assertion about such an unsettled question as the relative mental and physical powers of the Man and Woman, we can say that in those few cases where women have had equal chances of developing, the men have not always "beaten them in a canter." Caroline Herschel[1] and Jeanne Pascal[2] shared in the highest of their brother's calculations; Mrs. Somerville[3] (a self-taught genius, by the way) was ahead of many of the scientists of her day; since the London University Classes for Jurisprudence and Political Economy have been opened to both sexes, the traditionally weaker one has, in several instances, carried off the prizes; the first year that women had access to the Royal Academy School of Art, Miss Osborn[4] won the gold medal; of the eleven girls who went up for this year's London Matriculation, ten passed, and about half the boys failed; and we have, besides, to consider the great disadvantages under which most women labour, and the comparative smallness of the number of those who have, as yet, tried to cast off the yoke remaining from ages when physical power was almost always in the ascendant.

---

1   Caroline Herschel (1750-1847) is the first woman credited with discovering a comet. In her career assisting her brother William, a leading astronomer at Cambridge, she discovered a total of eight comets and three nebulae. She was awarded the Gold Medal of the Royal Astronomy Society in 1828, although her status as an astronomer was often discounted because of her gender.

2   Levy may be alluding to a sister of the seventeenth-century mathematician Blaise Pascal.

3   Mary Fairfax Somerville (1780-1872) was one of the most prolific science writers of the nineteenth century, with publications including *On the Connexion of the Physical Sciences* (1834) and *Physical Geography* (1848). The first known published use of the word "scientist" was in a review of her book *Connexion*.

4   Emily Mary Osborn (1828-1925), the Pre-Raphaelite painter, exhibited at the Royal Academy; her painting "Nameless and Friendless" (1857) depicts a woman artist attempting to sell her work. She also exhibited at the Grosvenor Gallery, mentioned in Levy's *The Romance of a Shop*.

I would now touch upon another point of your correspondent's argument; following out his idea that "women have their sphere," he would condemn all those to whom "work is not a pecuniary necessity," to the cares of domestic life and the performance of works of charity. But I doubt if even the great thought of becoming in time a favourable specimen of the genus "maiden-aunt"[1] would be sufficient to console many a restless, ambitious woman for the dreary performance of work for which she is quite unsuited, for the quenching of personal hopes for the development of her own intellect. To those who argue that she may find ample vent for herself in her own immediate circle, and with no definite aim in view, we point out the melancholy crowd of *femmes incomprises*,[2] so characteristic of the age.

★★★

—Yours obediently,
Amy Levy.
Brighton.

[In the 21 February 1879 issue the initial correspondent speculated on Levy's identity: "she is, I presume, an elderly lady who has seen much of the world, and whose grave experience gives weight to her expressions of opinion on this most important subject." This writer continues to question women's capabilities: "Why did not a woman discover electricity, or the manifold uses of steam, and why does she not even improve upon previously existing developments of science? Why has no female composer ever made people the richer by some sweet strains? Beyond Mrs. Browning, what great poetess has the sex given to us? Lady-novelists we have in plenty, but only one has been in the first rank,[3] and even she has been largely assisted by her constant association with two of the greatest thinkers of the age, Herbert Spencer and G.H. Lewes."]

"Jewish Women and 'Women's Rights,'" *The Jewish Chronicle* (28 February 1879): 5

To the Editor of the "Jewish Chronicle."
    Sir,—In your correspondent " 𝒲 's" letter of this week he has

---

1   Levy published in 1886 "Jewish Children (By a Maiden Aunt)."
2   Misunderstood women (French).
3   George Eliot.

again, unfortunately, shown a misconception of the question at issue. I did not in a former communication, nor do I at present, assert the equality of the male and female intellect; it is so evidently a question which has yet to be proved, that it would be idle to discuss it, such discussion could only be theoretical....

***

Following out his somewhat crude notions respecting the "sphere" and "mission" of women, " ѵ " hints at an ideal state of society, where man and woman have each their clearly defined functions, and are, in their mutual relations, like "perfect music unto noble words." Unfortunately, we do not live in Utopia; we have to deal with facts, not theories, and it is a great fact, that there has sprung up a large class of intelligent, capable women who are willing and able to perform work from which they find themselves shut out by the tradition of ages—women, who are destitute of their "natural protectors," or whose aims lie outside the circle which convention has marked out for them. The growth of such a class seems to point to the higher development of woman, to the fact that she is beginning to wake up to the sense of her own responsibility as a human being. All that she claims is freedom of competition; and I was not aware that she had, as yet, had a chance of "proving her incapacity for entering upon a competitive struggle with man." That society is beginning to acknowledge the justice of her claims, the rapidly increasing innovations in her favour testify: witness the opening of degrees to women at the London University, the establishment of Newnham Hall and Girton College, &c. I do not deny that your correspondent's ideal of woman is a noble one, nor that "there are thousands of women contented with their lot"; but we must not allow ourselves to be carried away by the beauty of the ideal from the claims of the actual. Because it is a grand and beautiful thing that woman should spend her life in self-sacrifice, we have no right to compel all women to do so, to regard as social outcasts those members of the sex who do not work in the old grooves. Your correspondent himself owns that we never hear of *un homme incompris*. This acknowledgment strengthens my argument; it is, I believe, the sense of cramped and restrained energies (energies which may lie in other directions than the domestic) which has given rise to the large class of *femmes incomprises*. I repeat the term—for me it has no unpleasant associations.

I fear that "ѵ " has fallen into the female error (as he considers it) of "letting out the gist of his letter" at its conclusion. When he alludes to women who are "delightful companions to men, and charming members of society, by reason of culture and intelligence," he appears to think that such have reached the whole aim and end of female education; he, like many others, has

"Misconceived the question like a man
Who sees a woman as the complement
Of his sex, merely 'He' forgets too much
That every creature, female as the male,
Stands single in responsible act and thought
As also in birth and death."[1]

Yours obediently,
Amy Levy.
Brighton.

2. "The Jew in Fiction," *The Jewish Chronicle* (4 June 1886): 13

[Levy also published an essay, "The New School of American Fiction" (1884), in *Temple Bar*, in which she critiqued recent American novels, particularly those of Henry James, as "a literature of decay.... where analysis supersedes narration" and as "small-beer chronicles of the soul." In contrast, Levy calls for "a better, fuller fiction than this self-conscious, half-hearted literature with its want of simplicity and moral greatness," a vision pertinent to her argument in "The Jew in Fiction." In the earlier essay, she cites George Eliot's characters in *The Mill on the Floss* (1860) and *Middlemarch* (1871-72) as models "for all time," but she does not discuss *Daniel Deronda* (1876) and its Jewish characters as she does in this essay.]

It is curious, that, while the prominent position of the Jew is recognised as one of the characteristic features of English social life of the present day, so small a place should be allotted him in contemporary fiction.

In finance, in politics, in society; in every branch of art and science, the English Jew is to be found in a position of more or less distinction. It is only in the novel, with one notable excep-

---

1 Elizabeth Barrett Browning (1806-61), *Aurora Leigh* (1857), book II, lines 434-39. Levy has slightly altered the wording.

tion, that his claims to consideration have been almost entirely overlooked. Rebecca, of York, with her hopeless love for the Gentile knight, and Isaac of York,[1] divided, like Shylock,[2] between his ducats and his daughter, remain to-day the typical Hebrews of fiction. Dickens, as might be expected, places himself on the crudely popular side, but tries to compensate for his having affixed the label "Jew" to one of his bad fairies by creating the good fairy Riah.[3] Thackeray has reproduced Jews in less romantic guise, as Mr. and Miss Moss[4] of the sponging houses, and to-day Mr. Baring-Gould[5] (a clergyman of the Church of England) slavishly follows the old Jew-baiting traditions in his absurd portrait of Emanuel Lazarus in *Court Royal.*

In *Daniel Deronda*,[6] it is true, a sincere and respectful attempt was made to portray the features of modern Judaism. But which of us will not acknowledge with a sigh, that the noble spirit which conceived Mirah, Daniel and Ezra, was more royal than the king? It was, alas! no picture of Jewish contemporary life, that of the little group of enthusiasts, with their yearnings after the Holy Land and dreams of a separate nation. Nor can we derive much satisfaction from the superficial smartness of such sketches as that of Jacob Alexander Cohen and his family. As a novel treating of modern Jews, *Daniel Deronda* cannot be regarded as a success; although every Jew must be touched by, and feel grateful for the spirit which breathes throughout the book; perhaps, even be spurred by its influence to nobler effort, and taught a lesson, sadly needed, to hold himself and his people in greater respect.

---

1 This Jewish daughter and father are characters in Sir Walter Scott's historical novel *Ivanhoe* (1819).

2 The Jewish moneylender from Shakespeare's *The Merchant of Venice.*

3 The Jewish character in Charles Dickens's *Our Mutual Friend* (1864-65).

4 Characters from William Makepeace Thackeray (1811-63), *Vanity Fair* (1847-48), chapter 53. Thackeray's novel *Rebecca and Rowena: A Romance Upon Romance* (1850) rewrites *Ivanhoe* by making Rebecca convert to Christianity and marry Ivanhoe.

5 Sabine Baring-Gould (1834-1924), a prolific writer of novels, poetry, an edition of *The Lives of the Saints*, a book on werewolves, and English hymns such as "Onward, Christian Soldiers." Levy refers to his novel *Court Royal* (1886) in which a poor girl is pawned to a Jew who also maintains mortgages he uses for revenge.

6 George Eliot (1819-80), *Daniel Deronda* (1876).

As for Lord Beaconsfield's[1] grandiloquent attempts in this direction, is not *Coningsby*[2] forgotten in *Codlingsby*, and which of us remembers the original of Raphael Mendoza?[3] In that clever, vulgar, unpleasant novel *Mrs. Keith's Crime*[4] we are presented with several specimens of Jewish portraiture, which at least make some attempt at realism. Perhaps, however, no outspoken picture of Jewish vice could be so offensive as the author's condescending acknowledgment of Jewish virtue. "The Sardine," (as, with characteristic refinement, he is called throughout the book) is an impossibly slangy Jew of wealth and position, who spends his time in doing good to ungrateful Gentiles. The patronising reception of his kindness on the part of the extremely unpleasant heroine, is enough to fill with wrath the honest Semitic bosom. However, as a concession, no doubt, to modern feeling, the despised Sardine is allowed to be happy with a woman of his own race and is not, as we had expected, left forlorn at the last; a male and modern Rebecca of York. There is far more cleverness in the sketch of the elderly Jewess in the same book, with her indolence and persistence; her indifference and tenacity of purpose; a sketch which for once shows real insight into Jewish character, not mere observation of outward peculiarities.

But these and kindred efforts are, when all is said, of the slightest nature. There has been no serious attempt at serious treatment of the subject; at grappling in its entirety with the complex problem of Jewish life and Jewish character. The Jew, as we know him to-day, with his curious mingling of diametrically opposed qualities; his surprising virtues and no less surprising vices; leading his eager, intricate life; living, moving, and having his being both within and without the tribal limits; this deeply interesting product of our civilisation has been found worthy of none but the most superficial observation.

There is yet to be done for him, the comparison inevitably

---

1   Benjamin Disraeli (1804-81). See *Reuben Sachs*, p. 87, note 3.
2   In Disraeli's novel *Coningsby* (1844), a mysterious Jew, Sidonia, inspires the title character to embrace a new Conservative idealism.
3   William Makepeace Thackeray parodied Disraeli's novel in "Codlingsby" (1847), where the character of Mendoza, based on Sidonia, claims the secret Jewish origins of many illustrious Christians, including the Pope.
4   Lucy Lane Clifford (1846-1929), *Mrs. Keith's Crime* (1885); the title character's crime is infanticide and euthanasia.

suggests itself, what M. Daudet[1] has done for the inhabitants of Southern France. No picture of English 19th century life and manners can be considered complete without an adequate representation of the modern son of Shem.

While writers and readers of fiction complain that *tout est dit*, producers and consumers, alike, sending forth an Athenian cry for something new, it is strange that a field at once so rich and so untrodden, should have been almost entirely overlooked.

We have, alas! no M. Daudet among us. His mingled brilliance and solidity; his wonderful blending of picturesqueness and fidelity, have no counterparts among our own contemporary novel-writers. It is in the throng of aspirants to fame that must be sought a writer able and willing to do justice to the Jewish question in its social and psychological aspects.

3. "Middle-Class Jewish Women of To-Day," *The Jewish Chronicle* (17 September 1886): 7

Conservative in politics; conservative in religion; the Jew is no less conservative as regards his social life; and while in most cases outwardly conforming to the usages of Western civilisation, he is, in fact, more Oriental at heart than a casual observer might infer. For a long time, it may be said, the shadow of the harem has rested on our womankind; and if to-day we see it lifting, it is only in reluctant obedience to the force of circumstances, the complex conditions of our modern civilisation.

What, in fact, is the ordinary life of a Jewish middle-class woman? Carefully excluded, with almost Eastern jealousy, from every-day intercourse with men and youths of her own age, she is plunged all at once—a half-fledged, often half-chaperoned creature—into the "vortex" of a middle-class ball-room, and is there expected to find her own level. In the very face of statistics, of the unanswerable logic of facts, she is taught to look upon marriage as the only satisfactory termination to her career. Her parents are jealous of her healthy, objective activities, of the natural employment of her young faculties, of anything in short which diverts her attention from what should be the one end and aim of her existence! If, in spite of all the parental efforts she fail, from want of money, or want of attractions, in obtaining a husband, her lot is a desperately unenviable one. Following out the old traditions,

---

1 Alphonse Daudet (1847-97), French novelist and short-story author.

the parental authority is strained to the utmost verge, and our community affords us many a half ludicrous, half pathetic spectacle of a hale woman of thirty making her way about the world in the very shortest and tightest of leading strings. It follows that as a society constructed on such a primitive basis, the position of single women, as rapidly improving in the general world, is a particularly unfortunate one. Jewish men have grown to look upon the women of their own tribe as solely designed for marrying or giving in marriage, and naturally enough, under the circumstances approach them with extreme caution. If a Jewess has social interests beyond the crude and transitory ones of flirtation, she must seek them, perforce, beyond the tribal limits. Within, frank and healthy intercourse between both sexes is almost impossible; the more delicate relations between men and women, the very flower and crown of civilisation, are not even understood. A natural attitude of self-consciousness, bred of the deplorable state of things, is almost inevitable between Jews and Jewesses. Once the all-important business of marriage and settlement over and done with, they find that they have nothing left to say to one another; that the degree of pleasure afforded by mixed social intercourse, never very high, has sunk to zero; just as a person whose sole educational aims are cramming and pothunting,[1] sits down blankly among his books when the degree is conferred and the fellowship won.

The inevitable result is that Jewish men and women of any width of culture, are driven to finding their friends of the other sex in the Gentile camp. That mixed marriages, comparatively frequent as they are, do not more readily accrue, must be set down either to the fact that, when all is said, our race instincts are strong; or to the less pleasing one that we are a wealthy nation and have not been educated to a high ideal of marriage.

Of course this state of things falls most hardly on the woman. As a matter of fact, so many of our men are absorbed in money-making, and are moreover each genuine Orientals at heart, that they scarcely feel the need of feminine society in its higher forms. Whereas the women, such of them as are beginning to be conscious of the yoke, are more readily adaptable, more eager to absorb the atmosphere around them; and by reason of their extra leisure, here in many cases outstripped their brothers in culture. Thus often, with greater social capabilities they have far less social opportunity. That this latter evil is common to all com-

---

1   Competing for the sake of prizes.

mercial communities, cannot be denied; and the same may be said of some other evils which have been pointed out in the course of this paper. But I maintain, that in the Jewish community they flourish with more vigour, more pertinacity, over a more wide-spread area, with a deeper root than in any other English Society.

It must be frankly acknowledged, that for all anxiety to be to the fore on every occasion, the Jew is considerably behind the age in one very important respect. That a change is coming o'er the spirit of the communal dream cannot be denied; but it is coming very slowly and at the cost of much suffering to every one concerned. The assertion even of comparative freedom on the part of a Jewess often means the severance of the closest ties, both of family and of race; its renunciation, a life-long personal bitterness. And the state of things is the more to be regretted, when we consider the potentialities of the women of our race. One of the most brilliant social figures of the century—the late Lady Waldegrave[1] may be claimed as a compatriot; and among distinguished women of to-day who are of Semitic origin we may mention that eminent journalist and writer on Schopenhauer, Miss Helen Zimmern;[2] that graceful poet and writer of *belles lettres*, Miss Mathilde Blind;[3] and that highly successful mathematical coach herself the inventor of a mathematical instrument, Miss Marks[4]

---

1 Frances Elizabeth Waldegrave (1821-79), daughter of a renowned Anglo-Jewish singer John Braham, married into the prominent Waldegrave family and came into possession of Strawberry Hill, a family estate outside of London, upon her second husband's death. Strawberry Hill became the site of her famous political hostessing during her third and fourth marriages to Members of Parliament.

2 Helen Zimmern (1846-1934) translated Friedrich Nietzsche's *Beyond Good and Evil*, wrote a book on the German philosopher Arthur Schopenhauer, as well as *George Sand* (1883) for the Eminent Women series of biographies (London: W.H. Allen and Co.). She and Levy were both members of the University Club for Ladies in London.

3 Mathilde Blind (1841-96), poet, novelist, and translator, also wrote *George Eliot* (1888) for the Eminent Women series. See Appendix C2.

4 Hertha Sarah Marks Ayrton (1854-1923), the first Jewish student at Girton College, Cambridge, was a mathematician and specialist in electricity, on which she published extensively. In 1899 she became the first woman elected as a member of the Institute of Electrical Engineers, and she was also the first woman to read a paper at the Royal Society of London. Like Levy, Ayrton belonged to the University Club for Ladies in London.

(now the wife of Professor Ayrton). Add to these an ever increasing roll of successful examination candidates, of writers in various branches of literature; examine the list of students at the High schools and Female Colleges, and we shall find good reason to hope for a better state of things.

But when all is said, to a thoughtful person thoughtfully surveying the feminine half of our society, the picture is depressing enough. On the one hand, he sees an ever increasing minority of eager women beating themselves in vain against the solid masonry of our ancient fortifications, long grown obsolete and of no use save as obstructions; sometimes succeeding in scaling the wall and departing, never to return, to the world beyond. On the other, a crowd of half-educated, idealess, pampered creatures, absorbed in material enjoyments; passing into aimless spinsterhood, or entering on unideal marriages; whose highest desire in life is the possession (after a husband) of a sable cloak and at least one pair of diamond earrings. Looking on them, it is perhaps hard to realize the extent of our undeveloped social resources; of the wickedness of our wilful neglects of some of the most delicately-flavoured fruits which the gods can make to grow. I for one believe that our Conservatism with regard to women, is one of the most deeply rooted, the most enduring sentiments of the race; and one that will die harder than any other; for die it must in the face of modern thought, modern liberty and, above all, of modern economic pressure.

4. "Cohen of Trinity," *The Gentleman's Magazine* 266 (May 1889): 417-24

The news of poor Cohen's death came to me both as a shock and a surprise.

It is true that, in his melodramatic, self-conscious fashion, he had often declared a taste for suicide to be among the characteristics of his versatile race. And indeed in the Cambridge days, or in that obscure interval which elapsed between the termination of his unfortunate University career and the publication of *Gubernator*, there would have been nothing astonishing in such an act on his part. But now, when his book was in everyone's hands, his name on everyone's lips; when that recognition for which he had longed was so completely his; that success for which he had thirsted was poured out for him in so generous a draught—to turn away, to vanish without a word of explanation (he was so fond of explaining himself) is the very last thing one would have expected of him.

I.

He came across the meadows towards the sunset, his upturned face pushed forwards catching the light, and glowing also with another radiance than the rich, reflected glory of the heavens.

A curious figure: slight, ungainly; shoulders in the ears; an awkward, rapid gait, half slouch, half hobble. One arm with its coarse hand swung like a bell-rope as he went; the other pressed a book close against his side, while the hand belonging to it held a few bulrushes and marsh marigolds.

Behind him streamed his shabby gown—it was a glorious afternoon of May—and his dusty trencher-cap[1] pushed to the back of his head revealed clearly the oval contour of the face, the full, prominent lips, full, prominent eyes, and the curved beak of the nose with its restless nostrils.

"Who is he?" I asked of my companion, one of the younger dons.

"Cohen of Trinity."

He shook his head. The man had come up on a scholarship, but had entirely failed to follow up this preliminary distinction. He was no good, no good at all. He was idle, he was incompetent, he led a bad life in a bad set.

We passed on to other subjects, and out of sight passed the uncouth figure with the glowing face, the evil reputation, and that strange suggestion of latent force which clung to him.

The next time I saw Cohen was a few days later in Trinity quad. There were three or four men with him—little Cleaver of Sidney,[2] and others of the same pattern. He was yelling and shrieking with laughter—at some joke of his own, apparently— and his companions were joining in the merriment.

Something in his attitude suggested that he was the ruling spirit of the group, that he was indeed enjoying the delights of addressing an audience, and appreciated to the full the advantages of the situation.

I came across him next morning, hanging moodily over King's Bridge, a striking contrast to the exuberant figure of yesterday.

He looked yellow and flaccid as a sucked lemon, and eyed the water flowing between the bridges with a suicidal air that its notorious shallowness made ridiculous.

---

1 A mortarboard academic hat.
2 Sidney Sussex College, like Trinity, is one of the colleges of the University of Cambridge.

Little Cleaver came up to him and threw out a suggestion of lecture.

Cohen turned round with a self-conscious, sham-tragedy air, gave a great guffaw, and roared out by way of answer the quotation from *Tom Cobb*:

"That world's a beast, and I hate it!"[1]

II.

By degrees I scraped acquaintance with Cohen, who had interested me from the first.

I cannot quite explain my interest on so slight a knowledge; his manners were a distressing mixture of the *bourgeois* and the *canaille*,[2] and a most unattractive lack of simplicity marked his whole personality. There never indeed existed between us anything that could bear the name of friendship. Our relations are easily stated: he liked to talk about himself, and I liked to listen.

I have sometimes reproached myself that I never grew fond of him; but a little reciprocity is necessary in these matters, and poor Cohen had not the art of being fond of people.

I soon discovered that he was desperately lonely and desperately unapproachable.

Once he quoted to me, with reference to himself, the lines from Browning:

... Hath spied an icy fish
That longed to 'scape the rock-stream where she lived,
And thaw herself within the lukewarm waves,
O' the lazy sea....
Only she ever sickened, found repulse
At the other kind of water not her life,
Flounced back from bliss she was not born to breathe,
And in her old bonds buried her despair,
Hating and loving warmth alike.[3]

Of the men with whom I occasionally saw him—men who would have been willing enough to be his friends—he spoke with an open contempt that did him little credit, considering how

---

1 W.S. Gilbert (1836-1911), *Tom Cobb; or Fortune's Toy* (1875), act I. Levy uses this same line in chapter 11 of *The Romance of a Shop*.
2 Riff-raff, the vulgar (French).
3 Robert Browning (1812-89), "Caliban upon Setebos; or; Natural Theology in the Island" (1864), lines 33-43.

unscrupulously he made use of them when his loneliness grew intolerable. There were others, too, besides Cleaver and his set, men of a coarser stamp—boon companions, as the story-books say—with whom, when the fit was on, he consented to herd.

But as friends, as permanent companions even, he rejected them, one and all, with a magnificence, an arrogant and bitter scorn that had in it a distinctly comic element.

I saw him once, to my astonishment, with Norwood, and it came out that he had the greatest admiration for Norwood and his set.

What connection there could be between those young puritans, aristocrats and scholars, the flower of the University—if prigs, a little, and *bornés*[1]—and a man of Cohen's way of life, it would be hard to say.

In aspiring to their acquaintance one scarcely knew if to accuse the man of an insane vanity or a pathetic hankering after better things.

Little Leuniger,[2] who played the fiddle, a Jew, was the fashion at that time among them; but he resolutely turned the cold shoulder to poor Cohen, who, I believe, deeply resented this in his heart, and never lost an opportunity of hurling a bitterness at this compatriot.

A desire to stand well in one another's eyes, to make a brave show before one another, is, I have observed, a marked characteristic of the Jewish people.

As for little Leuniger, he went his way, and contented himself with saying that Cohen's family were not people that one "knew."

On the subject of his family, Cohen himself, at times savagely reserved, at others appallingly frank, volunteered little information, though on one occasion he had touched in with a few vivid strokes the background of his life.

I seemed to see it all before me: the little new house in Maida Vale;[3] a crowd of children, clamorous, unkempt; a sallow shrew in a torn dressing-gown, who alternately scolded, bewailed herself, and sank into moody silence; a fitful paternal figure coming and going, depressed, exhilarated according to the fluctuations of his

---

1 Narrow-minded (French).

2 Compare with Leo Leuniger in *Reuben Sachs*. Levy also wrote a story "Leopold Leuniger: A Study" which was never published. See Linda Hunt Beckman, *Amy Levy: Her Life and Letters* (Athens: Ohio UP, 2000) 69-74.

3 An area of Northwest London with a lower middle-class Jewish community; mentioned also in *Reuben Sachs*.

mysterious financial affairs; and over everything the fumes of smoke, the glare of gas, the smell of food in preparation.

But, naturally enough, it was as an individual, not as the member of a family, that Cohen cared to discuss himself.

There was, indeed, a force, an exuberance, a robustness about his individuality that atoned—to the curious observer at least—for the presence of certain of the elements which helped to compose it. His unbounded arrogance, his enormous pretensions, alternating with and tempered by a bitter self-depreciation, overflowing at times into self-reviling, impressed me, even while amusing and disgusting me.

It seemed that a frustrated sense of power, a disturbing consciousness of some blind force which sought an outlet, lurked within him and allowed him no rest.

Of his failure at his work he spoke often enough, scoffing at academic standards, yet writhing at his own inability to come up to them.

"On my honour," he said to me once, "I can't do better, and that's the truth. Of course you don't believe it; no one believes it. It's all a talk of wasted opportunities, squandered talents—but, before God, that part of my brain which won the scholarship has clean gone."

I pointed out to him that his way of life was not exactly calculated to encourage the working mood.

"Mood!" he shouted with a loud, exasperated laugh. "Mood! I tell you there's a devil in my brain and in my blood, and Heaven knows where it is leading me."

It led him this way and that at all hours of the day and night.

The end of the matter was not difficult to foresee, and I told him so plainly.

This sobered him a little, and he was quiet for three days, lying out on the grass with a lexicon and a pile of Oxford classics.

On the fourth the old mood was upon him and he rushed about like a hunted thing from dawn to sunset winding up with an entertainment which threatened his position as a member of the University.

He got off this time, however, but I shall never forget his face the next morning as he blustered loudly past Norwood and Blount in Trinity Street.

If he neglected his own work, he did, as far as could be seen, no other, unless fits of voracious and promiscuous reading may be allowed to count as such. I suspected him of writing verses, but on this matter of writing he always maintained, curiously enough, a profound reserve.

What I had for some time foreseen as inevitable at length came to pass. Cohen disappeared at a short notice from the University, no choice being given him in the matter.

I went off to his lodgings directly the news of his sentence reached me, but the bird had already flown, leaving no trace behind of its whereabouts.

As I stood in the dismantled little room, always untidy, but now littered from end to end with torn and dusty papers, there rose before my mind the vision of Cohen as I had first seen him in the meadows, with the bulrushes in his hand, the book beneath his arm, and on his face, which reflected the sunset, the radiance of a secret joy.

III.

I did not see *Gubernator* till it was in its fourth edition, some three months after its publication and five years after the expulsion of Cohen from Trinity.

The name, Alfred Lazarus Cohen, printed in full on the title-page, revealed what had never before occurred to me, the identity of the author of that much-talked-of book with my unfortunate college acquaintance. I turned over the leaves with a new curiosity, and, it must be added, a new distrust. By-and-bye I ceased from this cursory, tentative inspection, I began at the beginning and finished the book at a sitting.

Everyone knows *Gubernator* by now, and I have no intention of describing it. Half poem, half essay, wholly unclassifiable, with a force, a fire, a vision, a vigour and felicity of phrase that carried you through its most glaring inequalities, its most appalling lapses of taste, the book fairly took the reader by storm.

Here was a clear case of figs from thistles.[1]

I grew anxious to know how Cohen was bearing himself under his success, which must surely have satisfied, for the time being at least, even his enormous claims.

Was that ludicrous, pathetic gap between his dues and his pretensions at last bridged over?

I asked myself this and many more questions, but a natural hesitation to hunt up the successful man where the obscure one had entirely escaped my memory prevented me from taking any steps to the renewal of our acquaintance.

But Cohen, as may be supposed, was beginning to be talked

---

1   Matthew 7.16: "Can people pick grapes from thorns, or figs from thistles?" The passage concerns false prophets.

about, heard of and occasionally met, and I had no doubt that chance would soon give me the opportunity I did not feel justified in seeking.

There was growing up, naturally enough, among some of us Cambridge men a sense that Cohen had been hardly used, that (I do not think this was the case) he had been unjustly treated at the University. Lord Norwood, whom I came across one day at the club, remarked that no doubt his widespread popularity would more than atone to Cohen for the flouting he had met with at the hands of Alma Mater. He had read *Gubernator*; it was clever, but the book repelled him, just as the man, poor fellow, had always repelled him. The subject did not seem to interest him, and he went off shortly afterwards with Blount and Leuniger.

A week later I met Cohen at a club dinner, given by a distinguished man of letters. There were present notabilities of every sort—literary, dramatic, artistic—but the author of *Gubernator* was the lion of the evening. He rose undeniably to the situation, and roared as much as was demanded of him. His shrill, uncertain voice, pitched in a loud excited key, shot this way and that across the table. His strange, flexible face, with the full, prominent lips, glowed and quivered with animation. Surely this was his hour of triumph.

He had recognised me at once, and after dinner came round to me, his shoulders in his ears as usual, holding out his hand with a beaming smile. He talked of Cambridge, of one or two mutual acquaintances, without embarrassment. He could not have been less abashed if he had wound up his career at the University amid the cheers of an enthusiastic Senate House.

When the party broke up he came over to me again and suggested that I should go back with him to his rooms. He had never had much opinion of me, as he had been at no pains to conceal, and I concluded that he was in a mood for unbosoming himself. But it seemed that I was wrong, and we walked back to Great Russell Street,[1] where he had two large, untidy rooms, almost in silence. He told me that he was living away from his family, an unexpected legacy from an uncle having given him independence.

"So the Fates aren't doing it by halves?" I remarked, in answer to this communication.

"Oh, no," he replied, with a certain moody irony, staring hard at me over his cigar.

---

1 Located in the heart of Bloomsbury, this is the street where the British Museum stands.

"Do you know what success means?" he asked suddenly, and in the question I seemed to hear Cohen the *poseur*, always at the elbow of, and not always to be distinguished from, Cohen stark-nakedly revealed.

"Ah, no, indeed."

"It means—inundation by the second-rate."

"What does the fellow want?" I cried, uncertain as to the extent of his seriousness.

"I never," he said, "was a believer in the half-loaf theory."

"It strikes me, Cohen, that your loaf looks uncommonly like a whole one, as loaves go on this unsatisfactory planet."

He burst into a laugh.

"Nothing," he said presently, "can alter the relations of things—their permanent, essential relations ... 'They *shall* know, they *shall* understand, they *shall* feel what I am.' That is what I used to say to myself in the old days. I suppose now, 'they' do know, more or less, and what of that?"

"I should say the difference from your point of view was a very great one. But you always chose to cry for the moon."

"Well," he said, quietly looking up, "it's the only thing worth having."

I was struck afresh by the man's insatiable demands, which looked at times like a passionate striving after perfection, yet went side by side with the crudest vanity, the most vulgar desire for recognition.

I rose soon after his last remark, which was delivered with a simplicity and an air of conviction which made one cease to suspect the mountebank; we shook hands and bade one another good-night.

★★★★★

I never saw Cohen again.

Ten days after our renewal of acquaintance he set a bullet through his brain, which, it was believed, must have caused instantaneous death. That small section of the public which interests itself in books discussed the matter for three days, and the jury returned the usual verdict. I have confessed that I was astonished, that I was wholly unprepared by my knowledge of Cohen for the catastrophe. Yet now and then an inkling of his motive, a dim, fleeting sense of what may have prompted him to the deed, has stolen in upon me.

In his hour of victory the sense of defeat had been strongest. Is it, then, possible that, amid the warring elements of that discordant nature, the battling forces of that ill- starred, ill-compounded entity, there lurked, clear-eyed and ever-watchful, a baffled idealist?

5. Poetry

[This selection of Levy's poetry includes "After Heine," verse that explores the influence of this German-Jewish Romantic poet (1797-1856) on Levy. Heine's attention to the fraught condition of diasporic Jewish identity is especially relevant to Levy's writing on Anglo-Jewry. "Captivity" suggests both the homelessness and strictures of modern Jewish and female subjectivity. The other poems consider the complexitites of love, sexuality, and gender and might be read in the context of Levy's own history as a Jewish and possibly lesbian "new woman." With the exception of "The Ballad of Religion and Marriage," none of these poems is currently in print.]

"After Heine," *The Cambridge Review* 7 (1886): 237-38

The stately sentinel cypress
    Stands out against the blue,
The world declares you wronged me,
    And I declared it too.

I've no blame left to utter,
    And no tears left to shed;
The joy, and the shame, and the sorrow,
    They, too, are done with and dead.

So long ago it happened;
    Long since my heart is stone;
And yet beneath the cypress
    I linger here alone.

Your friends forget: I scatter
    My flow'rs above your grave;
For you to me have given
    That which none other gave.

"New Love, New Life," A *London Plane-Tree, and Other Verse* (1889): 35

I.

She, who so long has lain
    Stone-stiff with folded wings,
Within my heart again
    The brown bird wakes and sings.

Brown nightingale, whose strain
     Is heard by day, by night,
She sings of joy and pain,
     Of sorrow and delight.
II.

'Tis true,—in other days
     Have I unbarred the door;
He knows the walks and ways—
     Love has been here before.

Love blest and love accurst
     Was here in days long past;
This time is not the first,
     But this time is the last.

"In the Night," *A London Plane-Tree, and Other Verse* (1889): 41

Cruel? I think there never was a cheating
     More cruel, thro' all the weary days than this!
This is no dream, my heart kept on repeating,
     But sober certainty of waking bliss.

Dreams? O, I know their faces—goodly seeming,
     Vaporous, whirled on many-coloured wings;
I have had dreams before, this is no dreaming,
     But daylight gladness that the daylight brings.

What ails my love; what ails her? She is paling;
     Faint grows her face, and slowly seems to fade!
I cannot clasp her—stretch out unavailing
     My arms across the silence and the shade.

"Captivity," *A London Plane-Tree, and Other Verse* (1889): 62-63

The lion remembers the forest,
     The lion in chains;
To the bird that is captive a vision
     Of woodland remains.

One strains with his strength at the fetter,
     In impotent rage;
One flutters in flights of a moment,
     And beats at the cage.

If the lion were loosed from the fetter,
       To wander again;
He would seek the wide silence and shadow
       Of his jungle in vain.

He would rage in his fury, destroying;
       Let him rage, let him roam!
Shall he traverse the pitiless mountain,
       Or swim through the foam?

If they opened the cage and the casement,
       And the bird flew away;
He would come back at evening, heartbroken,
       A captive for aye.

Would come if his kindred had spared him,
       Free bird from afar—
There was wrought what is stronger than iron
       In fetter and bar.

I cannot remember my country,
       The land whence I came;
Whence they brought me and chained me and made me
       Nor wild thing nor tame.

This only I know of my country,
       This only repeat:—
It was free as the forest, and sweeter
       Than woodland retreat.

When the chain shall at last be broken,
       The window set wide;
And I step in the largeness and freedom
       Of sunlight outside;
Shall I wander in vain for my country?
       Shall I seek and not find?
Shall I cry for the bars that encage me,
       The fetters that bind?

"A Ballad of Religion and Marriage"[1]

Swept into limbo is the host
    Of heavenly angels, row on row;
The Father, Son, and Holy Ghost,
    Pale and defeated, rise and go.
The great Jehovah is laid low,
    Vanished his burning bush and rod—
Say, are we doomed to deeper woe?
    Shall marriage go the way of God?

Monogamous, still at our post,
    Reluctantly we undergo
Domestic round of boiled and roast,
    Yet deem the whole proceeding slow.
Daily the secret murmurs grow;
    We are no more content to plod
Along the beaten paths—and so
    Marriage must go the way of God.

Soon, before all men, each shall toast
    The seven strings unto his bow,
Like beacon fires along the coast,
    The flames of love shall glance and glow.
Nor let nor hindrance man shall know,
    From natal bath to funeral sod;
Perennial shall his pleasures flow
    When marriage goes the way of God.

Grant, in a million years at most,
    Folk shall be neither pairs nor odd—
Alas! we sha'n't be there to boast
    "Marriage has gone the way of God!"

---

1   Twelve copies of this poem were privately printed by Clement Shorter
    and circulated in 1915.

Appendix C: Literary Contexts

1. From George Eliot, "The Modern Hep! Hep! Hep!," *The Impressions of Theophrastus Such*, *The Works of George Eliot*, vol. 20 (London: William Blackwood & Sons, 1878-83): 259-93

[This essay about Jewishness and anti-Semitism appeared in Eliot's last publication, following her last novel *Daniel Deronda* (1876). The 18 chapters are presented through the voice of Theophrastus Such, a middle-aged English bachelor who is also a writer, as Eliot crafts this image of her author-character of English culture with links back to the ancient Greek philosopher Theophrastus and also to the Hebrew Bible, Chinese poetry, and the Koran. "The Modern Hep! Hep! Hep!" of the title refers to the popular legend of the Crusaders's cry of "Hep!" (the acronym for *Hierosolyma est perdita*, or "Jerusalem is lost") as they attacked Jews, also invoked in the 1819 anti-Semitic student riots in Frankfurt. As with the other chapters in the collection, this essay considers the nature of contemporary community. Such sees modern nationalism as the resurrection of an ancient past, best typified by the idea of a modern Jewish nation with bonds to ancient traditions. The essay assails English Christian prejudice against Jews, also a central interest in *Daniel Deronda*. Typical of her era, Eliot understands "race" both as the general idea of a people, and in terms of the new scientific discourse of a fixed biological category. The excerpt that follows begins with a philosophical exploration of categories of social identities.]

To discern likeness amidst diversity, it is well known, does not require so fine a mental edge as the discerning of diversity amidst general sameness. The primary rough classification depends on the prominent resemblances of things: the progress is towards finer and finer discrimination according to minute differences.

Yet even at this stage of European culture one's attention is continually drawn to the prevalence of that grosser mental sloth which makes people dull to the most ordinary prompting of comparison—the bringing things together because of their likeness. The same motives, the same ideas, the same practices, are alternately admired and abhorred, lauded and denounced, according to their association with superficial differences, historical or actually social: even learned writers treating of great subjects often show an attitude of mind not greatly superior in its logic to that of the frivolous fine lady who is indignant at the frivolity of her maid.

To take only the subject of the Jews: it would be difficult to find a form of bad reasoning about them which has not been heard in conversation or been admitted to the dignity of print; but the neglect of resemblances is a common property of dulness which unites all the various points of view—the prejudiced, the puerile, the spiteful, and the abysmally ignorant.

★★★

It is certainly worth considering whether an expatriated, denationalised race, used for ages to live among antipathetic populations, must not inevitably lack some conditions of nobleness. If they drop that separateness which is made their reproach, they may be in danger of lapsing into a cosmopolitan indifference equivalent to cynicism, and of missing that inward identification with the nationality immediately around them which might make some amends for their inherited privation. No dispassionate observer can deny this danger. Why, our own countrymen who take to living abroad without purpose or function to keep up their sense of fellowship in the affairs of their own land are rarely good specimens of moral healthiness; still, the consciousness of having a native country, the birthplace of common memories and habits of mind, existing like a parental hearth quitted but beloved; the dignity of being included in a people which has a part in the comity of nations and the growing federation of the world; that sense of special belonging which is the root of human virtues, both public and private,—all these spiritual links may preserve migratory Englishmen from the worst consequences of their voluntary dispersion. Unquestionably the Jews, having been more than any other race exposed to the adverse moral influences of alienism, must, both in individuals and in groups, have suffered some corresponding moral degradation; but in fact they have escaped with less of abjectness and less of hard hostility towards the nations whose hand has been against them, than could have happened in the case of a people who had neither their adhesion to a separate religion founded on historic memories, nor their characteristic family affectionateness. Tortured, flogged, spit upon, the *corpus vile*[1] on which rage or wantonness vented them-

---

selves with impunity, their name flung at them as an opprobrium by superstition, hatred, and contempt, they have remained proud of their origin.

***

So far shall we be carried if we go in search of devices to hinder people of other blood than our own from getting the advantage of dwelling among us.

Let it be admitted that it is a calamity to the English, as to any other great historic people, to undergo a premature fusion with immigrants of alien blood; that its distinctive national character-istics should be in danger of obliteration by the predominating quality of foreign settlers. I not only admit this, I am ready to unite in groaning over the threatened danger. To one who loves his native language, who would delight to keep our rich and har-monious English undefiled by foreign accent, foreign intonation, and those foreign tinctures of verbal meaning which tend to confuse all writing and discourse, it is an affliction as harassing as the climate, that on our stage, in our studios, at our public and private gatherings, in our offices, warehouses, and workshops, we must expect to hear our beloved English with its words clipped, its vowels stretched and twisted, its phrases of acquiescence and politeness, of cordiality, dissidence or argument, delivered always in the wrong tones, like ill-rendered melodies, marred beyond recognition; that there should be a general ambition to speak every language except our mother English, which persons "of style" are not ashamed of corrupting with slang, false foreign equivalents, and a pronunciation that crushes out all colour from the vowels and jams them between jostling consonants. An ancient Greek might not like to be resuscitated for the sake of hearing Homer read in our universities, still he would at least find more instructive marvels in other developments to be witnessed at those institutions; but a modern Englishman is invited from his after-dinner repose to hear Shakespeare delivered under circum-stances which offer no other novelty than some novelty of false intonation, some new distribution of strong emphasis on prepo-sitions, some new misconception of a familiar idiom. Well! it is our inertness that is in fault, our carelessness of excellence, our willing ignorance of the treasures that lie in our national heritage, while we are agape after what is foreign, though it may be only a vile imitation of what is native.

***

And this is the usual level of thinking in polite society concerning the Jews. Apart from theological purposes, it seems to be held surprising that anybody should take an interest in the history of a people whose literature has furnished all our devotional language; and if any reference is made to their past or future destinies some hearer is sure to state as a relevant fact which may assist our judgment, that she, for her part, is not fond of them, having known a Mr. Jacobson who was very unpleasant, or that he, for his part, thinks meanly of them as a race, though on inquiry you find that he is so little acquainted with their characteristics that he is astonished to learn how many persons whom he has blindly admired and applauded are Jews to the backbone. Again, men who consider themselves in the very van of modern advancement, knowing history and the latest philosophies of history, indicate their contemptuous surprise that any one should entertain the destiny of the Jews as a worthy subject, by referring to Moloch[1] and their own agreement with the theory that the religion of Jehovah was merely a transformed Moloch-worship, while in the same breath they are glorifying "civilisation" as a transformed tribal existence of which some lineaments are traceable in grim marriage customs of the native Australians. Are these erudite persons prepared to insist that the name "Father" should no longer have any sanctity for us, because in their view of likelihood our Aryan ancestors were mere improvers on a state of things in which nobody knew his own father?

For less theoretic men, ambitious to be regarded as practical politicians, the value of the Hebrew race has been measured by their unfavourable opinion of a prime minister who is a Jew by lineage.[2] But it is possible to form a very ugly opinion as to the scrupulousness of Walpole, or of Chatham;[3] and in any case I think Englishmen would refuse to accept the character and doings of those eighteenth century statesmen as the standard of value for the English people and the part they have to play in the fortunes of mankind.

---

1   Semitic diety worshipped in biblical times and associated with death and child sacrifice, a practice abhorred and forbidden by Hebrew law.
2   Benjamin Disraeli (1804-81), novelist and statesman (Prime Minister in 1868 and from 1874 to 1880), was born Jewish and converted to the Church of England at age 12.
3   Sir Robert Walpole (1676-1745), statesman and Prime Minister, whose long-standing extramarital affair was satirized in John Gay's *The Beggar's Opera* (1728); William Pitt, first Earl of Chatham (1708-78), statesman who opposed measures taken against the American colonies.

If we are to consider the future of the Jews at all, it seems reasonable to take as a preliminary question: Are they destined to complete fusion with the peoples among whom they are dispersed, losing every remnant of a distinctive consciousness as Jews; or, are there in the breadth and intensity with which the feeling of separateness, or what we may call the organised memory of a national consciousness, actually exists in the worldwide Jewish communities—the seven millions scattered from east to west—and again, are there in the political relations of the world, the conditions present or approaching for the restoration of a Jewish state planted on the old ground as a centre of national feeling, a source of dignifying protection, a special channel for special energies which may contribute some added form of national genius, and an added voice in the councils of the world?

They are among us everywhere: it is useless to say we are not fond of them. Perhaps we are not fond of proletaries and their tendency to form Unions, but the world is not therefore to be rid of them. If we wish to free ourselves from the inconveniences that we have to complain of, whether in proletaries or in Jews, our best course is to encourage all means of improving these neighbours who elbow us in a thickening crowd, and of sending their incommodious energies into beneficent channels. Why are we so eager for the dignity of certain populations of whom perhaps we have never seen a single specimen, and of whose history, legend, or literature we have been contentedly ignorant for ages, while we sneer at the notion of a renovated national dignity for the Jews, whose ways of thinking and whose very verbal forms are on our lips in every prayer which we end with an Amen? Some of us consider this question dismissed when they have said that the wealthiest Jews have no desire to forsake their European palaces, and go to live in Jerusalem. But in a return from exile, in the restoration of a people, the question is not whether certain rich men will choose to remain behind, but whether there will be found worthy men who will choose to lead the return. Plenty of prosperous Jews remained in Babylon when Ezra[1] marshalled his band of forty thousand and began a new glorious epoch in the history of his race, making the preparation for that epoch in the history of the world which has been held glorious enough to be dated from for evermore. The hinge of possibility is simply the existence of an adequate community of feeling as well as widespread need in

---

1 Ezra (fifth century BCE), priest and scribe who crafted religious reforms for the new Judean commonwealth after the Babylonian exile.

the Jewish race, and the hope that among its finer specimens there may arise some men of instruction and ardent public spirit, some new Ezras, some modern Maccabees,[1] who will know how to use all favouring outward conditions, how to triumph by heroic example over the indifference of their fellows and the scorn of their foes, and will steadfastly set their faces towards making their people once more one among the nations.

2. From Mathilde Blind, "Daniel Deronda," *George Eliot*, Eminent Women Series (London: W.H. Allen and Co., 1883): 192-203

[Mathilde Blind (1841-96), from a Jewish German banking family, lived in England and published the poem "The Ascent of Man" (1889) about Darwinian theory, as well as other poems, biographies, essays; she translated from German *The Old Faith and the New* by David Friedrich Strauss. Like George Eliot, Blind was intensely interested in religious faith and doubt in the context of the new evolutionary sciences. Blind's *George Eliot* was one of 22 biographies of British, French, and American women in the "Eminent Women" series published between 1883 and 1895; subjects included Queen Victoria, Mary Shelley, Harriet Martineau, and Elizabeth Barrett Browning. The following comes from the last chapter, "Daniel Deronda," on Eliot's 1876 novel. Whether or not Eliot's views on Jews and Palestine are aptly summarized here, Blind does convey the reservations of some Anglo-Jews, including Levy, about separatist proto-Zionist ideals. However, many European Jews, including Joseph Jacobs, praised the novel's interest in restoring a Jewish state in "the East."]

'Daniel Deronda,' which appeared five years after 'Middlemarch,' occupies a place apart among George Eliot's novels. In the spirit which animates it, it has perhaps the closest affinity with the 'Spanish Gypsy.'[2] Speaking of this work to a young friend of Jewish extraction (in whose career George Eliot felt keen inter-

---

1 Judah the Maccabee (died 161 BCE), commanded Jewish rebels who liberated Jerusalem and reconsecrated the Temple, as commemorated in the Jewish festival of Hanukkah.

2 George Eliot (1819-80), *The Spanish Gypsy* (1868), a dramatic poem set in fifteenth-century Spain, about Spanish Christians, Moors, Jews, and gypsies, engages with questions of religion, nationalism, and gender.

est), she expressed surprise at the amazement which her choice of a subject had created. "I wrote about the Jews," she remarked, "because I consider them a fine old race who have done great things for humanity. I feel the same admiration for them as I do for the Florentines. Only lately I have heard to my great satisfaction that an influential member of the Jewish community is going to start an emigration to Palestine.[1] You will also be glad to learn that Helmholtz[2] is a Jew."

These observations are valuable as affording a key to the leading motive of 'Daniel Deronda.' Mordecai's ardent desire to found a new national state in Palestine is not simply the author's dramatic realisation of the feeling of an enthusiast, but expresses her own very definite sentiments on the subject. The Jewish apostle is, in fact, more or less the mouthpiece of George Eliot's own opinions on Judaism....

★★★

This notion that the Jews should return to Palestine in a body, and once more constitute themselves into a distinct nation, is curiously repugnant to modern feelings. As repugnant as that other doctrine, which is also implied in the book, that Jewish separateness should be still further insured by strictly adhering to their own race in marriage—at least Mirah, the most faultless of George Eliot's heroines, whose character expresses the noblest side of Judaism, "is a Jewess who will not accept any one but a Jew."

Mirah Lapidoth and the Princess Halm-Eberstein, Deronda's mother, are drawn with the obvious purpose of contrasting two types of Jewish women. Whereas the latter, strictly brought up in the belief and most minute observances of her Hebrew father, breaks away from the "bondage of having been born a Jew," from which she wishes to relieve her son by parting from him in

---

1 *Daniel Deronda* concludes with a group of characters planning to embark for "the East" to found a homeland for Jews. Throughout the nineteenth century there were sporadic agricultural settlements by European Jews and philo-Semitic Christians in Palestine, then a part of the Ottoman Empire, and some of these were funded by Sir Moses Montefiore (1774-1885), an Anglo-Jewish banker and humanitarian who visited Palestine several times.

2 Hermann von Helmholtz (1821-94), German physicist who developed theories of electric and magnetic forces.

infancy, Mirah, brought up in disregard, "even in dislike of her Jewish origin," clings with inviolable tenacity to the memory of that origin and to the fellowship of her people. The author leaves one in little doubt as towards which side her own sympathies incline to. She is not so much the artist here, impartially portraying different kinds of characters, as the special pleader proclaiming that one set of motives are righteous, just, and praiseworthy, as well as that the others are mischievous and reprehensible.

This seems carrying the principle of nationality to an extreme, if not pernicious length. If there were never any breaking up of old forms of society, any fresh blending of nationalities and races, we should soon reduce Europe to another China. This unwavering faithfulness to the traditions of the past may become a curse to the living. A rigidity as unnatural as it is dangerous would be the result of too tenacious a clinging to inherited memories. For if this doctrine were strictly carried out, such a country as America, where there is a slow amalgamation of many allied and even heterogeneous races into a new nation, would practically become impossible. Indeed, George Eliot does not absolutely hold these views. She considers them necessary at present in order to act as a drag to the too rapid transformations of society. In the most interesting paper of 'Theophrastus Such,' that called 'The Modern Hep! Hep! Hep!'[1] she remarks: "The tendency of things is towards quicker or slower fusion of races. It is impossible to arrest this tendency; all we can do is to moderate its course so as to hinder it from degrading the moral status of societies by a too rapid effacement of those national traditions and customs which are the language of the national genius—the deep suckers of healthy sentiment. Such moderating and guidance of inevitable movement is worthy of all effort."

Considering that George Eliot was convinced of this modern tendency towards fusion, it is all the more singular that she should, in 'Daniel Deronda,' have laid such stress on the reconstruction, after the lapse of centuries, of a Jewish state; singular, when one considers that many of the most eminent Jews, far from aspiring towards such an event, hardly seem to have contemplated it as a desirable or possible prospect. The sympathies of

---

1   Eliot's *The Impressions of Theophrastus Such* (1879) offers a collection of essays in the voice of Such, a fictional nineteenth-century English bachelor who specializes in modern thought. "The Modern Hep! Hep! Hep!" explores Jewishness and anti-Semitism. See Appendix C1.

Spinoza, the Mendelssohns, Rahel, Meyerbeer, Heine,[1] and many others, are not distinctively Jewish but humanitarian. And the grandest, as well as truest thing that has been uttered about them is that saying of Heine's: "The country of the Jews is the ideal, is God."

Indeed, to have a true conception of Jewish nature and character, of its brilliant lights and deep shadows, of its pathos, depth, sublimity, degradation, and wit; of its infinite resource and boundless capacity for suffering—one must go to Heine and not to 'Daniel Deronda.' In 'Jehuda-ben-Halevy'[2] Heine expresses the love and longing of a Jewish heart for Jerusalem in accents of such piercing intensity that compared with it, "Mordecai's" fervid desire fades into mere abstract rhetoric.

★★★

Soon after the publication of this novel, we find the following allusion to it in one of George Eliot's letters to Mrs. Bray:[3] "I don't know what you refer to in the *Jewish World*.[4] Perhaps the report of Dr. Hermann Adler's lecture on 'Deronda' to the Jewish working-men, given in the *Times*. Probably the Dr. Adler whom

---

1 All European Jews who advocated in theory or through practice secularization and assimilation through conversion and intermarriage. Baruch Spinoza (1632-77), Dutch philosopher that maintained an unfettered freedom of inquiry which was in opposition to traditional Jewish orthodoxy; he was excommunicated from the Sephardic community of Amsterdam in 1656. Moses Mendelssohn (1729-96), German philosopher, biblical scholar, and advocate of Jewish emancipation, is regarded as the leader of the Jewish Enlightenment, or *Haskalah*, in late eighteenth- and nineteenth-century Europe, to acquire secular knowledge. The composer Felix Mendelssohn was his grandson, who was raised as a Christian. Rahel Levin Varnhagen (1771-1833) hosted a salon of many prominent artists and intellectuals in Berlin; born Jewish she converted and married a Prussian diplomat. Giacomo Meyerbeer (1791-1864), German composer known chiefly for his operas. Heinrich Heine (1797-1856), a German Jewish writer who converted and whose poems were widely read and influenced many other poets, including Levy.

2 Yehudah ha-Levi (c.1075-1141), Jewish-Spanish poet and religious thinker who applied conventions of Arabic poetry to classical Hebrew. Levy translated his Hebrew poems from a German translation, and they appeared in Katie Magnus's *Jewish Portraits* (1888).

3 Caroline Bray (1814-1905), Eliot's friend and correspondent.

4 Weekly periodical of Anglo-Jewry.

you saw is Dr. Hermann's father, still living as Chief Rabbi.[1] I have had some delightful communications from Jews and Jewesses, both at home and abroad. Part of the Club scene in 'D. D.'[2] is flying about in the Hebrew tongue through the various Hebrew newspapers.... The Jews naturally are not indifferent to themselves."

3. From Israel Zangwill, *Children of the Ghetto: A Study of a Peculiar People* (Philadelphia: Jewish Publication Society of America, 1892)

[Israel Zangwill (1864-1926) was a noted Anglo-Jewish spokesman and writer, and author of the play *The Melting Pot* (1909) about Jewish acculturation in the United States. His novel *Children of the Ghetto* focuses on poor immigrant East End Jews in the first part, "The Children of the Ghetto,"and wealthy, Anglicized West End Jews in the second part, "The Grandchildren of the Ghetto." This excerpt comes from the first chapter, "The Christmas Dinner," in "The Grandchildren of the Ghetto." A dinner conversation ensues about a controversial novel of contemporary Jewish life, *Mordecai Josephs*, much like Levy's *Reuben Sachs*, which Zangwill clearly had in mind. "Edward Armitage" is a pseudonym concealing the authorship of Esther Ansell, who grew up in an impoverished East End family and has been adopted by the West End Goldsmiths. The entire scene is a studied commentary on the reception of *Reuben Sachs* and Julia Frankau's *Dr. Phillips* (1887), published under the name "Frank Danby." See Appendix A4, "The Deterioration of the Jewess." In this scene, "the dark little girl" is Esther Ansell.]

Hence, too, the prevalent craving for a certain author's blood could not be gratified at Mrs. Henry Goldsmith's Chanukah dinner. Besides, nobody knew where to lay hand upon Edward

---

1   Nathan Adler (1803-90) was born in Germany and moved to England, where in 1845 he was appointed Chief Rabbi of the United Synagogues of the British Empire. He was instrumental in shaping orthodox Jewry to resemble Anglicanism (see Eugene C. Black, *The Social Politics of Anglo-Jewry 1880-1920* [New York: Blackwell 1988] 26-29). His son Hermann (1840-1911) replaced his father as Chief Rabbi in 1880.

2   *Daniel Deronda*, chapter 42, where a number of working-class men along with Mordecai and Daniel debate the present and future of Judaism and English Jews.

Armitage, the author in question, whose opprobrious production, *Mordecai Josephs*, had scandalized West-End Judaism.

"Why didn't he describe our circles?" asked the hostess, an angry fire in her beautiful eyes. "It would have, at least, corrected the picture. As it is, the public will fancy that we are all daubed with the same brush; that we have no thought in life beyond dress, money, and solo whist."

"He probably painted the life he knew," said Sidney Graham, in defence.

"Then I am sorry for him," retorted Mrs. Goldsmith. "It's a great pity he had such detestable acquaintances. Of course, he has cut himself off from the possibility of any better now."

The wavering flush on her lovely face darkened with disinterested indignation, and her beautiful bosom heaved with judicial grief.

"I should hope so," put in Miss Cissy Levine, sharply. She was a pale, bent woman, with spectacles, who believed in the mission of Israel, and wrote domestic novels to prove that she had no sense of humor. "No one has a right to foul his own nest. Are there not plenty of subjects for the Jew's pen without his attacking his own people? The calumniator of his race should be ostracised from decent society."

"As according to him there is none," laughed Graham, "I cannot see where the punishment comes in."

"Oh, he may say so in that book," said Mrs. Montagu Samuels, an amiable, loose-thinking lady of florid complexion, who dabbled exasperatingly in her husband's philanthropic concerns from the vain idea that the wife of a committee-man is a committee-woman. "But he knows better."

"Yes, indeed," said Mr. Montagu Samuels. "The rascal has only written this to make money. He knows it's all exaggeration and distortion; but anything spicy pays nowadays."

★★★

"The whole book's written with gall," went on Percy Saville, emphatically. "I suppose the man couldn't get into good Jewish houses, and he's revenged himself by slandering them."

"Then he ought to have got into good Jewish houses," said Sidney. "The man has talent, nobody can deny that, and if he couldn't get into good Jewish society because he didn't have money enough, isn't that proof enough his picture is true?"

"I don't deny that there are people among us who make

money the one open sesame to their houses," said Mrs. Henry Goldsmith, magnanimously.

"Deny it, indeed? Money is the open sesame to everything," rejoined Sidney Graham, delightedly scenting an opening for a screed. He liked to talk bomb-shells, and did not often get pillars of the community to shatter. "Money manages the schools and the charities, and the synagogues, and indirectly controls the press. A small body of persons—always the same—sits on all councils, on all boards! Why? Because they pay the piper."

★★★

"The mental attitude you caricature is not so snobbish as it seems," said Raphael Leon, breaking into the conversation for the first time. "The temptations to the wealthy and the honored to desert their struggling brethren are manifold, and sad experience has made our race accustomed to the loss of its brightest sons."

"Thanks for the compliment, fair coz," said Sidney, not without a complacent cynical pleasure in the knowledge that Raphael spoke truly, that he owed his own immunity from the obligations of the faith to his artistic success, and that the outside world was disposed to accord him a larger charter of morality on the same grounds. "But if you can only deny nasty facts by accounting for them, I dare say Mr. Armitage's book will afford you ample opportunities for explanation. Or have Jews the brazenness to assert it is all invention?"

"No, no one would do that," said Percy Saville, who had just done it. "Certainly there is a good deal of truth in the sketch of the ostentatious, overdressed Johnsons who, as everybody knows, are meant for the Jonases."

"Oh, yes," said Mrs. Henry Goldsmith. "And it's quite evident that the stockbroker who drops half his h's and all his poor acquaintances and believes in one Lord, is no other than Joel Friedman."

"And the house where people drive up in broughams for supper and solo whist after the theatre is the Davises in Maida Vale," said Miss Cissy Levine.

"Yes, the book's true enough," began Mrs. Montagu Samuels. She stopped suddenly, catching her husband's eye and the color heightened on her florid cheek. "What I say is," she concluded awkwardly, "he ought to have come among us, and shown the world a picture of the cultured Jews."

"Quite so, quite so," said the hostess. Then turning to the tall thoughtful-looking young man who had hitherto contributed but one sentence to the conversation, she said, half in sly malice, half to draw him out. "Now you, Mr. Leon, whose culture is certified by our leading university, what do you think of this latest portrait of the Jew?"

"I don't know, I haven't read it!" replied Raphael apologetically.

"No more have I," murmured the table generally.

"I wouldn't touch it with a pitchfork," said Miss Cissy Levine.

"I think it's a shame they circulate it at the libraries," said Mrs. Montagu Samuels. "I just glanced over it at Mrs. Hugh Marston's house. It's vile. There are actually jargon words in it. Such vulgarity!"

"Shameful!" murmured Percy Saville; "Mr. Lazarus was telling me about it. It's plain treachery and disloyalty, this putting of weapons into the hands of our enemies. Of course we have our faults, but we should be told of them privately or from the pulpit."

"That would be just as efficacious," said Sidney admiringly.

"More efficacious," said Percy Saville, unsuspiciously. "A preacher speaks with authority, but this penny-a-liner."[1]

"With truth?" queried Sidney.

Saville stopped, disgusted, and the hostess answered Sidney half-coaxingly.

"Oh, I am sure you can't think that. The book is so one-sided. Not a word about our generosity, our hospitality, our domesticity, the thousand-and-one good traits all the world allows us."

"Of course not; since all the world allows them, it was unnecessary," said Sidney.

"I wonder the Chief Rabbi[2] doesn't stop it," said Mrs. Montagu Samuels.

"My dear, how can he?" inquired her husband. "He has no control over the publishing trade."

"He ought to talk to the man," persisted Mrs. Samuels.

"But we don't even know who he is," said Percy Saville, "probably Edward Armitage is only a *nom-de-plume*. You'd be surprised

---

1 A hack writer who contributes to journals for so much a line.

2 Hermann Adler (1840-1911) was Chief Rabbi and leader of orthodox Anglo-Jewry for the United Synaogues of Great Britain following his father Nathan's retirement from this post in 1880.

to learn the real names of some of the literary celebrities I meet about."

"Oh, if he's a Jew you may be sure it isn't his real name," laughed Sidney. It was characteristic of him that he never spared a shot even when himself hurt by the kick of the gun. Percy colored slightly, unmollified by being in the same boat with the satirist.

"I have never seen the name in the subscription lists," said the hostess with ready tact.

"There is an Armitage who subscribes two guineas a year to the Board of Guardians,"[1] said Mrs. Montagu Samuels. "But his Christian name is George."

"'Christian' name is distinctly good for 'George,'" murmured Sidney.

"There was an Armitage who sent a cheque to the Russian Fund," said Mr. Henry Goldsmith, "but that can't be an author—it was quite a large cheque!"

"I am sure I have seen Armitage among the Births, Marriages and Deaths," said Miss Cissy Levine.

"How well-read they all are in the national literature," Sidney murmured to Addie.

Indeed the sectarian advertisements served to knit the race together, counteracting the unravelling induced by the fashionable dispersion of Israel and waxing the more important as the other links—the old traditional jokes, by-words, ceremonies, card-games, prejudices and tunes, which are more important than laws and more cementatory than ideals—were disappearing before the over-zealousness of a *parvenu* refinement that had not yet attained to self-confidence. The Anglo-Saxon stolidity of the West-End Synagogue service,[2] on week days entirely given over to paid praying-men, was a typical expression of the universal tendency to exchange the picturesque primitiveness of the Orient for the sobrieties of fashionable civilization. When Jeshurun[3] waxed fat he did not always kick, but he yearned to approximate as much as possible to John Bull[4] without merging in him; to sink

---

1 See *Reuben Sachs*, p. 106, note 1.
2 The West London Synagogue of British Jews in Upper Berkeley Street reformed the religious service to resemble in some respects Anglican Church service. For more information, see *Reuben Sachs*, p. 64, note 3.
3 Deuteronomy 32.15. Jeshurun is a biblical name for Israel.
4 A personification for the English nation.

himself and yet not be absorbed, not to be and yet to be. The attempt to realize the asymptote in human mathematics was not quite successful, too near an approach to John Bull generally assimilating Jeshurun away. For such is the nature of Jeshurun. Enfranchise him, give him his own way and you make a new man of him; persecute him and he is himself again.

"But if nobody has read the man's book," Raphael Leon ventured to interrupt at last, "is it quite fair to assume his book isn't fit to read?"

The shy dark little girl he had taken down to dinner darted an appreciative glance at her neighbor. It was in accordance with Raphael's usual anxiety to give the devil his due, that he should be unwilling to condemn even the writer of an anti-Semitic novel unheard. But then it was an open secret in the family that Raphael was mad. They did their best to hush it up, but among themselves they pitied him behind his back. Even Sidney considered his cousin Raphael pushed a dubious virtue too far in treating people's very prejudices with the deference due to earnest reasoned opinions.

"But we know enough of the book to know we are badly treated," protested the hostess.

"We have always been badly treated in literature," said Raphael. "We are made either angels or devils. On the one hand, Lessing[1] and George Eliot,[2] on the other, the stock dramatist and novelist with their low-comedy villain."

"Oh," said Mrs. Goldsmith, doubtfully, for she could not quite think Raphael had become infected by his cousin's propensity for paradox. "Do you think George Eliot and Lessing didn't understand the Jewish character?"

"They are the only writers who have ever understood it," affirmed Miss Cissy Levine, emphatically.

A little scornful smile played for a second about the mouth of the dark little girl.

"Stop a moment," said Sidney. "I've been so busy doing justice to this delicious asparagus, that I have allowed Raphael to imagine nobody here has read *Mordecai Josephs*. I have, and I say

---

1 Gotthold Ephraim Lessing (1729-81), German writer who sympathetically depicted Jews in his plays, including *Nathan the Wise* (1779), based on his friendship with Moses Mendelssohn, leader of the Jewish Enlightenment in Germany.

2 See *Reuben Sachs*, p. 100, note 2. Also see Blind and Eliot in Appendix C.

there is more actuality in it than in *Daniel Deronda* and *Nathan der Weise* put together. It is a crude production, all the same; the writer's artistic gift seems handicapped by a dead-weight of moral platitudes and highfalutin, and even mysticism. He not only presents his characters but moralizes over them—actually cares whether they are good or bad, and has yearnings after the indefinable—it is all very young. Instead of being satisfied that Judea gives him characters that are interesting, he actually laments their lack of culture. Still, what he has done is good enough to make one hope his artistic instinct will shake off his moral."

"Oh, Sidney, what are you saying?" murmured Addie.

"It's all right, little girl. You don't understand Greek."

"It's not Greek," put in Raphael. "In Greek art, beauty of soul and beauty of form are one. It's French you are talking, though the ignorant *ateliers* where you picked it up flatter themselves it's Greek."

"It's Greek to Addie, anyhow," laughed Sidney. "But that's what makes the anti-Semitic chapters so unsatisfactory."

"We all felt their unsatisfactoriness, if we could not analyze it so cleverly," said the hostess.

"We all felt it," said Mrs. Montagu Samuels.

"Yes, that's it," said Sidney, blandly. "I could have forgiven the rose-color of the picture if it had been more artistically painted."

"Rose-color!" gasped Mrs. Henry Goldsmith, "rose-color, indeed!" Not even Sidney's authority could persuade the table into that.

Poor rich Jews! The upper middle-classes had every excuse for being angry. They knew they were excellent persons, well-educated and well-travelled, interested in charities (both Jewish and Christian), people's concerts, district-visiting, new novels, magazines, reading-circles, operas, symphonies, politics, volunteer regiments, Show-Sunday and Corporation banquets; that they had sons at Rugby and Oxford, and daughters who played and painted and sang, and homes that were bright oases of optimism in a jaded society; that they were good Liberals and Tories, supplementing their duties as Englishmen with a solicitude for the best interests of Judaism; that they left no stone unturned to emancipate themselves from the secular thraldom of prejudice; and they felt it very hard that a little vulgar section should always be chosen by their own novelists, and their efforts to raise the tone of Jewish society passed by.

Sidney, whose conversation always had the air of aloofness from the race, so that his own foibles often came under the lash of his sarcasm, proceeded to justify his assertion of the rose-color picture in *Mordecai Josephs*. He denied that modern English Jews had any religion whatever; claiming that their faith consisted of forms that had to be kept up in public, but which they were too shrewd and cute to believe in or to practice in private, though every one might believe every one else did; that they looked upon due payment of their synagogue bills as discharging all their obligations to Heaven: that the preachers secretly despised the old formulas, and that the Rabbinate declared its intention of dying for Judaism only as a way of living by it; that the body politic was dead and rotten with hypocrisy, though the augurs said it was alive and well. He admitted that the same was true of Christianity. Raphael reminded him that a number of Jews had drifted quite openly from the traditional teaching, that thousands of well-ordered households found inspiration and spiritual satisfaction in every form of it, and that hypocrisy was too crude a word for the complex motives of those who obeyed it without inner conviction.

4. From Vernon Lee, "A Dialogue on Novels," *The Contemporary Review* 48 (September 1885): 378-401

[Vernon Lee (Violet Paget) and Levy met in Florence in 1886 where Lee lived part of the year; the other half of each year she participated in the London literary scene. Her 1880 book, *Studies of the Eighteenth Century in Italy*, resulted in ties to many important men writers, including Robert Browning, Henry James, and Oscar Wilde. In this essay on the novel Lee uses the form of a conversation, a style employed by Henry James in his 1876 review of *Daniel Deronda*, "*Daniel Deronda*: A Conversation" (*The Atlantic Monthly* 38 [December 1876]) and later adopted by Wilde in "The Decay of Lying." This exchange between various artists and writers is set at Haworth in Yorkshire, where the Brontës lived; the discussion focuses on the capacity of novelists to draw a correspondence between characters and "real" people. These reflections on literary representation explore issues that Levy addressed the following year in "The Jew in Fiction."]

"After all," said Mrs. Blake, the eminent novelist, "with the exception of very few touches, there is nothing human in 'Wuthering Heights;'[1] those people with their sullenness and

---

1 Emily Brontë (1818-48), *Wuthering Heights* (1847).

coldness and frenzy are none of them real men and women, such as Charlotte Brontë[1] would have given us had she written the book instead of her sister. You can't deny that, Monsieur Marcel."

They had clambered through the steep, bleak Yorkshire village, which trickles, a water-course of rough black masonry, down the green hillside; past the inn where Branwell Brontë drank and raved; through the churchyard, a grim, grassless garden of blackened tombstones; under the windows of the Brontës' parsonage; and still higher, up the slippery slope of coarse, sere grass, on to the undulating flatness of Haworth Moor.

André Marcel, the subtle young French critic and novelist, who had come to Yorkshire in order to study the Brontës, listened to Mrs. Blake with disappointed pensiveness. Knowing more of English things than most Frenchmen, and with a natural preference for the exotic of all kinds, it was part of his mission to make known to the world that England really was what, in the days of Goethe,[2] Italy had falsely been supposed to be—a sort of exceptional and esoteric country, whence æsthetic and critical natures might get weird and exquisite moral impressions as they got orchids and porcelain and lacquer from Japan. Such being the case, this clever woman with her clever novels, both so narrow and so normal, so full at once of scepticism and of respect for precedent, gave him as much of a sense of annoyance and hostility almost as his placid, pessimistic, purely artistic and speculative nature could experience.

They walked on for some minutes in silence, Marcel and Mrs. Blake behind, Baldwin and his cousin Dorothy in front, trampling the rough carpet of lilac and black heather matted with long withered grass and speckled with the bright scarlet of sere bilberry leaves; the valleys gradually closing up all around; the green pasture slopes, ribbed with black stone fences, gradually meeting one another, uniting, disappearing, absorbed in the undulating sea of moorland, spreading solitary, face to face with the low, purplish-grey sky. As Mrs. Blake spoke, Dorothy turned round eagerly.

"They are not real men and women, the people in 'Wuthering Heights,'" she said; "but they are real all the same. Don't you feel

---

1 Charlotte Brontë (1816-55), author of four novels, including *Jane Eyre* (1847) and *Villette* (1853).

2 Johann Wolfgang von Goethe (1749-1832), German Romantic novelist whose writing influenced many Victorian writers, including George Eliot.

that they are real, Monsieur Marcel, when you look about you now? Don't you feel that they are these moors, and the sunshine, the clouds, the winds, the storms upon them?"

"All the moors and all the storms upon them put together haven't the importance for a human being that has one well-understood real character of Charlotte Brontë's or George Eliot's," answered Mrs. Blake, coldly.

"I quite understand your point of view," said Marcel; "but, for all my admiration for Charlotte Brontë and George Eliot, I can't agree that either of them, or any writer of their school, can give us anything of the value of 'Wuthering Heights.' After all, what do we gain by their immense powers of psychological analysis and reconstruction? Merely a partial insight into a certain number of characters—characters which, whatever the genius of the novelist, can be only approximations to reality, because they are the result of the study of something of which we can never completely understand the nature—because it is outside ourselves."

Mrs. Blake, who could understand of Marcel's theories only the fact they were extremely distasteful to herself, began to laugh.

"If we are never to understand anything except ourselves, I think we had better leave off novel-writing at once, Monsieur Marcel," she said.

"I don't think that would suit Marcel at all," put in Baldwin, "and he does not by any means condemn the ordinary novel for being what he considers a mere approximation to reality. All he says is, that he prefers books where there is no attempt at completely solving what he considers the inscrutable—namely, the character of every one not oneself. He perceives, more than most people, perhaps even too much, the complexity of human nature; and what to you or me is a complete moral portrait is to him a mere partial representation. I personally think that it is all the better for us if we are unable to see every little moral nerve and muscle in our neighbours: there are in all of us remains of machinery which belongs to something baser, and is little or not at all put in movement. If we could see all the incipient thoughts and incipient feelings of even the best people, we should probably form a much less really just estimate of them than we do at present. It is not morally correct, any more than it is artistically correct, to see the microscopic and the hidden."

"I don't know about that," said Marcel. "But I know that, by the fatality of heredity on one hand, a human being contains within himself a number of different tendencies, all moulded, it is true, into one character, but existing none the less each in its special nature, ready to respond to its special stimulus from without; on the other hand, by the fatality of environment every human being is modified in many different ways: he is rammed into a place until he fits it, and absorbs fragments of all the other personalities with whom he is crushed together. So that there must be, in all of us, even in the most homogeneous, tendencies which, from not having met their appropriate stimulus, may be lying unsuspected at the very bottom of our nature, far below the level of consciousness; but which, on the approach of the specific stimulus, or merely on the occasion of any violent shaking of the whole nature, will suddenly come to the surface. Now it seems to me that such complications of main and minor characteristics, such complications inherited or induced, of half-perceived or dormant qualities, can be disentangled, made intelligible, when the writer is speaking of himself, may be shown even unconsciously to himself; but they cannot be got at in a third person. Therefore I give infinitely less value to one of your writers with universal intuition and sympathy, writing of approximate realities neither himself nor yourself, than to one who like Emily Brontë simply shows us men, women, nature, passion, life, all seen through the medium of her own personality. It is this sense of coming really and absolutely in contact with a real soul which gives such a poignancy to a certain very small class of books ... and 'Wuthering Heights,' although an infinitely non-imaginative book, seems to me worthy to be ranked with these."

5. From Oscar Wilde, "The Decay of Lying: A Dialogue," *The Nineteenth Century* 25 (January 1889): 35-56

["The Decay of Lying" is often cited as Oscar Wilde's manifesto for the late-nineteenth century Aesthetic movement, which maintained that art was self-sufficient as the celebration of beauty and thus should be divorced from the political or social purposes of literary realism. In this essay, Wilde assails realism in modern literature as "the decay of lying." Like Lee's "A Dialogue on Novels," Wilde structures his critique in the form of a conversation between Cyril ("C") and Vivian ("V"), the latter espousing the "doctrine of the new aesthetics." Levy knew Wilde through the London literary network, and her short fiction, essays, and poems appeared in *The Woman's World* under Wilde's editorship. See his obituary of Levy in Appendix A6.]

C. Then we must certainly cultivate it at once. But in order to avoid making any error I want you to briefly tell me the doctrines of the new æsthetics.

V. Briefly, then, they are these. Art never expresses anything but itself. It has an independent life, just as Thought has, and develops purely on its own lines. It is not necessarily realistic in an age of realism, nor spiritual in an age of faith. So far from being the creation of its time, it is usually in direct opposition to it, and the only history that it preserves for us is the history of its own progress. Sometimes it returns on its own footsteps, and revives some old form, as happened in the archaistic movement of late Greek art, and in the pre-Raphaelite movement[1] of our own day. At other times it entirely anticipates its age, and produces in one century work that it takes another century to understand, to appreciate, and to enjoy. In no case does it reproduce its age. To pass from the art of a time to the time itself is the great fallacy of all historians.

The second doctrine is this. All bad art comes from returning to life and nature, and elevating them into ideals. Life and nature may sometimes be used as part of art's rough material, but before they are of any real service to art they must be translated into artistic conventions. The moment art surrenders its imaginative medium it surrenders everything. As a method Realism is a complete failure, and the two things that every artist should avoid are modernity of form and modernity of subject-matter. To us, who live in the nineteenth century, any century is a suitable subject for art except our own. The only beautiful things are things that do not concern us. It is, to have the pleasure of quoting myself, exactly because Hecuba is nothing to us that her sorrows are so suitable a motive for a tragedy.[2]

The third doctrine is that Life imitates Art far more than Art imitates Life. This results not merely from Life's imitative instinct,

---

1 The Pre-Raphaelite movement, initially constituted through the "Brotherhood" of artists, poets, and critics, including Dante Gabriel Rossetti (1828-82), John Everett Millais (1829-96), and William Holman Hunt (1827-1910), opposed the conventions of academic painting by returning to artistic themes and styles before the Italian Renaissance as a revolt against the ugliness of modern life. Both the Hellenistic arts of late-ancient Greek culture and the Pre-Raphaelite movement were influential sources for Aestheticism.

2 Shakespeare, *Hamlet* II.ii.559-560: "What's Hecuba to him, or he to Hecuba, / That he should weep for her?"

but from the fact that the desire of Life is simply to find expression, and that Art offers it certain beautiful forms through which it may realise that energy. It is a theory that has never been formularised before, but it is extremely fruitful, and throws an entirely new light on the history of Art.

The last doctrine is that Lying, the telling of beautiful untrue things, is the proper aim of Art. But of this I think I have spoken at sufficient length. And now let us go out on the terrace, where 'the milk-white peacock glimmers like a ghost,'[1] while the evening star 'washes the dusk with silver.' At twilight nature becomes a wonderfully suggestive effect and is not without loveliness, though perhaps its chief use is to illustrate quotations from the poets. Come! We have talked long enough.

---

1 Alfred Lord Tennyson (1809-92), *The Princess* (1847).

Appendix D: The Jewish Question in Victorian Culture

1. The Jewish Type: The New Race Sciences

a. From Robert Knox, "Of the Coptic, Jewish, and Phœnician Races," Lecture IV in *The Races of Men* (1862)

[Knox's ethnological study of race as biologically fixed and unchanging was influential in the new race science that emerged in nineteenth-century Europe. Knox's theory of race imagines Saxons, Celts, gypsies, Jews, and the "dark" races of the world playing out their biological fates, with Saxons as the superior race, evidenced by the spread of the British Empire across the globe. Opposing evolutionary theory, Knox maintains that race is a fundamental category of nature that determines all human destiny. However, his catalogue of racial characteristics blends in social habits and cultural prejudices. The following section on "the Jewish race" begins with Knox recounting his travels to different countries to classify "distinct races of men," although he acknowledges that "modern amalgamation" has obscured some racial traits.]

... [L]et me speak to you of another race I found in Holland, favourably placed for observation—the Jew. I had reached London, that compound of all the earth, and I had looked attentively at the Jewish physiognomy on the streets, as he perambulates our pavements, and with a hoarse, unmusical voice, proclaims to you his willingness to purchase the cast-off clothes of others: or, assuming the air of a person of a different stamp, he saunters about Cornhill[1] in quest of business; or, losing sight of his origin for a moment, he dresses himself up as the flash man about town; but never to be mistaken for a moment—never to be confounded with any other race. The women, too, were not forgotten; the beauties of Holywell-street;[2] there they are; the lineal descendants of those who fled from Egypt—spoiling the Egyp-

---

1 The section of the City of London where the financial district is located.
2 An 1850 London guidebook describes this street as "a narrow dirty lane" near the Strand, filled with "old clothesmen," a popular stereotype of poor Jewish buyers and sellers of used clothes.

tians—forgetting to replace what they had borrowed—but never returning to that land to which one might suppose them attached, though it does not really seem so—the land of promise.

But where are the Jewish farmers, Jewish mechanics, labourers? Can he not till the earth, or settle anywhere? Why does he dislike handicraft labour? Has he no ingenuity, no inventive power, no mechanical or scientific turn of mind? no love for war, nor for the arts of peace? And then I began to inquire into this, and I saw, or thought I saw, that the Jews who followed any calling were not really Hebrews, but sprung of a Jewish father and a Saxon or Celtic mother; that the real Jewess admits generally of no inter-marriage; that the real Jew had never altered since the earliest recorded period; that two hundred years at least before Christ they were perambulating Italy and Europe precisely as they do now, following the same occupations—that is, no occupation at all; that the real Jew has no ear for music as a race, no love of science or literature; that he invents nothing, pursues no inquiry; that the theory of "Coningsby"[1] is not merely a fable as applied to the real and undoubted Jew, but is absolutely refuted by all history.

★★★

As I attentively surveyed the Jewish population on the streets of London, I fancied I could perceive three different casts of features: the first, Jewish, *par excellence*, and never to be mistaken; a second, such as Rembrandt[2] drew; and a third, possibly darker, of other races intermingled. It seems to me, indeed, that almost every race shows, as it were, three forms of race which run into each other, connecting them possibly with others, so that this is not peculiar to the Jewish race. Of the first form I need say little to you, begging you merely to recollect that the contour is convex; the eyes long and fine, the outer angles running towards the temples; the brow and nose apt to form a single convex line; the nose comparatively narrow at the base, the eyes consequently approaching each other; lips very full, mouth projecting, chin

---

1 Benjamin Disraeli (1804-81), *Coningsby* (1844), a novel in which Jews are described as a foundational race of Europe, one of the "pure races of the Caucasus." Knox contends here that Disraeli fabricated a Caucasian race as a way to make Jews white, while in Knox's taxonomy Jews are fixed as one of the "darker" races.
2 Rembrandt van Rijn (1606-69), Dutch artist who painted many portraits of his Jewish neighbors in Amsterdam.

small, and the whole physiognomy, when swarthy, as it often is, has an African look. When fine, that is in the young person, with no exaggeration of any of the features; when the complexion is delicate, and neither passion nor age has stamped their traits on the face; before the energies of the chest and the abdomen, the stomach and the reproductive systems, have told on the features; before the over-development of the nose and mouth has indicated their sympathies with other organs than the brain, and dislocated by their larger development that admirable balancement of head and face, of brow and nose, eyes and mouth, cheeks and chin—constituting beauty in any face wherein it exists; before the eye of the observer is enabled to say at once, these features want proportion; that is, in a word, when youth prevails, then will you occasionally find in the Jewish face, male and female, transcendant beauty, provided your view be not prolonged. But why is it that you must not prolong your view? Why is it that the female Jewish face will not stand a long and searching glance? The simple answer is, that then the want of proportion becomes more apparent, and this is enough; but there is more than this; and I shall endeavour to explain it to you.

The living face cannot remain long unmoved; the play of the mind is at work on every feature; a passing thought kindles up the features, expands the nostrils, widens or contracts the mouth, dimples or furrows the cheeks, enlarges or diminishes the apertures of those glorious orbs through which the soul looks beamingly. Now to stand those changes, and remain beautiful, the proportions must be perfect so as to permit of change; but the Jewish woman's features do not admit of this; the smile enlarges the mouth too much, and brings the angles towards the ears; these are, perhaps, already somewhat too far back; the external angles of the eyes extend in the same direction, and the whole features assume a hircine[1] character, which the ancient Copt,[2] as I shall show afterwards, knew well how to caricature. If to these be added, as happens in the male face, that certain features display the internal structure, the skeleton of the face, then all beauty flies. A brow marked with furrows or prominent points of bone, or with both; high cheek-bones; a sloping and disproportioned chin; an elongated, projecting mouth, which at the angles threatens every moment to reach the temples; a large,

---

1 Goatlike.
2 Egyptians of the Hellenistic and Roman periods belonging to the early Christian Church.

massive, club-shaped, hooked nose, three or four times larger than suits the face—these are features which stamp the African character of the Jew, his muzzle-shaped mouth and face removing him from certain other races, and bringing out strongly with age the two grand deformative qualities—disproportion, and a display of the anatomy. Thus it is that the Jewish face never can, and never is, perfectly beautiful. I of course include not those rare exceptions which at times appear, nor those faces composed of two races which at times approach perfection. But, before I speak of this further, let me pursue my history of inquiry.

b. Joseph Jacobs, "The Jewish Type, and Galton's Composite Photographs," *The Photographic News* 29 (24 April 1885): 268-69

[Joseph Jacobs (1854-1916) was a Jewish social scientist, historian, and folklorist who began his career as an "Orientalist" scholar focusing on Jews, and published extensively on Anglo-Jewish history and "the Jewish Question." He compiled the catalogue of the 1887 Anglo-Jewish Historical Exhibition, the first large-scale display of Jewish culture in England. In this essay he describes how he assisted Francis Galton in devising his composite photographs to discern recognizable physical traits of the "Jewish type" (see pp. 222-23). Galton's theory of eugenics, the race science of improving humans by controlled breeding for desirable hereditary characteristics, was viewed as an antidote to degeneration, the morbid deterioration of racialized groups. Many of Levy's contemporaries and acquaintances were eugenicists, including Jacobs, whom she knew slightly, and Grant Allen, a better acquaintance of hers.]

Most people can tell a Jew when they see one. There is a certain expression in Jewish faces which causes them to be identified as such in almost every instance. Being engaged in some investigations into Jewish characteristics generally, I was anxious to discover in what this "Jewish expression" consists. It occurred to me that Mr. Galton's method of composite portraiture would enable us to answer this question with some degree of exactitude. I accordingly applied to him about two years ago, and he kindly consented to "compound" some Jewish types. I procured for him photographs of Jewish lads from the Jewish Working Men's

Clubs, and of Jewish boys from the Jews' Free School,[1] and he was good enough to compound them, with the results presented to the readers of the *Photographic News* this and last week. I am now to speak of them and their scientific value as representing the Jewish type.

Of the fidelity with which they portray the Jewish expression there can be no doubt. Each of the eight composites shown might be taken as the portrait of a Jewish lad quite as readily as any of the components. In some cases, indeed, *e.g., f3*, the portraits are less Jewish than the composites. The individuality and, I may add, on Mr. Galton's authority, the beauty of these composites are very striking. It is difficult, even for those who know the process, to grasp the fact that the composite E exhibited last week is anything but the portrait of an individual; and the same may be said of D, the composite of five older lads, whose portraits are not shown. A, again, the composite of the five *a*'s, reminds me of several Jewish youngsters of my acquaintance, and might be taken for a slightly blurred photograph of any of them. This is the more curious since A does not resemble very closely any one of its components. These facts are something more than curious: they carry with them conclusions of scientific importance. If these Jewish lads, selected almost at random, and with parents from opposite parts of Europe, yield so markedly individual a type, it can only be because there actually exists a definite and well-defined organic type of modern Jews. Photographic science thus seems to confirm the conclusion I have drawn from history, that, owing to social isolation and other causes, there has been scarcely any admixture of alien blood amongst the Jews since their dispersion.

These composites, there can be no doubt, give the Jewish expression. What do they teach us as to the elements which go to form it? The popular idea of a Jewish face is, that it has a long nose. But the full-face components exhibited this week have decidedly the Jewish expression, though the shape of the nose does not appear: and further, in composite H, as well as in co-composite G, which represents ten Jewish boys "rolled into one,"

---

1 Founded in 1874 by the Anglo-Jewish Member of Parliament Samuel Montagu, the Jewish Working Men's Club was the site for a variety of social gatherings including concerts, protest meetings, and public readings. For information on the Jews' Free School, see *Reuben Sachs*, p. 106, note 3.

the shape of the nose is markedly blurred, showing that there is no uniformity in this respect. The popular impression seems, then, to be disproved by these composites. Yet it contains a part of the truth, as do most of those rough averages which we term impressions. The nose does contribute much towards producing the Jewish expression, but it is not so much the shape of its profile, as the accentuation and flexibility of the *nostrils*. This is specially marked in the composite C. Take a narrow strip of paper and place it over the nose in this composite, and much, though not all, of the Jewish expression disappears. And in the profile *components* of last week it will be observed that every face has the curve of the nostril more distinctly marked than would be the case in the ordinary Teutonic face, for example.

A curious experiment illustrates this importance of the nostril towards making the Jewish expression. Artists tell us that the best way to make a caricature of the Jewish nose is to write a figure 6 with a long tail (fig. 1): now remove the turn of the twist as in fig. 2, and much of the Jewishness disappears: and it vanishes entirely when we draw the continuation horizontally as in fig. 3. We may conclude, then, as regards the Jewish nose, that it is more the nostril than the nose itself which goes to form the characteristic Jewish expression.

But it is not alone this "nostrility" which makes a Jewish face so easily recognizable. Cover up every part of composite A[1] but the eyes, and yet I fancy anyone familiar with Jews would say, "Those are Jewish eyes." I am less able to analyse this effect than in the case of the nose. The fullness of the upper lid, and the protuberance of the lower may be remarked, as well as the scantiness of the eyebrows towards the outer edges. The size, brilliance, and darkness of the iris are also well marked. Many persons have remarked to me that Jewish eyes seem set closer together, and this property is seen in composite A, D giving much of its expression to the latter. I fail to see any of the cold calculation which Mr. Galton seems to have noticed in the boys at any of the composites A, B, and C. There is something more like the dreamer and thinker than the merchant in A. In fact, on my showing this to an eminent painter of my acquaintance, he exclaimed, "I imagine that is how Spinoza[2]

---

1 See Composite Portraiture (p. 222), top image on left side.
2 Baruch Spinoza (1632-77), Dutch-Jewish philosopher who maintained an unfettered freedom of inquiry that was in opposition to Jewish orthodoxy; he was excommunicated from the Sephardic community of Amsterdam in 1656.

looked when a lad," a piece of artistic insight which is remarkably confirmed by the portraits of the philosopher, though the artist had never seen one. The cold and somewhat hard look in composite D, however, is more confirmatory of Mr. Galton's impression. It is note-worthy that this is seen in a composite of young fellows between 17 and 20, who have had to fight a hard battle of life even by that early age.

There remain the forehead, mouth, and chin to add their quota to the Jewish expression. The predominating characteristic of the forehead is breadth, and perhaps the thick and dark hair encircling it has something to contribute to the Jewishness of the face. The thickness of the lips, and especially a characteristic pout of the lower one, come out markedly in components and composites, both full face and profile. One may observe, too, the dimples (if one may use the term) which mark the termination of the mouth, and are seen in an exaggerated form in *a1*. Finally, the heavy chin, especially marked in the profile composites, confirms the popular association of this feature with the quality of perseverance, so ingrained in the Jewish nature.

We learn, then, from these composites that the Jewish expression is considerably more complicated than is ordinarily thought. If I have analysed it aright, the Jewish face has accentuated flexible nostrils, largish mouth, with ends well marked, and pouting under lip, heavy chin, broad forehead, with prominent superciliary ridges scantily covered with hair towards the outer extremities, and large dark eyes, set closely together, with heavy upper and protuberant lower lid, having a thoughtful expression in youth, transformed into a keen and penetrating gaze by early manhood. But words fail one most grievously in trying to split up into its elements that most living of all things, human expression; and Mr. Galton's composites say in a glance more than the most skilful physiognomist could express in many pages. "The best definition," said the old logicians, "is pointing with the finger" (*demonstratio optima definitio*); and the composites here given will doubtless form for a long time the best available definition of the Jewish expression and the Jewish type.

There is one consideration which lends an interest other than scientific to these composites of Mr. Galton. Most of the readers of this journal will be familiar with the portraits of spirits which gratify the curiosity of spiritualists, and cause ironical laughter among those who know the easy trick by which these plates may be manufactured. But here we have something more ghostly than a ghost, more spiritual than a spirit. The thing, person, spirit,

Francis Galton

Composites   Components

Illustrations of Composite Portraiture

[Figure 1]

ghost, idea, type, or what you will that looks at us in A has no bodily existence: and yet there is life in its eyes. And it has a definite expression which can only mean that it expresses something. In the present instance, as the components can in all probability trace back to a common ancestor, the composite face must represent, if it represent anything, this Jewish forefather. As the spectroscope has bridged over the abysms of space, and has told the composition of Orion's Belt, so the photographic lens seems, in these composites, to traverse the æons of time and bring up into visible presentment the heroes of the past. In these Jewish composites we have the nearest representation we can hope to possess of the lad Samuel as he ministered before the Ark, or the youthful David when he tended his father's sheep. Or, if this is saying too much, we may see in the composites the Jewish youngsters who "cooly appraised" the ancient prophet, as their components seem to have done with the modern scientist.

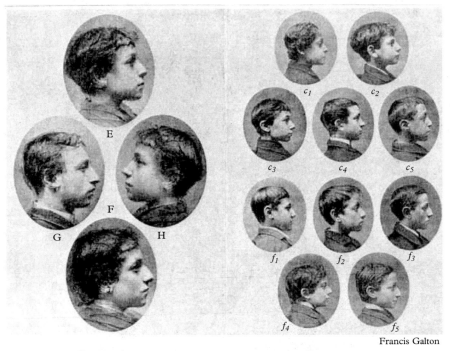

Francis Galton

Composites   Components

Illustrations of Composite Portraiture

[Figure 2]

Let me, in conclusion, recommend—of course with an eye to my own hobby—any photographer who intends taking up composite portraiture, to try his hand—but not his 'prentice hand—on composites of Jewesses. I am inclined to think that there is less variation in Jewesses than in Jews, so that the composite ought to be even more individual. Besides, in their case portraits can be taken at a later age without fear that any part of the face will be concealed from view, and we should thus be able to study the features when more set than in the case of the Jewish lads. The enterprising photographer who adopts my suggestion need have no anxiety about procuring components. I make bold to assert that my fair co-religionists are as constant visitors to photographic studios as any class of her Majesty's subjects. And if Mr. Galton has succeeded in producing such individual and beautiful composites of Jewish boys, not of a very refined class—well, my argument is obvious, and I leave some of the professional readers of the *Photographic News* to carry it into effect.

2. Political and Social Contexts

a. From Goldwin Smith, "Can Jews Be Patriots?" *The Nineteenth Century* (May 1878): 875-87

[Goldwin Smith (1823-1910) was a British historian who wrote extensively about what he called the perpetual "tribalism" of Jews as the cause of anti-Semitism, which could only be remedied by wholesale assimilation where Jews "de-nationalised" themselves. Although he called himself an anti-imperialist and professed many liberal social views, he staunchly believed in the supremacy of the British race. In this essay he raises the familiar accusation that Anglo-Catholics had divided loyalties between England and Rome, and that Jews cannot be English because they are a race apart. This essay comes from a series of exchanges on "the Jewish Question" between Smith and Hermann Adler, who became the Chief Rabbi of Great Britain, and Laurence Oliphant, an Anglo-Christian philo-Semite whose interest in Palestine anticipated the political Zionist movement.]

When a British nobleman proclaimed that he was an Englishman if we would, but before all things a Catholic, people said, 'Here is a political danger.'[1] They did not say that they wished to repeal Catholic Emancipation, because they knew that the advantage of that measure vastly outweighed its perils. But they said: 'Here is a political danger: at some critical juncture, when the interests of England clash with those of Rome, this man, and those who think as he does, may prefer the interests of Rome, and then we shall have to look closely to their exercise of political power.' This people said, and they were in the right, as was proved by the conduct of the Catholic priests and those under their influence in South Germany on the eve of the Franco-German war.[2]

So when we see that England is being drawn into a war,[3] which many of us think would be calamitous, and that Jewish

---

1 Sir John Acton (1834-1902) was a liberal Roman Catholic and a Member of Parliament (1858-65) who published on nationality and the modern nation-state.
2 The Franco-German War (1870-71) resulted in German unification and the establishment of the German Empire and the decline of French power on the European continent. Catholicism was the dominant religion in France, while Protestantism prevailed in Germany.
3 In the Balkan crisis of the 1870s between the Ottoman Empire and Bulgarian nationalists, British Prime Minister Benjamin Disraeli, Jewish

influence, which is strong both in the money-world and in the press, is working in that direction (as people on every side are saying that it is), we again note the presence of a political danger. We know, or think we know, that the ruling motives of the Jewish community are not exclusively those which actuate a patriotic Englishman, but specially Jewish and plutopolitan.[1] Therefore, while we do not wish to repeal Jewish any more than Catholic Emancipation, we promise ourselves, in the case of the Jews as in that of the Catholics, that we will watch rather closely the exercise of political power.

Judaism is not, like Unitarianism or Methodism, merely a religious belief in no way affecting the secular relations of the citizen; it is a distinction of race, the religion being identified with the race, as is the case in the whole group of primaeval and tribal religions, of which Judaism is a survival. A Jew is not an Englishman or Frenchman holding particular theological tenets: he is a Jew, with a special deity for his own race. The rest of mankind are to him not merely people holding a different creed, but aliens in blood. I speak now, as I spoke before, only of *genuine* Jews: I wish the American phrase "hard-shell"[2] were not slang; it would express my meaning better.

Dr. Adler thinks that in using the qualifying term I am providing myself with a loophole. I may be permitted to say that, if I had felt a loophole to be necessary, I should have preferred to remain silent. It can hardly have escaped Dr. Adler's notice that even among those who still profess Judaism there is now a division—I believe I may say a schism—between the stricter section and a section which is less strict. Not only so, but under the operation of the social and intellectual influences to which they are daily subjected, numbers of Jews are evidently putting off their Judaism and blending with the general element of European civilisation. The religion of these people is in fact nothing but Theism, into which the worship of Jehovah, from its pure and

---

by birth but a convert to the Church of England, supported the Ottoman Empire as a defense against Russian expansionism. Liberal opponents such as Smith viewed the "Eastern Question," as this crisis was dubbed, as a religious conflict between Christian Bulgarians and Muslim Turks, and felt that Disraeli's Jewish roots inevitably motivated his political views.

1 Possibly Smith's invention, "plutopolitan" literally means citizen of Pluto, a small, peripheral planet of the solar system. "Pluto" also derives from *ploutos* (Greek), for the wealthy.

2 Rigid, uncompromising.

exalted character as compared with other tribal conceptions of the Deity, passes by an easy transition. To speak either of the Liberal Jews or of those who have virtually ceased to be Jews at all as one speaks of the genuine, strict, or—to indulge in the Americanism once more—hard-shell Jew, would surely be irrational; and in observing the distinction we can hardly be said to lay ourselves open to the imputation of seeking a loophole. So rapid is the process of disintegration, especially in Germany, as to render it not improbable that in a few generations Judaism will cease to exist. One can hardly imagine, indeed, that anything palpably primaeval and tribal would very long resist the sun of modern civilisation, when a wise and tolerant policy once allowed that sun freely to shine upon it. Still there is at present a large body of strict Jews regarding the world outside the Jewish pale as Gentile, and acting towards it in accordance with that view.

b. From Hermann Adler, "Recent Phases of Judaeo-phobia," *The Nineteenth Century* (December 1881): 813-29

[Hermann Adler (1840-1911) became Chief Rabbi of Great Britain in 1880, replacing his father Nathan (1803-90) in this post. Here Adler responds to Smith's essays in the same magazine. For an earlier item in the many exchanges in this debate on the "Jewish Question," see the previous item in Appendix D.]

In the October number of this Review, Professor Goldwin Smith renews his onslaughts upon Jews and Judaism with an acerbity and virulence which I may be permitted to term Hamanic.[1] Each sentence is a barbed arrow; each barb is tipped with venom. I do not propose to traverse the ground already covered by my former replies to the Professor's attacks,[2] but shall mainly confine myself to the task of examining *sine irâ et studio*[3] the new charges which he brings forward, and of exposing his distortions of Judaism and his perversions of Jewish history.

The main argument, stripped of its side issues, is contained in

---

1 From the Book of Esther, Haman, the Chief Minister of King Ahasuerus of Persia, obtained a royal decree for the destruction of the Jews when a devout Jew named Mordecai refused to bow down to him. This name became synonymous with Jewish persecution.
2 *Nineteenth Century*, April and July 1878. [Note in original publication.]
3 Without anger and bias (Latin).

a narrow compass. Mr. Goldwin Smith discusses the anti-Jewish agitation prevalent in Germany, and justifies it on various grounds. He attributes the persecutions of the Hebrew, past and present, in the first instance to the tribal exclusiveness of the Jewish people. According to him the Jew makes a religious idol of his tribe. 'All the other races profess at least allegiance to humanity; they all look forward, however vaguely, to a day of universal brotherhood. The Jew alone regards his race as superior to humanity, and looks forward, not to its ultimate union with other races, but to its triumph over them all, and to its final ascendency under the leadership of a tribal Messiah.' I maintain that these statements are entirely opposed to fact. The great bond which unites Israel is not one of race, but the bond of a common religion. We regard all mankind as brethren. We consider ourselves citizens of the country in which we dwell, in the highest and fullest sense of the term, and esteem it our dearest privilege and duty to labour for its welfare. Is there aught incompatible with our devotion to humanity and with our patriotism, if, at the same time, we feel sympathy for those who profess the same religious faith and practise the same religious ordinances, whether they inhabit this country or other lands? If the bond which unites the Jew were, in truth, tribal, it would be a matter of perfect indifference to us what might be the religious belief or practice of our brethren in race. But the bare fact that we regard as apostates those of our fellow Jews who abandon their faith, is proof sufficient that religion is the main bond. So Mr. Goldwin Smith proposes, as his panacea, that the Israelite should abandon his tribalism, and 'all that separates him socially from the people among whom he dwells.' This means that he should give up his separate church, his religious rites and prayers, his seventh day Sabbath, and that in Turkey he should conform to Islam, in Russia to Greek orthodoxy—in other words, that he should cease to be a Jew; and in spite of this, the Professor claims that he upholds religious toleration and liberty of conscience. 'I will tolerate you Jews,' he would say, 'when you cease to be Jews; I will tolerate your religion when you reject it.'

Yet he himself demonstrates the worthlessness of his suggested remedy. For one would have thought that the late Lord Beaconsfield,[1] who adopted the dominant faith of this country, and

---

1 Benjamin Disraeli (1804-81). See *Reuben Sachs*, p. 94, note 1.

married out of the pale of his tribe, would have been a Jew after Mr. Goldwin Smith's own heart. Yet the ire of the historian pursues the statesman whose memory all England honours, and whose loss all Europe deplores, as though the author of *Lothair*[1] had been a 'hard-shell' Sarmatian.[2] In Berlin, the head-quarters of anti-Semitism, are numbers of Jews, who, according to the new nomenclature, would be classed among the Mollusks—men who have discarded every trace of tribalism and intermarried freely with the general population. But against these, even more loudly than against the consistent, observant, 'hard-shell' Jew, the modern 'Hep! Hep!'[3] is raised.

I emphatically contest the position that our objection to mixed marriages is the outcome of tribal exclusiveness. It is essentially a matter of religion. It is an indispensable condition of domestic peace and happiness, that two persons who have entered into a compact to pass their lives together should fairly agree in their views on religion, which, to those who possess any religion at all, is a paramount concern of life. Hence statistics show that in all religious denominations the parties who contract marriage usually belong to the same faith, and that, for example, alliances between Churchmen and Catholics are comparatively rare. Alliances between Christians and Hindoos, between Christians and Mahommedans, between Greek Christians and Protestants are still more rare, and probably in every case must practically (and especially for reasons connected with the religious education of the offspring) be attended with renunciation of faith by one of the parties to the marriage. Why, then, should the Jew specially be taunted and blamed for refusing intermarriage, seeing that it would practically necessitate the abandonment of a faith which he has ever felt dearer to him than life itself?

★★★

---

1 Disraeli's novel *Lothair* (1870) involves an anti-Catholic plot concerning the Garibaldi uprising and the popular resistance to Papal forces in the 1860s.

2 An ancient nomadic pastoral people of Eastern Europe who displaced other communities until they were eventually assimilated into German society around the third century CE.

3 Acronym for the Latin phrase *Hierosolyma est perdita* (Jerusalem is lost), supposedly a rallying cry of Christian Crusaders and later of anti-Semitic protesters. See Eliot's essay, "The Modern Hep! Hep! Hep!," in Appendix C1.

Mr. Goldwin Smith proceeds further to trace the persecutions of the Jews not to any religious fanaticism on the part of the oppressors, but to the peculiar character, habits, and position of the Jewish people. He stigmatises them as a wandering and parasitic race, without a country, avoiding ordinary labour, spreading over the world to live on the labour of others by means of usury and other equally discreditable pursuits. And he does not stay to investigate whether he may not be guilty of the crying injustice of making a whole community responsible for the wrong-doings of its black sheep. He does not stop to inquire whether any of these failings may not be due to a long-continued system of persecution unparalleled in the annals of humanity. No; he asserts that they are characteristics inherent in the Hebrew branch of the Semitic stock. 'Otherwise the Jews would not have adopted as a typical hero the man who takes advantage of his brother's hunger to buy him out of his birthright with a mess of pottage, or they would not record with exultation how they had spoiled the Egyptians by borrowing their jewels on a feigned pretext.' This is all that the Professor has to say in respect to the place occupied by the Jewish nation and the Jewish Scripture in the development of mankind, and such *suppressio veri*[1] may well justify the indignation with which a gifted writer[2] laments the abysmal ignorance prevailing concerning our people.

c. From Laurence Oliphant, "The Jew and the Eastern Question," *The Nineteenth Century* (August 1882): 242-55

[Laurence Oliphant (1829-88) was a British author and an avid Christian philo-Semite with a great interest in biblical lands who traveled extensively across the British Empire and founded a colony for Jews in Palestine. Although he died before the political movement of Zionism was launched in 1896, he was an advocate for establishing Palestine, then a part of the Ottoman Empire, as a Jewish state. This essay comes from the debate in the magazine *The Nineteenth Century* with Goldwin Smith and Hermann Adler on the condition of Jews in England.]

It is a remarkable circumstance that at the close of the nineteenth century the two political problems which press most urgently for

---

1   The suppression of truth (Latin).
2   George Eliot in *The Impressions of Theophrastus Such* (see Appendix C1).

solution should be essentially religious in their origin. Modern civilization has been startled by an outbreak of Christian fanaticism against Jews, and of Moslem fanaticism against Christians,[1] attended by outrage and violence which would have disgraced the middle ages, and threatening disaster still more serious. In the one case the diplomacy, and in the other the enlightened sympathy and benevolence, of the most advanced nations of the world have been invoked, and charitable committees and political conferences have been called into operation in the vain hope that moral pressure, backed in the case of Russia by large pecuniary donations, and in the case of Egypt by a naval demonstration, would suffice to grapple with difficulties which have their root in those passionate instincts of superstition and ignorance that defy all the panaceas of civilization, whether they be political or humanitarian. Either one of these politico-religious conflagrations recurring singly would have given Europe enough to do. The fact that they have burst forth simultaneously, and that the remedies tried have so far proved inadequate, has tended to complicate both, and render any satisfactory solution far more difficult than it would otherwise have been. That the Jewish and Moslem questions are destined to act and react upon one another has been already proved by the refusal of the Porte[2] to allow Jews to emigrate to Palestine. The experiences of the present century—during which the empire has been curtailed of its fair proportions, and one province after another has been severed from it on the nationality pretext—has not merely shaken the prestige of Islam among true believers, but has produced a profound feeling of national insecurity, and of animosity towards foreigners generally, of which we have recently had a striking instance in Egypt.[3] The first instinct

---

1   The Eastern Question of 1875-76 refers to the political unrest in the Balkans as Bulgarians opposed the Ottoman Turks, at which point Russia declared war on Turkey. The conflict was also perceived as a religious war between Christians and Muslims. In Britain, Disraeli's Conservative Party believed it was in British interests to back Turkey against Russian expansionism, but the Liberal Party opposed this stance and painted Disraeli as siding with Muslims because of his Semitic origins. The "Christian fanatacisim against Jews" may refer to the revival of the blood libel, stemming from the accusation that Jews were responsible for the death of Jesus Christ, against Hungarian Jews in 1882 over the disappearance of a Christian girl.

2   The Ottoman Empire.

3   British troops occupied Egypt in 1882; with the opening of the Suez Canal in 1869, Egypt was of strategic importance to British colonial interests in Asia and Africa.

of the Government, therefore, upon hearing that an emigration of Jews from Russia was about to be directed upon a province to which they might some day put forward a national claim likely to enlist strong foreign sympathy, was instantly to prohibit any such immigration; and this not merely on grounds of political, but also of religious, expediency, based upon certain predictions connected with the return of the Jews to the Land of Promise. Indeed, if we examine into the forces at work in the opposing monotheistic forms of belief, which are as intensely antagonistic to each other as they are to Christianity, it will be apparent that, as the political and social issues of the three religions become more and more sharply defined, the collisions which they will produce, exasperated by prejudice, will become more inevitable.

Morever, in their common Semitic origin, Jews, and the majority of Moslems, possess a racial bond which separates them widely from the Aryan peoples of Europe, and which tends, in the case of the Jews, to attract them to those Eastern lands from which they have sprung, and to which all their earliest religious and historical associations are attached. That they should have developed into conditions which contrast so widely with other nations of Semitic origin, is due partly to the exigencies of that destiny which has pursued them ever since they lost their national character, partly to the influence of the religion of Moses as compared with that of Mahomet.

★★★

… The orthodox Jew believes, and is no less supported in that belief by the assurances of his sacred books, that those ruins are destined to prove the foundations of his future greatness and triumph; but in order to this consummation he feels that the tribal distinction and religious exclusiveness of his race must be preserved. Hence it is that the orthodox Jews of Russia and the east of Europe have manifested a strong opposition to the desire of their more advanced western co-religionists to promote a mass emigration to America, and have inaugurated a counter-movement in favour of a return to the East, which has seized upon the imagination of the masses, and produced a wave of enthusiasm in favour of emigration to Palestine, the force and extent of which only those who have come in contact with it, as I have done, can appreciate.

The causes of this wide divergence of sentiment are not very far to seek. The object of the Western, or 'modern,' Jew is to identify himself as much as possible with the country of which he is a citizen. He desires to have no interests or nationality apart from the people among whom he is settled. He becomes a fervent patriot, feeling that in a free country all careers are open to him, all positions of power or authority are possible to him, and he shrinks from becoming identified with aspirations attached to an obscure province in Asia, and which possesses a certain national character apart from the people among whom he dwells. Unlike the Irishman who, when he becomes an American, becomes with characteristic inconsistency an enthusiastic patriot of two countries, he eagerly repudiates one in favour of the other; and to him there is no more disagreeable prospect, or more inconvenient theological dogma, than the advent of a Messiah, which should compel him to turn his back upon the fleshpots of the land of his adoption, and return to that of his forefathers. Hence it is that one of the members of the most opulent of Western Jewish families is credited with the saying that, 'if ever the Messiah came, he would apply to be appointed Palestinian ambassador in London.'[1]

The orthodox Jews, on the other hand—living in countries to which all careers are closed by law to them, who are debarred from holding land, from engaging in certain trades, and are placed under all sorts of legal disabilities; who are subject to contempt, ignominy, injustice, and persecution, culminating in murder and rapine on a terrible scale—have naturally no such attachments to the land in which they are ill treated. With them there is no temptation to indulge in any sentiments of patriotism; they can afford to cling to the hope of a Messiah, and of a restoration to their ancient home. The Jew of the West, living in countries where a growing scepticism threatens to sap the foundations of the Christianity by which he is surrounded, is, unconsciously to himself, infected by the materialistic tendency which pervades the literature and taints the society of which he forms part; in the country of his adoption the ancient theological landmarks become slowly obliterated with him, as with the Christian; he wishes his bigoted co-religionist of the East to share in the blessings of the civilisation which he enjoys, and participate in the privilege of that free and independent thought which accompa-

---

1   Apparently many versions of this quip circulated later in the early Zionist movement. In Israel Zangwill's novel *Children of the Ghetto* (1892), one character comments on the idea of a return to Palestine, "It would be too chaotic! Fancy all the Ghettos of the world amalgamating. Everybody would want to be ambassador to Paris, as the old joke says."

nies it; and he believes conscientiously that he is consulting his highest interest better by sending him to America, where he may become an enlightened millionaire, than by aiding him to go to a country endeared by traditions inconsistent with the progress of the age, and where his religious prejudices are likely to be strengthened by the associations by which he is surrounded, while the material advantages which it offers under Moslem rule are at best doubtful.

Appendix E: The New Woman Question

1. From Clementina Black, "On Marriage: A Criticism," *Fortnightly Review* 53 (April 1890): 587-94

[Clementina Black (1854-1922) was a social activist largely on behalf of working-class women in London, and she was an organizer of the Women's Trade Union League. She was good friends with Amy Levy, whose first novel, *The Romance of a Shop* (1888), is loosely based on the all-woman London household of the Black sisters. Levy left the posthumous earnings of her publications to the Women's Trade Union League. Here Black is replying to Mona Caird's critique of marriage, summarized in the passages below. Mona Caird (1854-1932) also knew Levy and likewise was a novelist of the "new woman" in which she represented marriage as an oppressive institution and explored possibilities for women beyond the domestic sphere.]

Mrs. Mona Caird's article in last month's *Fortnightly* seems to have shocked some people very much. It seems to have been considered very daring and very revolutionary. But having read the article carefully more than once, I will venture to affirm—at the risk of seeming offensive and patronising—that it contains much less that is novel, and much more that is sensible, than might at first appear, or than evidently does appear to many readers.

***

The article begins with the thesis that a married woman should be economically independent, and that therefore a woman should have a legal claim to a salary when she works in her husband's business. Mrs. Caird goes on to say that because married women are economically dependent they become mothers of far too many children, and this in many cases in spite of their own wishes. She is very eloquent upon the sufferings entailed both on mothers and children by the existence of large families; and in this connection she makes an admission which seems to me to give away her case, and which I for my part believe to be erroneous. "The mother of half-a-dozen children who struggles to cultivate her faculties, to be an intelligent human being, nearly always breaks down under the burden or shows very marked intellectual limitations." If I believed with

Mrs. Caird that a woman by becoming the mother of more than three or four children, let us say, must become permanently disabled for the cultivation of her faculties, or for being an intelligent human being, then I for one should feel compelled, however regretfully, to say: "Perish the faculties and the intelligence rather than the children," and I should, I fear, feel tempted to indulge in bitter and unprofitable complaints about the cruel injustice of nature towards women. Experience, however—and in using that phrase I mean, in effect, as we all do, merely my own experience—does not confirm the statement. I do, it is true, observe a considerable intellectual supineness in many mothers of large families, but I observe a similar supineness in many spinsters of the same time of life—and for that matter, in many bachelors and husbands too.

Mrs. Caird proceeds to ask, in terms which must, I am sure, greatly alarm the average Philistine, whether the institution of marriage may be so altered as to make it a companionship of equals without any predominance on either side. That, at least, I gather to be the substance of her question; and she seems to involve, as an essential part of this equal companionship, its easy dissolubility. As immediate steps she desires: less rigid divorce laws, equal for the two sexes, and the right of the mother to control her children; and she looks forward to "contract-marriage under certain limitations" as the next stage to follow upon the practical recognition of equality between the sexes. Finally she discusses the present condition of children, and declares that, "If only for their sakes, the present marriage system stands condemned."

★★★

To sum up the whole position, marriage, like all other human institutions, is not permanent and unalterable in form, but necessarily changes shape with the changes of social development. The forms of marriage are transitional, like the societies in which they exist. Each age keeps getting ahead of the law, yet there are always some laggards of whom the law for the time being is ahead. The main tendency of our own age is towards greater freedom and equality, and the law is slowly modifying to match. At this moment the statute book and the prayer-book are both in the rear of the feeling and conduct of the younger generation at least of the more cultivated class in England; and this fact tends more or less to hinder marriage in that class. At present the strict letter of the law denies to a married woman the freedom of action which more and more women are coming to regard not only as their just right but also as their dearest treasure; and this naturally causes a certain unwillingness on the part of thoughtful women to marry. Moreover, the customs of education and social intercourse are, taken on the whole, such as to render rather difficult the preliminary steps of such marriage as alone satisfies the most highly civilised. That law and custom should alike enlarge so as to suit the growing ideal is evidently desirable; it is also, if that growth continues, inevitable, and the best way to secure the advance is to foster and promote the growth and spread of that better ideal. We must also bear in mind, however much we may prefer to forget it, that there are dangers in allowing the law to outrun the general feeling; and that even freedom is a dangerous weapon in the hands of those who have no sufficing inward law to guide them.

But to do our best towards improving the customary ideal is at least safe. We can all of us influence custom a little, since custom, after all, is only made up of many individual examples. We can all promote in our own small sphere a fuller and freer intercourse between men and women of all sorts, and thus help to enlarge that opportunity of friendship between man and woman which is also the opportunity of the best and most enduring kind of love, and of the happiest marriage. But no opportunity and no form of marriage that can be devised can make beautiful or civilised the relations of those who are themselves unbeautiful and uncivilised; nor can any machinery of law or custom avert the suffering brought on human beings by their own faults and follies, or by the faults and follies of those who stand nearest to them. Even as marriage stands now, it remains substantially true, in spite of striking exceptions, that men and women reap as they sow. In this, as in every department of life, to enter rashly upon serious undertakings is to invite ruin. In marriage, as in other relations, peace, confidence, and affection can only be bought by paying justice and gentleness in return. In this, as in every other affair of life, faultiness and folly bring, and will continue to bring, their own retribution; but in this, even more conspicuously, perhaps, than in others, it is folly of which the retribution is the more certain and the more severe.

It is not, I think, mitigation of the penalty at which the reformer should aim, so much as alteration of the environment in which faults and follies naturally grow. Easier divorce may be necessary, but the opportunity of making wiser and happier marriages is more necessary still—partly, though not chiefly, because in that direction lies the only safe path towards less stringent legal conditions.

2. From Grant Allen, "The Girl of the Future," *The Universal Review* 7 (1890): 49-64

[Allen's writing, both fiction and essays, reflects his belief in eugenics. His essay "Plain Words on the Woman Question" appeared a month after Levy's death in October 1889 in *The Fortnightly Review*, but it is in this essay that he alludes to Levy's suicide. He also wrote a poem on the same topic, "For Amy Levy's Urn."]

High up in the front rank of social problems which engage the minds of thinking people in this age of transition, I suppose we may place the fundamental problem of how the Community may best be provided in future with constant relays of sound and efficient citizens. The Marriage Problem, most people call it, with illogical glibness; for that phrase begs the question from the very outset by tacitly taking for granted the continued existence in time to come of the institution of marriage. The Sex Problem, I dare say Miss Schreiner[1] and Mrs. Caird[2] would call it—thumbscrews will not drive me to violate the genius of our mother tongue by describing this last lady as "Mrs. Mona Caird": but to speak of it as a problem of Sex rather than as a problem of Paternity and Maternity is to fall into the besetting sin of women who lightly meddle with these high matters—the error of treating marriage or its substitute mainly from the point of view of the personal convenience of the two adults involved, and very little indeed from the vastly more important and essential point of view of the soundness and efficiency of the children to be begotten. Were I to choose a name for it myself, I would call it rather the Child Problem, or if we want to be very Greek, out of respect to Girton, the Problem of Paedopoietics.

★★★

... [I]t must be clear at once to every sensible mind that if any good thing is ever to come out of the present ferment, the opin-

---

1 Olive Schreiner (1855-1920), author of *The Story of an African Farm* (1883), an early "New Woman" novel.
2 Mona Caird (1854-1922), novelist and essayist whose 1888 essay "Marriage" in the *Westminster Review* spurred a controversy over the marriage question.

ions of men who have thought much upon these subjects, and the opinions of women (if any) who have thought a little, should be openly collated, compared, and debated upon. It is only by such frank sifting of the very best and fullest thought—the product of long and earnest study—that advance has ever been made in any direction. And if it be objected that no advance is here needed, the answer is obvious. You can't stand still. Change is in the air: change is close upon us: revolutionary ideas as to marriage permeate our society, and what is specially important, our women in particular. The wife is beginning to clamour for easier divorce: the spinster is beginning to kick against lottery wedlock.

★★★

It isn't the Quantity but the Quality of our fresh material that is now at stake. The East End and the scrofulous pensioners will pullulate in a thousand garrets as of yore: the nervous woman will still bring forth abundantly her rickety offspring with great regularity at measured intervals of twenty-four months: even the broken-down product of the Oxford Local Examination[1] system will continue to produce on an average two congenitally hysterical and anaemic infants before she finally fades away into thin air at her third childbed. But the question is, will our existing system provide us with mothers capable of producing sound and healthy children, in mind and body, or will it not? If it doesn't, then inevitably and infallibly it will go to the wall. Not all the Mona Cairds and Olive Schreiners that ever lisped Greek can fight against the force of natural selection. Survival of the fittest is stronger than Miss Buss,[2] and Miss Pipe,[3] and Miss Helen Gladstone,[4] and the staff of the Girls' Public Day School Company,

---

1 Introduced in 1858, these rigorous examinations, taken at the end of a course of study, were intended to elevate middle-class secondary education for persons not entering academic professions. Levy passed the Cambridge local examinations in 1878.

2 Frances Mary Buss (1827-94), advocate for women's rights who fought for the admission of women to Cambridge University.

3 Hannah Pipe (1831-1906) founded Laleham Lodge, a boarding school for girls in Clapham from 1856 to 1908.

4 Helen Gladstone (1814-80), the younger sister of the statesman William Ewart Gladstone, rebelled against her father and brothers who tried to control and restrain her "aberrant" behavior.

Limited,[1] all put together. The race that lets its women fail in their maternal functions will sink to the nethermost abyss of limbo, though all its girls rejoice in logarithms, smoke Russian cigarettes, and act Aeschylean tragedies in most aesthetic and archaic chitons. The race that keeps up the efficiency of its nursing mothers will win in the long run, though none of its girls can read a line of Lucian[2] or boast anything better than equally-developed and well-balanced minds and bodies.

✱✱✱

One of the most striking among the innumerable inconveniences of our existing marriage system is the fact that it makes practically no provision for what Mr. Galton aptly terms 'eugenics'—that is to say, a systematic endeavour towards the betterment of the race by the deliberate selection of the best possible sires, and their union for reproductive purposes with the best possible mothers. On the contrary, it leaves the breeding of the human race entirely to chance, and it results too often in the perpetuation of disease, insanity, hysteria, folly, and every other conceivable form of weakness or vice in mind and body. Indeed, to see how foolish is our practice in the reproduction of the human race, we have only to contrast it with the method we pursue in the reproduction of those other animals whose purity of blood, strength, and excellence has become of importance to us.

✱✱✱

There has been of late years a great movement in England and America for the Higher Instruction of Women. Colleges have been opened; High Schools have been started; Senior Classics have been led like lambs to the slaughter; our girls have been crammed with Mathematics like Strasbourg geese with Indian meal, till they are bursting with vast stocks of unassimilated knowledge. The raw material has been pushed in at one end of the mill with indiscriminate zeal, and has come out at the other,

---

1 The Girls' Public Day School Company was established in 1872 for the purpose of providing girls with a rigorous and nondenominational academic education similar to public school programs for boys. Levy attended the Brighton High School for Girls, one of the first schools established by this organization.

2 Lucian of Samosata (120-190 CE), Greek satirist.

turned and shaped to pattern, with wooden regularity. All life and spontaneity, to be sure, has been crushed out in the process; but no matter for that: our girls are now 'highly cultivated.' A few hundred pallid little Amy Levys sacrificed on the way are as nothing before the face of our fashionable Juggernaut. Newnham has slain its thousands, and Girton its tens of thousands; the dark places of the earth are full of cruelty. But still, in spite of all its hideous and inhuman errors, 'the movement' has this at least of good augury in it—that now for the first time in the history of the world, mankind has begun to think about the upbringing of its women.

Appendix F: Map of Levy's London from Bacon's New Map of London *(1885)*

Locations from Levy's Life:
1. 11 Sussex Place, Regent's Park (residence 1872-84)
2. 26 Ulster Place, Regent's Park (1884-85)
3. 7 Endsleigh Gardens, Bloomsbury (residence 1885-89)
4. British Museum
5. University Club for Ladies, 31 New Bond Street
6. West London Synagogue, Upper Berkeley Street

Locations in *Reuben Sachs*:
7. Lancaster Gate (Reuben Sachs' mother's home, ch. 1)

244   APPENDIX F

8. Portland Place (Solomon Sachs' home, ch. 8)
9. Kensington Palace Gardens (Leunigers' home, ch. 2)
10. Westbourne Grove (Whiteley's, ch. 6)
11. Walterton Road (Judith Quixano's parents' home, ch. 10)
12. Bayswater Synagogue, Chichester Place (Solomon Sachs and the Montague Cohens, ch. 7)
13. Spanish and Portuguese Synagogue, Bryanston Street (Quixano family, ch. 7)
14. St. John's Wood Synagogue, Abbey Road (Samuel Sachs family, ch. 8)
15. Chancery Lane, Lincoln's Inn (Reuben's chambers, ch. 10)
16. Albert Hall Mansions (Judith and Bertie's home, Epilogue)

Select Bibliography

Works by Amy Levy

Novels

Reuben Sachs: A Sketch. London and New York: Macmillan and
Co., 1888.
The Romance of a Shop. London: T. Fisher Unwin, 1888;
Boston: Cupples and Herd ("The Algonquin Press"), 1889;
ed. Susan David Bernstein. Peterborough, ON: Broadview
Press, 2006.
Miss Meredith. London: Hodder and Stoughton, 1889; serialized
in *British Weekly* (April-June 1889).

Poetry

"A Ballad of Religion and Marriage." Privately printed and cir-
culated by Clement Shorter, 1915.
Translations of poems by Jehudah Halevi and Heinrich Heine.
Jewish Portraits. By Lady Katie Magnus. London: Routledge,
1888.
A London Plane-Tree, and Other Verse. London: T. Fisher Unwin,
1889.
A Minor Poet and Other Verse. London: T. Fisher Unwin, 1884.
Xantippe and Other Verse. Cambridge: E. Johnson and Co., 1881.

Short Fiction [This is a partial chronological list of Levy's
magazine fiction in the 1880s.]

"Mrs. Pierrepoint: A Sketch in Two Parts." *Temple Bar* 59 (June
1880): 226-36.
"Euphemia: A Sketch." *Victoria Magazine* 36 (August-Septem-
ber 1880): 129-41, 199-203.
"Between Two Stools." *Temple Bar* 69 (1883): 337-50.
"The Diary of a Plain Girl." *London Society* 44 (September
1883): 295-304.
"Sokratics in the Strand." *The Cambridge Review* 6 (February
1884): 163-64.
"At Prato." *Time* 19 (July 1888): 68-74.
"Griselda." *Temple Bar* 84 (September 1888): 65-96.

"The Recent Telepathic Occurrence at the British Museum." *The Woman's World* 1 (1888): 31-32.
"Cohen of Trinity." *The Gentleman's Magazine* 266 (May 1889): 417-24.
"Addenbrooke." *Belgravia* 68 (March 1889): 24-34.
"A Slip of the Pen." *Temple Bar* 86 (1889): 371-77.
"Eldorado at Islington." *The Woman's World* 2 (1889): 488-89.
"Wise in her Generation." *The Woman's World* 3 (1890): 20-23.

Essays [This is a partial chronological list.]

"The New School of American Fiction." *Temple Bar* 70 (March 1884): 383-89.
"The Ghetto at Florence." *The Jewish Chronicle* (26 March 1886): 9.
"The Jew in Fiction." *The Jewish Chronicle* (4 June 1886): 13.
"Jewish Humour." *The Jewish Chronicle* (20 August 1886): 9-10.
"Middle-Class Jewish Women of To-Day." *The Jewish Chronicle* (17 September 1886): 7.
"Jewish Children." *The Jewish Chronicle* (5 November 1886): 8.
"The Poetry of Christina Rossetti." *The Woman's World* 1 (1888): 31-32.
"Women and Club Life." *The Woman's World* 1 (1888): 364-67.
"Readers at the British Museum." *Atalanta: Every Girl's Magazine* (April 1889): 449-54.

Secondary Reading on Levy

Beckman, Linda Hunt. *Amy Levy: Her Life and Letters.* Athens: Ohio UP, 2000.
Beckman, Linda Hunt. "Leaving the Tribal Duckpond: Amy Levy, Jewish Self-Hatred, and Jewish Identity." *Victorian Literature and Culture* 27.1 (1999): 185-201.
Cheyette, Bryan. "From Apology to Revolt: Benjamin Farjeon, Amy Levy and the Post-Emancipation Anglo-Jewish Novel." *Transactions of the Jewish Historical Society of England* (January 1985): 253-65.
Francis, Emma. "Amy Levy: Contradictions?—Feminism and Semitic Discourse." *Women's Poetry, Late Romantic to Late Victorian: Gender and Genre.* Eds. Isobel Armstrong and Virginia Blain. Basingstroke: Macmillan, 1999. 183-206.
Jusová, Iveta. "Amy Levy: The Anglo-Jewish New Woman." *The*

New Woman and the Empire. (Columbus: Ohio State UP, 2005) 131-77.

Nord, Deborah Epstein. "'Neither Pairs Nor Odd': Women, Urban Community, and Writing in the 1880s." *Walking the Victorian Streets: Women, Representation and the City*. Ithaca: Cornell UP, 1995. 181-206.

Parsons, Deborah L. "The New Woman and the Wandering Jew," *Streetwalking the Metropolis: Women, the City, and Modernity*. Oxford: Oxford UP, 2000. 82-122.

Rochelson, Meri-Jane. "Jews, Gender, and Genre in Late-Victorian England: Amy Levy's *Reuben Sachs*." *Women's Studies* 25 (1996): 311-28.

Scheinberg, Cynthia. "Amy Levy and the Accents of Minor(ity) Poetry." *Women's Poetry and Religion in Victorian England*. Cambridge: Cambridge UP, 2002. 190-237.

Vadillo, Ana Parejo. "Amy Levy in Bloomsbury: The Poet as Passenger." *Women Poets and Urban Aestheticism: Passengers of Modernity*. London: Palgrave, 2005. 38-77.

Valman, Nadia. "'Barbarous and Medieval': Jewish Marriage in Fin de Siècle English Fiction." *The Image of the Jew in European Liberal Culture, 1789-1914*. Eds. Bryan Cheyette and Nadia Valman. London and Portland, OR: Vallentine Mitchell, 2004. 111-29.

On Anglo-Jewish Literature, Culture, and Related Topics

Cheyette, Bryan. *Constructions of 'the Jew' in English Literature and Society: Racial Representations, 1875-1945*. New York: Cambridge UP, 1993.

Endelman, Todd M. *Radical Assimilation in English Jewish History, 1656-1945*. Bloomington: Indiana UP, 1990.

Endelman, Todd M. and Tony Kushner, eds. *Disraeli's Jewishness*. London and Portland, OR: Vallentine Mitchell, 2002.

Feldman, David. *Englishmen and Jews: Social Relations and Political Culture, 1840-1914*. New Haven and London: Yale UP, 1994.

Freedman, Jonathan. *The Temple of Culture: Assimilation and Anti-Semitism in Literary Anglo-America*. New York: Oxford UP, 2000.

Galchinksy, Michael. *The Origin of the Modern Jewish Woman Writer: Romance and Reform in Victorian England*. Detroit: Wayne State UP, 1996.

Galchinsky, Michael. "'Permanently Blacked': Julia Frankau's Jewish Race." *Victorian Literature and Culture* (1999): 171-83.

Gilman, Sander. *The Jew's Body*. New York: Routledge, 1991.

Jacobs, Joseph. *Jewish Ideals and Other Essays*. London: David Nutt, 1896.

Lewis, Reina. *Gendering Orientalism: Race, Femininity and Representation*. London and New York: Routledge, 1996.

Novak, Daniel. "A Model Jew: 'Literary Photographs' and the Jewish Body in *Daniel Deronda*." *Representations* 85 (Winter 2004): 58-97.

Picciotto, James. *Sketches of Anglo-Jewish History*. Rev. and Ed. by Israel Finestein. London: The Soncino Press, Ltd., 1956.

Potter, Beatrice. "The Jewish Community." *The Life and Labour of the People in London*. Vol. 3. Ed. Charles Booth. London: Macmillan and Co., 1892. 166-92.

Ragussis, Michael. *Figures of Conversion: 'The Jewish Question' and English National Identity*. Durham: Duke UP, 1995.

Rosenberg, Edgar. *From Shylock to Svengali: Jewish Stereotypes in English Fiction*. Stanford: Stanford UP, 1960.

Scheinberg, Cynthia. "Introduction: Re-Mapping Anglo-Jewish Literary History." *Victorian Literature and Culture* (1999): 115-24.

Valman, Nadia. "'A Fresh-Made Garment of Citizenship': Representing Jewish Identities in Victorian Britain." *Nineteenth-Century Studies* 17 (2003): 35-45.

Zangwill, Israel. "English Judaism: A Criticism and a Classification." *The Jewish Quarterly Review* (July 1889): 376-407.

Zatlin, Linda Gertner. *The Nineteenth-Century Anglo-Jewish Novel*. Boston: G.K. Hall, 1981.

On the "New Woman" in Late-Victorian Literature and Culture

Ardis, Ann. *New Women, New Novels: Feminism and Early Modernism*. New Brunswick, NJ, and London: Rutgers UP, 1990.

Cunningham, Gail. *The New Woman in the Victorian Novel*. London and New York: Harper & Row, 1978.

Heilmann, Ann. *New Women Fiction: Women Writing First-Wave Feminism*. New York: St. Martin's Press, 2000.

Ledger, Sally. *The New Woman: Fiction and Feminism at the Fin de Siècle*. Manchester and New York: Manchester UP, 1997.

Nelson, Carolyn Christensen, ed. *A New Woman Reader: Fiction,*

Articles, and Drama of the 1890s. Peterborough, ON: Broadview Press, 2001.

Richardson, Angelique. *Love and Eugenics in the Late Nineteenth Century: Rational Reproductions and the New Woman*. Oxford and New York: Oxford UP, 2003.